MAPPING MURDER

MAPPING MURDER

BY WILLIAM D. ANDREWS

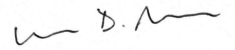

ISLANDPORT PRESS

ISLANDPORT PRESS
P.O. Box 10
Yarmouth, Maine 04096
www.islandportpress.com
books@islandportpress.com

Copyright © 2017 by William D. Andrews
First Islandport Press edition published in May 2017

ISBN: 978-1939017-98-7
Library of Congress Card Number: 2015945260

Book jacket design by Teresa Lagrange / Islandport Press
Publisher Dean L. Lunt

Also from William D. Andrews:

Breaking Gound
Stealing History

Also from Islandport Press:

Old Maine Woman: Stories from The Coast to The County
by Glenna Johnson Smith

Where Cool Waters Flow
by Randy Spencer

Contentment Cove and *Young*
by Miriam Colwell

Windswept, Mary Peters, and *Silas Crockett*
by Mary Ellen Chase

My Life in the Maine Woods
by Annette Jackson

Shoutin' into the Fog
by Thomas Hanna

Nine Mile Bridge
by Helen Hamlin

In Maine
by John N. Cole

The Cows Are Out!
by Trudy Chambers Price

Hauling by Hand
by Dean Lawrence Lunt

Down the Road a Piece: A Storyteller's Guide to Maine
by John McDonald

Live Free and Eat Pie: A Storyteller's Guide to New Hampshire
by Rebecca Rule

Not Too Awful Bad: A Storyteller's Guide to Vermont
by Leon Thompson

A Moose and a Lobster Walk into a Bar
by John McDonald

Headin' for the Rhubarb: A New Hampshire Dictionary (well, sorta)
by Rebecca Rule

At One: In a Place Called Maine
by Lynn Plourde and Leslie Mansmann

Dahlov Ipcar's Farmyard Alphabet
by Dahlov Ipcar

The Cat at Night
by Dahlov Ipcar

My Wonderful Christmas Tree
by Dahlov Ipcar

CHAPTER 1

After living in Maine for nearly five years, Julie Williamson thought she had a solid grasp of the Pine Tree State's varied geography: the low mountains and river valleys around where she lived in Ryland; the dramatic coast and islands running from Penobscot Bay to the Canadian Maritimes; Katahdin and the other rugged mountains around Baxter State Park; Portland's gracious Casco Bay; Mount Desert Island, with its breathtaking combination of mountains, lakes, and ocean. She loved the incredible range of sights, and the differing experiences each made possible.

People "from away"—the standard description of folks like her who came from anywhere but Maine, and one she found herself applying to others with increasing frequency—thought they had Maine fixed. Paddling the Allagash to see moose, a whale-watching cruise off Portland, a hike to the top of Cadillac to see the ocean off Mount Desert, skiing in the Mahoosucs near Ryland—each defined Maine for the person who experienced it. But in her time of living in the state, she had come to believe that the essence of its appeal was that each time you thought you knew Maine, it surprised you.

And surprised was how Julie felt as she moved through the rolling hills, picturesque farms, and apple orchards of interior York County. She was attending a conference at Willowbrook Village in Newfield. The area felt more like southeastern Ohio, where she had grown up, than Maine: tame, domesticated, unthreatening, and, on this mid-October day with its brilliant foliage, downright dazzling.

Willowbrook was a nineteenth-century village lovingly re-created by someone from away to allow tourists and local schoolchildren to celebrate the rural values of another era. Julie was there because it was the venue for one part of the annual meeting of the Maine History Network, the association of local historical societies she had joined when she became the executive director of the Ryland Historical Society. Privately, Julie always thought of it as the Maine Old Boys Network, since she was one of only a handful of women members. Although the gender disparity continued to bother her, she also believed it had helped her to be elected to the Network's executive committee in only her second year as a member. If that was tokenism, she had decided then, so be it; she valued outcomes over motives. And, for the most part, it was a good group to belong to, composed as it was of committed, often eccentric, and occasionally knowledgeable people who simply loved local history.

This year's meeting was based in Portland, but in keeping with the Network's goal to familiarize members with the many historical societies and museums around the state, today's session was held at Willowbrook. The seventy-five or so participants had made the forty-five-minute trip on school buses through the gentle fields that so surprisingly but pleasantly reminded Julie of Ohio.

Her seatmate on the ride was Daniel Dumont, the executive director of the Mountain Valley Historical Society in Farmington. Julie had visited his museum not long after she arrived in Maine but had only a passing acquaintance with him. "Not like our part of the woods," Dumont remarked as they watched the gentle hills unfold outside the bus window.

"No, but quite pretty. And surprising—at least to me. I hadn't realized there was an area like this in Maine. It reminds me a lot of where I grew up."

"Mountains and rocky coast—that's what everyone thinks. Where did you grow up?"

"Southeastern Ohio, on the river, but the area north of us looked just like this. You're a Mainer, aren't you, Dan?"

"Born and bred, with more generations behind me than I care to count. But I'm a tolerant type, willing to chat with a flatlander now and then." Julie laughed. "I'm looking forward to your paper," Dumont added.

"It's not really a paper, just some comments. They said to keep it casual. There are two others on the panel, so I hope they do the same. I'd hate to be the only one without something formal prepared."

"It's your experience we want to hear about. That was a pretty amazing situation."

Indeed it had been, Julie thought, as she closed her eyes for a moment and remembered her introduction to the Ryland Historical Society. Valuable items, including a letter from Abraham Lincoln and muskets from Benedict Arnold's Kennebec Expedition, were discovered to be missing within weeks of her arrival as director. At the time she had likened it to the Whac-A-Mole game: Every time she turned around, a new artifact had disappeared. And then the former director of the Society was murdered. As it turned out, there was no connection between the thefts and Worth Harding's brutal murder—except for the Ryland Historical Society. And because she was the director, she was at the center of it all, credited eventually with solving the murder.

Such events were very big news in a small town like Ryland, but Julie had been amazed at her first meeting of the Maine History Network when she'd discovered that all of her fellow directors knew about the events, down to the grisly details of Worth's death and the sad story behind it. Of course, as a former president of the Network, Worth Harding had been well known to the group, but Julie had still been surprised at the notoriety the affair had given her among her fellow directors. Indeed, she was sure the invitation to participate in this panel on museum security had resulted directly from those events in her first weeks on the job. She had learned a lot about museum security in the meantime, however, and was happy to share that knowledge with her colleagues. That she had been involved in solving another murder just a year later must have been known, but since it wasn't directly related to missing items, it rarely came up in conversation at the Network meetings.

"You'll really liven things up," Dumont said, startling Julie out of her quiet thoughts. "Museum security sounds so dull, but I'm sure you know all about the consequences of not having good procedures in place." He paused, and then resumed hesitantly. "In fact, I'd like to talk to you about a couple of things along those lines, but it looks like we're here. Maybe we can get together later—back in Portland. Want to have a drink after the banquet?"

"Maybe you'll change your mind after the panel."

"Don't think so. We can talk later about a time," he said. "Do you know where the panel is?"

"No. I've never been here before. The program says visitors' center—is that where we are?"

"Yeah. There's a space inside where they do the welcomes. After the panel we'll get a tour; I'm surprised you haven't been here before. It's a great little place."

"I'm looking forward to seeing it," she said. "I really should catch up with the others, though."

Dumont joined two others from the bus and stood chatting with them while Julie entered the barn-like structure with the WELCOME TO WILLOWBROOK VILLAGE sign. Inside, the two colleagues she was to share the panel with were talking. A heavyset man in his sixties came up to them and said brusquely, "Showtime, guys."

James Hartshorn, the current president of the Maine History Network, was exactly the type Julie had in mind when she referred to the group as the Old Boys Network. He headed the Down

East Historical Society, a house museum and archive in one of the small towns very far down the coast whose name Julie always forgot. She had never visited his museum, but she had talked with him at meetings enough to know that she would not rush to see it. Hartshorn wasn't a historian, a fact she had at first found curious, since she assumed all her colleagues had at least the minimum academic credentials. He had returned to his hometown when he retired from what Julie gathered had been a very successful career as an engineer at IBM in the New York City area. His profession didn't bother Julie—her father, after all, was a professor of math—and the fact that he valued local history enough to volunteer to lead the Down East Historical Society was in his favor.

What bothered her about James Hartshorn was that he was, as she succinctly described him to herself, a number-one sexist. That fact became evident when they had met at Julie's first Network meeting and Hartshorn had said he was happy to see "so many smart girls in the business." Julie had considered but then rejected several pointed responses, telling herself it was unwise to pick fights unnecessarily. Over the four years she had known him, Hartshorn's language and behavior hadn't improved, but her self-confidence had, so when he referred to Julie and the two men on today's panel as "guys," she decided to respond.

"Guys and woman, did you mean, James?" she asked tartly.

"I was thinking guys and gal, but I don't suppose that would make you happy either," he answered.

Instead of responding further, Julie just looked at him, holding his eyes with hers.

"No," he said, "I guess it wouldn't. So, gentlemen and lady, let's get going."

He was so infuriating, Julie thought, as she followed the three men into the room. Why does he think lady beats girl or gal? Hartshorn stopped and came back to her and said, "So, Dr. Williamson, I think you should lead off."

Doctor! That title, Julie knew, was the ultimate put-down among the old boys of the Network. She didn't go out of her way to use it, even though her PhD in museum studies made it perfectly apt; indeed, she didn't think of herself as Dr. Williamson, and bristled when her secretary insisted on it. Rather than a mark of respect, as the title was in the academic world, in the smaller universe of local historical societies—and in Maine, generally, she acknowledged—it was said with a slight but malicious smile. It translated roughly as "You may think you are, but you're not a real doctor, the kind that sets bones and prescribes medications." Since she didn't use it, someone like Hartshorn who did was clearly putting her down. And so she said, "Thank you, Mr. Hartshorn," dragging out the "Mr." for emphasis. "I'll be happy to start."

Although she was still bristling, especially after Hartshorn made a point of highlighting her doctorate when he introduced the panel, once she started talking, Julie became the calm professional she prided herself on being. Running the Ryland Historical Society, she had learned a great deal about security issues facing small museums—and not all of it related to the missing items she had discovered when she began. She had attended museum conferences on the subject, visited sites to observe best practices, read widely, and talked with experts, so she felt she had a pretty good understanding of the issues, and how even small museums with limited staffs and budgets could address them.

Glancing only occasionally at her notes as her PowerPoint presentation proceeded, she spoke about electronic security devices, rotation of artifacts, storage and preservation, staff and volunteer training, and general risk management programs, concluding—in exactly the twenty minutes allotted to her, she saw as she looked at her watch—with a slide listing websites with additional information.

"I have a paper copy of this list of websites for anyone who would like it," she said, thanking her audience before sitting down at the table with her colleagues. The applause was, she felt, more than polite.

James Hartshorn stepped to the podium, thanked Julie in a tone she admitted seemed genuine, and reminded the audience that questions would follow when the other presenters had finished.

The other two panelists glanced at each other and leaned together to talk briefly, after which, one—Brent Cartwright, from the Portland Historical Society—said to the audience, "After Julie's presentation, we're not sure we have much to add, so maybe we could have a roundtable discussion now." Cartwright looked at Hartshorn, who frowned but said, "Whatever your pleasure. That okay with you, Dr. Williamson?"

Embarrassed, Julie said, "I'd love to hear from my colleagues before the Q and A." She smiled at them, and they nodded back. Cartwright went to the podium and spoke for five or six minutes, after which Ted Korhonen, from the Finnish Historical Society of Maine, did the same. Then the questions began, and Julie was once again embarrassed by the proportion of them directed to her. She tried to hand them off to Cartwright and Korhonen, but they deferred most back to Julie.

After nearly forty-five minutes, James Hartshorn stood and said, "We've gone far over our time here already, and I know you're all as eager as I am to have a tour of Willowbrook before our picnic lunch. I'm sure our panelists will be happy to make themselves available for more questions then. So let's give them a nice round of applause." He cut it short and said, "We'll meet outside this building in ten minutes. Boys' and girls' rooms are just inside the door."

Several dozen of the audience members came forward to request copies of Julie's handout and lingered to ask questions. Out of the corner of her eye, she saw Cartwright and Korhonen by themselves, and said to one of her questioners, "Ted knows a lot more about that than I do." Then she directed another questioner to Brent, and soon she had cleared the crowd and was able to move away herself—in search of "the girls' room" Hartshorn had mentioned.

After the tour, during which she remained the object of both praise for her talk and further questions, Julie was happy to sit at one of the picnic tables grouped in the yard beside the visitors' center and contemplate lunch, and some peace and quiet. Dan Dumont, her seatmate from the bus, came by and said, "Great job! Can I join you?" He put his paper plate piled with cold cuts and salad on the table and, noticing that she hadn't gone through the buffet line yet, offered to get something for her.

"Oh, I'll go in a minute," Julie replied. "It feels good just to sit for a minute. It was quite a tour."

"It's a big place," Dumont said. "All the grounds and buildings—security must be tough here."

Museum security was the last thing Julie wanted to talk about now. "They really keep up the facility well, don't they? I'm so glad to get a chance to see this place." Dumont followed her lead and talked about Willowbrook, and after a bit Julie decided she was ready to line up for lunch. When she returned to the table, she was happy to see that Brent Cartwright and Ted Korhonen were sitting with Dan Dumont. She hadn't had the chance during the tour to talk with them more than to praise their presentations. She wanted to apologize for monopolizing the panel, but didn't know how to introduce the topic without drawing too much attention to the fact that she had so upstaged them, wholly unintentionally.

Korhonen saved her. "We should take this show on the road, Julie. You can talk and answer questions, and Brent and I will carry your papers and provide comic relief. You were great!" His tone told her he really didn't mind what had happened.

Julie laughed and said she was sorry to have been the first, since she probably went too far.

"I'm glad you were first," Cartwright said. "You put everything out there and framed the discussion, and Ted and I didn't have to do more than jump in with a few additions. It was really a great session—one of the best the Network's had, I think."

Dumont agreed, and Julie was happy that the plates of picnic food before them drew the three men away from the conversation and into the heart of any good scholarly conference: eating.

CHAPTER 2

The evening banquet continued the emphasis on dining that Julie called the Food for Thought motif of Network conferences. It was held at the Westin Harborview Hotel, the beautifully restored old gem formerly named the Eastland Hotel in Portland, the central site of the conference where most of the participants stayed. After the excursion to Willowbrook, her well-received talk, and the walking tour, Julie was glad to be able to exit the banquet and retire peacefully to her room. Tomorrow she would go for a run, but tonight she was looking forward to an early sleep. But as she was heading to the elevator, Dan Dumont came up to her and said, "The view from the top is supposed to be pretty good; do you want to meet there in, say, fifteen minutes or so?"

She had completely forgotten Dumont's earlier invitation to have a drink after the banquet. Alas, he had not. Julie looked at her watch, which said nine-fifteen, and then at Dumont, hoping he would agree that it had been a long day, and the drink could be postponed. Instead, he consulted his own watch and said, "Nine-thirty okay?" It wasn't, but she agreed.

When she entered the small bar at the top of the hotel, appropriately named 'The Top of the East,' her spirits improved. The view was indeed very good. Portland didn't offer skyscrapers, but the view over a few relatively tall buildings toward Casco Bay seemed to her adequate compensation. She wasn't at all a city person. In the five years she had lived in Ryland, however, she had come to value Portland as the kind of small city she could get to like. With Casco Bay as the background, the low-scale brick buildings of the Old Port were charming, as were the close-by neighborhoods of the leafy West End and trendy Munjoy Hill. Julie planned to take her morning run through one of those two, to be determined by her mood. But for now she was content to view the city from the glassed-in bar area at the top of the hotel.

Dan Dumont spotted her and waved, and she joined him at a table in front of the window on the east side.

"I grabbed this for the view—hope it's okay," he said.

"Terrific. I've never been up here before."

"Me neither, but I heard it was impressive. What would you like to drink?"

She ordered, and once her wine had arrived, Dan said, "So, do you know much about maps?"

She took a sip and looked at him.

"Sorry," he said. "I'm not being subtle, but I know it's late, and I don't want to keep you, so I thought I should just jump in. The thing is, two maps of Franklin County—1857 and 1883—are missing."

"From your museum?"

"Right. I was trying to answer a question from a researcher and went to get the maps, and they weren't there."

"Where?"

"Oh, in the archive. We have pretty good humidity control there. Maybe you remember—the room at the back of the main building?"

Julie tried to recall the tour of the Mountain Valley Historical Society Dumont had taken her on back when she was new to Maine and getting acquainted with other organizations. She closed her eyes and re-created the scene, her strong visual sense bringing it in front of her like an image on a screen. The building came into view, and then the interior layout, and finally, the large archive room at the rear.

"Yes, I can see it," she said.

"Well," Dumont went on, "I pulled out the drawer of the map case where those two should have been, and they weren't there. I went through all the other drawers, and I even checked some places where no map should be kept, but nothing. They're gone."

"When was this?"

"Two weeks ago."

"Did you report the loss?"

"Not yet. Not even to the volunteers, or my board. Actually, Julie, I was hoping they would just reappear somewhere, but when after a week they didn't, I knew I had to do something. I realized the Network meeting was coming up and knew you were speaking about security, and I thought, well, I'd just wait and talk to you about it, since you're an expert."

"An expert on items missing from historical societies?" Julie asked, and laughed. "I've had some experience, Dan, but I'm hardly an expert."

"Hey, come on; I heard your talk today, remember? You know a lot about this. What do you think I should do?"

Of course Julie was flattered, just as she had been earlier when her talk had brought such a positive response. It was nice to be known as an authority on something, almost anything, and if being a security specialist in small historical societies happened to be her role, so be it, she thought. Rich O'Brian—she still thought of him as her boyfriend, even though he was actually her fiancé—kidded that she should set herself up as a consulting detective. With apologies to Sherlock Holmes, he always added. While Julie had become well known among her Maine colleagues because of the thefts, she knew her career would be better served by publishing a book, or even some scholarly articles. She was working in that direction. But Dan Dumont wasn't consulting her on her project to document the effects of the Depression on rural Maine; he was asking for her help about missing maps.

"You're going to have to," Julie said, abruptly enough that her companion seemed startled. "Report it," she added. "To your board, and to the police. And soon. A couple of weeks of delay is okay, since you can say that you thought you'd find them, but if you wait any longer people will be unhappy—and suspicious."

"Suspicious? They'll think I took them?"

"Dan, the vast majority of thefts from historical societies are inside jobs. I hate to say this, but it's true. And the longer you wait to tell them, the more suspicious the cops will be, because they're used to people reporting thefts immediately, not two weeks after the fact."

Dumont looked troubled, and Julie regretted alarming him. Or, did his look mean more? Maybe he had taken the maps and was now using this conversation with her to cover it up? Julie didn't know him well enough to know if that was possible, but she did believe that people were rarely what you perceived them to be, even when you had a lot more familiarity with them than she did with Dumont.

"But you can do that when you get back," she said, steering the conversation in another direction. "What do you think the maps are worth?"

"We don't carry the kind of insurance that requires a specific valuation, but after they disappeared, I checked some auction sites on the web. No Franklin County, Maine, maps, I'm happy to say, but maps of similar period and size seem to be fetching in the thousands."

"Easily," Julie said. "And these are in good condition?"

"Excellent."

"Okay, tell me exactly what happened, and all about your arrangements—locks and alarms, who gets access to the room, that sort of thing."

Dumont told her when the maps had last been used, how and where they were stored, and described the security he had in place, helped along by questions from Julie. When he had finished, he asked, "Do you see something here?"

"What I'm mostly seeing is myself getting more tired and having trouble concentrating. I don't mean to end this, but it is getting late. I'd like to think about what you said when my mind's a little fresher. Can we talk again tomorrow?"

Dumont agreed. After he'd paid the bill, they took the elevator, Dumont exiting at the fifth floor, Julie at the fourth. The clock by her bed said ten-thirty, but it felt like midnight to her. Too late to call Rich in Orono, but just enough time to get in a good night's sleep, one she felt she had more than earned.

⌁

The alarm she had set the night before brought her sharply out of the dream she was having about maps, and for an instant she mistook it for a security alarm and sat up quickly to locate its source. She smiled when she realized she was in her hotel room in

Portland, that it was six a.m., and that she could take that long, challenging run she had fantasized about before falling asleep the night before.

"Seems chilly for such short shorts," a man's voice said as she started across the lobby toward the door. She turned to see James Hartshorn, looking her up and down.

"Running warms you up pretty fast," she replied crisply, and kept walking.

"Well, don't get too hot," he said as she went out the door to the street.

Sexist pig, she said to herself. She didn't miss the double entendre. Well, she wasn't going to let Hartshorn get under her skin. She turned left on Congress Street and headed toward Munjoy Hill, the eastern end of the Portland peninsula, preferring the water views in that direction to the tamer streets of the West End. At the top of Congress, she came onto the Eastern Promenade and stopped to admire the sun rising over one of the islands in Casco Bay. Rich, a runner long before she was, had taught her to stop from time to time to take her pulse and be certain she was elevating it enough for good aerobic effect. Having such a spectacular scene before her made this seem the right place to do so.

After she descended the hill toward the boat launch, she found her mind drifting from the view to her conversation with Dan Dumont. In summary, the two now-missing maps had been on display at an exhibit that had run from May through the end of August, at which time they had been returned to the map case in the archive and duly logged in on the record. The room itself was locked, and only Dan and two volunteers had keys. The electronic security system for the building was alarmed only at night and on weekends. That was what she remembered.

She still had a lot of questions that she would've asked the night before if she hadn't been so tired, like, did Dan trust the two volunteers? Did he check the part of the archive to which other items from the summer display had presumably been returned? Were other maps on display then, and if so, were they in their proper storage place now? How many maps did the museum own? Was there a record of archive visitors who wanted to see the maps, before or after the exhibit? Had anyone ever shown any particular interest in the missing ones?

She had other questions, too, but now, as she came off the walking path and back onto the street, she regretted that she had concentrated on Dan's missing maps rather than drinking in the lovely views of the water. She decided to concentrate on the brick warehouses along Commercial Street, sturdy structures whose utilitarian function in the nineteenth century gave them an authenticity she admired, despite their current use as souvenir shops and restaurants.

She checked her watch at the top of High Street and was happy to see she had gotten in a full hour of exercise. She could feel the run's effect in her legs, but that problem was more than offset by the high she was experiencing. Rich had been right about running, she thought, as she entered the hotel lobby and took the elevator to her room. "And I should have called him last night," she said aloud as she entered the room. She had phoned him yesterday afternoon to tell him about her talk, and she'd intended to call again after the banquet, but had gotten distracted by her conversation with Dan Dumont and the exhaustion that had set in afterwards.

She picked up her cell phone and saw she had two messages. Both turned out to be from Rich, one at ten o'clock the night before, the other, at six-forty-five this morning.

"I told you, you should always take your phone when you're running," Rich said when she explained where she had been. "You never know if you're going to take a tumble or something and need help."

15

Julie realized that Rich's scolding tone resulted not from her forgetting her phone on her run but from his worrying over why she hadn't answered last night or this morning.

"I know, I know, you're right—but I hate to be tied to that thing. I'm sorry I didn't call last night. It got to be late, and I was beat after yesterday. But I had a fantastic run just now; we'll have to do it together sometime. Portland is a really fun place."

"So, how was the banquet and the Old Boys' Network?"

"I'm fine, and the old boys are old, and boys. I'll tell you more about everything tomorrow."

Julie planned to leave on Saturday morning after the last session and drive to Orono, where Rich taught, and lived, during the week. On weekends they traded visits, he coming to Ryland one and she to Orono the next. The route from Portland to Orono to Ryland was a long triangle, but this was her weekend to see him, and she didn't mind the extra driving. She did mind the shortened weekend, however; because of the conference, she wouldn't get to Orono till Saturday afternoon instead of the usual Friday evening, and would still have to return to Ryland Sunday night.

"I'm sorry it's going to be such a short weekend," Rich said just as Julie was thinking the same.

"I know, but I really need to go to this is conference. It's only once a year."

"Right. Anyway, I can't wait to see you. We have so much to talk about."

Julie knew what he meant: the wedding. They had gotten engaged last spring, and he had wanted to marry over the summer. For reasons she never fully articulated to herself, Julie wanted to wait till the next summer. That delay, she knew, made Rich angry, and there were times when she regretted insisting on it. It wasn't that she was unsure about marrying Rich; she was very sure she wanted to. She just wasn't sure how their life together was going to unfold in a practical way. Would it mean more commuting? A change of jobs? A move to jobs somewhere else where both could be employed in the same place? It was just more than she wanted to contemplate, so she had persuaded Rich to delay the wedding until the coming summer. That had once seemed a long way off, but from October it was only seven or eight months away, depending on what date they set.

And she was sure that setting the date was what Rich meant when he said they had a lot to talk about this weekend.

"Well, I'm planning to take off as soon as the last session ends at noon. So how long will it take me?"

"Let's see, from Portland, about three hours, depending on how heavy your foot is. But don't take chances; I'd rather see you safe and sound at four o'clock than—"

"—than to have to come to Waterville to bail me out of jail for speeding," Julie finished for him, substituting an outcome that she thought lighter to talk about than what Rich might have said. He was very nervous about her driving, not without reason, and sometimes suggested he do two trips to Ryland for one of hers to Orono, to spare her the heavy truck traffic on Route 2 from Ryland to the interstate south of Orono.

"Exactly," he said, preferring her version. "But now that I think about it, it might take more than three hours—so don't set that as your goal."

"Okay, my goal will be just to see you."

"Just?"

"You know what I mean! I should hop in the shower now and see if I can get breakfast before the first session. I'll call you this afternoon after your two o'clock class."

After they had hung up and she was luxuriating in the shower, finding it a fit reward for the exertion of her run, Julie felt glad she hadn't told Rich about the business of Dan Dumont and

17

his missing maps. She knew what Rich would have said: "Don't get involved, Julie. You're the director of the Ryland Historical Society, not a detective." And she would have said, "I thought you wanted me to follow in Sherlock's footsteps." And of course he would have laughed. Still, she was glad she hadn't brought up the matter at all.

CHAPTER 3

Never for a moment did Julie think Rich's attitude toward her driving was sexist. The phrases he had used to describe it ranged from inattentive to careless to reckless, and he described his own state of mind when he knew she was on the road as nervous, concerned, or—in moments of special candor—terrified. But Julie never took his words as a reflection on her gender. They were simply true. She knew she was a terrible driver, not because she was mechanically inept, but because she was easily distracted.

The distractions were often inside her head, because she had developed the habit of using road time to think. But they were equally likely to be external—the color of a field, the shape of a barn, the changing sky. Color, line, shape, dimension—physical attributes grabbed her attention and focused her. In elementary school, her teachers had always cited her strong visual sense, and it was surely her love of objects and fascination with their appearance that took her through college as an art history major, and eventually to graduate school in museum studies. She loved to touch an artifact, feel its shape and texture. And she loved to imagine its origin—who made it; when, where, and for what purpose? She worked back from the thing to the world that created it and the ways it helped shape others. That she was drawn to puzzles—fitting together jigsaws, finding hidden objects, figuring out what had led someone to do something—stemmed naturally from her visual orientation, and was another reason she had studied history and how museums display and explore it.

She'd left after the last session, as promised, and had just driven onto the Maine Turnpike when she called Rich from her cell phone to report she was on her way..

"Just pay attention to the traffic," he said.

"I will," she replied. "It's such a gorgeous fall day—the colors down here are dazzling. What's it like in Orono?"

"Past peak, but still pretty. If you get here in time we can take a walk. But don't rush. And pay attention to the road," he said again.

She promised to, and for the most part she did, reminding herself that the truck loaded with logs in the lane ahead of her was more than the source of a geometric pattern. It was a long ride, and she vowed both to enjoy the scenes it presented and to spend some time thinking about the two odd conversations she had had at the Network meeting.

Dan Dumont's tale of his missing maps was one. The other had occurred just this morning over breakfast. Betsey Bowers, the director of Two Rivers Museum in York County, had approached her in the buffet line at the hotel and asked if they could sit together. She had talked to Betsey a few times at other meetings, but didn't feel she knew her well, and so welcomed the chance to get to know another woman. But Betsey's purpose was more focused: She wanted to talk about missing glassware. Two Rivers apparently had a large and valuable collection of glassware and pottery produced locally in the late eighteenth and early nineteenth centuries. In preparation for a large exhibit planned for next summer, Betsey had been working to identify prime objects in the collection when she discovered that a number of pieces were missing.

"We looked everywhere," Betsey had told Julie, "and they're just gone. I feel terrible about this, and I thought maybe you could suggest something."

Julie had listened and asked a few questions, but in the end didn't have anything to suggest beyond what she had told Dan Dumont: Report the loss to the board and to the police. At the end of breakfast, Betsey had asked if Julie would consider coming to the museum in the next month to help her evaluate security. Julie had agreed, but with the warning that she couldn't be expected to solve the mystery of the missing items, but instead to give advice on current conditions. Although Betsey had accepted that, Julie had the strong sense she was still expecting her to play detective, and to be truthful, she didn't entirely mind. If she could help, she would; and if trying to figure out what had happened to the bowls and mugs presented her with an interesting puzzle to solve, even better.

What Rich would say when she told him about the two incidents and her agreement to look into them wasn't something she had to guess at. He would at first warn her off, repeating that she wasn't a detective and should stick to her job as director of the Ryland Historical Society, and especially, to continuing her research on the effects of the Depression on rural Maine. She would say he was absolutely right, and then go on to describe the background of the two cases, and he would start to ask questions, and as she answered she would hook herself further and bounce ideas off him, a pattern he would lamely try to resist. Would everything in their life be so predictable, she wondered. She smiled as she contemplated the years ahead of them, the conversations and even disagreements they would have, the walks and runs and hikes during which those conversations would occur, the quiet time when he read and she did jigsaws at the table.

And the meals! She realized that although the yogurt she had eaten in the car as she was leaving Portland was appropriate after her large buffet breakfast, it had left her eagerly imagining one of Rich's dinners. At his request, she had picked up halibut from a fish store off Commercial Street and had it packed in ice for the trip. Rich was an imaginative and energetic cook, and she hadn't asked what he intended for the two large filets she was bringing because she probably wouldn't have understood. But she did look forward to whatever he produced.

The highway sign told her she was approaching Bangor, and she reached for her phone to report her progress. As he'd predicted, she drove up his street an hour later. Rich was standing in the yard in front of the house he rented near the University of Maine campus. He was beside the car when she emerged, and they embraced and kissed with the urgency both felt when their weekends together finally began.

"I'd better get the fish," Julie said as they drew apart.

"Always thinking about your next meal?" he kidded.

"Not always, and not the only thing I'm thinking."

"Let me guess: You need to use the bathroom after your drive? You want to take a walk? You want to see if I finished reading my students' papers?"

"All of those, but first things first," Julie said, and raised her eyebrows in a campy way.

⤜᳚⤛

After they left the bedroom, Rich said he had forgotten all about the halibut, and hurried to the kitchen to put it in the refrigerator.

"We still have time for a walk if you want," he said when she followed him into the kitchen. "We can debrief that way—unless you'd rather take a run."

Julie opted for the walk, in part because her legs still felt yesterday's long run, but mostly because the walk would give them a better chance to do their debriefing, as Rich always called it, filling each other in about what they had done in the week they had been apart. They called it "Your Turn." The person who had made the drive came first, and then the other would take a turn, and in an hour or so they would feel they had caught up on the past week and were free to enjoy the present, looking forward to the rest of their time together before the next drive. It wasn't perfect, but the approach usually worked pretty well to compensate for the obvious drawbacks of their commuting relationship.

They began the walk in silence, drinking in the beauty of the foliage, now past peak, as Rich had reported, but appealing in its darker, winter-predicting way. Julie thought that it would be easy to see Orono as a sort of in-between place—larger than Ryland, smaller than the city she had just visited, and therefore, sharing some of the charm of both. Instead, she had to admit, she just didn't care for it. Ryland felt authentically small-town, and Portland felt authentically urban, notwithstanding its modest population. But Orono felt . . . well, not like much; maybe most like Newark, Delaware, the university town where she and Rich had met in graduate school. She had found neither charm nor authenticity in Newark, and felt the same about Orono.

But Rich was here, and they were walking together. Your Turn began with her account of the conference, during which she snuck up on what she really wanted to talk about: the missing artifacts. She was more than surprised when, after her story, Rich enthusiastically endorsed the idea of her helping her two colleagues.

"You mean that?" she said. "You really think I should?"

"Absolutely. Who better? You know so much about museum security, and you love to solve puzzles. Why shouldn't you—"

"—play consulting detective," she finished for him.

"Right. Haven't I said that before?"

"But you were kidding."

"Not really. Look, Julie, Ryland Historical Society is booming because of you. The new wing is completed, the visitor count is up, the board loves you, you hired a new assistant, and volunteers are coming out of the woodwork to be a part of things. Face it: You've really built the place, and now you can think about the future."

"Think about another job, you mean?" she asked suspiciously, aware they were verging on difficult terrain now because of their upcoming wedding and how they would live as a married couple.

"Not necessarily," Rich said. "That's a bigger issue, but doing some consulting on security would give you something new and exciting to focus on, something to keep you satisfied while you think about the next step."

"You mean, something I could do as Mrs. Richard O'Brian, living here?" She stopped and gestured toward the small, shabby houses around them.

"That's unfair. I don't expect you to change your name—that was never part of the program as far as I'm concerned. Julie Williamson is more than fine with me, and I'll be happy to hyphenate my name—maybe a nice Wasp addition to my Irish one!" He laughed, and she did too, at what had been a long-standing joke between them. "All I'm saying, Julie," he resumed, "is that doing some projects like this would be good for you—give you a chance to try something different."

"What I should be doing is more work on Depression-era Ryland, and specifically, the Tabor papers. I seem to just nibble away at that, never finding the time to really dig in."

The Tabor papers consisted of boxes of diaries and correspondence written by a Ryland doctor that his descendants had given to the historical society, and which Julie had been slowly reading with the idea of writing about how the Depression had affected rural Maine. The papers had been useful in helping Julie resolve a difficult situation two years ago, which included the bloody murder of a Ryland Historical Society trustee. She knew the papers were a gold mine, and Rich, who had more interest in that sort of historical research, had been urging her on. But somehow she couldn't focus squarely on the project, and she sensed that Rich was now shifting to support the idea of her doing some security consulting as an alternative.

Before she could say that, he said, "You've got all the time in the world to work on the Tabor papers and that project. It'll keep, but these thefts are right in front of you; they need attention now."

"I didn't say thefts, Rich. The maps and glassware are missing; that's all I know. Could be they're just misplaced."

"So you're interested in finding out. That's good. But now, isn't it My Turn?"

She said it was, and for the next ten or fifteen minutes, after they'd reached the end of the town sidewalks and had started on the walking path that looped back toward the university, Rich filled her in on his week, ending with a funny story about a senior professor in his department whose interest in undergraduate students was well known, and the frequent topic of rumors.

"So," he concluded, "the beat goes on."

"Old guys and young girls," Julie said, uncomfortable when she realized that she sounded like James Hartshorn.

"Something like that," Rich said, "but my guess is that this young girl is beginning to think about dinner, and this young guy—if I may say so—has some plans. Shall we head back?"

The chill of the afternoon had settled into Rich's rented house, and Julie agreed with his decision to turn up the heat. "You really need a fireplace," she said.

"Well, you've got a couple to spare."

Rich loved the three fireplaces in the house where Julie lived in Ryland. It belonged to the historical society, and Julie lived there as partial compensation for her work.

"And I'm having wood delivered this week," she said.

"So I can plan on stacking next weekend?"

"Only if you insist. And of course, you can light a fire."

"Sounds good, but right now I should light a fire in the oven and get to work. You said you like halibut, right?"

"Love it. Anything I can do to help?"

"I think just your usual role—looking beautiful and anticipating my culinary handiwork. Want a glass of wine?"

She did, as he did, and after she came to the kitchen for it, he told her to enjoy the living room while he started dinner. Knowing Rich liked to be alone so he could concentrate, she took her glass and returned to the living room, where the jigsaw puzzle she had begun two weeks ago awaited her. She had never known Rich to work on one of her puzzles in her absence, and she was glad he didn't. She felt about puzzles the way Rich felt about cooking: It was something to be done on one's own.

CHAPTER 4

The drive into Ryland from the south—the route from Portland Julie would have taken had she not added Orono to the triangle—presented one of her favorite views: a teasing glimpse of Mount Washington across the valley, just as you started down the gentle hill toward the Androscoggin. The view she had late Sunday afternoon as she wound her way southwest on Route 2 was equally appealing, if less dramatic—not the Presidentials, but the tamer Mahoosucs, off to her right. The foliage here was still bright, just reaching its peak. Each mile she drove from Orono brought crisper colors, and more traffic, the RVs and other vehicles with out-of-state plates that made up the seasonal parade of leaf-peepers who came to Maine for the fall colors. So it was turning out to be a slower trip than she had hoped, though still rewarding for the foliage, and now, as she came closer to Ryland, the low mountains and glistening Androscoggin.

After the three days in Portland and the shortened weekend with Rich in Orono, Julie found herself truly excited about returning to the small mountain town she now called home. When she had moved to Ryland from Delaware to become the director of the historical society, Ryland had struck her as quaint. As she had come to know its people and its ways, she still used that adjective, though in an increasingly positive and even protective way.

Julie turned off the highway and up the street toward Ryland's gracious Common. It was fronted by Victorian houses like the one she lived in, and it anchored the town both physically and socially. You could stroll across the Common to have breakfast or lunch at the Ryland Inn and run into just about anyone you needed to do business with: trustees of the historical society, volunteers who gave tours or worked in the archives, painters or other craftspersons doing work—or at least promising to—on one of the Society's buildings, workers from Clif Holdsworth's hardware store or Ryland Groceries. She was still surprised at how many people she had come to know and how accepted she now felt, still someone from away, but welcomed into the community of like-minded souls who found Ryland a stable center in a perplexing world.

Harding House bore the name of the person who had donated it to the Ryland Historical Society—Worth Harding, the Society's founder and long-serving director, whom Julie had succeeded. In the first months of living there, Julie had maintained a very distant relationship with the physical spaces, still spooked by having discovered Worth's body in the front parlor. But over the years that memory had receded, replaced by a sense of domestic comfort, an at-home quality that always struck her most forcefully when she returned to the house after being away. How long, she wondered as she carried her bags through the kitchen door and up the stairs to unpack in her bedroom, would Harding House continue to be home? She and Rich hadn't talked about that directly, concentrating instead on the practical matter of establishing a firm date and place for the wedding.

She didn't share her parents' preference for holding the wedding in the Ohio town she had grown up in, and where they still lived. Newark, Delaware, remained an option, since that's where Julie and Rich had met, and they still had friends there from graduate school. But a midsummer wedding in the tropical dampness of the Delaware Valley held no appeal for either of them. Orono was not even Rich's choice, since his life there was transient; and Boston, his hometown, seemed an undue burden to place on family and friends who would be invited to the celebration.

Ryland seemed so obvious that Julie didn't even remember much discussion about it; somehow, they had simply talked about whether to have the ceremony in one of the historical society buildings and the reception at the Inn, or vice versa. Since one way or another the Inn would figure into it, they had agreed Julie had to check there first about availability before setting the date. She planned to go over to talk to the manager in the morning to see which, if any, July weekends would work. Then she would have to call her mother to break the news, a conversation she dreaded. While her mother had been enthusiastic when Julie had called last spring to say she and Rich were engaged, Julie knew that her father remained ambivalent about Rich, and that his views affected his wife's attitude, putting her, as always, in a brokering position between Julie and her father. He had apparently come to accept the fact of the marriage, but it was around details like date and place that he could continue to stir trouble.

But that was for tomorrow, Julie told herself after she had unpacked and come downstairs to the kitchen to see what sort of meal she could concoct from what was in the refrigerator. Rich had roasted a chicken for their midday meal and packed the leftovers for her, but she wanted to save it for Monday. The refrigerator yielded no good alternative, and the can of tuna she found in the cupboard didn't appeal, so she decided to walk to Ryland Groceries. Looking at her watch, she verified she still had time since it was open on Sunday till eight p.m. And stretching after the drive appealed to her.

Waiting in front of the deli counter for her sliced ham, Julie heard "Well, the return of the native," and turned to see Dennis Sutherland behind her. "Return of the person from away," she replied with a smile. "You're the native, Dennis."

"Now that you mention it," he said. "But welcome back anyway."

That Dennis Sutherland was a Ryland native had actually troubled Julie when she had hired him last year as the Society's curator and assistant director, a position that had been vacant for far too long after the former incumbent left under very clouded circumstances. Julie had kept the position open for an uncomfortable length of time—uncomfortable because she herself had had to handle many of its duties, even as she continued to work on the new Swanson Center and determine what sort of staffing its additional space would require. When that was done, she had advertised in all the professional journals and interviewed three finalists.

Dennis was without doubt the best, and the fact that he was from an old Ryland family was seen by her trustees as a great plus. But she had feared that his family's position in the Ryland firmament would combine with his experience elsewhere, along with the fact that he was a year older than her, to make everyone think he was the director and she his assistant. She acknowledged that his experience at a local historical society in upstate New York and his unquestioned knowledge of Ryland were rational reasons to select him, but it took her weeks of agonizing to get over the fear that he would somehow supplant her. In the nearly six months he had been on the job, she'd had no reason at all to retain that fear, and in fact, in every way possible he was proving to be a perfect fit for the job. Moreover, she had come to like him as a person because of his relaxed manner, good humor, and unfailing willingness to work hard.

"Good conference?" he asked. "And did you get your urban fix down there in the big city?"

"Terrific conference. I'll tell you all about it tomorrow if you want to hear, and, yes, I did enjoy Portland. But, you know, it's great to be back in Ryland. Walking down from the house just now, I felt so at home and comfortable."

"Tell me about it! I never thought I'd be back here—or happy to be. But I'm going to Portland next weekend myself."

"The lure of the big city," Julie said, even though she knew the real attraction for Dennis was a young resident at Maine Medical Center, a woman he had met when she was in medical school in Rochester. The fact that coming to Ryland brought him closer to her in Portland hadn't come out until he had been on the job for a few months, but when it did, it helped relieve her fears about his motive. It also established a bond between them because of their commuting relationships, although Dennis's with Ellie Mukowski was at a much earlier and less secure stage than hers with Rich.

"If that's okay," Dennis continued. "I mean, about going away next weekend."

"Of course. It's my turn to take Saturday; you covered yesterday—and the other three days, for that matter. Everything okay?"

29

"Oh, we had to shoot a guy trying to steal some furniture, and then there were the kids who smashed the windows in the Swanson Center, and of course, the chairman of the board . . ."

The fact that he didn't laugh as he recited the fictional litany of what had gone wrong in her absence reflected one part of what she so liked in his personality.

"Sounds normal to me," she said. "I assume you took care of it all—dragged off the body, slapped the kids, told Howard Townsend to go home and mind his own business."

"Just following your orders, Dr. Williamson, like always."

"Anything else?" the deli clerk asked as she handed Julie the plastic bag.

"No, thanks. Your turn, Dennis."

He stepped up and placed his order, and as the clerk pulled out the cheese to slice for him, Dennis continued. "How did the talk go? Brilliantly, I'm sure."

"So they tell me. Actually, it was terrific, Dennis. I really enjoyed it, and there were so many questions that the moderator— old Hartshorn; you haven't met him—had to stand up and put a stop to it."

"Well, it's on everyone's minds, isn't it—museum security. And you know a lot about it."

"More than I did before. The other panelists were good, and some of the participants had stories of their own." Julie was reluctant to mention Dan Dumont and Betsey Bowers and their requests for help. She would do that eventually, but since it raised the question of whether she was going to take on the assignments they offered, she wasn't ready to do so now.

Dennis retrieved his order from the deli clerk and the two of them walked to the registers at the front of Ryland Groceries to check out, leaving the store together. Dennis offered her a ride, but Julie was happy to stroll back up Main Street in the gathering dusk.

As she passed the buildings of the Ryland Historical Society, she was tempted to stop at her office, but decided that if anything required immediate attention, Dennis Sutherland would have told her. She had plenty of time tomorrow to catch up on what had happened in her absence. Preparing the final agenda and related documents for the quarterly meeting of the board of trustees scheduled for Thursday was her only big project, but she didn't feel like starting it now.

So she continued on to Harding House and let herself in through the kitchen door, observing the New England custom of never going onto the porch and in through the front entrance. It was amazing how readily she had adapted to local culture. She understood she was and always would be from away, but that didn't diminish how happy she felt to be living in Ryland, Maine. How long she would be doing so wasn't a topic she intended to think about at the moment.

CHAPTER 5

"Mr. Townsend asked you to call," Mrs. Detweiler said from where she stood at the door between her office and Julie's. No "Good morning," no "How was your meeting?," no "Did you have a good time in Portland?"

Fortunately, her secretary's abrupt style and cold tone had long since ceased to trouble Julie. Mrs. Detweiler was an efficient typist and keeper of the accounts. She was always on time, handled phone calls and took messages reliably, and seemed to have a good rapport with volunteers and trustees. That she continued, after five years, to call Julie "Dr. Williamson" and never hinted that she herself had a first name that Julie might one day be allowed to use was one concrete problem she hoped eventually to solve. But Julie had resigned herself to overlooking these things, focusing instead on valuing Mrs. Detweiller's strengths, and accepting her for what she was.

"I hope you had a good weekend," Julie replied cheerfully. After Mrs. Detweiller nodded in response, she continued: "I'll call Howard right away. Anything else I should know about after being away?"

The secretary paused, apparently trying to decide if Julie's reference to her absence required any response and then concluding it didn't. "I'm sure Dennis will fill you in," she said. "He should be in shortly. Do you want me to send him in?"

"I'll find him after I call Howard. Isn't it a gorgeous fall day, Mrs. Detweiller?"

"I suppose so, but I have to say, I'm looking forward to the end of the foliage season. All these tourists . . . well!"

Well, indeed, Julie thought as Mrs. Detweiller turned abruptly and closed the door behind her. Those tourists represented visitors to the museum, and while her drive among their RVs and campers yesterday remained a less than pleasant memory, she was perfectly prepared to accept the inconvenience in return for the business they brought to Ryland. You can't have it both ways, she said to herself, and then laughed when she realized she could also be referring to her secretary.

As always, Howard Townsend answered on the first ring. Or at least he'd always done so in the year and a half since he had retired as president of the bank and set up an office in his home at the top of Granders Hill Road. Julie imagined that Mrs. Townsend was unhappy to have him around the house, and glad he could be contained in his own space with a separate phone that only he answered. Besides chairing the Ryland Historical Society Board of Trustees, Howard remained active in a number of local and state organizations, so Julie guessed his home office worked well for his transition from the bank.

Although she had found Howard stiff and cold in their earliest dealings, she had come to admire his dedication to the community, his steady hand, and his ability to intimidate and control those trustees who threatened to stray into Julie's realm of authority. She appreciated that as a former CEO, he understood that the boss was the boss—even though the boss of the historical society happened to be a woman, a circumstance, Julie admitted, that Howard had only grudgingly accepted.

"Hope your conference was good," Howard said when he picked up and heard Julie's voice. "I expect you'll want to report on it at the board meeting Thursday. That's why I called, in fact."

Julie made a mental note to add a brief report on the Maine History Network meeting to the agenda, silently thanking Howard for the suggestion, since it gave her a chance to demonstrate her statewide status to the board.

"I'm planning to work on the agenda today," Julie replied. "I'll put down a brief report on the conference, and of course, we have the usual: minutes, treasurer's report, update on membership and the annual fund."

Howard's silence suggested she was missing something, so she asked if he had anything else to add.

"Well, there's that business Wayne's been bringing up. I think we agreed we'd defer it to this meeting. But perhaps I'm wrong."

Howard Townsend rarely was, and Julie immediately answered, "How could I forget? Sorry, Howard—though, to tell you the truth, maybe I was trying to forget."

A laugh from Howard was rare; the nearly full-throated one he gave in response to Julie's comment was beyond her imagining, and she found herself joining in. "Well, you know what I mean," she said when they both finished.

"Indeed," Howard said. "But I don't really think we can avoid it, do you?"

Much as she wanted to, Julie agreed. The topic that Wayne Reiter had been raising at every trustee meeting since he had joined the board sounded simple enough: collections policies, and especially what museum people called de-accessioning. Julie always used that term, though Reiter insisted on saying, "Call it what you like. I call it selling excess inventory. But then, I'm just a business guy."

Actually, he wasn't. Wayne Reiter was a retired professor from Harvard Business School, and Julie suspected he had never been in business himself. He just liked to talk about it. His family had a ski house at the mountain, and when he retired two years ago, Wayne and his wife had moved there permanently from Boston. Howard had met him through some connection and had brought up his name for the board, no doubt on the assumption that the magic of the Harvard Business School could thereby rub off on the Ryland Historical Society.

Julie was enthusiastic at the time, welcoming an academic presence on the board, but she had come to regret Wayne's presence when she realized he was a different sort of academic from what she had in mind. She liked to think of Rich as the perfect type: smart and knowledgeable, but modest and subtle, leading his students toward understanding instead of bludgeoning them. The latter approach, she guessed, had been Wayne Reiter's as a professor, since it was definitely the way he approached board business. At his first meeting, he had questioned what artifacts the Society owned, how it had acquired them, what use it put them to, and what it did about what he called "excess inventory"—what Julie translated in museum language as "redundant holdings."

She admitted, both to him publicly and to herself privately, that Wayne had a good point. Too many small museums just hung on to things, adding lamps and buttons and spinning wheels and whatever items people chose to give because they considered them valuable, or at least interesting. Some were, some weren't, but accepting donations often seemed to Julie more a means of pleasing donors than a rational way to build a collection. It was a complicated topic, and a very sensitive one, especially because so many trustees of the Ryland Historical Society had been generous donors of artifacts from their own families.

Howard Townsend and Clif Holdsworth, longtime trustees, were noteworthy in that regard, as was Ann Gibbons, who had joined the board the same year Wayne Reiter had. So any discussion about de-accessioning became personal. To remove an item from the collection that had been given by someone like Clif amounted to saying that it was without value—and with the further implication that having accepted it in the first place had been a mistake. So, as Julie always said to herself when Wayne raised the question, "There be dragons."

"We can't really ignore it," Howard said to end Julie's silence.

"And he's got a fair point," Julie added.

"Right. So just put that on the agenda, something neutral like 'collections policy' should cover it, I think. And perhaps you could assemble some documents for us—museum standards, that sort of thing."

Something to distract Wayne, Julie said to herself. And to Howard she said, "Good idea. There's lots of material on this. I'll pull together a packet."

"Excellent. Well, let me know if I can do anything more, Julie," he said, and abruptly ended the call.

After being away from the office, Julie had a pile of work on her desk: payments to authorize, correspondence to answer, research requests to pass along to Tabby Preston in the library, or to Dennis, purchase orders—the bits and pieces of administration that she found far from boring because they allowed you to mark your progress, concrete testimony to running the show. Today's pile was naturally higher than normal, and she decided to pace herself through the paperwork, attacking a third of it before taking a break to catch up with Dennis Sutherland on the past week's activities.

At the end of their conversation, he again inquired about her presentation at the panel discussion, and she again deferred, explaining that she really needed to work on the board agenda. She ate a yogurt at her desk and worked into the middle of the afternoon, first clearing the rest of the paperwork and then preparing the agenda. She assembled the documents on collections policy Howard had suggested, and had Mrs. Detweiller copy them for mailing.

"I'll drop them at the post office on my way," the secretary said, when at her usual departure time of four-thirty p.m., she gathered her purse and coat and exited without another word.

"Have a nice evening," Julie said to the secretary's retreating figure. And then, out loud, added to herself: "You, too." She laughed, but decided to take herself up on the offer. She was tired, stiff from sitting so long, but satisfied that she had cleared her desk and pulled together what she needed for the board meeting on Thursday. She considered rewarding herself with a run, but noticed that it was drizzling lightly, so opted to go home, pour a glass of wine, work on a crossword puzzle, and consider how to best reheat the chicken dinner Rich had sent home with her.

After she closed up and entered the code to activate the security system, she glanced to her right at the Ryland Inn across the Common and realized she had not gotten there to check on dates for the wedding. Well, tomorrow, she told herself.

"But you said you would do it today," Rich said plaintively when she mentioned to him on the phone that she hadn't gotten to the Inn.

"I know, but I just had so much to catch up on at the office that I didn't make it there today. I'll go tomorrow, Rich; I don't think it will make any difference." Silence from his end told Julie that was not the way Rich saw the situation. "I'm sorry," she said. "It's just not a big deal." Further silence. "Are you there, Rich?" He grunted. "Are you mad at me?" she asked.

Phone conversations, Julie knew, were a poor substitute for being together, but their commuting relationship made regular talk on the phone critical. Sometimes they duplicated face-to-face contact, but sometimes they turned awkward, a situation that could have been easily corrected if they'd been together in person and could use a gesture—a touch on the arm, a smile—to redirect the conversation. This was apparently one of those awkward times.

"Are you mad, Rich?" she asked again.

"Not exactly mad. Maybe disappointed. I guess sometimes I don't think this whole thing is as important to you as it is to me," he added slowly.

"This whole thing means the wedding—or us?" she asked.

"It's the same thing, isn't it?"

"No, it's not. There's us, our relationship, our marriage. Then there's the wedding, the event, the party we're putting on for our family and our friends. I'm glad we are, Rich; don't misunderstand. I want to have a really fun wedding. But that's not as important to me as you are." She knew her logic would catch him up.

"Of course," he said. "But there is at least a tiny bit of a connection between the wedding and our marriage, and sometimes I don't think you're quite ready. For either one."

Now he was mad, and she knew it. One side of her wanted to just end the conversation, to suggest they were headed into a hole and should stop before it got deeper, and to call back later. But another side, the self-confident and even aggressive side she knew was a part of her personality, wanted to persist, to settle this now.

"I think you've got that way wrong," she said. "I love you, Rich, and I want to marry you, but I don't want to feel like this is some sort of game, something we have to win by putting on a big show. We have to cool it, not let ourselves get into a competition to produce a big wedding just to . . . just to—"

"To prove we're normal?"

"What does that mean? Of course we're normal. I don't understand what you're saying here."

"What I'm saying is that we don't exactly have a normal relationship—living together like most couples we know. It's hard, Julie. It's been hard all along, but I thought everything would get straightened out, and we'd . . ."

"We'd have a normal relationship—me sitting around Orono, going to faculty dinner parties as Mrs. Rich O'Brian, helping you with your research. Is that what normal means to you?"

"This is going nowhere fast. I never, ever said that I expected you to be like your mother, or like mine. Give me a break, Julie. I think maybe we should just cool off and come back to this when we've both calmed down."

She hesitated before saying, "Look, I admit I'm upset. You jumped all over me because I didn't get to the Inn today, and I said I'm sorry and that I'll go first thing tomorrow. No, don't say anything. Just let me blow off steam for a minute. I'm probably just tired—it really was a long day, getting caught up. So let me go have that delicious chicken dinner you made, and I'll call back later. Okay?"

"I love you, Julie."

"And I love you, Rich. Later, okay?"

CHAPTER 6

Although the call to Rich just before she'd gone to bed had eased the tension between them, it hadn't fully cleared it. She realized when she awoke at six on Tuesday morning that her sleep had been shallower and less satisfying than she needed, but she was awake and the sun was out. Despite the autumn chill apparent when she got dressed, a long run seemed the right way to put last night's quarrel, and the edgy sleep it induced, behind her.

As she began her usual route from Harding House past the buildings of Ryland Historical Society, she couldn't help but contrast the scene with that of her most recent run, last week in Portland. No brick buildings, no Casco Bay views, no traffic to watch for at intersections, but the modest Victorian houses, arching trees vibrantly sporting their seasonal colors, open lots, and the gentle hill that took her down toward the river suited her just fine. She laughed to herself as she imagined the odd looks she would get from her trustees or Mrs. Detweiller if she told them how proprietary she felt about Ryland, and how settled she felt here. The paved stretch by the Androscoggin was Julie's favorite part of the route, not just because it was flat—though that had a lot to do with it—but because it offered glimpses through the trees and meadows of the nearby low hills and, at one spot where she always slowed, the looming Mahoosuc Range. The foliage was spectacular.

Coming up the hill toward the Common and the Inn that faced it opposite the historical society, Julie was tempted to stop in to check on available summer dates. She wanted to get that done so she could call Rich and tell him, putting that source of irritation behind them. But it was only seven a.m., and she doubted the manager would be in. So she continued past the Inn and up Granders Hill Road for a quarter of a mile or so, turning where

the steep stretch began. Just over an hour, she told herself with
satisfaction when she reentered the house—not too shabby for a
thirty-seven-year-old.

"Bastille Day!" Rich said when she phoned him later that
morning after her meeting with the manager of the Ryland Inn.

"You're right; how did I miss that?" she said. "I guess I was just
so glad they had an available weekend. So is July fourteenth okay
with you, despite the fact that it's Bastille Day?"

"Perfect. Overthrowing the monarchy, freeing the prisoners—
seems appropriate to me."

Julie was relieved by Rich's lighthearted response, glad to have
last night's unpleasantness buried by the concrete reality of a fixed
date for the wedding.

"Maybe we should have a French theme," she said. "You know,
for the food."

"'Let them eat cake'? Well, we'll have a wedding cake, so that
should do. Did you book it?"

"No, because I wanted to talk to you, and I'll have to call my
mother, but he's holding it for us. We just need to make a deposit
in a week or so."

"Is this just for the reception—or for everything?"

"I left it open, Rich. I'm still thinking the ceremony could be
here at the Society, but they're holding all the public areas at the Inn
for Friday through Sunday of that weekend. We can work it out."

"And your mom will have an idea about that?"

"Lots of them, I'm sure. Oh, Rich, can you hold on a minute?
What is it, Mrs. Detweiller?" she asked her secretary, who was
standing at the door between their offices.

"That Mr. Dumont again. He called when you were out, and
he's on the phone now. Says it's very important—sounds upset."

Julie told Rich she'd call him back later and took Dan
Dumont's call. Mrs. Detweiller had been right about his mood.

"I just can't believe this!" he said as soon as Julie came on the line. "This is the third one."

"Third what?"

"Map. Sorry; I'm really flustered. A third map is missing—a really old one, late eighteenth century."

"That's terrible, Dan. How did you find out?"

Dumont told the story, prompted by Julie's questions. She could tell that he was quite flustered, and she sympathized, but it took a while to get a clear picture. Once she had it, she asked, "Do you have any theories?"

Dumont's long pause alerted her that he was not being entirely open.

"Not really a theory," he finally said. "More like a worry."

"That someone at your place might be the one stealing the maps?"

"Not exactly. Maybe I better explain. After we talked at the Network meeting, I started asking around—you know, just casual questions to some of the other directors. I could tell a couple of other folks were also worried. Maybe they had stuff go missing, too; they didn't say, but there was a certain level of worry about this. And someone—I can't even remember who it was now, because I was trying to be very casual—someone said maybe we ought to establish a sort of statewide register of valuable items, with a blog or something, so we could all keep in touch in case anything happened."

Julie paused to consider it. A register of valuable items sounded to her like a wish list for thieves, a perfect way for someone to identify valuable items to steal. But she reserved the thought and asked Dumont if he could remember who had made the suggestion.

"I'll think about it, but right now I'm not sure. Might have been Hartshorn. Or maybe that new guy at Bath. Anyway, it seemed to me a good idea, but I didn't do anything. I figured it was something we could take up at a future Network meeting. I didn't realize I was going to have another missing map!"

"Have you told your board?" Julie asked, remembering her admonition to Dumont last week not to keep the missing items a secret.

"I told my board chair, as soon as I discovered the new one, and then I explained about the others. That was good advice, Julie; I really should have kept her informed. She's very supportive. She's going to handle the rest of the board, and I reported it to the police."

"That's good. They might come up with something fast. In the meantime, can we go back to this idea of a register?"

Dumont still couldn't remember who had suggested it, and he didn't seem as troubled as Julie did that such a listing could become a to-steal list. Still, Julie sensed that Dumont was suspicious—about something or someone—and if not the register itself, then perhaps the person responsible for the thefts.

She pressed him. "Can you think of anyone at your museum who might have taken them?"

"Not necessarily at the museum."

"Someone around town, then?"

"Farmington's a small place, but because of the university, it draws a lot of people coming and going—students, of course, but their friends and families and, well, people who want to be near college students."

"To sell drugs?"

"Probably—or to steal things in the dorms. I really don't know, but I'm sure the police will look into that. You'd have to know the value of maps, know which ones are worth something and which aren't."

"So you think professionals were involved?"

"Professional thieves?"

Julie paused. Of course, she said to herself, she meant thieves. But what other kind of professional was Dumont thinking about? So she said, "Well, people who know about values—could be in the business one way or another."

"The museum business?" Dumont asked, with what Julie sensed was caution.

"On one side or another! Look, Dan, do you think someone from another museum could have done this?"

"It's worth thinking about, isn't it? I have to run now, Julie. A police officer just arrived, and I need to talk to her."

Dumont hadn't said anything directly, but Julie felt he had been close to doing so, and she regretted that the appearance of the officer had ended their conversation. She asked him to call her if he had any further ideas.

There wasn't anything concrete she could put her fingers on, but she had a sense that Dumont did indeed have some thoughts, but was reluctant to share them—at least, for now. So, there was no more for her to do on that front. It was time for her to get back to work, reading and rereading the documents on collections policies and de-accessioning she had assembled for Thursday's board meeting. She laughed when she realized that Dumont had experienced a kind of de-accessioning, trying to concentrate on the other meaning of that term: to sell or give items from a collection when they were redundant, or of low quality, or somehow didn't fit the museum's mission. The more she read, the more complicated she realized the topic was—and how contentious it would likely be at the board meeting, since Wayne Reiter was an articulate and dogged person.

As she thought about him, she remembered the advice her old mentor from graduate school had given her about how to deal with strong-minded trustees: get to them before public discussion, make them feel you especially valued their views, try to get them on your side—or at least, think you're on theirs. Why not, she thought as she dialed Wayne Reiter.

"Just looking at the documents you sent," Reiter said. "Very helpful. I always like to get the big picture, see how things fit together." Before Julie could respond, he added, "It seems to me these museum associations are like an old aunt of mine who doesn't believe in getting rid of anything. Ever."

"I wouldn't go that far. The guidelines allow for de-accessioning as long as—"

"As long as more stuff replaces it," Reiter finished her sentence with his own construction. "The outcome's the same, and it's outcomes I focus on, Julie. Just my business background."

Wayne Reiter's purported "business background" was the cudgel with which he beat Julie and the trustees routinely, but in this case, she decided to turn it back on him.

"You're exactly right," she said. "The American Association of Museums forces us all to focus on outcomes. That's really the purpose of the guidelines—to make sure museums keep their eye on achieving their goals. Building and protecting, and, when necessary, pruning the collection, is central to what we do in programs and exhibits."

"Well, of course," he interrupted, "but my point is . . ."

He then proceeded to bang away on the need to "clean up" Ryland Historical Society's collection. Julie was well aware that Reiter had no idea at all about the collection, having found excuses not to take the tour she gave as part of the orientation for new trustees. Ignorance, she had come to understand, was no bar to his pronouncement of truths, a pattern that made her question, not for the first time, the value of a Harvard MBA.

When his lecture ended, Julie said that he had certainly raised some interesting points, and that the full board would no doubt benefit from what he had to contribute to the discussion at the upcoming meeting. Then, without thinking, just to change the topic, Julie abruptly asked if Wayne Reiter knew anything about theft.

"Stealing?" he asked.

"Yes, but not like teenagers shoplifting CDs or something. I mean organized theft. I gave this talk last week to our state association about museum security, and it just struck me afterwards that there must be some research on systematic thefts in the field—you know, like gangs that target valuable items and sell them through fences or something. It's really a business, or it might be, and I was wondering if you were aware of any literature on the subject. I should have talked to you before, but . . ."

Without having planned it, Julie realized that she had hit on a perfect way to deflect Wayne Reiter from his obsession with collections and de-accessioning—or perhaps to redefine what de-accessioning meant. She could sense from the brief silence that greeted her question—silence rarely being Reiter's mode—that she had hooked him.

"Very interesting," he responded. "Of course, one could approach museum thefts as a systematic business: willing agents, transaction systems, problems of valuation, organizational patterns, barriers to entry, and so forth. Indeed. Well, let me look into that. I can do a bit of research online and perhaps contact a few of my old colleagues at the B-school. I think you may be on to something. I'll let you know."

As she replaced the receiver, Julie smiled and congratulated herself. Although she hadn't intended to, and still didn't quite know how she'd managed it, she had achieved two "outcomes," as the good professor surely would have observed: She had deflected Reiter from his obsession, at least for now, and she had put him on to some research that might help her meet her promise to advise Dan Dumont on the map thefts. She reminded herself that she really needed to get back to Betsey to arrange a time to visit Three Rivers Museum. Who knows, she thought, as she let her mind run—maybe Wayne Reiter would actually learn something that would help her, at least with another talk or paper, if not in solving the two thefts her colleagues had put before her.

"Lunch?" Dennis Sutherland said from where he stood at the door to Julie's office. "Mrs. Detweiller said you were on the phone when I came by earlier to ask. She's gone now, and I didn't hear you talking. Just wondered if you'd like to have lunch at the Inn?"

Julie thought of the yogurt and fruit she had brought from home and put in the small refrigerator near the coffee machine— same as her lunch the day before.

"Why not?" she said.

CHAPTER 7

When she first took the job of director at the Ryland Historical Society, Julie had been anxious about board meetings. Nothing in her formal training as a museum specialist, or any direct experience, had prepared her for them. As a result, she had overprepared, spending far too much time reviewing the agenda, practicing what she would say, and trying to anticipate questions and the direction of the discussion.

Now, with four years of board meetings behind her, Julie told herself she could relax about them. Nevertheless, as she sat in her office early Thursday morning, she found herself once more taking notes on her yellow pad, editing them to get the right words to use in response to the comments and questions she guessed her trustees would raise. Except for her, Swanson House was empty, Mrs. Detweiller not due for another half-hour, so when the phone rang, Julie instinctively reached for it—and then checked herself. We're not officially open till nine, she thought; if it's important, the caller can leave a message.

There was a brief pause after the fourth ring, but the tape giving the hours and inviting the caller to leave a message didn't come on, so Julie assumed the person would call later. When Mrs. Detweiller arrived shortly thereafter, Julie asked her to hold all calls except any from Rich, so she could concentrate on preparing for the board meeting.

"It's quite unusual," Mrs. Detweiller said—not in response to Julie's instruction about the phone, but from her own thoughts, which rarely overlapped with Julie's. "We've never had a luncheon meeting before," the secretary continued.

"The board wanted to try something different," Julie said. "It was actually Howard's idea to meet from eleven to two, with lunch. I think it'll work out fine."

"Well, that remains to be seen. I'll need to go over to the Center and organize the lunch. So much could go wrong."

Especially if you want it to, Julie thought to herself as Mrs. Detweiller left.

The Center to which she was bound was the Mary Ellen and Daniel Swanson Center, the addition built just under two years ago. Swanson House, the site of administrative offices and the Society's library and archives, had been named earlier for the same family, creating confusion among both staff and visitors, the former of whom settled the matter by calling the new building simply the Center, and this, Swanson, or sometimes Swanson House.

In addition to climate-controlled storage, the Center also included a classroom that was set up with a conference table and chairs for board meetings. It had a small kitchenette that could be used as a staging area for events like today's lunch. Julie had been surprised when Howard Townsend, the board chair rarely given to new ways of doing things, suggested meeting in the middle of the day rather than at the long-standing time of four p.m., and her surprise turned nearly to shock when he had added that they could serve a light lunch in the middle of the meeting. "Have to shake things up now and then," he had said when he proposed the idea.

Julie had later guessed that the plan resulted from the advancing age of Howard and several other trustees and their consequent desire not to drive after dark. Whatever the reason, the idea appealed to her, and though it took a bit of work to guide Mrs. Detweiller through the business of ordering lunch from a local restaurant, Julie had meant it when she told her secretary she was sure it would work out. If, of course, Mrs. Detweiller didn't sabotage the arrangements.

"It's almost ten-thirty," the secretary said to Julie later as she stood at the open door between their offices. "You asked me to remind you," she continued. "And you had a call earlier, but you didn't want to be interrupted. Mr. Hartshorn. I told him you were in a meeting, which of course wasn't really true. He asked you to call back when you finished."

"Thanks, Mrs. Detweiller. I'll call after the meeting."

Although she had time, Julie felt no urgency to return Hartshorn's call, which she assumed was a belated thank-you for her talk at the Network meeting. Instead, she gathered her papers and walked to the Swanson Center to take a final look before the meeting. Outside the building, she stopped to admire it—her first real project. Simple and understated in the New England way that she had come to like so much, the new wing carried out the lines of the adjacent Ting House, making a neat closure to the space that formed the rear of the historical society's campus. If you didn't know, you'd think it was original to the site, an effect the board's planning committee had worked hard to achieve.

"Seems to be holding up," a voice said from behind her.

Julie turned to face Dalton Scott, the architect turned bed-and-breakfast owner who had chaired that very committee.

"That's exactly what I was thinking, Dalton. What a coincidence you appeared just now!"

"Not really a coincidence. We do have a board meeting, don't we?"

"Of course. I just meant that I was looking at the Swanson Center and remembering all those planning meetings with poor Mary Ellen, and how perfectly you handled her and kept us on track. It seems so long ago now, doesn't it?"

"And still strange to think of Mary Ellen," Scott added.

"Yes." Julie paused, recalling all too vividly Mary Ellen Swanson's bloodied body on this very site, under the tent set up for the ground-breaking. "Well, I guess it's silly to say so, but I think Mary Ellen would be very pleased with the result."

"It's working out okay. How about the storage area?"

"It's great, and adding a classroom that we could use for meetings was really clever of you."

"Was that my idea?"

"Don't be so modest, Dalton. This couldn't have happened, or turned out so well, without you."

"Always happy to oblige," he said, taking a mock bow.

"Admiring your handiwork, Dalton?" a tall and rangy man said as he walked toward them.

"I'd say it's as much yours as anyone's, Howard," Scott said. "You led us through the whole project as chairman of the board."

"And the Swanson money didn't hurt, did it?" Townsend said with a grin, then added what had become an automatic tag to mark the murder of the building's principal donor: "Poor Mary Ellen." With only the slightest pause, he continued, "Well, we should enter the Mary Ellen and Daniel Swanson Center and commence our meeting. Are the others here, Julie?"

49

"I just got here," she replied. "I was going to check things out, but we can do that together."

Julie, Howard Townsend, and Dalton Scott were alone when they got to the meeting room, but within minutes the rest of the board appeared. It was a small board—only seven trustees—but Julie actually thought of it as three boards. One consisted of Howard Townsend and Clif Holdsworth, both in their late seventies, both very much Ryland old-timers, which meant not just that they were natives, but that their parents and grandparents and ancestors, heaven only knows how far back, had also been born there. Howard chaired the board, and Clif, owner of the hardware store that bore his name, served as treasurer.

Julie labeled a second group "the young professionals," with the proviso that in their case, young was a relative term, since she guessed they were in their late forties or early fifties. Loretta Cummings, principal of Ryland High School, was energetic, irreverent, and full of good ideas for expanding the reach of the historical society to schoolchildren and tourists, an audience whose existence the old-timers recognized, but whose actual presence in the buildings they found disturbing.

Dalton Scott was a special favorite of Julie's in this group. He described himself as a recovering architect who gave up his practice, and what Julie assumed was an unsuccessful marriage in Boston, to buy, renovate, and run a charming bed-and-breakfast in Ryland called the Black Crow Inn. His live-in companion, Nickie Bennett, was a smart and athletic young woman who ran a ski shop on the road to Ryland Skiway. Rich and Julie had enjoyed many social and recreational times with Dalton and Nickie. Henry LaBelle, secretary and clerk of the board, had a solo legal practice in Ryland and a large brood of children he regularly complained about, while clearly adoring them and his role as father.

Then there were what Julie called "the newbies," because both had joined the board since Julie had become director: Wayne Reiter, the retired business professor, and Ann Gibbons, a real estate broker about whom Julie hadn't yet gotten a clear picture. Ann was in her 40s, always well dressed, and like other members of her profession, inexhaustibly positive and cheerful, certain that home prices could only go up, that hard work and long hours would be handsomely rewarded, and that tomorrow would be better than today, though easily bested by the next day.

As she mentally reviewed the characteristics of her trustees, they appeared and took their accustomed places around the table. Howard Townsend, following his inevitable custom, checked his watch, brought his fist down on the table, and announced in formal and sonorous tones the commencement of the regular quarterly meeting of the Ryland Historical Society Board of Trustees. "No need to declare a quorum," he then said, "since we have perfect attendance."

"Drawn by lunch, Howard," Loretta said impishly. "Feed them and they will come."

Howard smiled. "You underestimate us, Loretta. Duty brings us here, and I'm delighted that you're all present today. I believe we have a solid agenda to accomplish, and we'll try to do that before we eat. Minutes of our last meeting were circulated. Are there any questions or amendments? If not," he said, before anyone could consult the minutes in the pile of papers before them, "I'll accept a motion for approval." The motion was duly made, seconded, and approved. Townsend continued: "Clif, your report is next, I believe."

Belief, Julie thought, has nothing to do with it. Clif Holdsworth's treasurer's report always followed consideration of the minutes. It was just as likely to be at another spot on the agenda as a snowstorm on the Fourth of July. Holdsworth picked up several pages, squared them carefully, glanced through each silently, and then said, "Those of you who have served on the board over the years will know that the first page of my report contains a summary of financial activity for the quarter. You have that right there," he said to Ann Gibbons, who was paging through the pile of papers in front of her. "Perhaps Professor Reiter may find my little accounting not up to his high standards, but I believe our longer-serving colleagues have come to consider it useful."

"Looks fine to me," Reiter said,.

"Good, good," Holdsworth resumed. "Now, I wish I could say the reality of our situation was as clear as the way in which I've presented it here."

Although hardly a numbers person, Julie understood the finances of the Society well enough to know they were solid, helped by growing visitorship, attendance at programs, and the several successful grant proposals she had written. But she also understood that Clif Holdsworth had the instinctive talent to spot an impending thunderstorm on any sunny day.

"It seems to me we're in solid shape," Wayne Reiter said. "I've sat on a few boards in my time, and I've never seen a better balance sheet or income statement. What's the problem, Clif?"

"I didn't say we had a problem, exactly," the treasurer responded. "I just want to add a note of caution here. Our current situation seems reasonably secure, I admit, but as treasurer I'm obliged to look into the future, and I don't want anyone to think I'm wearing rose-colored glasses as I do so."

Heaven forbid! Julie thought. An optimistic Clif Townsend—that was indeed unthinkable.

"And I'm sure we all appreciate your realism, Clif," Townsend said. "Now, would you like to review any of these details for us?"

Holdsworth was quite happy to do so, in the line-by-line pattern he favored. As she glanced around the room, Julie noticed the fog spreading over the group. Only Wayne Reiter seemed to be following along as Clif recited the numbers.

"Very good, Clif," Townsend finally said to end their agony. "As always, you've given us a clear picture of what appears to me a very solid financial situation, though of course we also appreciate your caution about the future. Would anyone care to offer a motion here?"

Julie tried not to look at Henry LaBelle, because she knew he would do what he always did at this moment: move to approve the treasurer's report. And then, just as inevitably, Holdsworth would say that a motion to accept the report was really more in order than one to approve it, the distinction between the two actions as clear to Holdsworth as it was irrelevant to everyone else. The dance proceeded according to custom, LaBelle graciously acknowledging his error and accepting Holdsworth's correction, then making the motion for acceptance, which found a quick second and passed unanimously. Julie, like the others, experienced a palpable sense of relief as this particular form of torture ended and the real business of the meeting could begin.

"Now, our principal work today concerns collections policies, I believe," Townsend announced. "If there are no objections, I propose we hear Julie's overview on this matter and then proceed to a working luncheon. Let's hear from our director, bring our food to the table, and have our discussion as we eat."

CHAPTER 8

It had actually gone very well, Julie thought, congratulating herself as she walked back to her office a little after two-thirty p.m. She had lingered after the formal close of the meeting to chat with the trustees and make sure that no one had any concerns that had gone unspoken during the wide-ranging discussion about the collections. Although Reiter had made his usual case about the need to clean up the holdings, the materials Julie had sent ahead of the meeting seemed to have had a good effect in moderating the passion with which he had previously attacked the status quo.

Julie was pleased with the overall thoughtfulness of the discussion, and especially with the formal outcome: the decision to appoint a small working group to review the current policy based on a review of best practices in the field. Loretta Cummings had agreed to lead the group, and besides Julie, it also included Reiter and Ann Gibbons. Reiter was an obvious choice, and Julie was happy to have him contained within a group she felt confident Cummings would manage skillfully. Gibbons was still an unknown to Julie, but her presence on the committee would give her the chance to get to know the woman better. With two upbeat members, Cummings and Gibbons, the group had a good chance of overwhelming Reiter's tendency to find fault. In all, it had been a positive discussion with a good result, and Julie was pleased with the meeting, as tiring as all such events were to her as the person responsible to the board.

"He called again," Mrs. Detweiller announced when Julie opened the door to the office. Waiting for a further word on the caller's identity, Julie paused before following her secretary's practice of speaking without context or clue.

"We had a very good meeting," she said. "The lunch worked perfectly, and Howard asked me to tell you how pleased everyone was. Thank you for handling that, Mrs. Detweiller."

"Well, I think it all depends on getting the right people, don't you?"

That it had been Julie who had suggested which restaurant to call on for the catering seemed lost on the secretary now.

"They do a nice dinner there," she continued, "so I assumed they could handle lunch for us."

This was almost word for word what Julie had said when she'd suggested the restaurant to Mrs. Detweiller a few weeks ago, but she decided to let it go, saying, "You were certainly right about that. Who was it that called, by the way?"

"Mr. Hartshorn. You remember he called this morning. I told him you were in a meeting till two o'clock, and it wasn't five past when he phoned again. Very impatient. I said the meeting was still going on, but that you'd call him as soon as you could."

Talking to James Hartshorn, even if simply to hear his thanks for her talk, didn't appeal to Julie as an ideal way to conclude what she viewed as a very successful day. So she spent the rest of the afternoon filing papers from the meeting, taking notes on follow-up actions, and drafting a tentative schedule for the collections group, per Loretta Cummings's request.

When Mrs. Detweiller put her head into the room to announce she was leaving for the day, Julie was surprised that these tasks had consumed so much time. She glanced again at the WHILE YOU WERE OUT note on her desk with Hartshorn's message: "Please call him. Urgent. Use home number after five p.m." Well, Julie thought, it wasn't quite five, and she could probably still reach him at his office at Down East Historical Society, but somehow the "Urgent" status seemed to her to be just the man's way of drawing attention to himself. Tomorrow, she thought, as she cleared her desk and headed for the door at, for her, the unheard-of early hour of four-forty p.m.

⁓⁓

"Sorry to call you at home," James Hartshorn said, interrupting her after-dinner crossword puzzle. Before she could respond, he said, "It's a terrible tragedy, and I wasn't sure if you'd heard."

"Heard what?"

"Dan Dumont. He's dead."

"Dead?!" she practically screamed. "When . . . how . . . what happened?"

"Yesterday. Or at least they found his body yesterday. I guess they don't know when he died, or exactly how it happened. A hunting accident, I gather. I've been trying to reach all the folks in the Network to let them know before they see it in the paper. I tried you first, this morning, but your secretary said you were in an all-day board meeting or something. I'm sorry if I shocked you, but I know you were working with Dan on something, and didn't know if perhaps you might have any information."

"None at all. This is a complete shock." Julie carried the phone with her from the living room and sat down at the kitchen table to collect herself. "How did you find out?"

"I phoned Dan yesterday afternoon to talk about some Network business, and his secretary said he was out of the office for the day. So I left a message, and then last night I got a call from the State Police. Apparently they were trying to figure out Dan's schedule yesterday, people he might have talked to, whatever. They saw that I had phoned, so they called me, and that's how I found out."

"What did they tell you? A hunting accident, did you say?"

"When he said Dan was dead, I of course asked when, and what happened, but all he said was that they were investigating, and that they assumed it was a hunting accident."

"I didn't know he was a hunter."

"I don't know if we ever talked about that. Lots of people in rural Maine hunt. Farmington's in the sticks, so I'm not surprised."

"Ryland's in the sticks, too, so I know that hunting season doesn't start till the end of the month. So . . ."

"That's deer hunting, though, right? There are other kinds."

"I guess. Anyway, I'm still surprised Dan hunts. Hunted. God, this is so terrible. I still can't believe it."

"I agree. Sorry to be the bearer of bad news, but like I said, I knew you and Dan were working on something, so I wanted to get in touch with you right away to see if you knew anything, or if you didn't, then to let you know what happened."

"Thanks. I appreciate that. I just have to get my head around this." She paused to calm herself and then said, "Did Dan tell you what we were working on?"

"Not exactly. I think I heard from someone last week at the meeting that the two of you had a project together or something."

Julie wasn't inclined to reveal the nature of their conversations, as it really wasn't Hartshorn's business that Dan's museum had been robbed. But she did wonder if he might know about it, since Dan might have consulted him, too.

"Actually, Dan asked for some advice on a problem he was having," she said, to lure him out.

"What kind of problem?"

"Dan was keeping it under wraps. I'm not sure—"

"You don't need to say anything else. If it was confidential, that's between you and Dan."

"Not anymore," Julie said, letting the words sink in. "But I still don't think I should talk about it until we get more information about what happened."

"I see. That's fine. Well, I'll let you go, Julie, and again, let me say how sorry I am to bring you such bad news."

The call ended, and Julie got up and walked to the living room, then back to the kitchen, then into the living room again. It didn't make any sense, but choosing and following a course of action seemed like a way to gain some control over the situation.

Dan Dumont wasn't really a friend, but he was a professional colleague, someone she had warm feelings for, obviously reciprocated, since he'd trusted her enough to confide in her about the thefts and ask for her help. She hadn't meant to sound so mysterious to James Hartshorn. She knew this could backfire, as he was the kind of person who would poke around to find out more about the problem Dan had discussed with her. She just didn't think it would be fair to Dan to tell others when he had spoken to her in confidence.

Back in the kitchen, headed again for the living room, Julie checked the clock and saw that it was not quite time for Rich's usual call. But that didn't matter; talking to him would be better than pacing. She was sure their quarrel was behind them, and she needed to hear his voice.

"I was just getting ready to call," he said when he answered. "But I'm glad you did. I'm so happy about the plans, Julie, and I just wanted to say how sorry I am about being such an ass the other night. I hope—"

But she stopped him and quickly told him about Dumont.

"That's horrible," he said. "You read about hunting accidents all the time around here, but this was someone you actually knew—and liked. I'm really sorry, Julie. Is there going to be a service or something? Do you want me to come?"

She explained that she didn't know any more than Hartshorn had told her, which didn't include funeral plans. "You know, I don't have any idea if he has a family. He never talked about a wife or kids or anything, but I really didn't know him all that well. I guess I can call his museum in the morning and see what's happening. There may have to be an autopsy, and that would delay things. It's really just shitty, Rich. I had to talk to you."

But she found it was not talking but listening she needed. She really had no more to say about Dan's death, and what she wanted was to hear Rich's calm voice, an influence on her mood not unlike her earlier pacing. She brought the subject back to their wedding plans, then encouraged him to talk about his classes, and when that came to a slow end, she answered his questions about that day's board meeting. There was nothing specific she wanted to know or say; it was the call itself that mattered, the coming together, even if electronically. And it worked. After half an hour, she knew she would be able to sleep that night without thinking about Dan Dumont. And Rich was coming tomorrow for the weekend!

Julie poured herself a glass of wine, sat at the kitchen table to once again tackle the crossword, and told herself that in fifteen minutes she would be ready for that deep sleep earned by a successful board meeting. She hoped that concentrating on the mundane would keep at bay the thoughts about Dan's death that threatened to overwhelm her. It didn't work; she was still on edge when the phone rang again, surprising her, at nine-thirty p.m.

"Dr. Williamson? I hope I'm not calling too late."

The voice was so familiar that Julie had to tell herself it couldn't be Mike Barlow, seeing as he'd left Ryland almost a year ago. She had heard his voice many times during the course of two years—and two murder investigations—so it didn't seem likely she could confuse it with someone else's.

"Mike Barlow," he said.

"Of course! I thought I recognized your voice, but it's been so long."

"Almost a year to the day," he said. "How have you been?"

"Fine. And you? How's the job?"

"Better on some days than others, but that goes with the territory. Being in a big outfit like the State Police is a lot different from being chief of police in Ryland, but it's working out. We'll see how it goes. Maybe you can guess that I'm calling today in my new capacity."

"Detective lieutenant, isn't it?"

"Let me just check the badge. Yeah, that's what it says."

"What's up, Mike?"

"Well, it's sort of strange, but I'm looking into another death involving a historical society."

"Dan Dumont?"

"I thought Ryland was a small place; guess I should have realized that Maine's the same."

Julie explained about James Hartshorn's call.

"And you were working with him, I gather. That's what Mr. Hartshorn told me today, and that's why I'm calling."

"What happened, Mike?"

"I can't really go into the details, Julie—guess you know that more than most people! He was found in the woods near Farmington. We have to do an autopsy, but it's pretty clear he died of a gunshot wound."

"A hunting accident—that's what Hartshorn said."

"To be determined. I'd like to ask you a few questions, but I know it's late. I'm based in Augusta now, but I'm up here in Farmington tonight, and thought I could swing over to Ryland in the morning. Not exactly on the way back, but I'd really like to talk to you about Mr. Dumont. Think you could work me into your schedule tomorrow? Maybe lunch at The Greek?"

"Like old times. Sure, I can meet you there at noon, if that's okay."

He agreed, said good night, and hung up.

Sleep, Julie knew, wasn't going to be quite so easy now. Mike Barlow's sudden reappearance in her life brought back a flood of memories, starting with this very house, where Julie had found Worth Harding's body in the front parlor—what, in defiance of the former owner, she now called the living room, to banish the memories.

Just a few more minutes on the puzzle, she told herself. Maybe she'd finish it, in an effort to tire herself out. Going back to the living room on her way upstairs didn't appeal to her at all now.

CHAPTER 9

It was raining lightly when Julie awoke at six on Friday morning. The rain more than the light sleep made her decide to forgo a run. With the prospect of a diner lunch ahead, she decided to limit breakfast to toast and juice. Even after a long shower and some indecision about how to dress, she saw it was just seven-thirty as she passed through the kitchen toward the back door. She stopped when she saw the rain was now heavy, and went in search of an umbrella.

She liked to get to her office early to take advantage of the quiet, but today was early even for her. She didn't mind, though, since now she would have time to review what she knew about Dan Dumont, away from the house and the thoughts it evoked of the Harding murder. Talking with Mike Barlow about Dan didn't trouble her, since it was obvious her agreement to keep the matter of the thefts to herself no longer held.

She pulled a file folder from her desk drawer and leafed through the notes she had made after their talk in Portland. At eight-thirty, she was interrupted by Dennis Sutherland.

"Hard to beat the boss in," he said pleasantly from where he stood at the door.

Julie laughed and said, "Especially when the boss lives two doors away. How are you, Dennis?"

"Fine, despite the weather—but then I guess after the gorgeous stretch we've had, it's time to pay the piper. Am I disturbing you?"

"No, just looking over some stuff. I planned to catch up with you sometime this morning to let you know how the board meeting went yesterday. If you have time, we can talk now."

"As long as it's okay with you. You look like you were working on something pretty engaging."

"More troubling than engaging, I'm afraid. Maybe I should tell you about it first; then we can discuss the meeting." Julie told Dennis about Dumont's death and her talk with Mike Barlow.

When Mrs. Detweiller arrived at her accustomed hour, they exchanged brief greetings before she closed the door to Julie's office.

"So you think there's some connection?" Dennis said. "Between the thefts and his death?"

"I don't have any reason to, but I'm sure that's something Mike Barlow will ask. He knows the way my mind works! You weren't here when . . . when the other things happened, but Mike and I got pretty close then, almost like partners on the case."

"Oh, I know Mike. We overlapped a couple of years in school, and then he went off to the army or whatever. I heard he ended up back here as chief of police, but he was gone before I returned."

"That's right. Last fall. In fact, he mentioned last night that it's been just about a year since he left. It seems longer."

"And he's a state cop now, right?"

"Detective lieutenant. Funny, he always used to say he wasn't much of an investigator, but I guess the State Police realized he was just being modest, because they worked really hard to recruit him. He was reluctant to leave Ryland, but it was a good step for him. I think he needed to get into a bigger world."

"Unlike those of us trying to get into a smaller one."

"Right. Well, that's all I know about Dan and the maps. Thought I should mention it to you, but please keep it to yourself. Dan had asked me not to tell anyone else, but of course, now that he's . . . now that he's dead . . . I guess that no longer holds. Still, the business about the missing maps isn't public knowledge."

"Mum's the word with me, boss. So, about the board meeting?"

After Julie brought her assistant director up-to-date on the outcome of the meeting and the plan to review the collections issue, she busied herself with paperwork. Checking purchase orders, signing checks, scheduling school visits and the like were all part of the daily routine that she had come to find useful as a means of satisfying herself that she was doing the job the trustees had hired her for. This was the smallest, least significant part of the job, but doing these tasks was like doing a crossword puzzle: You knew you had achieved something when you were done, however trivial.

⌘

When she had first come to Ryland, Julie had been mystified when people referred to The Greek. Mike Barlow had been the one to explain: In Barlow's youth, the diner just north of Ryland had been run by a Greek family. Both ownership and name had changed many times since, but old Ryland people still called it The Greek.

As she pulled into its parking lot just before noon, Julie laughed to realize she wasn't even sure of its current name. But she knew the owner, Bert, and would have been prepared to guess it was named for him. It was, she saw when she glanced at the neon sign to the left of the front door. The robin's-egg-blue Ford she parked beside had no seal on the door, no lettering, and no roof bar for lights, but anyone who had driven in Maine for more than a few weeks would recognize it as a State Police vehicle. Typical, Julie said to herself, that Mike would be early.

He was leaning over the counter, talking with Bert. A blue blazer and gray slacks had replaced the khaki uniform he'd worn as Ryland's chief of police, but otherwise Mike looked just as he always had—trim and sinewy rather than imposing, a man you immediately sensed you could trust, whether to offer good advice or fight off an attacker.

"Julie!" he said, turning to her. "It's great to see you. I could pick you out of a lineup any day!"

"You, too," she said, leaning toward him, not sure if a hug was appropriate, but readying herself for one in case he did. He didn't. Instead, he gripped her hand and shook it vigorously, the pat he gave her arm signaling the friendship that had grown around their professional relationship.

"Let's take a table back there—that okay, Bert?" Barlow asked.

"Wherever you like, Chief. Good to see you, Dr. Williamson," the proprietor added.

"Hard to know what to order," Barlow said after they seated themselves at a table near the restroom in the back, a choice Julie realized was deliberate to give them privacy for the interview. "For lunch, I mean," he added. "Seems like you and I specialized in breakfasts here in the past."

Julie laughed. She found Mike Barlow a very easy person to be with, and realized how much she'd missed him as a character in the rich life of the town. His replacement as chief of police, a young man new to Ryland, seemed capable, but Julie had spoken to him only a few times, and would have been hard-pressed even to come up with his name. But then, she hadn't worked with him yet on a crime—and planned to keep it that way.

Some catching up was in order. When she told him of her impending marriage, Barlow was effusive in his congratulations, and when he described his life in Augusta—and the new girlfriend who seemed to be at its center—Julie was equally congratulatory. She would have liked to continue the conversation in this vein, but when their sandwiches arrived, she reluctantly gave him the opening to change the topic.

"It's really terrible about Dan Dumont," she said. "I don't know what I can tell you—I really knew him only as a colleague. Funny, but I don't even know if he was married."

"No. Divorced before he came to Farmington. I talked to his ex, down in Massachusetts. She was upset, but she said they hadn't been in touch in years. She's remarried, has a kid."

"Will there be a funeral or memorial service?"

"That's up to his parents. They're retired and living in Florida, so I had to talk to them on the phone, which is one hell of a way to break the news. My sense was they're pretty old and not quite with it, but they told us he has a sister still in Maine. One of our guys met with her, and she said she'd handle things for the family. Anyway, it'll be a while, because we have to do an autopsy."

"I was going to call the historical society there today to see if anything is being planned, but I suppose I should wait."

"Up to you. So, what did you know about him, Julie?"

She explained about meeting Dumont when she'd first come to Maine and gotten involved in the Network, and then accepting his invitation to visit Mountain Valley Historical Society.

"So we've been professional colleagues for a few years, but it was only last week that I really had a chance to talk with him much." She couldn't withhold the information about the maps now, and Barlow seized on it.

"How many?" he asked.

"When we talked last week, he said two maps had disappeared—nineteenth-century maps of Franklin County. But he called me on Tuesday to say a third one was missing, an older one, probably more valuable."

Barlow was silent for a moment, fixing Julie with a look she interpreted as meaning We've been here before, haven't we?

"Mind if I take a few notes?" he asked as he opened the leather folio he had put on an empty chair at their table. "You know me—can't remember anything if I don't write it down. You happen to remember the dates?"

Because she had reviewed her notes earlier, Julie said, "The first two maps were from 1857 and 1883. But he just said late eighteenth century for the third one."

"Okay. I can check that out. Did others know, at his museum?"

"I asked him that last week, and he hadn't told anyone then. You know how it is, Mike; you don't want to raise an alarm until you're sure. People don't like to think that stuff can go missing at a historical society."

"I do remember something about that," he said, and laughed.

"But I urged him to talk to his board about it, and when he called on Tuesday he said he had told the chair about all three missing maps. She was very supportive, and agreed to let the rest of the board know. He also reported it to the police; in fact, he had to break off our call because he said a cop had just arrived."

"I'll check on that, too. It was probably a theft report to the locals on behalf of the museum, so it might take a bit for them to connect it to Dumont. And Mrs. Marshall is the board chair. I haven't talked to her yet—another thing on my to-do list. You have any sense of the value of these maps?"

"No, but old maps always fetch good prices; I can check if you want me to. I guess I'm confused. You think Dan's death wasn't an accident, and that it had something to do with these missing maps?"

"Did I say that?" he asked, looking around as if appealing to an unseen audience.

"Not in so many words, but . . ."

"You have a tendency to connect missing items and murders. Like I said, we've been there before. It's pretty weird, really."

"Okay, Mike, you can't get away with that! You know more than you're telling me. I know you can't say anything right now, but my hunch is you think Dan was murdered. I have to admit, I was surprised when Hartshorn said it was a hunting accident, because Dan didn't seem like a hunter to me."

"Come on, Julie. You've said you didn't know much about him—didn't know he had been married, for example. And don't forget that a lot of people who grow up in Maine go hunting. That's not something people from away recognize."

Julie smiled even though she felt the sting of Mike's description of her.

"True," she admitted. "Well, you won't know for sure till the autopsy. When is it being done?"

"Just about now," he said, consulting his watch. "I'm expecting a call soon. I should probably get going. You've been real helpful, as always, and I'm very happy for you and Rich. When did you say the wedding is?"

Julie told him.

"Should be a good time for it. Well, let's keep in touch." He reached for the bill, saying it was a business expense. "Have to treat my sources well," he said.

As they walked to the front counter to pay, a shrill buzz from inside Mike's pocket stopped him. He withdrew his phone and identified himself. Julie moved ahead toward the counter to give him privacy, but she was close enough to hear him say, "Right. Thanks. Not surprised, but good to have it confirmed. I was heading to Augusta, but I think I'd better go back to Farmington now. Just email it. Thanks again."

At the counter, she looked at him to see if he would tell her about the call.

"Can't say anymore now, Julie, but I'll get back to you. You're going to be in Ryland this weekend?"

Julie said Rich was coming this afternoon and they would be home.

"I'm sure you'll hear it on the news, but I'll try to give you a ring anyway after it's public. Thanks again, Julie; it was great to see you. Ryland's still my favorite place."

With those words, he walked quickly through the door and down the steps and slipped behind the wheel of his car before she could respond.

As she opened the door to hers, she took a deep breath and said out loud: "So Dan was murdered."

CHAPTER 10

Although Julie felt grateful to Rich for introducing her to running, hiking was the activity she was most happy to have discovered through him. You could run anywhere, but the mountains around Ryland offered so many interesting trails with spectacular views that Julie was especially happy Rich had insisted, early in their time in Maine, that she would be a fool not to take advantage of them.

Where she had grown up in southeastern Ohio, hiking was something you read about people doing elsewhere; it sounded fun, but the flat trails along the Ohio River didn't give you a chance to really find out. The Mahoosucs and White Mountains were a different matter, and in the three years since their first ambles up Mount Will, she had willingly followed Rich's lead in pursuing longer and more difficult trails. Because of the mosquitoes and blackflies so common and so annoying in the Maine woods, they reserved hiking for the fall. For this Saturday, Rich had proposed a daylong hike along part of the loop trail in Grafton Notch, and Julie had welcomed the prospect, partly for the sheer fun of the hike, and partly because it would give them a long stretch of time together to patch up the tears in their relationship that wedding planning had induced.

So it was the prospect of Rich's late arrival on Friday and their hike the following day that helped Julie push from her mind further thoughts of Dan Dumont—that, and the usual paperwork that she had allowed to accumulate around the board meeting. With her desk cleared, Julie felt no hesitation in accompanying Mrs. Detweiller through the door at four-thirty. She set the security alarm and walked to Harding House to await Rich's arrival.

❧

"It was on the news," Rich said. "I forgot to mention it earlier."

While they didn't always begin their weekends together in bed, on this Friday afternoon, after their quarreling earlier in the week, both had silently signaled their desire to do so. They had drifted into a light sleep after making love, and once they started to wake up, Rich had twisted to face her and they began to talk. When he said he was sorry to hear about Dumont, Julie had asked what he'd heard.

"You know how Maine Public Radio is, reading news stories off the wire? It was just something like, 'State Police are investigating the death of Daniel Dumont, whose body was found in the woods north of Farmington.'"

"Did they say it was suspicious?"

"Yeah, I think so—maybe something about suspecting foul play, or one of those expressions that means they know more than they're saying."

"Did they mention the autopsy?"

"Julie, I'm sorry to say I didn't memorize the story; I was trying to keep my mind on the road. Maybe it's on their website. Do you know for a fact that they performed an autopsy?"

Julie explained about her lunch with Mike Barlow, the call he'd received, and his comment that she'd hear more on the news.

"So why don't you check out the website while I start dinner? You won't be satisfied till you find out."

"Here it is," Julie said a few minutes later, sitting in front of her laptop at the kitchen table while Rich chopped vegetables for the stir-fry. "No, don't drop your peppers and onions on my computer," she said as he moved toward her. "I'll read it to you: 'Maine State Police reported this afternoon that an autopsy performed by the state medical examiner in Augusta confirmed that Daniel Dumont of Farmington died of a gunshot wound. His body was discovered Wednesday in an isolated forest north of Farmington. Dumont was the executive director of the Mountain Valley Historical Society. State Police spokesperson Steve McCauslin said the State Police investigation, in cooperation with Farmington and Franklin County authorities, is continuing, and that the death is being treated as a possible homicide.' Suspicions confirmed," Julie added, as she leaned back from her laptop.

"Your suspicions?" Rich asked.

"And Mike's. I guess I know him well enough to understand that's what he was saying. It was murder."

"I'm sorry, Julie. I know Dan Dumont was a friend."

"No, like I told Mike, I didn't really know him all that well. But I did like him, and I was flattered that he asked me to help him with his missing maps."

"And you think the maps are somehow connected to his death?"

"I think it's a strong possibility, and I think Mike does, too. He said he'd call over the weekend. Wonder if I should get in touch with him now?"

"I think what you should get in touch with is the lovely veggie stir-fry I'm about to present you with. And before that, I think we should both get in touch with a glass of wine. And then after that I think we should get in touch with our plans for tomorrow's hike."

Laughing, Julie went to the refrigerator to retrieve the bottle of sauvignon blanc she had chilled for dinner, following his instructions. "Want to do the honors?" she asked, extending the bottle to him.

Tired and, Rich admitted, a bit done in by the second bottle of wine they had had with dinner, they went to bed at ten o'clock, cuddling under the extra blanket she had insisted on when she realized how cold the bedroom was.

The bright sun streaming into the window woke them at six-thirty on Saturday morning. While it didn't provide enough warmth to ease the prospect of getting out of bed, Rich suggested an alternative way to warm up, and it wasn't until after seven-thirty that they made their way downstairs for a quick breakfast. Afterwards, Rich packed a lunch for the trail, and by ten a.m. they had parked and started up the west side of the loop trail below Grafton Notch.

If she had been responsible for planning the day, Julie would have aimed to complete the loop. But Rich was in charge, and his realism and experience prevailed to confine their hike to the eastern portion, up the new trail on Puzzle Mountain to where it joined the Appalachian Trail.

"The views won't be like the ones on Old Speck," he explained as they slogged along an old logging road just above the parking area. "But the guidebook says there's a decent place about an hour or so from here. Let's book it to there."

Rich was waiting, propped against a rock, when Julie made it to the lookout. It bothered her to fall behind on the trail, but after some tense moments on previous hikes, they had agreed to follow their own pace. She had accepted that he was both more experienced and stronger, and he was good about pausing to limit the gap between them. Still, when she reached him, she felt obliged to apologize.

"Hello, hare," she said. "The tortoise has arrived."

"Welcome, tortoise. By the way," Rich said as he stood up and kissed her, "did I tell you today that I love you?"

"That rings a bell," Julie said. "Me, too."

"And did I tell you that I'm so glad you made the arrangements for the wedding? And that I'm sorry I was so crappy about all that?"

"Yes to the first; and to the second, you don't have to say any more. I'm so glad it's settled."

"And you talked to your mother?" he asked hesitantly, not eager to scratch the wound.

"Yes, she's okay with it. I think she's just happy to have a date so she can get to work."

"Well, I'm sure we'll have to get to work, too, but let's not spoil the hike. We can talk about plans tonight. Unless you were thinking about flower arrangements and table settings on the way up?"

"I have to confess that I wasn't," she said with a laugh. "Actually—and don't start in on me about this—I was thinking about Dan Dumont."

"Why should that surprise me? What were you thinking?"

Julie felt that Rich's easy acceptance of the topic opened the door, and she walked through it with pleasure. "What I was thinking, Rich, is that I didn't tell Mike about the blog."

"What blog?"

"I think I mentioned this before, but maybe not. Dan told me that someone, he couldn't remember who, had suggested to him that the Network should sponsor a list or a blog or something— I'm not sure which, but it doesn't matter anyway—some kind of statewide listing of valuable items held by historical societies."

"Why?"

"So other directors would be aware of things that could be targets for theft, to sort of keep an eye out for valuable stuff that might resurface elsewhere."

"Well, that seems reasonable."

"Maybe, but it's really like a to-steal list, isn't it? That's what I told Dan, but I'm not sure he got the point. In any case, I should have told Mike about it."

"Does it exist—the blog?"

"Not as far as I know, but I think it's important. Whoever suggested it to Dan may have been trying to find out where the valuable items are. Mike ought to know, and if he can find out who it was, maybe—"

"Maybe he'll find out who killed Dumont? That seems like a huge leap to me."

"It's curious that he was killed after discovering that the third map was missing," Julie said, ignoring Rich's comment on the possible significance of the blog.

"Why?"

"Well, if his murder is related to the thefts, it took the third one to bring it about. Why not earlier? Because," she continued before Rich could answer, "Dan must have figured out who was stealing the maps, and if it was the same person who suggested putting together the statewide list, well, there you have it!"

"I wish I could unravel these mysteries the way you do, but I'm just a history professor looking for some weekend escape from reading papers and talking to sleeping students. Should we get moving?"

Julie laughed and stood up. "Lead on. See you at the next stop. And I promise: I won't think any more about Dan's murder."

Rich's chuckle didn't persuade either of them that he actually believed her.

It was after four o'clock, with the sun rapidly setting, when they emerged from the trailhead to sink with relief into the seats of the car.

"That was fantastic!" Rich exclaimed. "What do you think?"

"At the very least, fantastic; maybe even unreal! I'm totally beat, Rich, but I enjoyed every minute of it. You're right that the views aren't as good as on Old Speck, but they were good enough. And I more or less kept up, didn't I?"

"More or less. You really enjoyed it?"

"Absolutely!"

"And you didn't spend any more time thinking about Dumont's murder?"

"What's the dinner plan?"

"Okay, change the subject; see if I care. Dinner . . . hmm, I'll have to see what Ryland Groceries has to offer. Mind if we stop on our way?"

⁓⋛⁓

Rich told Julie she could be first in the shower while he prepared a marinade for the chicken breasts he'd bought at the store. But the blinking light on the answering machine was too strong a lure for her. They both stood silently as Mike Barlow's message played: "I'm sure you've heard by now. You can give me a call later if you like—at home." He gave the number. "I can't really tell you more than we've released, but I do want to ask you a couple of questions—just routine stuff about historical societies. And I can tell you about the plans for the memorial service. I'll give you a ring tomorrow if I don't hear from you. Have a good evening."

"Well, if you're going to be on the phone I might as well jump in the shower ahead of you," Rich said when the message ended. "I assume you're planning to call him now."

"I suppose I might as well," Julie said.

Rich laughed and said, "Why am I not surprised? If you finish while I'm still in the shower, don't hesitate to join me."

Julie, already punching in Barlow's phone number, nodded. "I'll be right up."

CHAPTER 11

Tuesday was the fifth straight day of perfect late-autumn weather: bright blue skies, with temperatures in the low sixties during the day, then dropping close to freezing most nights. Although the foliage was well past its peak, the occasional clusters of yellow leaves seemed all the more beautiful for being on their own, the last bits of fall that would soon enough yield to winter.

As she drove along the river toward Rumford, headed to Farmington for Dan Dumont's memorial service, Julie felt both the obvious connection between the waning of the season and Dan's death and the sharp contrast of today's beauty with the impending service. She didn't look forward to it. At what she now thought of as her first "official" Ryland Historical Society funeral—Mary Ellen Swanson's—Henry LaBelle had told her she should get used to such events because of the advanced years of so many Society trustees and members. But Dan Dumont wasn't in that category; she wasn't sure of his age, but guessed he hadn't been more than five or six years her senior.

She tried to focus on the beauty of the drive, but her thoughts were elsewhere. Mike had told her on Saturday that the memorial service was scheduled for noon on Tuesday, and that he wanted to interview her following the service, along with the local officer. Julie hadn't been sure if Mike had understood the significance of the valuable-items listing, because he'd said they could pursue that when they met. She hoped to get them to see that Dan's murder must be connected to the thefts. When she asked herself why she believed that, her only answer was instinct—a gut sense. She hadn't put together the pieces; in fact, she didn't even know what the pieces were yet. But why else would he have been murdered?

She admitted that she didn't know Dan well enough to confidently dismiss other possibilities. From Mike she had learned he was divorced, and that fact opened up other possible explanations, since failed relationships often left hard feelings and ugly emotions. Would his ex-wife be there? His family? She hoped attendance would be respectable, a tangible mark of Dan's significance.

When she turned off Farmington's main street past the university campus, Julie was happy to see that the parking area at the Mountain Valley Historical Society was already full, a half-hour before the service was to begin. She had to park farther along the street, behind Mike's cruiser and a black-and-white with FARMINGTON POLICE DEPARTMENT on the door. The cars were empty, but as Julie started back down the street toward the historical society, Mike Barlow called out to her from where he was standing on the sidewalk.

"Sergeant Tara Bolduc," he said to Julie, gesturing toward a heavyset young woman wearing tan slacks and a blue blazer. "She was working the thefts."

"Pleased to meet you, Dr. Williamson," Bolduc said after Barlow's introduction. "Lieutenant Barlow told me about your relationship with Mr. Dumont. I hope we can talk after the service."

"I'll be happy to. Looks like quite a turnout," Julie said. "I'd better make sure I get a seat."

"See you in there," Barlow said. "We'll stay at the back, try not to intrude."

A large room inside had been set up with chairs, a table with a podium at the front. Julie made her way past a handful of people she didn't know—members of Mountain Valley, she guessed—and toward a familiar face: Betsey Bowers, from Two Rivers Museum.

"So sad about Dan," Betsey said as they embraced. "He seemed like such a nice guy. I wish I had known him better; he was so pleasant at Network meetings." Julie agreed. "But I guess you knew him pretty well," Betsey continued.

"Not really," Julie said, still reluctant to reveal the nature of their recent conversations. "But he was nice to me when I started, and I always enjoyed talking with him at meetings."

"I heard you were helping him with a project, something like the situation I'm facing."

Julie realized her effort to conceal the thefts wasn't going to work.

"I've been meaning to call you about that, Betsey, and you're right that Dan talked to me. But I'm wondering who told you about it."

"Maybe it was Dan," Betsey said, pausing. "Or maybe not, now that I think about it. Maybe James Hartshorn? You know, I'm not sure. But there were some thefts here, too, right?"

"I'm not really comfortable talking about it—especially now. Dan confided in me, and I feel I have to keep it to myself right now. But I do want to follow up on your situation. Maybe we can talk later. Looks like the service is starting."

A young man was moving about the room, gesturing for people to be seated. At the front, a formidable-looking woman of sixty or so, wearing a tailored woolen suit and pearls, was standing at the podium.

"Thank you for finding a chair," she said crisply, and loudly, and then continued while some of the stragglers were still searching for chairs at the back. "I'm Harriet Marshall, and as many of you know, I'm the chair of the trustees of Mountain Valley Historical Society. On behalf of our board and members, I want to welcome you to this memorial service for our beloved executive director, Daniel Dumont." She paused and said, "There are some seats available here. Please do come forward."

As the speaker pointed toward several empty chairs in the front row, Julie saw Mike Barlow and Tara Bolduc sheepishly slipping into them. So much for Mike's desire to stay out of the way, Julie thought.

"Dan's sister, Marcia Callahan, would like to say a few words," Mrs. Marshall continued as the two police officers took their seats. "Marcia?" she prompted.

A woman in her late forties or early fifties rose from her chair in the front row and, clutching some pages in her hand, stepped forward to the podium. Julie thought she looked distressed, and the long pause that followed before she began to speak confirmed it. After one start that was interrupted by a flood of tears and subsequent drying of her eyes, the woman found enough strength to speak.

An only child, Julie couldn't imagine how painful it would be to stand in front of people and talk about your dead—in fact, murdered—brother. But she could guess. The gestures and pauses and tears from Marcia confirmed her pain, and Julie felt as much sympathy for her as she did for Dan.

When Dumont's sister had finished, Mrs. Marshall introduced a staff member, the curator, who spoke in a lighter tone of Dan's eccentric ways, inducing the relief of laughter in the audience. Mrs. Marshall finished with a well-crafted eulogy, a bit formal and distant, but an effective conclusion. As she was inviting the guests to adjourn to the next room for food and socializing, a voice from the back of the room said, "I'm sorry to interrupt, but I wonder if I might say a word about Mr. Dumont on behalf of his fellow historical society colleagues."

Flustered but gracious, Mrs. Marshall immediately consented, and Julie, with the others, turned to see James Hartshorn moving to the front of the room. While Julie had realized that others from the Network would be there, she and Betsey had been so absorbed in their conversation earlier that she hadn't even looked for them. Now she saw, in the row from which Hartshorn rose, Brent Cartwright and Ted Korhonen, along with several others she knew less well. That's good, she thought; a nice tribute to Dan Dumont.

And what a tribute James Hartshorn delivered. As Julie listened, she tried to ignore her feelings about Hartshorn and concentrate on the words of praise he directed toward their deceased colleague. She turned slightly to watch the others, wondering if any of them also knew about the missing maps. Might Dan have consulted them, too? And might that have led to . . . But, no, Julie decided this was neither the time nor place for such speculation. She turned back to follow Hartshorn's eulogy.

When he concluded, Mrs. Marshall renewed her invitation to move to the other room. Julie made a point of walking alongside Hartshorn to thank him for his kind words about Dan.

"I thought it was appropriate," Hartshorn replied. "I would have thought someone from here would have asked his professional colleagues to participate, but so be it. I think I spoke for all of us."

Julie felt she had no alternative but to agree that he had.

"Good turnout of the Network," he continued as they walked toward the table of refreshments. "Important to show the flag, though of course, you were probably closer to Dumont than any of us, helping with his problems here."

Julie saw this as a chance to inquire about who else knew of Dan's "problems," but before she could do so, Hartshorn turned away and began talking with Mrs. Marshall.

Ted Korhonen stepped beside her and said, "Nice words from James, I thought." Julie agreed. "It's interesting that everyone was tiptoeing around it, though, wasn't it?"

"Around what, exactly?"

"That Dan was murdered. I mean, that's amazing, isn't it? I know you've had some experience with murders, Julie, but for most of us, a murder—especially of someone we actually know—is pretty strange. Are you on the case, so to speak?"

"They are," she replied, nodding in the direction of Mike Barlow and Tara Bolduc, who had come into the room together and were standing away from the others.

"Cops?" Korhonen asked.

"He's State Police, and she's Farmington. Actually, he used to be the police chief in Ryland," she added, "so I should go and say hi." She didn't think it was any of Ted's business to know about her conversations with Barlow, or her upcoming one with both officers.

"You going to be here for a bit?" Barlow asked when she walked over to them.

"I should talk to some of the others, but not for too long. When do you want to meet?"

"Is one-thirty okay?"

Julie glanced at her watch and saw that this gave her about thirty minutes; she really wanted more time, and Mike agreed to two-thirty. "At the Farmington station," he said. "You know where it is?" She didn't, but Sergeant Bolduc gave her directions.

Julie resumed her circuit of the room, beginning with Mrs. Marshall.

"It's very kind of you to come," the board chair said after Julie had introduced herself. "Of course, Dan told me that he'd discussed the situation with you. That's something we'll have to deal with down the road. The main thing now is to determine how the terrible accident happened."

"Accident?" Julie asked.

"Dan's. Oh, I know they're saying it was a possible homicide, but that's just speculation at this point. I'm sure they'll confirm it was a horrible accident—someone jumping the gun on hunting season. As I said, we'll have to deal with the missing maps in due course, and perhaps then we might call on you for help."

"I told Dan I'd be happy to, but I don't really know much about the circumstances. I'm sure the police are handling that now."

"They have their hands full, don't they? Oh, here's Marcia Callahan; have you two met?" Julie expressed her sympathy and thanked Marcia for her talk.

"It wasn't easy," Marcia said. "I guess everyone could tell that. I wish I could have been funny or said something uplifting, but . . ."

"It was very appropriate," Julie said. "I really didn't know your brother that well, so what you said helped to fill in the picture of his life."

"I should have said something about his ex-wife, I guess, but that didn't seem right to me. And our parents—I really should have said why they couldn't be here. They're in Florida, and in frail health; this was all too much for them. But I should have said that. Oh, I wish I could do it over again. No, I don't really mean that. I'm sorry . . . thank you for coming."

Marcia put a handkerchief to her running eyes and walked away.

Julie wanted to talk to the curator who had told the touching stories about Dan, but as she was making her way in that person's direction, Brent Cartwright came up to her.

"Good to see you, Julie," he said, "though I wish the circumstances were different."

Julie agreed.

"It's so sad. He was such a nice guy," Cartwright said.

"Yes. I didn't know him all that well, but he was certainly a good guy. He invited me up here to see his museum right after I got my job."

"I thought you two were working on something together," Cartwright said. "Some kind of inventory of stolen items?"

Startled, Julie looked at him for a few seconds before responding. "Where'd you hear that?"

"Not sure, now that I think of it," Cartwright said, looking away. "Probably from Dan. Or, no, maybe it was Ted. Yeah, I think Ted told me. But you know, I'm not sure."

"We can ask him," Julie said, and looked over where she had last seen Korhonen leaning over the refreshment table.

"He's probably gone," Cartwright said. "He told me he had to be back to pick up his kid at day care. Anyway, what difference does it make? Were you and Dan working on something?"

"Just talking about matters of mutual interest, the way we all do." Julie really wanted to probe further to discover what Brent Cartwright knew—and how he found out—but she was reluctant to show her interest before she could think through a strategy. "I should be going, too."

"Hey, before you do, Julie, I just wanted to say again what a great talk you gave at the Network conference. I'd really be interested in talking to you more about it; the board at Portland Historical has been pressing about security, and I don't know enough to determine whether they're right, or just being fussy. Could I pick your brains someday? Lunch in Portland, if you'd like."

"Give me a ring, Brent, or send an e-mail with some dates. I'd be happy to talk."

Happy to talk about the thefts, she thought as she walked from the room, and even happier to find out what he knew about Dan Dumont's—or someone's—scheme for a listing of valuable items.

CHAPTER 12

The fact that Mike Barlow didn't seem to share her interest in the matter of a statewide listing of valuable items in historical society museums was something Julie had to keep reminding herself as she drove down the street and turned up the main drag toward the Farmington police station. But she was sure she could stimulate his interest.

"Why do you think that's so important?" Mike asked after he, Bolduc, and Julie had sat down at the conference table and Julie had jumped into the topic.

"Oh, you take cream, don't you?" he added, and excused himself to go for some. Julie didn't have the chance to tell him black coffee was fine with her—a change in taste induced through Rich's tutelage.

"You knew the lieutenant in Ryland?" Bolduc asked as they waited for his return.

"Yes, and we miss him. He's a terrific guy."

"That's what everyone says. This is my first case with him."

"How long have you been on the force?" Julie asked, sensing she was a newbie, and then regretted it, seeing Bolduc's blush. She guessed the officer to be in her mid-twenties, and had been surprised earlier when Mike had introduced her as Sergeant Bolduc.

"This is my second year in Farmington—will start my third in a couple of months, in fact. But I was military police before that. Got credit for it toward my rank," she added.

It happened all over rural Maine, Julie knew: Smart kids from poor families who couldn't afford college went into the army or another branch of service, got some training and a profession, and then returned to civilian life to practice it. Mike Barlow had done the same, she remembered.

"So," Barlow said as he returned and handed Julie her coffee, "I think I was asking why you think this statewide listing is important. To the murder, I mean."

After Julie explained, it was Tara Bolduc who said, "Does that tie the death to the missing maps?"

"Yes. What else could it be tied to?"

"Hunting accident," the young officer responded. "Happens all the time. And since deer season hasn't opened yet, a person out in the woods at the wrong time who's made a mistake might be pretty reluctant to come forward. They might not even know that their shot killed Mr. Dumont. Or, if it was deliberate—and we really don't know this for sure—it might have something to do with his personal life, not with the missing maps or anything else at all connected to his job," she added.

"True," Julie admitted. "I know it's a leap to make the connection, but there was something in Dan's voice that made me worry. It just seems too convenient to be a coincidence. He was—" she paused for a moment trying to recall Dan's tenor of voice when she last heard from him. She shrugged a little. "I just know there's something there."

"Coincidences do happen," Barlow said, joining the conversation after having observed the back-and-forth between the two women. "Of course, as I've told the sergeant, you are something of an expert on the connection between murders and items that are missing from historical societies."

Although Julie heard the lightness in his tone, she wasn't sure if he was dismissing her idea. "You think I'm jumping to conclusions?"

"Didn't say that. Why don't you walk us through your thinking—on how the death could be related to the missing maps, assuming for the sake of argument they're connected."

"Okay. First, Dan could have found out who stole the maps and confronted the person; then the thief could have lured him into the woods and killed him. Or, second, Dan could have realized that whoever was trying to set up this listing might really be interested in identifying items to steal. And, again, confronted him. Or, third, both of the above: Dan realized that the person trying to start the listing had already stolen the maps."

"Let's go back to the timing, Julie," Barlow said. "The last time you talked to him—"

"—was Tuesday. In the afternoon."

"About the maps, or the listing?"

"Both. He had just discovered that a third map was missing, and he seemed to be connecting it to the listing. He said he couldn't remember who had suggested it; he was vague, but stressed, maybe even a bit scared."

"About someone who had taken the maps?"

"Yes, but also—I think—about starting the listing. I know this sounds lame, Mike, but I just had the sense he knew more than he was telling me—about both the maps and the listing—and that he was making a connection between the two."

"Okay, that was on Tuesday afternoon. Then Wednesday morning, he's found dead. What happened in between, Sergeant?"

"I haven't gotten all the facts yet, but it looks something like this: Tuesday after lunch he told his secretary he wanted to work alone in the archives—didn't want to be disturbed. She left at five, and he was still there. I can't find anyone who saw him leave, but he was at home on Wednesday evening, because he made some calls. We're getting the records."

"Good. Landline or mobile?"

"Landline. He left his cell at the museum, and there's nothing on it for the whole day Tuesday."

"Funny that he didn't have it with him on Wednesday. If he was meeting someone, you'd think he'd carry his cell."

"If he was meeting the person who killed him, that person wouldn't want to make contact by phone, would he?" Julie asked.

"I wouldn't, but then, I'm not a murderer. Just trying to think like one. Even if I wasn't going to call the person, if I was going into the woods I'd want to keep my cell handy."

"True," Julie said. "I'll have to think about that."

"Anyway," Bolduc continued, "we don't have any witnesses to his movements on Wednesday morning, but we've put out a public request for anyone who might have seen his car to get in touch with us. Nothing yet."

"So," Barlow summarized, "Tuesday afternoon he talked to Julie, told her about the third map being missing, closed himself in the archives all afternoon, went home, made one call—or maybe more from there; we'll know more when we get the phone records—went into the woods sometime on Wednesday, and was found dead later that day."

"That's it, for now," Bolduc said. "And when did you find out, Dr. Williamson?"

"James Hartshorn phoned me. He's the head of our professional association. As I remember, he said the police called him because he had tried to call Dan on Tuesday."

"That's right," Bolduc said. "One of your troopers," she said to Barlow. "We were trying to figure out his movements, and his secretary said he had a call from this Hartshorn, but that was when he was alone in the archives in the afternoon. So your guy called him to verify, and told him why."

"It'll be interesting to see if Dan called Hartshorn from home on Wednesday," Julie said.

"Why?" Bolduc asked. "If he got the message that Hartshorn had called, wouldn't it be logical that he'd return the call at night from home?"

"Maybe. Anyway, when we get those records—"

"You mean, when we get those records, Julie," Barlow said with a laugh, pointing to Bolduc and then himself. "Didn't realize you'd joined the State Police. So assuming for a minute that you're still an interested citizen helping us, let's talk more about that conversation you had with Dumont last Tuesday. Can you recall exactly what he said about maybe having an idea as to who might have stolen the maps?"

"Like I said, Mike, he kind of mixed up the maps with the listing."

The policeman nodded for her to continue.

"I asked him if he thought professionals were involved, and—I'd almost forgotten this—he said something like, did I mean professional thieves. I guess the implication of that is that he may have been thinking about museum professionals."

"At his place?"

"Maybe, or maybe directors from other places—like, whoever had suggested the listing in the first place. But then he also said something about Farmington having funny people around, people involved in drugs. I'm not sure why he brought that up."

"Hey," Bolduc said, "this is a college town; although the city fathers wouldn't like me to say it, drugs are a normal part of the scene. Are you saying Mr. Dumont thought the maps may have been stolen to finance drug deals?"

Julie paused before saying, " I'm not sure. I'm just mad that I didn't take some good notes when we talked. I had so much going on, getting ready for a board meeting and dealing with a difficult trustee. I listened to Dan, and I think I've told you the gist of what he said, but I really can't be more specific."

"That's okay; you've been real helpful, as always," Barlow said. "If anything else occurs to you, I have a funny feeling you won't be shy about letting us know." Julie and Mike laughed as Bolduc seemed to be studying them. "We've got a lot to do with phone records and trying to trace Dumont's movements, so we'll be busy here. Thanks for all your help, Julie."

The policeman rose to signal the meeting was over, but, still seated, Julie said, "You talked about phone records, but what about Dan's computer? If he heard about the proposed listing, it might have been in an e-mail."

"We've got that, Dr. Williamson," Bolduc said. "His laptop—used the same one at work and at home. Lieutenant Barlow and I are going to be looking at it now."

"I could stay," Julie said. "I can help you identify the people in the Network."

"You can do the latter, but not the former," Barlow said. "Just give us the names and I'll put them in my notebook. This one," he added, holding up the leather folio Julie remembered him using back in their Ryland times. Taking out his pen, he said, "Go ahead. The Network."

Julie started with the museum directors who had been at the memorial service: James Hartshorn, Betsey Bowers, Ted Korhonen, Brent Cartwright. "They were all here today," she explained. "I don't know all the others, but I can send you a list."

"That would be helpful," Barlow said.

"Or you could start in on Dan's e-mail now? I'll just sit over there quietly and you can ask me about specific ones if there are messages from them."

"That list will be great," Barlow said. "Have a safe trip home."

Julie knew Mike well enough to realize further words would not change his mind, and so she shook hands with the two police officers and walked out of the station to her car. As she opened the car door she remembered that she was supposed to call Betsey Bowers about the proposed statewide list, as well as the thefts Bowers herself had experienced. It was too late now, so Julie reluctantly set off toward Route 2 and the drive back to Ryland, making a mental note to call Bowers at home that night.

CHAPTER 13

It was only fair that the schedule had come together so readily, since the pieces of the jigsaw puzzle Julie had spent a frustrating hour on before bed that night had not.

Indeed, the schedule worked perfectly. When Julie reached her at home that night, Betsey Bowers had suggested Julie visit Two Rivers Museum the coming Friday. Julie was at first reluctant to take another weekday away from the Ryland Historical Society, but then Betsey had reminded her that Friday was Halloween, and that the Portland Historical Society was having its annual costume party that night, an event Julie had heard of but not attended before. She was due to drive to Orono for the weekend, but a call to Rich led to a quick change of plans. He said he would welcome an urban fix, and told her he would make reservations at a B&B in Portland's West End that he'd heard about from a colleague. So in a matter of minutes it all came together: Julie would drive to York County early Friday, visit Betsey's museum and offer advice on their missing items, and then meet Rich in Portland for the Halloween event and a leisurely weekend.

Was she indulging herself, Julie wondered—or shortchanging the Ryland Historical Society? Maybe so on both counts, she decided, but she was eager to learn more about what had happened at Two Rivers—partly because she liked her emerging role as an advisor on missing items, but also because she sensed a link between Dan Dumont's murder and the disappearance of items from his, and apparently Betsey's, museum. That puzzle she hoped to have more luck with than the jigsaw she'd left in pieces on the kitchen table when she went to bed.

Two Rivers Museum consisted of an eighteenth-century house fronting the York River and a low, modern structure behind it facing the road that led from Route 1 to York Village. As Julie parked in the visitors' lot next to the new building, she noticed the river off to right and the lovely historic house, but she couldn't see a second river, and made a note to herself to ask Betsey Bowers about the name.

Conversations at Network meetings had provided Julie's only knowledge of her colleague, but she had found her agreeable: cultured and professional, but also warm and direct. Betsey was in her late fifties, Julie guessed, and had been at Two Rivers for a long time. More than that she didn't know, but hoped to find out today.

The receptionist in the visitors' entry told her Mrs. Bowers was expecting her, and picked up the phone to alert the director to her visitor's arrival.

Mrs., Julie thought. The title had become so rare among her professional colleagues that Julie realized she had assumed only people like Mrs. Detweiller used it.

"So good to see you," Betsey Bowers said when she came out of a hallway behind the receptionist and greeted Julie. "And so good of you to come on such short notice."

"It all worked out," Julie replied. "I'm glad you reminded me about the Halloween party. I've never been, but I've heard it's fun."

"You're going, then?"

"Yes. My fiancé is coming down from Orono, and we're spending the weekend in Portland."

"Dear, I didn't realize you were engaged," Betsey said. "Who's the lucky man—if you'll forgive my old-fashioned way of putting it?"

Julie briefly told her about Rich, their graduate-school relationship, his job at the university, their commuting pattern, the planned wedding.

"That's wonderful," Betsey said. "I thought I was probably the last married woman in the profession. Seems like most of our colleagues are married to their jobs, but I can assure you, it is possible to have both a career and a marriage. That's not why you're here, though, is it? Let's go back to my office and talk a bit, and then we can look around. You haven't been here before, have you?"

Betsey turned businesslike as soon as they entered the small office and took seats at a round glass-top table. "I made a list for you," she said, and handed Julie a sheet of paper with a numbered list:

1. CLAY MOLASSES JUG; PORTLAND, 1884; 42 X 20 CM
2. CERAMIC PITCHER; YORK, 1802; 28 X 30 CM
3. CREAMWARE PLATE (OCTAGONAL); YORK, 1770; 2.3 X 19 CM
4. GLAZED REDWARE FLOWER POT; ?, 1840; ??
5. CERAMIC COMMEMORATIVE PITCHER; ENGLAND, 1804; 21 X 21 CM (COMMODORE EDWARD PREBLE'S ROLE IN BATTLE OF TRIPOLI)
6. CREAMWARE AND CERAMIC PITCHER; ENGLAND, 1798; ?? (SHOWS THE PACKET PORTLAND)

"That's the basics," Betsey said as Julie scanned the list. "I didn't indicate inventory numbers or acquisition details, but I can give you all that if you need it."

"Value?" Julie asked.

"Again, I can give you insurance estimates, but as you know, prices are always in flux. I did some checking on various websites when I realized the extent of the missing items and figured the total value is probably $35,000 to $50,000. The last two are the most valuable, of course. Are you familiar with these sorts of things, by the way—ceramics?"

"Not in any detailed way," Julie admitted. "We have a fair number of ceramic items in our collection, and of course, I worked with pottery of various kinds in grad school courses, but I can't say I'm at all an expert."

"What you're an expert on is finding out what happened to missing items," Betsey interjected. "That's why I wanted you to come here. It's really very distressing, and quite frankly, I'm too embarrassed to report this."

Ignoring the comment about her expertise, Julie asked, "Then you haven't called the police?"

"No. Haven't even told my board, except in a very roundabout way. I think I mentioned to you the other week that we're planning a big exhibit for next summer, featuring local ceramics. It was when I was working through the inventory to start lining up the artifacts that I noticed these six were missing. I've hinted to the board that I'm having trouble locating everything I'd like to display, but I haven't said more than that. I was waiting till you could advise me."

Why was it, Julie wondered, that museum directors seemed to find it so hard to come clean with their boards? Oh, she understood how cranky and difficult trustees could be, but the lesson she had learned from her old mentor at Delaware—if you treat trustees as friends and supporters, they will be—had been reinforced for her several times over at Ryland. So she said, "My first advice, Betsey, is to tell your board what you found out. Right away. And then call the police."

"I'm sure that's the right thing to do, but frankly, my fear is that the stuff will turn up—misplaced somewhere, put on the wrong shelf, labeled as something else. You know how it is when you rely so much on volunteers; they're well-intentioned, but they're not professionals, and they do make mistakes."

While Julie understood, she was adamant. "That's true, but I assume you've poked around enough to determine that these six items really are missing."

"Touché. I guess it's just that I don't want to look bad in front of the board."

Betsey's frankness encouraged Julie to follow suit. "You'll look bad, Betsey, if the museum loses $50,000 worth of ceramics and the board doesn't have a clue."

Betsey sat silently for a moment and then said, "You're right. I'll call my board chair this afternoon, after we've finished, because then I can tell him that I've had you in to consult on this, and that you and I agree on what happened."

Julie understood that serving as cover was one of the benefits she provided in these circumstances, so she agreed.

"Now, can we talk about when you discovered the items were missing?" she asked. "If you don't mind, I'll just take a few notes, to make sure I'm getting it right."

This technique was actually one she had learned, or intuited, from Mike Barlow: Pulling out a notebook to record comments had a way of encouraging brevity and accuracy. Julie made notes as Betsey spoke quickly and directly.

Betsey had been on vacation for two weeks in late August, and when she returned after Labor Day she began reviewing the ceramics inventory to determine what items to display the following summer. A week later, she started looking through the archives to match the items with her tentative list, and within two days, she had discovered that six of the items were not where they were supposed to be. She took another few days to investigate possible alternative sites, but by the end of September, she'd come to the conclusion that the six pieces were indeed missing.

Julie asked how the archives were organized and protected, and who had access. Betsey explained the procedures, which seemed standard. Users had to register with the curator, indicating what artifacts they wanted to see, and why. If the items were not overly fragile or rare, they were brought into the main archive area and examined under the curator's supervision and then returned to their storage location.

"Who's the curator?" Julie asked.

"Lucy Bodewell. I've encouraged her to come to Network meetings, but she hasn't been able to yet. She has a three-year-old, and has such a tight schedule that it's been hard for her to become professionally active." So much for career and family, Julie thought, but didn't say. "And of course, she has to cover for me here when I attend meetings, so you wouldn't have met her. But she's very good—well educated, quite knowledgeable about museum practices. I trust her completely."

"And you've talked with her about these items?"

"Yes! In confidence, of course, and she's as upset as I am. We just can't figure it out. I imagine you'd like to talk to her?" Betsey continued, rising as if she were going to go and find the woman in question.

"I would, but I have a couple of further questions." Betsey sat back down. "Has anyone shown any special interest in the ceramics? You know, a volunteer or trustee, or a visitor with a special interest?"

Betsey thought for a few moments and then said, "Not that I can recall. But we might ask Lucy about that."

"Okay. How do you record visits, especially people who look at the catalog?"

"Well, you know what a sensitive topic that is with museum people—trying to balance access with security, making sure we know who comes and goes, but without discouraging them. We do ask visitors to sign the register, and if anyone uses the catalog, we absolutely require them to sign in—just like anyone who wants to view an item in the collection."

"So you have records of who visited this summer, and who consulted the catalog and maybe asked to see an item?"

"Certainly. Shall I get them? Oh, and some coffee, too, or tea? I should have asked earlier."

Coffee gratefully in hand, Julie studied the general visitor register while Betsey Bowers made herself busy in the reception area. Pretty impressive visitorship, she thought, as she paged through the book; but then York was in the direct line of summer tourists to Maine's southern coast, whereas Ryland was a bit off the beaten path. Still, the numbers made Julie admire the Two Rivers operation, and the extent and diversity of its audience.

Nothing else in the general register struck her, so she turned to the one that recorded what museum people called "users"—not the casual ones who drop in on a rainy day to see what's on display, but the scholars, genealogists, and others with a specialized interest. It was the last two weeks of August that most interested Julie, the period when Betsey had been on vacation. Eight names were listed, one twice. Their subjects—or, at least, what they reported as such—ranged from "family history" to "York Co. tools of the early nineteenth century." None listed ceramics. Julie jotted all the names in her notebook for later review.

When Betsey returned to see how she was getting on, Julie said she was ready to get up and stretch, and that she'd enjoy the promised tour of the museum. They began with a quick look at the exhibits in the building and a viewing of the introductory video, and then proceeded to the house museum. Throughout the tour, Julie reminded herself of her immediate purpose—to figure out how artifacts could disappear from the museum—but at the same time, she found herself making mental notes on little features she could adopt at Ryland, like the large and appealing labels that seemed so much better than the cramped ones at her home institution. She especially liked the video, something she had been talking about for two years but had so far not been able to achieve.

Lucy Bodewell was waiting for them in the archives. Julie had asked that this be the last stop on their tour so she could spend an hour or so there, to get a good understanding of the layout and procedures. Much as she tried to avoid stereotyping professional colleagues, especially women, Julie immediately recognized Lucy as a type common in the museum world: late twenties, athletic and attractive but not conventionally pretty, dressed sensibly in a wool skirt and cotton blouse, and though not aggressive, quick to extend a hand and say warm words of welcome. Art history major at Smith, Julie guessed to herself.

Consistent with the type Julie couldn't help seeing in her, Lucy Bodewell got right to the point in answering Julie's questions about security, storage, climate control, inventory management, and procedures for users. She seemed on top of her game, familiar with the jargon but, like her boss, clear and direct. When Julie showed her the list of users who had signed in during the last two weeks of August, Lucy admitted that although it had been a slow period, she didn't have strong impressions of any of them.

"With Betsey away, I had to do double duty then," Lucy said, "like covering out front while supervising the archives. Of course, I always stayed here with the users. I just can't remember anything specific about these folks."

"One came twice," Julie said. "Timothy Brothers."

"I don't think I know him," said Betsey. "You don't remember anything in particular about him, do you, Lucy?"

Julie sensed that the younger woman felt slightly defensive in responding: "Well, I do vaguely recall that he was interested in lithographs, I think."

Julie guessed that Lucy had prepared herself for this interview by reviewing the users' register before Betsey had brought it in for Julie's inspection. But that showed initiative, and Julie didn't want Lucy to think she was being criticized.

"I know what it's like," she said, "with folks coming and going. It's not our job to take notes on them—just to make sure they get what they need."

Lucy seemed relieved. "That's right, and I do remember he looked at a couple of early lithographs of York County towns. Let me just check that." The register had been returned to the archive room, so Julie made a further guess that Lucy had consulted it again while the tour was in progress. "Yes, both times. Two items the first time, and then the same ones again, plus three others, when he came back four days later."

"Stoughton, Mass.," Julie said. "That's what he listed as his address. But nothing more than the town. I can check that out."

"Do you think that's important, Dr. Williamson?" Lucy asked. "I mean, is he a, well, suspect, or whatever it is you'd say?"

Julie laughed. "I'm not a detective, Lucy—but I am Julie, by the way. Please. And it's far too early to think about suspects. All I want to do today is to get a good feel for your procedures and facilities, to understand how artifacts are handled so I can begin to piece together how some things may have gone missing."

"You said may have gone missing," Betsey interjected. "Do you think they're actually here somewhere? That they weren't stolen?"

"That's an option you always have to consider. I'd like to take some time just to walk around. I'd be happy to do that on my own, if you don't mind. Say, an hour?"

"And then we'll have lunch," Betsey said. "I made reservations at a wonderful new place in town for one o'clock. Hope that's not too late."

"Perfect," Julie said.

CHAPTER 14

"I asked for a table at the back, so we can talk," Betsey Bowers said as the hostess led the two women up three stairs and toward an alcove far removed from the dozens of late-lunch diners. Julie was struck again by the contrast with Ryland. There, at one p.m., at best a handful of people would be left in any restaurant—and there weren't any as fancy as this one. She had to remind herself that they were on the coast; just as the museum drew from that rushing stream of tourists, so did the restaurants.

"Of course they have pumpkin soup today," Betsey said after glancing at the chalkboard with the daily specials. Julie nodded, not following. "It's Halloween!" her companion said.

"Right. I had almost forgotten—but then, we're going to the party at Portland Historical tonight. Thanks again for reminding me about it. I gather it's costumes optional; I didn't bring anything. Are you going?"

"Not this year. We've done it a few times, and you needn't worry about costumes. Very few people besides the staff have them. You know Brent Cartwright, don't you?" Julie nodded. "My prediction is, he'll have an outlandish costume. Well, we should order. I know I'm starting with the pumpkin soup."

Julie did, too, and both had the broiled scallops to follow. Seeing that they really were quite separated from the rest of the diners, Julie asked if Betsey would mind talking about what she decided to call "the situation."

Betsey was eager to. "How did things look to you?" she asked.

"You have excellent storage facilities, and I'd say you're following sound procedures. I don't think it's likely that anyone could have removed the items through a routine visit. You have all the right safeguards in place. These aren't maps or bits of paper someone could conceal, and besides, they would have had to be retrieved from storage by a staff person and then returned to that person. There's no way someone could stash them in a bag without a staff person noticing."

"So what do you think happened?"

"Assuming they're not misplaced—and I can't rule that out, though I gather you've checked pretty carefully—"

"Multiple times!" Betsey said, before Julie could complete the thought.

"Yes, I'm sure you have, but I'll just do some more poking when I get back. But as I was saying, if they're really not there, then you have to assume it was one of two things." Julie uttered the last words so softly that Betsey leaned across the table. Julie noticed the waitress moving in their direction and didn't continue till after she had cleared the soup and placed the scallops before them. "Two possibilities, I should say: Someone inside took them, or someone broke in."

"Not possible! Our staff is very good, and so is our security system."

"Well, as someone said, when you eliminate the impossible, you have the likely. Or something like that. The point is you have to explain the situation one way or another. I'm only listing the possibilities as I see them. Perhaps you see another?"

Betsey looked at her scallops and then back at Julie, saying nothing in words but conveying her acknowledgment that Julie had to be right—and her wish that this wasn't so.

"Well, I've thought a lot about all this, and I have to confess that I came to the same conclusion. It's logical, really, but I hate to . . ."

"Hate to what, Betsey? By the way, these are excellent—perfectly done."

Ignoring both Julie's comment about the scallops and her own plate of them, Betsey continued: "I just hate to think that someone on staff would do this, and although I know our security system is good, it's not perfect. So . . ."

"I'll do some checking on the system. I recognize the brand and agree it's good, but at some point you'll still need to talk to the company. Or the police will."

"Yes, well, I'm waiting till next week to do anything about that. I'll talk to my board chair after you've left today, and then we'll see about the police. But as far as staff, it's obvious that Lucy is the primary person to consider."

"She's in direct contact all the time with the collections, so of course you have to start there. But I'd like to talk about all the others—volunteers, too."

"I can make a list when we get back and go over it with you. I have to say that as much as I've thought about this, I can't see any of them stealing something—or how they'd do it. Lucy really is on top of the archives."

"So we should talk about her," Julie said.

"A wonderful young woman; I couldn't ask for a better curator. I hired her almost two years ago, and there's never been a day when I regretted it."

"Where was she before?"

"She worked at The Museum of Fine Arts in Boston—a fairly low-level position, but appropriate for a first job out of college. Tom, Lucy's husband, was doing his residence at Brigham and Women's. It was just our great fortune that he joined a practice here in York and Lucy was available to come to the museum."

Married to a young doctor, mother of a three-year-old, Julie thought—she was a busy young woman.

"No," Betsey said in a louder voice than she had used before, "no—there's no way Lucy could be at fault here."

Julie didn't think so either, and she didn't think pursuing the topic would be worthwhile.

"I'll look forward to talking to you about the rest of the people this afternoon, but remember, Betsey, that a break-in is still very much a possibility. When I look around further I'll try to see if there's some likely way for that to happen. Anyway, there's one more thing I'd like to ask you before we go back: Do you have any idea why these particular items might be missing?"

"I hadn't really thought about that," Betsey answered.

"What would you say they have in common—if anything?" Julie probed.

"Besides being ceramics? Well, I'm not sure they do have anything else in common."

"Would you say they're the most valuable ceramics in your collection?"

Betsey paused to think, mentally reviewing the collection.

"I'd hate to give you a definitive answer on that without looking at the catalog," she said after a few moments. "I rather think there might be a few items worth more, but I'd like to check."

"That's fine," Julie said. "You can let me know. How about their historical significance—aside from monetary value. It seems to me they're kind of scattered in that way, from the late eighteenth to late nineteenth centuries; some English, some American; some local, one from Portland."

"That's true. No, I can't see any historical link. But coming back to the value, I guess I was assuming that thieves always take the most valuable stuff."

"Not necessarily. You'd be surprised how many times a thief leaves a very valuable letter, for example, and instead grabs a couple of old augers."

"Because they don't know about values?"

"Perhaps. Or just because they want certain stuff—they like tools rather than manuscripts. But there's also another reason, and I'm wondering if it might be the key here: location."

"Where the items are stored?"

"Right. You store items together, so if I'm a thief, I don't see a more valuable, say, shawl, if I'm in the ceramics collection."

"That assumes someone broke in; if it was someone on the inside, they could pick and choose, maybe working from a list of valuable items—some ceramics, some books, some maps, whatever."

"Exactly, though I'm still not willing to conclude it was a break-in, or even someone from the outside who got access without actual breaking in."

"Oh, Julie, I'm so happy you're working on this! You know so much, have so much experience. I would never have looked at this from so many angles the way you are. I'm sure you'll figure it out."

"I hope so, Betsey, and thanks for saying that. But remember: You've got to report this to the police. They may figure it out right away based on something we don't even know about."

"After I talk to my board chair. But you'll work with them, won't you?"

"The police? Of course. But they're not going to like the fact you had me in first."

"I'm going to tell them the same thing I'll tell the chair—that I had to have an expert confirm the losses before I could report them. Anyway, there was one thing I wanted to ask you before we leave: Is this going on all over the place, or at least, all over Maine?"

"Thefts from museums and historical societies?"

"Yes. I was wondering if someone singled us out, or if it's common."

"I don't think it's common, but I really have no way of knowing except when someone like you comes to me."

Julie recognized this as the moment she had been waiting for: a chance to find out if Betsey Bowers was aware of the blog or statewide item list that Dan Dumont had mentioned.

"Maybe," she began tentatively, "maybe that's what this statewide listing is all about."

"James's blog, or whatever it is?"

"James Hartshorn?" Julie asked quickly.

"Well, I assumed he was behind it, since he's a computer person, isn't he? I haven't been contacted about it, but I did hear from someone—I can't really remember who it was—at one of our meetings. The one in Portland, I think. Anyway, it was just some general talk."

"About?"

"Well, about starting some kind of computerized listing—is that a blog? I'm so old-fashioned! Some kind of listing of missing items, or valuable ones. I'm not sure which. It was all so vague. But you must know about it; after all, you're the expert!"

Julie had thought about this more than once. She may not be "the expert," but she was, after all, pretty well known around the state for her involvement with missing items. That's why both Dan and Betsey had contacted her. So why hadn't this person—James

Hartshorn, or whoever it was—talked to her about this list? And what, exactly, did the list entail?

Her reply to Betsey wasn't meant to be evasive, though she did plan to conceal the Dan Dumont business.

"I'm like you in that I don't know much—just some vague comments here and there. Anyway, I suppose it's worth talking to James about. But to come back to your point about whether items are going missing all over the state, have you heard about others?"

"No. That's why I asked. But remember, I'm not tied in to the Network the way you are. I don't always hear what's going on elsewhere because I'm busy just trying to keep Two Rivers going. And speaking of that . . ." She reached for the check and then went to take care of it.

⌘

The two women returned to the museum a short time later. As Julie entered the archives area, Lucy Bodewell stood up and said abruptly, "I thought I should review the register for the whole year. I hope you don't mind, but I know you were looking at the weeks Betsey was on vacation. So I went back through the whole year, and here's what I found."

Julie glanced at the piece of paper Lucy thrust into her hand. It listed, by month, the number of persons who had registered to see items in the collection. For each month, it also noted the ones interested in ceramics, and the total of those: eighteen up to the middle of August. At the bottom was listed "Holly Davis: March and May (3), June (2), July (4)."

"Other than Miss Davis," Lucy said before Julie could speak, "the only repeat visitor was Timothy Brothers, but as you know, he listed lithographs as his area of interest."

"And Miss Davis?"

"Frankly," Lucy answered with a low laugh, "a nutcase. But please don't say I said that! It would be better if Betsey told you about her."

Julie wondered if Lucy was embarrassed by her description of the woman, or if she had some reason to put off saying more. So she pressed. "I'll ask Betsey, but I'd like to know what you think of Miss Davis. I assume she styles herself that?"

"Insists on it. No Ms., and she always calls me Mrs. Bodewell. But that's a generational thing. I suppose you'd call her a colorful character. She's local; lives right in town, actually. She comes in dressed to the nines one day and then in jeans and a torn sweatshirt the next, and always—even when she's in a dress and dripping with jewelry—wears beat-up sneakers. She carries a briefcase, a big one like lawyers use, and when she sits down to work, she opens it and pulls out files and notebooks and dozens of pencils. I don't think I've ever seen her write anything down, but she fills the desk with all her stuff.

"Then she asks to see things—plates, pots, bowls; always ceramics. I always keep an eye on her, but she never even asks to touch—just looks them over, stands up and walks around them, shakes her head, sighs, whatever. Then I put them back and she piles all her stuff into the briefcase and leaves. Always very polite; she seems quite cultured. She never fails to say 'please' and 'thank you'—real old school, if you know what I mean."

Julie nodded, having some experience with the type.

"Anyway, the reason I said what I did about her earlier—I know, I really shouldn't have—is that when she's done and ready to leave, she comes over to my desk and leans down and whispers crazy things."

"Like what?" Julie asked.

"Oh, it's always different, but along the lines of 'I'm getting closer now,' or, 'I think I've got it figured out,' or 'I'll get there soon.' Things like that."

"I see." Julie was torn between two instant interpretations: Either Miss Davis was responsible for the missing items, or she was a harmless eccentric of the kind that museums drew like cats to a bowl of milk. "So on balance," she said to Lucy, "do you think she has anything to do with the missing items?"

"No! I can't imagine her being compos mentis enough to do anything practical."

"But she has an interest in ceramics—at least in the items we have here."

Lucy considered this for a few seconds before responding. "It may seem that way, but the truth is, I don't think she has any real interest in them. They're just something she hit on. It could have been anything—an excuse to come in and go through this routine. But you really should talk to Betsey about her."

"I will. Thanks for your observations, and for running through the registers for me. I planned to do that, but you saved me a lot of time. And speaking of time, I have just an hour or so left, and I'd like to walk through the storage area again. Could you join me?"

As Lucy was unlocking the door at the back of the main archive room, Julie thought about Holly Davis as a suspect. Without even seeing the woman, or talking to Betsey about her, Julie felt she knew the type of eccentric she represented, but it would be too easy to dismiss her out of hand. Even if she was, as Lucy said, incapable of a practical act like stealing ceramics, she might have hired someone else to do it. No, she couldn't be ruled out—not yet.

"Is there anything particular you'd like to see?" Lucy asked when they were inside the first of the storage rooms and she had locked the door behind them.

"I want to do a little walking around and thinking on my own to get the general feel of things, but what I wanted to ask you about is the location of the missing items. Well, I mean, where the items were before they went missing. Were they all stored together?"

"Sort of. Back here"—she gestured toward a small room that led off the larger one they were standing in—"is where the ceramics are. So it's correct to say the missing items were together."

Lucy led the way into the room, Julie following. Floor-to-ceiling shelves on the walls were filled with plates, cups, bowls, and pots.

"But it's not like those six were together; they were distributed all over. We basically store by date of acquisition, since that means you don't have to keep rearranging things the way you would if it were done by date, or place of manufacture or whatever."

Julie nodded. This was a familiar problem, and the solution pretty typical, at least in small museums.

"Anyway, you can see from the empty spaces here, here, there—the items we can't find were in different spots."

"So it wasn't likely a case of someone just grabbing pieces that were next to each other?" Julie asked, and then realized the question was directed to herself rather than Lucy. So she answered it: "They would have had to know what they were looking for, and then check the acquisition dates on the cards to find them."

"Well, that, or they could have just looked around and taken things they liked, I suppose."

"True, but what do the items have in common?" Julie said. "They are of different dates, types, and places of manufacture."

"I guess I assumed they were worth a lot," Lucy said. "Isn't that usually why things are taken?"

"From what you know, are these the most valuable ceramics in your collection?"

"I'm not at all sure; ceramics aren't really my specialty. Betsey is checking on the values now. Do you mind if I ask what you think they have in common?"

"Well, it might turn out that their value is the common link. It may sound flip, but the fact is that at this point, what they have in common is that they're all missing. Which is sort of the end of the puzzle. Now I've got to go back to the beginning. Thanks for your help, Lucy. I'll just look around in here for a bit longer."

It was almost four in the afternoon when Julie finished in the archives, said good-bye to Lucy, and stopped in at Betsey Bowers's office. An hour after that she was on the road to Portland to meet Rich.

Driving gave her a chance to review her day's work. The facilities and access procedures of Two Rivers Museum seemed sound and conventional, but the reliance on the electronic security system to prevent break-ins was, she knew, seldom warranted. All it took was one person with the code to facilitate a late-night visit. She had found no evidence of forced entry, and she doubted anyone inside the museum could have spirited away such hard-to-disguise items during working hours.

Betsey had confirmed that Miss Holly Davis was a familiar eccentric presence and not a likely thief herself, although possibly capable of hiring someone else to do the work. Doubtful, but possible. The two visits of Timothy Brothers of Stoughton, Massachusetts, had gotten Julie's attention, and she planned to try to identify him.

Finally, there was the matter of the common linkage between items. Betsey's review of values confirmed what Julie had guessed: The missing six items were by no means the most valuable ceramics in the collection. The guess of $35,000 to $50,000 for the whole group still seemed right to Betsey, but she had identified another half-dozen items whose total value was two to three times that.

And that, Julie thought, as she slowed her car out of respect to a State Police car at the side of the turnpike just ahead, directed her back to the assumption she had been working on: that the missing items had not been stolen because they were the most valuable, or because they just happened to be sitting together when the thief entered. They had been stolen because someone wanted those particular items. Someone, she felt sure, who was filling the holes in a personal collection, or acting on behalf of a collector who was. Someone who knew exactly what the Two Rivers Museum offered—and knew how to bypass the security system or hire someone to do it.

A professional. Or several.

CHAPTER 15

When Rich had suggested they stay at the hotel where the Portland Historical Society was holding the Halloween ball, Julie had at first agreed. Then she realized it was that hotel, the one that put "By the Bay" after its generic name. The one whose cement-panel construction contradicted the brick that characterized Portland architecture. The one that managed to blight the city's modest skyline without, Julie was convinced, offering views of Casco Bay. The one more suitable for an interstate off-ramp in the Midwest than in the middle of a New England seaport.

No, she couldn't stay there. She could swallow hard and attend the ball, since it was a fund-raiser for the historical society—and she guessed the hotel's ballroom was the only one big enough for the event—but stay there? No way.

So Rich booked them into a cozy Victorian B&B in the West End that he'd heard about from a colleague. He was there when she arrived, stretched out on the canopied bed with a pile of student papers at his side. Julie entered the room, slid in beside him without taking off her coat, and pressed her face to his for a kiss. As she started to remove her coat as the first step of getting undressed, Rich unexpectedly stopped her.

"Before . . . well, before anything . . . you're going to kill me," he said.

"Because it's Halloween? I wasn't planning to."

"You will. I can't stay tomorrow. I have to go back to Orono, and I'm so pissed because I was looking forward to our weekend."

"What happened?"

"The dean. She came by my office this morning after class just as I was getting ready to leave. She's never done that before. Maybe someone told her she needed to get out of her palace and meet the faculty—management by walking around, or whatever it's called. Anyway, she's giving a brunch on Sunday for some visiting professor and invited me. It's a command performance. I'm so sorry. You can stay, but I really have to get to Orono by tomorrow night, because the brunch is at ten on Sunday."

"You're right," Julie said.

Rich nodded. "You agree I couldn't have said no?"

"I meant you're right: I'm going to kill you. But not right now."

⟡

Walking to the hotel for the party that night, Julie said, "Of course I'm disappointed, Rich, but I do understand. We just have to be flexible. You'll be coming up for tenure next year, and turning down an invitation from the dean would be really dumb. We know that commuting means being able to change our plans . . . So."

He stopped and pulled Julie toward him for a kiss. "Thanks. I'm glad you're not going to kill me."

"Well, the timing would have been terrible. But don't get confident. After all, this is a Halloween party we're going to. Anything can happen."

"Well, I just want to say you're being very good about this. I owe you."

"Maybe we're even, since you agreed to come to this Halloween party."

"Why did you decide to go?"

"It's a fund-raiser for Portland Historical Society—a good cause, though not as good as Ryland Historical."

"And you just might do a little sleuthing while we're here?"

"Are you suggesting it?"

"I don't think you need a nudge from me. You're still thinking about Dumont's murder; you spent all of today at that other museum that had some thefts; and tonight, most of the state's historical society directors will be here. So let's just say you plan to do a bit of investigation."

"And I thought I was the detective!"

Under other circumstances, being greeted by James Hartshorn the minute she and Rich entered the hotel ballroom would have made Julie cringe. But under the present circumstances, he was exactly the person she wanted to see first.

"Jim, I'm not sure if you've met my fiancé, Rich O'Brian," Julie said breezily as Hartshorn came toward them and extended his hand to Julie.

"Heard you were getting married," Hartshorn said. "So this is the lucky man. Nice to meet you, and congratulations. Julie's a peach!"

Julie wished she could roll her eyes and groan aloud. Instead, she said, "Glad we're not the only ones who aren't in costume," gesturing toward Hartshorn's gray suit, white shirt, and paisley tie.

"It's sort of a costume," he said. "When I worked for IBM, back in the day, everyone dressed like this. I don't have to now, so I thought it would be fun tonight to drag out the old suit. Have you eaten? The buffet looks wonderful. Maybe we could find a table together and I can talk to the groom."

The fact that Hartshorn was so eager to join them surprised Julie, but it fit her plan to pin him down about the statewide register, and so after making their way through the buffet line, she and Rich went to the table at the back of the room where Hartshorn was seated, waving them over.

"Quiet here—good chance to get acquainted, Rick," he said.

"Rich," Julie quickly corrected him.

"Sorry. Rich. And what do you do, Rich? When you're not courting lovely Julie, I mean."

Julie saw in Rich's eyes the same desire she felt to land a not-so-gentle punch on James Hartshorn's nose. But his ironic mode kicked in.

"Well, that's a full-time job in itself, Jim, as you can imagine. But in my spare moments I teach history at Orono."

"Another historian! How convenient. When's the wedding, by the way?"

"Bastille Day," Rich said. "We figured two American historians should marry on Independence Day, but there was no room at the inn, so we settled on the next best date."

Hartshorn laughed just heartily enough to suggest that he wasn't sure if he was being teased.

"Of course, of course," was all he said. "Does that mean you'll be moving to Orono, Julie?"

"No," Rich answered emphatically before Julie could. "Ryland can't spare her."

"You young folks have it figured out," Hartshorn said. "My poor wife followed me all over the country. You know what we used to say: IBM means I've Been Moved. But that was another era. Well, good for you. Careers for both. Fine with me. Now, Julie, I heard you and Betsey Bowers have a little project going."

So that, Julie thought, explains Hartshorn's desire to talk: He seemed to be tracking her activities, using almost the same words he had used when he'd asked what she and Dan Dumont were doing. She decided to ignore his question and pose her own: "Betsey mentioned to me that you're starting some kind of statewide register of valuable items in local museums and historical societies. I don't remember that coming up at Network meetings."

She paused and watched Hartshorn's face. It was as blank as his white shirt. After a few seconds he responded. "Don't think it's been mentioned there. Probably should be. But it's not really my idea, and it's in a preliminary form."

"Whose idea is it?" Julie blurted out more quickly than she'd intended.

"Well, that's funny," he said, scratching his face and looking out into the room. "Now that you ask, I'm not sure I know. It's one of those things that just surfaced. Brent may have told me about it. No, I'm not sure it was him. Maybe Dan. Yes. I think it was poor Dan. So tragic. I don't suppose you've heard more on that?"

Julie saw that Hartshorn was slick at changing directions, but she couldn't decide if he was lying. Although she was pretty good at reading people, she couldn't quite penetrate Hartshorn's bland smile.

"The police are investigating," she replied. "Rich," she said turning to him, "I don't think you've met Brent Cartwright. He's over there in the nineteenth-century getup. Let me introduce you. Good to talk with you, Jim."

"Longfellow, I presume," Hartshorn said, referring to Brent's costume.

"Of course," Julie said. "Well, we'll see you around later." She rose from the table, and Rich followed.

"So did you get what you wanted?" Rich asked as they made their way across the room.

"What I wanted, frankly, was to get away from Hartshorn. He's such a slime."

"Seems like it. But I thought you were trying to get something out of him."

"I was, and, no, I didn't get it. This whole business of a state-wide register is so murky. No one seems to remember—or be willing to say—who thought of it, and I'm not even sure it's in place. Hartshorn sort of confirmed that. But what's so strange is that on the one hand I can't pin anything down, and on the other, no one seems to be very concerned about it."

"Why should they be?"

When Mike Barlow had expressed a similar sentiment, Julie had concluded that she was the one who just wasn't getting it. Rich's question reinforced that sense.

"Maybe it's just me, Rich, but it seems like this kind of register is basically a to-steal list—a perfect way to identify valuable items without going to the bother of digging into the collections. You're sort of asking directors to put their best things on eBay."

"I don't think that's how eBay works, Julie."

"Okay, fine. I really don't know how it works, and I don't care. All I'm saying is that if I wanted to go around Maine grabbing valuable stuff from vulnerable little museums, I'd sure like to get my hands on a statewide register."

"Don't get mad at me. I was just trying to understand."

"Sorry, Rich. I'm frustrated because I can't figure out how the pieces fit together."

"You're going to illuminate me, I assume."

"Later. Here's Brent. Mr. Henry Wadsworth Longfellow," she said to the man in the frock coat. "So nice to see you again."

"Ah, my dear, there's nothing a dead poet enjoys so much as meeting a lovely young woman. How are you, Julie?"

Julie handled the introductions and complimented Brent Cartwright on his costume.

"It seemed appropriate," Cartwright said, "since we use his house. I wanted to wear a suit of his that we have there, but my boss didn't think that was a good idea. This is as close as I could get. You approve?"

Cartwright turned to display himself, and Julie said he looked smashing. "We opted out of costumes this time," she said, adding, "but I wish we hadn't. Maybe next year."

"And what would you wear?" he asked.

"Have to think about that. Rich would probably come as Cotton Mather, or maybe Jonathan Edwards. He's a colonialist."

"Are you?" Cartwright asked Rich, who had been standing silently as the other two bantered.

"That's what I teach, at Orono," he said.

"A long way from Ryland. How do you and Julie know each other?"

Julie hadn't introduced Rich as her fiancé like she had with Hartshorn, so now she explained, skipping quickly through to their graduate-school days in Delaware to avoid the automatic congratulations on their engagement.

But Cartwright wasn't distracted. He congratulated them, happily omitting the seemingly obligatory "lucky man" description. He did ask them if they had a wedding date, and Rich supplied the answer.

"Bastille Day," Cartwright repeated. "Don't think I'd want to revisit the original one, but a July wedding in Maine sounds lovely."

Julie hadn't paid attention to Cartwright before, but studying him now she was struck by the sharp, fine features of his face. A

115

woman with them would be called pretty, but Cartwright exuded a strong masculinity, despite his short, thin body. She didn't think he resembled Longfellow, at least not the portly old gentleman whose portraits she had seen, but he had a certain celebrity quality to him. And, to be blunt, Julie thought, he's very sexy.

"Are you staying in Portland, Julie?" Cartwright suddenly asked. "Remember I said I'd like to get together and pick your brains about museum security. If you're going to be around, maybe we could meet tomorrow. With Rich, of course, if it wouldn't bore you," he added.

"We're leaving tomorrow, but maybe I can take a rain check," Julie said.

"Sure. Just let me know when it's convenient. By the way, what do you think about this statewide register?"

Julie wasn't exactly stunned, but surprised was an accurate description.

"What do you think?" she asked, to gain some time.

"Sounds like a good idea. But then, you know a lot more than I do about stolen items. I still think of your talk last month—really terrific. You should have heard it, Rich; Julie knocked our socks off."

"Even my leather ones," a voice from behind said.

Julie turned to see Ted Korhonen in a costume she recognized at once.

"Natty Bumppo!" she said. "How nice to see you."

"Well, I'm not sure if I'm James Fenimore Cooper or Natty, but either way, they wouldn't let me bring my gun."

"Reasonable enough," Julie said. "I don't think you two know each other," she added, and introduced Ted and Rich.

"Actually near Ryland," Ted said in response to Rich's question about the location of the Finnish Historical Society of Maine. "Finns settled all over that part of the state. They must have felt right at home. First time I went to Finland I thought I was in Oxford County—lakes, low hills, heavily forested. So anyway, lots of them came, and they're keen to preserve their heritage. Voilà, the Finnish Historical Society of Maine. It's nothing like Ryland Historical—one building, one half-time director, one very small budget. Anyway, how about you, Rich?"

After the conventional narrative, the three stood silently for a few moments before Julie raised the matter of the statewide register.

"I thought it was your idea," Korhonen said. "I mean, you're the expert on thefts of valuable items; I'd assumed you thought up the idea of a place to keep track of them."

Julie explained that far from being the source of the idea, she was in the dark about it, hearing only rumors and not being able to sort out exactly what it was, and whether it even existed.

"Not yet," Korhonen said. "As far as I know, it's just in the talking stage. But I'm not really tuned in; like I said, I'm really only a half-time director."

"I hadn't realized that," Julie said.

"I'd say I'm in the majority when it comes to Maine historical societies, Julie. Most of us are small, and run by volunteers or part-timers."

She wasn't sure it was exactly delicate to ask, but Julie was too curious to resist: "So what fills up the other half of your life, Ted?"

"Whatever it takes," he responded, laughing. "That could be the Maine motto: Folks lucky enough to live here do whatever it takes to get by. Me, I have a pretty big woodlot, I do some organic gardening and sell at farmers' markets, I paint a house now and then. And of course, I get my deer! Like I say, whatever it takes."

Julie was happy that Rich jumped in quickly to carry on the conversation with Ted, whose revelation about his odd-jobs life she found embarrassing. She hadn't known. But then, she really didn't know Ted well at all, especially considering that his institution was indeed a half-hour drive from Ryland.

"I like that expression," she heard Rich saying to Ted. "A guy at the garage in Orono asked me the first fall I was in Maine: 'Get your deer?' To me it sounded like one word: getchadeer, like some kind of cheese, I thought."

Korhonen laughed. "That's how we keep folks from away in their place—speaking in tongues."

"So did you?" Rich asked. "Getchadeer?"

"Not yet. Hunting season opens tomorrow. The museum's open since it's Saturday, but I'll be out there first thing Monday morning."

Still on the side, listening to the dialogue between the two men, Julie was suddenly struck by the realization that, among the many things she hadn't known or guessed about Ted Korhonen, the latest piece of information was the most intriguing: He was a hunter. Like Dan Dumont.

CHAPTER 16

"Spray, or real?" Julie asked, as she and Rich descended the stairs and entered the breakfast room the next morning.

It was a game they had begun a year or so back after staying at B&Bs around New England. It had started when Rich said he was sure the odor of cinnamon buns in the breakfast room of a B&B in Belfast, Maine, came from a spray.

"They sell it," he had said. "B&B suppliers sell spray—cinnamon bun, blueberry muffin, cranberry scone—whatever you want, they have it. This way, B&Bs can decide what atmosphere they want to create."

The more Julie laughingly resisted his notion, the further Rich carried it, and as a consequence, the running joke between them now required that one or the other pose the question—Spray, or real?—when they stayed at a B&B.

Julie had taken the initiative this morning, and Rich answered, "spray."

But it turned out to be real, the enticing odor of freshly baked cinnamon buns wafting from the kitchen through the dining area and up the stairs.

"Wrong!" Julie said as the chipper proprietor placed two large buns on their table and took their beverage order.

"Probably enhanced with spray," Rich said as he cut into his. "But damned good anyway," he added, taking the first bite. Julie tried hers and agreed. When their coffee came, he said, "So what's the plan? Hope we can still make a day of it. I don't have to leave till late afternoon."

They agreed on a long walk through the West End, and then the museum. Julie said she needed to do some shopping at L.L. Bean, so they decided to drive in separate cars to Freeport, have lunch there, and then go their separate ways after shopping—Rich to Orono, Julie to Ryland.

Julie was quiet after they'd agreed on the day's schedule.

"I'm really sorry about having to go back early," Rich said.

"I understand."

"You seem somewhere else this morning," he said. "Are you mad at me?"

"No. I mean, I'm sorry we can't stay another night, but I do understand. I was just thinking about last night."

"It was fun."

"It was. Actually, I'm surprised, because I don't usually enjoy that kind of thing, but I actually did last night. Thanks for coming. Did you enjoy it?"

"I did. And it was nice for me to meet some of your fellow directors. It's good for me to meet the folks you talk about so often, have faces to put with the names. But why do I think you're on another wavelength?"

She laughed. "Just trying to put some things together."

"What things?"

"Oh, starting with my visit to Two Rivers yesterday—I still haven't digested all that. And then last night, I wanted to pin down this business about the statewide register—like, who started it, first of all; and if it has been started, why no one told me about it in the early stages; and finally, how it works."

"No luck?"

"Not really. I keep sensing it's a big secret, but then people just say casually they know about it—even though no one can tell me who's behind it. It's just frustrating!"

"You think it's tied in to Dumont's death, don't you?"

"Yes, and to the missing items at Two Rivers. But I can't connect the dots. And then there's Ted Korhonen. He's a hunter, Rich, which sort of links him to Dan Dumont."

"Him, and a couple of hundred thousand other Mainers! Just because someone hunts doesn't make him a killer."

"Of course, I know that! But look: Ted hunts; Dan was shot. Ted and Dan are museum directors. Ted's job is part-time, and he does all sorts of other things to make a living."

"Like stealing items from other museums?"

"Possibly. He'd be well positioned to do it—knowing how museums work, finding out what's valuable, using his own place to dispose of things he steals elsewhere."

"I don't think I follow that," Rich interrupted.

"Getting rid of stolen items is the hardest part, but if you're the director of a museum, you could use that as a cover: You tell a buyer it belongs to your museum and you're de-accessioning it. Makes it a lot easier than just appearing with an old map or a ceramic bowl."

"Yeah, that makes sense. What else do you know about Korhonen?"

Before Julie could respond, the ring tone of her cell phone startled her.

The proprietor appeared at their table before she could reach into her purse to retrieve it. He pointed to a sign that said PLEASE RESPECT YOUR FELLOW GUESTS—ALL CELL PHONES OFF.

Julie nodded guiltily and jumped up to leave the room, but the call ended before she could reach the hallway. If it was important, she told herself, the caller would leave a message. So she returned to the dining room, apologized to the proprietor, and accepted more coffee.

"Not much," she said, and, seeing Rich's curious expression, added: "About Ted. I really don't know much at all about him. Everything he said last night was news to me, so I'll have to do some more research."

Rich nodded, and reminded her that it was time to check out of the B&B.

"They were good to let us drop tonight's reservation, so I promised we'd be out early," he said. "Still up for a walk and a visit to the Portland Museum of Art after that?"

"Of course," she said, slipping her hand into his.

After checking out, Julie realized she was cold and returned to her car to retrieve a fleece vest.

"What happened to fall?" she asked.

"That was yesterday," Rich replied. "I heard it might actually snow this evening."

"I like changes in seasons, but that seems a bit too fast."

"Well, hunters like it."

Julie stopped and looked at him.

"Snow makes it easier to track deer," he said.

"I'd forgotten what an expert hunter you are. Got your deer?"

Rich laughed. "You gotta work on your pronunciation. Hey, if you're looking to find out more about Korhonen, you can call him on Monday and ask if he did. Now say it this way: Getchadeer?"

By the time they had worked their way south through the neighborhoods of substantial houses and come out on the Western Promenade, the chilly wind was blowing steadily into their faces.

"On a clear day you can see Mount Washington from here," Rich said, pointing over the high bluff, but the only thing they could see was a distant smokestack of a now-abandoned paper mill in the suburbs. Beyond that were clouds, growing heavier. They picked up their pace, happy to be turning away from the wind, and when they arrived at the art museum they entered quickly to take advantage of the warmth.

❧

It wasn't till later, driving to Freeport, that Julie remembered the phone call she had missed at breakfast. Tempted though she was, she decided not to try to check for a message while she was driving. They had lunch at a small restaurant close to the large L.L. Bean store; remembering the admonitory sign at the B&B, Julie decided not to check for messages there. But after they had finished and walked down the street to the store, she told Rich she had to check. Sheltering from the dropping temperatures near the covered entrance to one of Freeport's many outlets, she dialed her voice mail while Rich seemed to be giving his full attention to the window display.

"Damn it!" she said as she came up behind him.

"Sorry. Just browsing," Rich replied.

When she looked at him blankly, he pointed to the window, and she realized he had been studying a lingerie display.

Julie laughed. "As long as you're just browsing," she said. "I wasn't commenting on that—I'm just mad that I missed the call. It was from Mike Barlow, and he said he had some interesting news, but that he's going to be away from cell towers this afternoon. So I'm supposed to call him this evening when he's back in range."

"Hunting."

"What?"

"Hunting. I'm sure our police officer is off sharpening his artillery skills in the woods. Doesn't he hunt?"

Julie said she had no idea, adding that she was getting tired of talking about hunting.

"Then we better not use the entrance back there," Rich said. "That goes through the hunting section. Let's go in the other way."

They agreed to shop separately, since Julie had a mental list of exactly what she needed, whereas Rich practiced what he called "opportunistic shopping," which meant he wandered around and bought something he might (or might not) need if it struck his fancy. Rich's style drove Julie to distraction, and he found hers amusing, if perhaps more effective. They arranged to meet at the exit by three-forty-five p.m.

Rich was waiting when she got there. She had two large bags, and he was carrying a small one.

"Successful?" he asked.

"It always is here. They have just what I want, and I know where to find it. I stocked up on blouses, two pairs of tan slacks, and a flannel shirt. How about you?"

"Interesting book," he said, holding out his small bag. "Animal tracking."

"For hunting?

"It's not for hunting; it shows you how to identify animal tracks in the snow. It'll be good for when we go snowshoeing. So, you got what you wanted, then?"

"Yeah. All set."

Neither of them liked departures, or handled them well. So when their weekends together ended, they had learned to simply leave. But today both were leaving, and it complicated matters. Back in the parking lot, their purchases tucked into their cars, they kissed quickly, but the usual custom of one waving while the other drove off wasn't going to work.

"So," Rich said, "who wants to be first?"

"Go ahead," Julie said. "I want to check the directions."

"Can I help?"

"That's why they created GPS" she said, holding up her cell phone.

"Just show me where you're going."

She recognized it as a stalling tactic, but didn't mind. "It's too cold to stand out here," she said. "Let's get in and I'll start the heater while I show you what I was thinking."

There was a route from Freeport to Ryland that would rather quickly put Julie on the main Portland-Ryland road, but to reach it she would have to travel several smaller roads in a southwesterly direction. Ryland was northwest, and Julie liked straight lines. So she had found a route on the Maine atlas that met her need to move directly, even though it included more secondary roads, none of which she knew.

"You're right that it's pretty direct," Rich said as they examined the atlas. "But you'll have to be sure to catch all those turns. If you miss one, you'll end up in Skowhegan."

"Perish the thought! I can follow the directions on GPS, Rich."

"Okay, it's your call, but a couple of these roads look pretty small, and they're probably curvy. Just be careful. It's going to be raining—maybe even snowing."

"Don't worry; it'll still be a pretty drive. I haven't seen that part of the state yet. You be careful, too. The turnpike is a lot more dangerous. Call when you get in, or I will."

She leaned over to kiss him again, and he quickly exited. She didn't wait for him to leave but instead put the car in gear and pulled out of the parking lot.

CHAPTER 17

Objects intrigued Julie because museums use them to tell people about history—although museum people always call them artifacts. Cars, however, were not among the things Julie found interesting; she saw them as wholly utilitarian—a means to get you where you wanted to go. The Volkswagen Jetta that she'd bought, used, when she had started graduate school had served her well then, and continued to do so after she moved to Maine. But a year ago it had begun to exhibit problems, minor at first, but escalating to the point where Rich said he didn't feel comfortable with her driving it between Ryland and Orono.

More to stem the growing cost of repairs than to placate him, she had traded it in for a VW Passat. It was larger and more powerful, and while its front-wheel drive didn't offer the same traction as the four-wheel-drive SUV Rich had urged her to consider, it was still a good car for Maine winter driving. To her surprise, Julie had found herself taking a more-engaged attitude toward the car. In fact, she liked it, and liked driving it, comfortable with its handling and confident it could get her through whatever conditions Maine's roads presented.

As she left Freeport and found the first of the several state routes she would be following, snow was not among the conditions she anticipated her zippy car dealing with today. A little drizzle looked likely, but that presented no problems, so she decided to relax and enjoy the ride, which now took her along the banks of the Androscoggin River. It was funny to see the river that ran through Ryland, and that she and Rich had canoed and kayaked so often, at this end of its route to the ocean.

Maybe it was the sight of the Androscoggin that triggered thoughts of Two Rivers Museum and her visit there. She hadn't had time to sort through what she had learned. When she got home, she planned to review the few notes she had been able to make and to expand on them with later thoughts, but she felt sure she'd reach the same conclusion she had tentatively come to the day before: that one or more persons had targeted Three Rivers to steal the specific items found missing. It was definitely, she told herself, a professional job.

Which led her to think of the statewide register and the likelihood that it was being developed as a way to identify items for theft. She wished she had been able to get to the bottom of the register in the conversations she had had last night with Hartshorn, Cartwright, and Korhonen. But just in asking about it, she realized, she had drawn attention to the fact that it interested her. Was that a mistake, she wondered? In advertising her interest, was she alerting the person or persons behind the register, and perhaps behind the thefts—and Dumont's murder?

A cup of coffee, she decided, would keep her alert. As she entered Auburn, she decided to pull into a fast-food place to get one. Disliking drive-throughs, she parked to go inside, but then realized she was going to be soaked by the rain that was now falling steadily, driven by the same strong wind she and Rich had encountered earlier that morning on their walk. So she pulled out of her parking spot and proceeded to the drive-through.

As she moved between the order window and the pickup window, she noticed that her windshield had glazed over. In just seconds, rain had become ice; how long before it got to snow, she didn't know, but snow would definitely be better. She pumped up the defroster after getting her coffee, cleared the windshield, and resumed the drive, dropping her speed to accommodate what she now feared would be treacherous conditions, and thus, a slow ride. Maybe the other route on a larger highway would have been better, she thought. At the very least, it would have been less curvy. The route she had turned onto twenty minutes outside of Auburn must have been laid out by someone whose straight ruler had broken. More likely the road followed old cattle or horse paths, she decided.

What came from the sky was sometimes ice, sometimes very wet snow. Nothing was accumulating on the road, but to feel safe, Julie slowed to a crawl. Luckily there was no traffic, she thought— right before a set of headlights appeared behind her, seemingly out of nowhere but rapidly closing in. Her instinct was to speed up, but she checked it because of the icy road. Pull over? she wondered. There was no space for that, at least just now; maybe a side road or driveway ahead would offer her an escape. But it couldn't come too soon because the vehicle—a large pickup truck, she now realized—was directly behind her, its headlights on high beams. To slow even more would risk an immediate collision, but speeding up was equally unattractive. For no good reason, Julie hit the horn, just once but then repeating it. She had no idea what good it would do. None, as it turned out.

Then she glanced to the side mirror, not wanting to take her eyes off the road but sensing a presence there. The truck pulled toward the passing lane, and Julie felt instant relief. But it stayed there, a few feet off her rear, and then turned as if trying to ram her. She had no choice now but to push the gas pedal, thinking that putting even a dozen feet between her and the truck would be better than having it riding so tightly on her. But the truck kept pace, and she decided she now had no choice. Just ahead was a slightly wider spot off to her right—not a road, but at least a place she could pull into, if she could do it fast and avoid being hit. It might have worked had the road been dry, but the icy covering afforded no traction, and her quick turn became a spin. The Passat seemed to tilt as she pulled the wheel sharply. She braked, harder than she knew she should, but the fancy antilock braking system kicked in at once, and she could feel the several jolts that brought her to a complete stop, ten feet or so off the road, and turned around so that she was facing the way she had come.

But she was safe! The truck roared past, not pausing to check on her, not even beeping to say good-bye. What she felt then was a mix of utter pleasure and utter exhaustion. Yes, she was safe; and her car was safe, its engine still running and its wipers making comfortingly routine sweeps across the windshield. "I'm okay," she said out loud. I'm okay; really I am. And the car is safe and everything is okay. But I feel like I've been run over by a train, she thought. Or a truck! Thinking of it she became angry, wishing she had at least saluted the driver with her middle finger as he raced on, oblivious to what had happened.

But was he? Was it just some kid having fun? Or a redneck eager to get to the nearest bar? Because of the height of the cab, Julie hadn't seen the driver, and so didn't even know if it had been male or female.

Despite the heat pouring out of the dashboard, Julie felt oddly cold, shaking. Shock, she told herself. But even though it was colder out than in, she wanted to get out—partly to check that her car was indeed okay, but also to move, to shake the imprisoned sense she had felt as the truck had tried to ram her. Walking around the car, satisfied that it seemed intact, Julie had another thought: Maybe it wasn't an accident. Maybe whoever it was had wanted to harm her—or at least, to scare her. Well, he—she had decided, based on no evidence, that it was indeed a he—had certainly succeeded. She really was scared. And standing on the side of a country road in the middle of an ice and snow storm didn't diminish that feeling.

So she got back in the car, pulled out on the road, and slowly resumed her trip. The only vehicle she encountered in the next half-hour was a small car going in the opposite direction. She stayed on high alert for a pickup, even though she had been driving around Maine long enough to realize that seeing a pickup truck would not qualify as a rare sighting. She was pretty sure it was tan, but it could have just been dirty white. One side of her wished she'd see it again so she could get the license number; the other side hoped she would never see it again.

The back road she was on eventually brought her back to the main highway. After a few minutes, she stopped at a convenience store to use the bathroom. Anger had replaced fear now, and Julie wanted to do something, take some action to offset the feeling of powerlessness the incident had induced. She considered calling Rich, but realized he would still be on the road; he couldn't do anything, and she didn't want to distract him with worry. She would wait till she got home and call him from there.

She decided to call Mike Barlow. He had told her to call later, but when his message came on she guessed he was still out of range—maybe hunting, as Rich had said. So she left a message, asking him to call her on her cell or at the house. Would it do any good to report what had happened? Couldn't hurt, she decided, and so called 911.

"This isn't really an emergency," she told the young woman who answered, "but someone tried to run me off the road, and I wanted to report it. Maybe that's silly," she added.

"Not at all. We take all incidents seriously. I need to transfer you to the county sheriff. Please hold."

The young deputy who took the information was polite, but Julie didn't sense that he was taking the matter quite as seriously as the 911 dispatcher had. Without a license plate, Julie felt she had little to offer, and regretted making the call. At least she had done something, she told herself as she left the parking lot to continue the drive. She was glad she hadn't mentioned the thought that had been growing in her mind over the past hour: that the driver of the truck was sending her a message. What that message was, exactly, she couldn't put in a simple sentence, but she knew it included items stolen from museums, a statewide register of valuable artifacts, and a murder. And at its heart: Stay away!

CHAPTER 18

The first thing Julie did when she got home was to turn up the thermostat. When she had left on Friday morning, a beautiful Indian summer day, she hadn't thought about moving it from its summer setting. Now, shivering as she carried her bags upstairs, she wished she had. This early appearance of winter had caught her by surprise. In the basement, the oil burner responded almost instantly, and its comforting growl persuaded her to stay home rather than go to the office. As she boiled water for tea, she convinced herself she could already feel the heat.

When she got Rich's answering machine, she realized that he would still be on the road. She left a message saying she was home, and hoped conditions on the turnpike were better than they'd been on the back roads she had traveled. She didn't mention anything more about her trip, saving that for their conversation. Then she dialed Mike Barlow's cell phone, but at the last minute decided against leaving a message when his voice mail kicked in.

As she was investigating her typically bare refrigerator and pondering whether to head to Ryland Groceries for something to eat, Rich called. She relieved his concern about driving conditions, but then, as casually as she could, told him about what she called a "little adventure."

She listened in silence as Rich denounced smart-ass kids, rednecks, owners of pickup trucks, and the entire driving population of southern Maine. When he was done, he asked a few questions about what she had seen, trying to identify which of those on his list most deserved his anger. When she told him she hadn't been able to see the driver, he asked about the license.

"Whoever it was just raced off," she said, "and by that time, I was facing the other direction anyway. I did report it," she added, "but it was a bit later, so I'm sure there's nothing they can do."

Rich kept questioning her about her condition and the Passat's, and when he seemed satisfied, she allowed a few more seconds of silence on her end.

"You're thinking something, Julie," he said. "I can tell. What is it?"

"It's just this sense I have—don't ask why; there's really nothing concrete—this sense that, well, it was deliberate. A warning."

"Shit! That's not what I wanted to hear."

"Look, I don't have any real reason to think it, but I just felt the guy was telling me to back off, to stay away from all this business of thefts and Dan Dumont's murder."

"This guy?"

"Generic—I don't know that for sure, but somehow I can't imagine a woman driving like that, coming after me that way. But who knows?"

"What I know is that I'm scared. For you. If you're right—and you know I can't always follow your thinking, even though I respect it—if you are right, then you're in danger, and you've got to be careful. Are you home or at the office?"

Julie's off-and-on fear of being alone in the big old house where she had discovered Worth Harding's bloody body two years ago had been, recently, mostly off, but she wasn't ashamed to admit to Rich that the house, which had also been broken into while she slept a year ago, remained a source of anxiety. Not fear, but certainly worry. Admitting that right now wouldn't help Rich—or herself.

"Home, and everything's locked. My only worry is about being cold," she fibbed. "God, it was so cold when I got here, but the heat's on now, and it's getting better. I'm in the kitchen, and you know how it always seems warmer because of the pilot lights on the stove burners. Do you have snow there?" she asked abruptly, to change the subject.

"No. It rained as far as Waterville, with a little icing, but beyond there it was just cloudy. Is there snow in Ryland?"

"Maybe a dusting, but it's more like a heavy frost. I guess it was more coastal."

"Yeah. Look, Julie, getting back to your 'little adventure,' what are you going to do?"

"You mean, if it was a warning, am I going to back off?"

"That's exactly what I mean. And I hope the answer is yes."

"Well I wasn't planning to do anything now except get warm and fix dinner. And I still haven't gotten ahold of Mike; when I do, I'll tell him what happened and see what he thinks."

"You know as well as I do what he'll say: that you should leave the detective work to the people like him who get paid to do it."

Julie laughed. "You do a good imitation."

"He's right, and I'm right. Promise me you won't do anything more about all of this—that you'll talk to Barlow and let him handle things."

She promised, and meant it—or at least meant that she'd tell Mike what had happened. Then Rich extracted promises that she'd recheck all the doors and windows and find something to eat at home so she wouldn't have to go out to the store.

"And you'll call me again before you go to bed—I'm home all night. Just check in, okay?"

Keeping to her promise not to go to the grocery store proved Julie's first challenge. She simply couldn't follow Rich's instructions for making an omelet, but she could at least scramble eggs. Those and a salad made her meal. When she'd finished, she tried Mike again. He answered on the first ring.

"Got your message, but I just got back to civilization and hadn't had a chance to call you back yet."

Julie decided not to ask if being away from civilization meant he had been hunting.

"You can call later if it's more convenient," she said, and got the response she was hoping for.

"Now's fine. Some interesting stuff I'd like to run by you, if you have a minute. Let me just walk to the other room to get my notes. You were in Portland, right?" he asked.

"And Two Rivers Museum on Friday. I need to tell you about that, as a matter of fact; and then Friday night, Rich and I went to a Halloween party at the historical society. I'll tell you about that. And another thing."

"You want to go first?"

"No, tell me what you called about. Calls from Dan's house, I'm assuming."

"Actually, no calls."

"So he didn't call Hartshorn last Tuesday night?"

"It would have been a toll call, and they'd have records. A local call won't be noted, so he might have talked to someone in Farmington, but there's no record of anything from his landline on Tuesday or Wednesday morning. Not sure what that proves."

"Not much, I guess. But what did you find that you said was interesting?"

"Well, that's where I could use your help. And remember, Julie, that's why we're talking—so you can help me solve this; not so I can help you!" She laughed and agreed. "Anyway, we went through Dumont's laptop. Thought we'd do that on Tuesday, but other things came up, and we didn't get to it till yesterday. We found a file called 'Maps.' It's full of notes about the missing items—descriptions, dates, that sort of stuff. Then a note that says . . . here, let me read this to you: 'Visitors: all known, except one in late August—Timothy Brothers; no address; no indication of research interest. Check this.' That's it. Make any sense to you?"

Julie paused before responding, stunned by the name.

"Mike, I just mentioned that I spent yesterday at Two Rivers Museum. Well, they've also had some items go missing, and the director asked me to come in and talk to her and look around. I can give you all the details later, but when they checked the register of people doing research, the only one they didn't know was Timothy Brothers."

"You're kidding! Any address or anything?"

"Stoughton, Mass. But that's it. I was going to Google him, but haven't had a chance. I can do that."

"Don't. I'll take it from here, Julie. Did anyone there remember him?"

"No."

"So what are they missing?"

Julie gave a brief summary.

"Very interesting," Barlow said. "Well, I'm going to have to talk to them. Give me the director's name and contact info, if it's handy."

Julie's notebook was on the table, and she gave Mike the information.

"I'd like to call Betsey first if you don't mind," she said, "to alert her that you'll be in touch."

"But don't say anything about Dumont. Just tell her I'm following up on something. Has she reported the thefts?"

"Not as of yesterday. I told her to, but she might not get around to it till after the weekend."

"You said you wanted to tell me about the Halloween thing," Barlow said. "Is that relevant to this?"

"I don't know. But if you have a few more minutes, I'll explain."

When she had finished her narration, ending with the road incident, there was silence on his end.

"You there?" she asked.

"Sorry; just thinking. You're connecting all this, aren't you—the missing items, the murder, the folks at the party, and then being run off the road?"

"It's not that I'm connecting them, Mike. I just think they are connected. Doesn't it make sense?"

"My mind doesn't work like yours, Julie. I see that something happened and try to find what caused it. Connect the dots, you know. But what you're describing is a whole bunch of dots, and it just doesn't seem like they have to be connected. Like the incident on the road . . . You okay, by the way?"

She said she was, and told him she had reported it.

"But you didn't get the plate?" he asked.

"No."

"That makes it pretty hard. Likely just some dumb teenager out to have a little fun. Stupid, but not necessarily deliberate. Really not much the sheriff can do. Tell me again why you think it was—what did you say—a warning?"

She explained that it was only a feeling, nothing she could pin down.

"Well, one thing I've learned about you is that your feelings are sometimes right on the mark."

"Only sometimes?"

"Well, maybe more often than not. But this is pretty complicated, and I've got to think it through. You're sure you're okay? Feel safe being by yourself?"

She said she did, half meaning it.

"Okay, just make sure everything's locked—you have a double bolt on that door, don't you?"

She said she did.

"Well, use it, and check the windows and everything. I need to sit down and review all of this with you. Are you free on Monday? I could come over then and we could go through it."

Julie said she would make sure she was, and they agreed that he would come to Ryland late morning.

When they had finished talking, she phoned Rich, who repeated Mike Barlow's cautions and arranged for another call before she went to bed. Considering that she didn't feel at all sleepy, she told him that it might be late.

"So what are you going to do in the meantime?" he asked.

"Oh, probably work on a puzzle or something to relax."

"Make it a jigsaw," he said.

She agreed. Although her notes about Two Rivers tempted her, she chose instead to do a fiendishly tough jigsaw of a moose that she had picked up at L.L. Bean. It was almost midnight when, nearly halfway through the puzzle, she finally threw in the towel for the night, called Rich, and headed to bed. After rechecking the doors and windows.

CHAPTER 19

The swirling snow made it hard for Julie to focus on the yellow center line that she was using to guide her way, but she was determined to keep focused on it as she slowly made progress through the storm. She was surprised by the speed at which the rain had yielded to ice and the ice to the heavy, wet snow that was now making her drive so demanding. But if she just persisted, slowly, carefully, she thought . . . and then behind her came the headlights, so bright they seemed like spotlights, and she could hear the straining engine of the truck as it edged up alongside. If only she could take her eyes off the center line, she thought, she would turn quickly to see if she could tell who was driving the threatening vehicle that was now directly beside her. She had to keep focused, she reminded herself.

But how could she, with that bell ringing? What bell? Was it a warning device on her car? Some mysterious alarm under the control of the all-powerful computer chips that she knew controlled the vehicle?

Julie rolled toward it and realized it was her phone—and that she was in bed, obviously dreaming crazily about the incident during her trip home. The phone on the stand was emitting its third ring. The clock beside it said one-forty-five.

"Hello?" she yelled when she picked it up. "Hello?" she repeated when the response was silence. That was broken with a voice, male and muffled: "Maine winter driving is not for everyone. 'Specially folks from away. I'd be careful if I was you. Real careful."

She heard the line go dead but continued to scream obsceni-
ties into the mouthpiece, words she knew more from reading than
from speaking them. In a flash she was back in the condo at the
Ryland Skiway right after her move. Late-night hang-up calls then
had tried to warn her off pursuing her investigation of valuable
items missing from the historical society. They hadn't worked
then, and they weren't going to work now.

She had had caller ID installed then, at Mike Barlow's suggestion, and did the same when she'd moved to Harding House.
What it told her now was that the number of the call was 'unavailable.' Great help there! Probably an unlisted cell number. It didn't
matter. Although she admitted some measure of fear, it was mostly
anger she felt—anger for the violation that such a call represented,
and anger for her inability to do anything about it.

Julie got up, pulled on her heavy robe, and put on all the lights
in the bedroom. She went to the top of the stairs and listened for a
minute or so to be sure she was alone. When she was satisfied she
was, she went back and sat on the bed beside the phone, thinking
of whether she should call anyone. Although it would be comforting to hear Rich's voice, he was a grueling two-hour drive away,
and could hardly come spend the rest of the night with her. Mike
Barlow? He was in Augusta. The Ryland Police station was just
two blocks away, and a cop on patrol might get to her quickly. But
what would be the point?

I just have to work through my options, she thought. And why
not? She knew she wasn't getting back to sleep anytime soon.

She went downstairs, turning on every light along the way,
and settled in at the table where last night's puzzle remained
incomplete, one of the moose's antlers beginning to emerge. Before
she attacked it, she took a pad and pen and recorded the call
as best she could. She was pretty sure she got it right. Then she
added: "Male. Hard to tell age—not a teenager. Muffled voice,

like maybe he was holding something over his mouth to disguise it. Didn't remind me of anyone. Sounded rushed—like he was trying to get the call over with."

She kept the pad beside her in case anything else occurred that would be worth noting. But it was the jigsaw puzzle itself she focused on, studying the pieces with the same care she had applied to watching the center line in her dream. Focus and move forward, she said to herself. And just before three a.m., she finished, snapping the last piece of the moose's antler into place. She stood to admire the whole: a peaceful riverside scene in autumn colors with a grand bull moose gazing at her. If I'd known I was going to finish it so fast, she thought, I would have bought another. But then, I didn't realize I'd be sitting here in the middle of the night. Could she get back to sleep? It was worth a try.

❦

When she woke at seven-thirty, Julie was surprised at how rested she felt. No further dreams had disturbed her sleep. No phone calls. No squeaks on the steps or rustling branches against the house. She had slept deeply and felt refreshed enough to go for a run before breakfast. She was happy it was Sunday and she didn't have to open the historical society till noon.

She was coming up the hill toward the Common after forty-five minutes, and decided that was enough. She returned to the house, and as the coffee brewed, she remembered today was the start of standard time, so instead of eight-thirty, it was now seven-thirty. She reset her watch and went around the house, doing the same with the clocks. The extra hour was already beginning to wear on her; it was going to be a longer day than she wanted.

Over coffee she considered calling Rich to remind him about the time change, so he wouldn't show up early for the dean's brunch that had forced their change in plans. But she knew Rich, of all people, would be on top of that. Just then her phone rang.

"Hope I didn't wake you," Rich said. "I just wanted to remind you to reset your clocks."

She laughed and explained that she'd just been thinking about calling him, but realized he wouldn't need the reminder.

"You're okay?" he asked.

"Fine. Just came back from a short run. What's the weather like up there?"

Julie was aware she didn't really care about his answer; she was buying time for herself to decide whether or not to tell Rich about her late-night phone call. While he described the bleak conditions in Orono, Julie made her decision: There was no reason to worry him; after all, what could he do but worry?

Still, she felt guilty, which continued after the call as she ate breakfast, washed the dishes, took a shower, and dressed for her afternoon at the museum. It was only ten-thirty, new time, when she realized she was ready. Although the historical society didn't open till noon, she decided to go to her office first to catch up on anything that had accumulated during her absence on Friday and Saturday. And to make another call—to Betsey Bowers.

At first Betsey was nervous about the prospect of State Police involvement, but Julie assured her that Mike Barlow was discreet.

"So this is bigger than Two Rivers?" Betsey asked.

"Well, it might be. That's not yet clear, but I suggested to Mike that he should talk to you directly so he can decide for himself if there's something going on."

"But that means you think there is, Julie."

"Just a hunch I want to test."

"Is this related to Dan Dumont's murder?" Betsey asked. "I assume that's what the State Police are investigating. Did Dumont have anything go missing?"

"I'm not really able to go into things like that, Betsey, but let's just say that Dan and I talked about museum security, and that's what Mike Barlow is interested in. So when I mentioned my visit to Two Rivers, he said he'd like to talk to you, and that's why I'm calling."

"Okay. I don't mean to be difficult, Julie; of course I'll talk to him, and tell him whatever he wants to know. But if you hear or think of anything I should know, please call me. Frankly, this is making me nervous."

Julie tried to persuade Betsey that she had nothing to be nervous about, beyond the obvious fact that some items seem to have been stolen from her museum, but by the end of the call, she wasn't sure she had succeeded. Before hanging up, she told Betsey to get in touch if anything in her call with Barlow caused her concern, and promised to call again in a few days if she didn't hear from Betsey.

This less-than-satisfying call behind her, Julie spent the next hour reading the mail and call-back slips left in her absence. One note from Mrs. Detweiller indicated that the pile of papers it covered had been delivered by Wayne Reiter, who also confirmed their meeting on Monday. When she glanced at the papers, reluctant because she assumed they were more about collections policies and de-accessioning of items, she saw they were instead copies of scholarly articles about what one called "the business of theft." She had almost forgotten that she had asked Reiter about this topic, partly to divert him from his usual obsession.

She decided she was glad she had asked, because it was possible that somewhere in what she guessed would be the dense and jargon-laden prose of these academic papers, she might find some hints to focus her thinking about the stolen items. Or might not. In either case, reading them would have to come later, since it was time to open the doors to the Ryland Historical Society.

Sundays were always slow, especially in the fall and winter, but Julie had resisted Dennis Sutherland's suggestion that they open only one Sunday a month during this slow season. Whatever reasons she had marshaled then escaped her now as she sat alone at the desk in the visitors' entrance at two-thirty, having seen no one in the past two and a half hours except the volunteer staffing the museum shop. Good museum practice, Julie knew, frowned on staff members reading on the job when performing such a public function as welcoming visitors, but the prospect of sitting idle and greeting no one trumped good practice in this case, Julie convinced herself as she read the academic papers about theft.

She had to hand it to Reiter; he had located at least a dozen such papers, and while she admitted that what more than half of them said baffled her, with their quantitative analysis and lengthy footnote references, even her rapid skimming produced some basic conclusions. One was that crime did pay. A lot of thieves got away with it, undetected and unpunished. Petty crime in particular seemed to be successful more often than not. Did that mean that the thefts she was investigating were unlikely to be solved?

Another conclusion she found less disturbing and more helpful was that systematic thefts of objects were rarely accidental. People who stole art and other valuable artifacts didn't just wander into museums and select items of interest. More often, they were guided by what one author called "shopping lists," typically made by collectors and given to thieves to carry out the work. Thieves rarely wanted the items for themselves, but instead pursued them on behalf of those who did. The one article that developed this case most carefully subjected it to "artificially induced demand source analysis"—a phrase Julie couldn't help but quarantine inside quotation marks, even though its author didn't. What he seemed to mean was that people who wanted things artificially created demand for them by asking thieves to steal them, and so just as the demand for the items was inflated by the quirks of collectors, so the supply of the items was artificially increased, placing them beyond their natural market-clearing price. Or, as Julie phrased it for herself: Things people steal for others bring higher prices than things people don't want. That sounded perfectly reasonable to her, although she didn't necessarily trust her ability to translate academic jargon into simple prose.

A voice startled her, and Julie dropped the page she was reading.

"I'm sorry," she said to the woman standing in front of her, circled by three children. "I didn't hear you come in."

"That's okay," the woman said pleasantly. "I was wondering whether it's too late to see the Halloween exhibit. Maybe it's already been taken down? It's just that we got so busy with costumes and all that, we didn't get here before. The kids really wanted to see it."

"That's wonderful," said Julie. "The exhibit is still up—through the end of the month, actually—but this is a good day to see it."

Julie directed them to the room at the rear where the "Ryland Halloweens of the Past" exhibit was located. "Museum admission is always free on Sunday," she said, when the woman reached into her handbag.

The woman insisted on making a contribution anyway, and Julie thanked her.

"Are you a member?" she asked, and when the woman said she wasn't, Julie gave her a membership brochure. You never knew who might join—no one, if you didn't ask, Julie always reminded volunteers during training sessions.

Marking "1 adult, 3 children" in the visitor book, Julie resumed her thoughts on the business of theft. Although it wasn't good for the Ryland Historical Society that the total audience for the afternoon was covered by that single entry, Julie found she was happy for the quiet reading and thinking time.

In one sense, nothing she had read in Reiter's papers had offered any new insight, but taken together, they sparked something—the beginnings of a theory, and a good one at that.

CHAPTER 20

Sitting in her office Monday morning as Mike Barlow moved quickly through his list and took notes, Julie thought he was even more efficient now than when he had served as chief of police in Ryland. She had admired his directness and focus then, but either she had forgotten just how skilled he was, or his State Police experience had honed it.

On Timothy Brothers, she had little to add to what she had told him Saturday night.

"Still checking," he said, when she asked if he had located anyone of that name in Stoughton, Massachusetts. "You didn't find anything?" he asked.

"I thought you said you'd pursue it."

"I did, and I've started, but I know you well enough to assume you'd be doing the same. Maybe our inquiries crossed on Bing."

Julie laughed. "I'm still on Google."

"They're about the same," Barlow said, "but even though we have a few more tools in law enforcement, so far, nothing. I'm guessing he's not from Stoughton, just like that's not his real name. 'Timothy Brothers' doesn't mean anything to you?"

"Nothing. Did you talk to Betsey Bowers? I told her you'd be in touch."

"Not yet, but I hope to get to that this afternoon. Do you think there's any more coffee out there?"

Julie took both their mugs to the outer office and refilled them. Barlow took a sip and then asked if Julie had anything to add about the incident on the road Saturday.

"As a matter of fact," she began, and then told him about the hang-up call.

"That sounds a bit familiar. You should have told me yesterday. Weren't you scared?"

"More mad than scared. You know what I mean: It's such an invasion, someone pushing into your life like that, and you don't have any defense."

"That's why they do it. So how did he sound?"

Julie pulled out the sheet on which she had taken notes about the call and read them to him. He took notes, rapidly.

"Did your phone show a caller ID?"

"No, the screen said 'Unavailable.'"

"Move on to your theories about this statewide register and who's behind it. I'm not saying it's connected, but I want to understand it better."

After Julie had summarized her feelings that such a listing of valuable items would make a perfect to-steal list, Barlow asked who she thought was behind it.

"You mean, who might be behind the thefts—and the murder?"

"I think you've got a suspect list, Julie. Tell me who's on it, and let me decide what they might be up to."

She started with James Hartshorn, and Barlow made notes: president of the Network, computer background. "But he's way the hell Down East, isn't he?"

"True, but with the Internet, that doesn't matter."

"I mean, as far as Dumont's murder and your being run off the road. He's pretty far away to be involved in those."

"So you do think all this is connected?"

145

Barlow stood up, stretched, and circled the table. Smiling at Julie, he said, "One of the best training courses the Staties provide is preparing you to testify in court. You learn what not to say when a lawyer is trying to get you to connect a couple of things you might think are related, but can't prove. They teach you how to respond, to resist what the lawyer is trying to get you to say while still answering the question. I found that really useful."

"I get the point, Mike. I won't badger you to agree, but you know what I think."

He laughed and came back around to his chair and sat down. "So who's next on your list?"

"In no particular order: Brent Cartwright, at the Portland Historical Society."

Barlow took notes as she described him.

"And why is he on your list?"

When she said she didn't have anything concrete to link him to the thefts or the murder, Barlow said, "I'll just put down 'Julie's instincts.' Who else?"

"Well, I think it's more than my instincts on this one. Ted Korhonen is a hunter, so he has a gun. His job is part-time, and he needs money. He told me he does all sorts of odd jobs to keep afloat. He's a lot closer to both Mountain Valley and Two Rivers, and not far from where I was run off the road. He could have easily followed me there on his way home."

"Interesting."

The long pause that followed reminded Julie of earlier times when Mike's response annoyed her—and prompted her to speak instead of letting his silent thought advance. Now she knew better, and though it was still hard to sit quietly, she did so until he broke his own silence.

"With the others, I have to say it seems a stretch, Julie, but Korhonen might just have the holy trinity—you know, motive, opportunity, and means. Needs money, lives not far from the scenes, owns and uses a gun." He paused again, but this time Julie didn't wait.

"But really, Mike, Ted seems to me the nicest of them all. I mean, somehow not like Hartshorn or Cartwright, despite the holy trinity."

"You like him and you don't like them. What does that prove? Anyway, you put him on your list."

"Maybe I'm wrong on that."

"Maybe, but you got my interest. You don't happen to know if Korhonen owns a truck, do you?"

"As a matter of fact, he does. He mentioned he had an old truck that needed repairs or something. I forgot that; guess that's another part of opportunity."

"Could be. You think one of these guys might be Timothy Brothers?"

Julie hesitated. "I don't think so . . . No, I just don't see how that's possible."

"Why not?"

"They're all known to other directors. This Timothy Brothers signed in at Two Rivers during the summer, when Betsey was away, but I don't think if he was one of the three he would take the chance of being recognized by Betsey's assistant. We don't know when Timothy Brothers visited Mountain Valley, but again, I can't see one of these three taking such a risk. The museum world is small, Mike, and in a place like Maine, it's really small."

"So you're saying that we've got at least two people involved— one of your guys as mastermind, and then someone who goes out and does the thefts?"

"To tell you the truth, I hadn't thought of that, but you're absolutely right: At least two people are involved."

"Well, I need to do some checking, so I better leave you to your work. Everything here going okay?"

Julie realized he was referring to the historical society, and told him things were in great shape.

"Glad to hear it. You've done a terrific job. I can remember when this place seemed on its last legs, with Worth Harding presiding over his private museum. But it sounds like the place is humming now, thanks to you. Sometimes folks from away can get the job done," he said with a wink. "And I should be doing mine. I'll be in touch."

Mrs. Detweiller knocked and entered. "After all that time with Chief Barlow, you're running behind. I just wanted to remind you that Mr. Reiter is coming in."

"Detective Barlow." Julie couldn't stop herself from correcting her secretary, perhaps as a return shot for the implied criticism that she had spent society time on outside business.

"Well, I knew that, but I'll always think of him as Chief. We all miss him. He was so much better than that young man who calls himself chief now."

Since Julie barely knew the young man in question, she didn't feel compelled to defend him, despite the nearly constant impulse she felt to resist whatever Mrs. Detweiller said.

"Mike was a great chief, but he seems to be thriving now in the State Police."

"I'm sure," Mrs. Detweiller responded unconvincingly. "Do you have those papers Mr. Reiter sent? He's coming to talk to you about them, as I said."

"Yes, thank you, Mrs. Detweiller. They're right here. I've read them, so when Wayne comes, send him right in."

It was true that Julie had read the articles on the business of crime, along with the various policy statements on collections management and de-accessioning that she knew he wanted to focus on. When Mrs. Detweiller knocked and ushered Wayne Reiter into Julie's office a few minutes later, Julie thought she was ready for him.

Though short and burly, Reiter moved with speed, taking the chair across from her and launching into his subject, much as he'd probably done when commanding the podium in a large class-room at Harvard Business School.

"I'm quite glad you raised that point last time we were to-gether," he said. "It was a connection I frankly missed."

Julie looked at him blankly, trying to remember their earlier interview. What connection, she wondered?

"You might call it 'involuntary de-accessioning,'" he contin-ued, oblivious to her lack of understanding.

"Call what 'involuntary de-accessioning'?"

"Thefts, of course. You see, when thieves remove items from a museum collection, they're in effect de-accessioning, but not in the way we talk about when we discuss collection management. Quite the opposite, really; thieves go for the most valuable stuff, whereas we cull from the collection to remove the least-useful items—although I suppose the matter of value is relative, isn't it?"

Julie felt a gentle throb above her eyes, what she knew was the beginning of a headache. Much as she enjoyed solving problems, trying to trace the order of Wayne Reiter's thinking presented problems of a different magnitude from assembling the parts of a grazing moose into a completed jigsaw puzzle. She decided not to try, but instead, to shift the conversation to what most interested her: "I was quite taken by the article on 'induced demand.' I think that was the term."

"Yes, indeed. Actually it's artificially induced demand, if I remember correctly."

You always do, Julie added silently.

"Normal demand, or what economists consider normal, comes about when potential seekers after a good or service are pursuing normal needs," Reiter said, "for food or shelter or what have you. But demand can be induced—by, say, advertising, which tries to make you want something you didn't know you needed—and probably don't. BMWs come to mind," he added.

Julie was aware that Wayne Reiter roared around Ryland in a red BMW convertible, but decided not to mention it.

"In any event," he continued in his professorial way, "inducing demand artificially can take various forms. In the article you reference, the source of the demand is what you might call an order. Let's say someone desires lithographs of butterflies. Well, there isn't a huge demand for that ordinarily, I'd guess, but this person's passion leads him, or her, to seek such lithographs, and as a consequence, the value of them rises beyond what one would expect in a so-called normal market. You see that?"

Julie felt she should be taking notes, but the throbbing above her eyes was increasing, and she didn't know how long she could hold off the full-blown headache that was surely coming.

"Yes, I see that," she said. "What interests me is how this applies to thefts from museums."

"Of course, of course. That's our focus, isn't it? Or yours. Yes, a collector who wants something that a museum has instructs an intermediary to obtain it, and as a consequence, the value of the item rises. Here, let me show you."

He took a thick Montblanc pen from the inner pocket of his tweed sport coat and drew lines on the back of a page from one of the articles that were neatly stacked on the desk.

"This is the normal supply, you see, and this is the normal demand. Here's where the lines cross—the market clearing price, we call it. Now, if I shift the demand line higher, artificially induced by the collector's out-of-normal desire, you see what happens: Voilà! Up goes the clearing price!"

Julie wanted to say that all of this seemed to be common sense, but instead she tried to study the lines on the page as if they revealed some deep secret that the good professor had kindly shared with her.

"Yes, that makes a lot of sense," she said. "I think I see it now. Thank you."

"Indeed. A little sketch can often illuminate something rather profound, don't you think? A trick I learned early in my teaching career. Now, I sense you find all this quite applicable to our situation here."

This was where Julie knew Reiter was going to redirect the conversation to his favorite topic: the need for Ryland Historical Society to de-accession some of its artifacts. Her headache was in full bloom now, so she found it easier to try to listen than to say more. And listen she did, for the next forty minutes, as Reiter lectured her on collection management, pulling documents from the pile to make his points. She felt bludgeoned by his endless talk, but did her best to nod from time to time to show she was following, and agreed with him.

"It sounds like we're in sync on this," he said. "I think we need to convene the collections group and present a plan. Do you agree?"

Julie had lost the thread again and wasn't at all sure what it was Reiter was proposing to present, but the numbness she felt left her no defense.

"Yes, I think so, Wayne. How soon do you think we should meet?"

"Immediately, I would say. No time to lose, really. Later this week, perhaps, depending on your schedule. You'll notify the others? Let's say Friday at two o'clock. I can make myself available then."

Julie glanced at her calendar and saw that she was free. She reminded Reiter that Loretta Cummings was appointed to head the working group on collections that had been set up at the last meeting. "Shouldn't we check with her first?" she asked.

"If you like. Then have your secretary phone the others. We've made good progress here. I'll see you Friday."

When he shot off and exited the office, Julie put her aching head on her desk and wondered what she had let herself in for.

CHAPTER 21

The e-mail from James Hartshorn had been sent Monday evening, but Julie did not see it till Tuesday morning when she came to her office early.

A few months ago she had adopted a policy of not doing e-mail from home except on weekends, an approach she realized she needed to take in order to tamp down the anxiety that being constantly online, or at least feeling she needed to be, had induced. The new approach was one part of Julie's pledge to herself that with everything running so smoothly at the historical society, she needed to pull back and relax into her success. The world, she had been pleased to discover, was in no danger of ending if she didn't clear her e-mail every night before going to bed, and spending a half-hour on it at the beginning of each workday provided a nice start to the day.

When she logged in on Tuesday morning at the office, Hartshorn's message, third in the queue, was a particularly good kickoff:

As most of you know, there has been quite a bit of informal talk among Network members about the desirability of beginning a blog through which we can communicate with each other about the various doings of our museums. Foremost among these is security, a topic about which we had an excellent presentation at the last state meeting, and which all of us are concerned about. Because access to the blog is strictly limited to members, you can feel secure using it to communicate about your collection and to alert others to problems. I'm happy to say that with help from several on the executive committee, we now have our Network blog up and running!

Hartshorn went on to provide the link, and instructions for accessing the blog, including how to register with username and password.

Julie shut down her e-mail immediately, went to the web, located the blog, and registered. The first posting was of course from Hartshorn. It elaborated on the matter of security, and proposed that members could, with safety, use the blog to register items of value in their collections as a means, he wrote, "of keeping track of holdings that may be vulnerable."

"This information," his posting continued, "will help all members work together to prevent or resolve problems when we are presented with the gift or purchase of valuable items."

Julie's translation was more direct: We can check to see if something we're offered has been stolen from another museum. Or, she thought, decide what we might like to steal!

Why now? Julie wondered. She had been hearing talk over the past month about such a blog, but hadn't been able to find out anything concrete. Was its appearance now related to the Mountain Valley or Two Rivers thefts? To Julie's conversations at the Halloween party—and her subsequent little road problem? Or merely a coincidence?

Julie pondered those questions as she went to the outer office to see if the coffee machine she had started earlier had done its job. It had, so she poured herself a cup and was heading back to her office when Dennis Sutherland appeared.

"Just what I was looking for," he said, gesturing to the coffee machine. He walked over to fill his mug. "Glad you're not one of those bosses who waits for the secretary to start the coffee," he added.

Julie smiled. Mrs. Detweiller's personality was a frequent topic of conversation between them.

"If I did," Julie said, "we'd be having coffee with lunch."

"Or maybe tea at teatime," Dennis countered. "So what's up, boss?"

"Something you might want to see. Come inside and I'll show you James Hartshorn's latest."

Dennis pulled up a chair beside hers and read the screen with Hartshorn's introductory message.

"Sounds like a good idea," he said when he'd finished reading. "Good way to make contact about sensitive things without e-mail or phone calls. It's limited to Network users, I gather." Julie said it was. "Something you can check if an item is offered, to be sure it didn't start out somewhere else." Julie agreed, albeit without much enthusiasm. "One thing I don't follow, though, is why it's limited to museums in Maine. I mean, if you took something from an in-state museum, wouldn't you try to sell it somewhere else—any-where else, really?"

Julie paused before responding. It was a good point—and it reinforced the feeling she had that the new blog wasn't intended to prevent or solve thefts, but rather to facilitate them. She wasn't sure she wanted to share that with Dennis, so she said, "I see what you mean. I'll mention that to Hartshorn. Maybe there's a way to expand it, or tap into other state blogs—if any exist."

"I'll leave you to it then," he said. "I've got a busload of middle schoolers coming in ten minutes. Better finish this coffee and get ready. By the way," Dennis said, as he took his last gulp of coffee, "how was the Halloween party?"

With all that had happened since, Julie had nearly forgotten the event. "Fun," she said. "The usual crowd—in costumes, of course."

"Ellie and I went by the hotel," he said, naming the girlfriend whose work in Portland had prompted him to apply for the job at the Ryland Historical Society. "We were heading back after dinner and saw folks going in. Probably we should have gone ourselves, but with Ellie's schedule at the hospital, it's hard to plan. So it was fun?"

"You were in Portland?" Julie asked.

"Just Friday night—came back here early Saturday, before the snow. Guess it was pretty tricky driving later, but you got back okay."

Before she answered, Julie had an odd thought: Dennis Sutherland had traveled from Portland to Ryland on Saturday, and Dennis has a pickup truck. But that's silly, she said to herself.

"Tricky, that's true. But no problems."

"Good. Well, I'd better get over there and greet the kiddies. Thanks for the coffee."

After he left, Julie sat at her desk and recounted all the reasons she shouldn't think of Dennis Sutherland as a suspect. She was glad she had talked to Mike Barlow before she knew about Dennis's weekend; putting him on her list would have been really, really dumb, she was sure. What she needed to think about was what Dennis had said about blogs. I really ought to know that sort of thing, she told herself. Despite the attention she got from her peers in Maine about museum thefts and security, she didn't delude herself into thinking she was a true expert. If she were, she would have known about blogs and other web-based tools to enhance security.

Mrs. Detweiller interrupted her thoughts, saying, "You have a light schedule today."

As always, Mrs. Detweiller had a deft way of making a statement into an accusation. Julie had planned her "light schedule" because she'd wanted to return to the work she had been doing in the archives. Whether her secretary would accept research as a substitute for sitting at her desk, or see it as an excuse for not doing Society business, Julie didn't know—and didn't care, she told herself before responding.

"I'm planning to do some research today, Mrs. Detweiller. As soon as I finish a few things here, I'm going up to the library. I want to get in some good work there before lunch."

"I'll hold your calls, then."

"Please. Unless, of course, it's really important." In order to define important here, she specified that she meant calls from a trustee, Rich, or Mike Barlow.

A few minutes later, Julie gathered her folders with the extensive notes she had made over the past two years and nodded to her secretary as she passed through the outer office to climb the stairs to the library.

Tabitha Preston was already on duty, seated at her desk at the far end of the room. Julie's entrance had the effect on the older woman that the presence of another person in the quiet environment of the library always elicited: surprise. Tabitha took off her reading glasses, glanced up from the cards spread on her desk, looked down again, reached for her other glasses, and then said, "Oh, Dr. Williamson. It's you."

"Yes," Julie responded, feeling as she always did when Tabitha greeted her this way: that confirmation of her existence—or at least, her identity—wasn't really necessary.

"How are you, Tabitha? I didn't mean to startle you."

"Oh, I was just trying to sort out these cards from the inventory. I think those high school students who were here the other day mixed them up, and now they're all out of order."

One of Julie's recent initiatives had been to encourage use of the Society's materials by students to engage them in history and to widen the museum's audience. Not everyone agreed with the approach. Volunteer librarian Tabitha Preston was among those with doubts, but, being compliant, she went along with the plan, and helped high school teachers develop research assignments.

If it had stopped there, Tabitha would probably have been able to accept the concept, but the actual presence of gangling, loud adolescents in her space took the matter a step too far for her taste. The teachers who were supposed to oversee the students were not, in Tabitha's estimation, much better at understanding proper library procedures. Horror of horrors, one even insisted on taking notes with a ballpoint pen—surely, in Tabitha's mind, the ultimate sin, since three signs clearly announced PENCILS ONLY.

But Tabitha wasn't a complainer, and she had never spoken directly to Julie about her concerns. She had talked to Dennis Sutherland about them, and Dennis had relayed them to Julie. Sympathetic as Julie was, she had decided not to deal with the matter openly, hoping that in the long run the small problems would be worked out. But now the fact of the disordered inventory cards had to be addressed. Julie began by admitting that she knew the student work created additional problems, but hoped that Tabitha could put up with them, since her knowledge and experience would be so helpful to the students for whom the idea of historical research was quite foreign.

"I try, Dr. Williamson," the librarian said with a sigh. "I do understand it's important for young people to do real research, but they're so unprepared, and, frankly, the teachers aren't much better. Well, I'll just straighten these out now, if that won't disturb you."

Julie understood that the topic was now closed.

"Not at all," she responded. "I've been so negligent about the Tabor papers, but I blocked off this morning to work on them. I hope I'm not disturbing you."

"Of course not. Do you know which box you want? I'll be happy to bring it out."

Julie opened a folder to remind herself of where she had left off in her slow and often interrupted process of working through the papers, box by box. When she saw where she should begin today, she was tempted to say she would retrieve the box herself, but thought better of it when she glanced at the closed metal door of the vault that held the archives. She had once been an involuntary occupant of that vault, and entering it, even for the brief time required to retrieve a box of papers, always triggered a sense of panic, marked by sudden sweating and the beginning of a tremor.

"That's good of you," she said. "I was halfway through number six, so I'll pick up there and try to finish it this morning."

Tabitha Preston rose stiffly from her desk and shuffled to the vault, unlocked it, swung the heavy door open, and entered. Better her than me, Julie thought, feeling guilty that she had put the older woman to such a chore. But it was no more than a minute before Tabitha carried the box to the table and put it down.

"Hope this will be interesting," she said.

"Me, too. I'm so grateful to you for getting me involved in the Tabor papers, Tabitha. Every box is different; you never know what you'll find."

The librarian accepted the thanks with a smile that Julie knew was genuine; Tabitha really did enjoy putting people on to interesting items in the collection—provided, of course, they were over the age of twenty-one and carried pencils. Julie fit both criteria.

As she consulted her notes to find her place, Julie paused to think about what the papers represented. They were, she felt, the best counter to Wayne Reiter's endless complaints about how much "stuff"—his usual word—the Society owned. In her mind, collecting defined what it meant to be a museum; for Reiter, collecting was a bad habit that an outsider like him could help the Ryland Historical Society overcome. The Tabor papers, at least in Julie's way of thinking, refuted his argument.

She shuddered to imagine what might have happened if Wayne Reiter had been on the board when Dr. Samuel Tabor's relatives appeared at the museum with eighteen boxes of materials. Since that had happened over a year before Julie had assumed her job, she hadn't been responsible for the decision, but she silently blessed her predecessor, Worth Harding, who had gratefully accepted the gift. And what a gift it was! Tabitha Preston had, almost by accident, alerted Julie to the papers several years ago, and since then she had slowly been working her way through the boxes—not quite a third of the way through, she realized.

Dr. Tabor had been Ryland's town physician for almost forty years, from just past the beginning of the twentieth century until just before the end of World War II. He was a packrat, incapable of discarding anything on paper. So the boxes contained, in no particular order, pages from medical journals, agendas from town government committee meetings, programs for plays and musical performances, photographs—and letters: from friends, relatives, and patients, and copies, on carbon paper, of typewritten letters Tabor wrote to them.

It was the letters that Julie so treasured, because they painted vivid pictures of life in Ryland over the nearly forty years of Dr.

Tabor's residence. When she first dipped into the papers, Julie had had no clear purpose, other than getting an overview of what the boxes held, but at Rich's urging she began to focus on the letters, particularly those written in the 1930s. Rich had pointed out that little was known about how the Depression affected small towns like Ryland, and Tabor's descriptions of town events helped to fill that gap.

When asked, Julie told people she was working on a scholarly article she had tentatively titled "Down and Out in Ryland, Maine: The Depression in Small-Town America." And she was working on that. But in the meantime, she was also simply enjoying thumbing through the documents and immersing herself in the gritty details of Ryland life that emerged from the disparate materials—made possible because Ryland Historical Society collected such items, preserved them, and made them available to anyone. That, she almost shouted, is what we do; so there, Wayne Reiter!

Had she indeed shouted? Fearing that she had, Julie looked toward Tabitha, but found she was still hunched over her desk, sorting through the inventory cards left in disarray by the high school students. A small price to pay, Julie thought, for introducing young people to the wonders of historical research, with real documents written and saved by real people. Putting aside those satisfying but slightly irrelevant thoughts, Julie tucked into box six of the Dr. Samuel Tabor papers. Reading, sorting, making notes, she was soon lost in her work, and when she heard Tabitha say she was taking her lunch hour, Julie realized the morning was gone.

While Tabitha returned the box to the vault, Julie reluctantly gathered her folders. The two walked down the stairs together.

"You seemed pretty absorbed," the librarian said when they parted at the bottom. "The papers are still interesting?"

"Wonderful! I just wish I could spend more time with them; maybe I can find another morning next week."

"Just let me know and I'll get what you need. I'm glad you find it so fascinating to work with old materials. It's really the reason we're here, isn't it? The historical society, I mean."

"Yes it is, Tabitha. You're absolutely right."

Back in her office, Julie felt very satisfied with her morning. The papers really were terrific. There was something else, however—something more specific that she felt about the collection, but she couldn't pinpoint it. She spent a few moments trying and then gave in to the realization that it was well past noon, and she had eaten very little for breakfast.

She decided to go home for lunch, the nagging thought of that elusive something accompanying her home and remaining with her throughout her lunch break.

CHAPTER 22

"We have our ways," Mike Barlow responded when Julie asked how he managed to check the alibis—and so quickly. They had talked on Monday, and he phoned Thursday morning with the information. "You don't need to know the little stories I make up to get the info I need. Might shake your faith in the police if you did."

"I do remember your MO," Julie said. "Seems to me you con-cocted a few stories to check alibis for a couple of folks in Ryland a few years ago." She knew she didn't need to say more about how Mike had handled the investigation of the Swanson murder that Julie herself had effectively solved. Their history of cooperation pleased her, and she believed Mike felt the same.

"Maybe so," the policeman continued. "Although I'm reluc-tant to reveal information to the public, since this concerns you directly, I'm willing to tell you a bit—confidentially, of course."

"Of course," she said. His willingness seemed to confirm that he, too, enjoyed their joint approach.

Julie took notes during their brief call, as Mike Barlow summarized what he had learned about the three figures. He said he'd keep her informed, and asked her to let him know anything that came up on her end.

The nagging thought that had entered her head while working on the Tabor papers on Tuesday hadn't taken firm-enough shape for her to even mention it as something that might interest Mike. She told herself he'd be the first to know if it mattered—when and if it became clear.

After the call, she reviewed her notes:

Name	Truck	Alibi: road incident	Alibi: Dumont murder
Korhonen	Yes	hunting	working at the museum
Cartwright	No	in Boston w/friends	working at PHS
Hartshorn	No	driving home Hist. Soc.	working at Down East

Only Korhonen appeared to be a possible suspect in both running Julie off the road and murdering Dumont, although he might be able to prove he was, as he said, working at the museum when Dumont was killed. Mike had cautioned her that he hadn't tried to verify anything at this stage; he was just reporting what he had learned from the men themselves. Hartshorn's assertion that he was driving home at the time of Julie's incident on Saturday was unlikely to be supported by anyone else, but then, he didn't have a truck. Cartwright's Boston friends could corroborate his alibi for the road incident, but then he, too, didn't have a truck. Assuming the incident and the murder were done by the same person, only Ted Korhonen seemed possible.

Of course, there were lots of people with trucks in Oxford County. There was also the fact that someone calling himself Timothy Brothers seemed to be linked to the thefts. And if the thefts were linked to the murder and to Julie's road incident, then Timothy Brothers had to be the prime suspect—although Timothy Brothers could actually be Ted Korhonen!

Happy as she was to have Mike's information, Julie realized it didn't prove anything—and didn't lead her anywhere. She was glad she hadn't mentioned Dennis Sutherland as a suspect; he just didn't make her list. Although she now had some pieces of the puzzle, its shape just wasn't getting clearer for her. Maybe, she decided, that was because she was thinking too much about it and not enough about her real job. If she could just focus on the Ryland Historical Society, maybe the part of her mind that functioned on its own, out of her immediate awareness, would do its job and tell her what it had figured out about Dumont and the thefts and the road incident. Or maybe not.

In any case, she did have RHS work to do, especially preparing for Friday's meeting on collections and the fight she expected with Wayne Reiter. Okay, she told herself; I'll work on that and let the rest go for now.

The reading and note-taking and thinking Julie did Thursday afternoon and Friday morning made her feel prepared for the meeting at two o'clock. But then, she hadn't fully reckoned with Wayne Reiter. On Monday, when he had, to put it bluntly, instructed her to call the meeting, she had pointed out that Loretta Cummings chaired the group. Reiter had gone along with her suggestion to consult the appointed chair before calling the meeting. Julie had tried to fudge the matter with Loretta, but years of listening to adolescent stories in her service as principal of Ryland High School provided Loretta with a reliable fudge-detector.

"So Wayne is getting itchy," Loretta had said when Julie phoned on Monday. "That's okay. It's time we meet. I can cut out early for it. Go ahead and call the others."

So now they were all assembled in the Swanson Pavilion conference room. Wayne Reiter had arrived first, before Julie—and she always tried to be in place at least ten minutes before the start of every meeting. Like a professor preparing to administer an exam, Reiter had distributed stacks of papers on the table in front of four chairs.

"No need to waste time passing these out later," he told Julie when she looked at his handiwork. "We're four, aren't we?" he asked.

"I invited Dennis Sutherland to join us," Julie said. "But I brought handouts, too," she added, lifting the box of papers she'd asked Mrs. Detweiller to prepare for the meeting. Reiter apparently missed the point that it was her job, not his, to supply the group with materials.

The next arrival was Ann Gibbons, elegantly turned out in a wool skirt, pink blouse, nicely contrasting dark silk scarf, and tweed jacket. Gibbons had joined the board at the same time Reiter did, when the trustees acted to fill the vacancies left by Worth Harding's and Mary Ellen Swanson's deaths, and Martha Preston's confinement for murdering Harding.

Clif Holdsworth, treasurer and resident curmudgeon, had objected at the time that it was dangerous to appoint two people "from away," but Howard Townsend, the board chair, argued that Ann's marriage to Russell Gibbons, scion of one of Ryland's oldest families, was a mitigating factor. Julie harbored a distrust of real estate agents in general, but she had had no dealings with Ann, and so nothing to say against her appointment. In fact, Clif's opposition rather led her to be supportive just on principle, but in the end it didn't really matter, since the trustees didn't offer her a consistent voice on matters of board membership.

Since she'd come on, Ann Gibbons seemed dutiful and serious, and her annual fund gift of $1,000 had a slightly shaming effect on the other trustees, who had been content to consider their own $500, $200, and, in Clif's case, $100 annual checks quite generous. So on the whole, Julie was inclined to be happy with Ann Gibbons's presence.

"I thought I was going to be late," Gibbons said. "I was showing the old Howell farm to a nice couple from Massachusetts, and they took longer than I expected."

"You're right on time," Julie said. "We're still waiting for Dennis and Loretta."

"Count me in," Dennis Sutherland said as he came through the door. "And I saw Loretta parking, so she'll be right along."

Glancing at his heavy Rolex, Reiter said, "Then perhaps we can begin."

Much as she hated to put herself in opposition to the formidable professor, Julie felt she had to step in.

"Howard asked Loretta to chair the working group," she said.

"For my sins," Loretta Cummings added as she entered. "Sorry to be late. Looks like we're all here."

Julie was happy that Loretta's self-confidence and experience in running meetings made her a fit foil to Wayne.

"Since we're a working group rather than a formal committee, I didn't prepare an agenda," Loretta continued, taking a seat at the head of the table that Julie was sure Wayne had planned to assume. "I see we have plenty of handouts to discuss, but perhaps Julie can frame the discussion. What would you like us to do today?"

How rare that trustees asked that question! Julie thought. Blessings on Loretta for understanding that the purpose of the trustees was to help the director. And just how rare that understanding was, was immediately reinforced with Wayne's interruption: "Julie and I have been working through this," he said. "These documents in front of you pretty well explain the need for a policy of de-accessioning. We've got to get a handle on all of the items we own, and the most effective way to do that is to have a formal policy. You'll see in the first handout—"

"I know you've been talking with Wayne about this," Loretta intervened, turning the focus back to Julie by looking at her rather than the professor, "so for the benefit of the rest of us, why don't you give us an overview."

Julie began by saying that Ryland Historical Society had a collections policy, and that while it might bear review, it was at least a good starting point. "What we don't have," she said, "is a formal collections committee, which both our own policy and best-practices standards require. So I hope one of our outcomes today will be a recommendation to the board to create a committee. Wayne's right that de-accessioning needs to be a part of our work, something that's also covered in the current policy."

"Rather obliquely, it seems to me," Wayne said. "It's on page eight, I think, of the top document. Now in my humble opinion, that statement doesn't go far enough. The second document— from the Massachusetts Historical Society, which the director there, a dear old friend of mine, kindly provided—seems to me much better. I'd like to move that we revise the current policy by adopting in whole the de-accessioning statement from MHS's policy. Would anyone care to second that?"

Loretta's patience, honed by hours of parent conferences, seemed to Julie near the breaking point. But she was polite if firm when she said, "Let's hold off on formal actions, Wayne, till we work our way through the issues. Remember, we're a working group, not a committee, and I'd prefer to frame our work today in the form of a report to the board."

"That's fine," Wayne said, in a tone that suggested exactly the opposite. "As long as our report carries specific recommendations, I have no objection."

"Good," Loretta said, meaning it. "Now, Julie, why don't you continue with your overview."

With Loretta keeping Wayne on a tight leash—at least most of the time—Julie was able to outline her ideas about collections management. Dennis Sutherland added a few pertinent points based on his day-to-day experience overseeing the collections in his role as curator. Ann Gibbons asked one or two good questions, answered more often by Wayne than by Julie. But in the end, Julie got what she wanted: a recommendation to the board to revise the policy, addressing de-accessioning more fully, as Wayne wanted, and to create a formal collections committee to oversee implementation of the policy.

Julie was uncertain whether Wayne got what he wanted from the meeting. At least he had the chance to vent, even if his broad accusations about over-collecting were nicely qualified by specific points from Dennis and Julie, both of whom had the hands-on experience with the collections that Wayne lacked. In the end, he seemed resigned to the direction of the discussion, and even to Loretta's suggestion that Julie draft the report.

"Of course I'll circulate it to all of you after I've looked it over," Loretta said. "But writing a report by committee rarely works. So after you've reviewed it and made suggestions, Julie and I will put the finishing touches on it and send it to the full board. I think we're done here," she said, adding, "Thanks to all of you for the good work, and especially to you, Wayne, for bringing this to our attention and to assembling all of these useful documents."

"Happy to help," he said, clearly mollified by Loretta's crediting of his work. "If we move expeditiously, I think we can get started by the spring."

"Get started on what?" Ann Gibbons asked.

"Clearing out the attic, as I call it. Maybe have an auction or something. Kill two birds with one stone: Rationalize the collections, and make a little money for the Society while we're at it. It's being done everywhere, I believe."

Julie was familiar with other museums that auctioned duplicates and irrelevant items from their collections, but she was equally familiar with the difficulties inherent with such an approach—in public relations, but also in making sure such actions met museum standards. That was a whole new topic she just didn't want to get into today, and she silently cursed Wayne Reiter for introducing it so late in the discussion, and without any warning to her. Her response was intended to close the door for now: "Wayne's right, of course, but I think we're getting pretty far ahead of ourselves until we do the work on the policy and set up a committee. An auction is a possibility, but we'll have to look to the new committee to consider that—along with other approaches."

"Like theft," Wayne said.

The silent stares that met his comment at first didn't seem to register, but then he said, "I know that sounds crazy. It's just something Julie and I were discussing—the fact that thefts are a kind of involuntary de-accessioning. Heavens, I'm not suggesting we invite the thieves in!"

"Well, that's reassuring, Wayne," Loretta said. "But then if we do have theft, we'll know whom to suspect," she added with a laugh that quickly spread to everyone except Wayne.

"It's a deeper topic than that," he said, with a hint of impatience for those he obviously deemed incapable of dealing with deep topics. "But Julie and I can discuss that further. Not really something for our group at this time."

"Then I'll repeat myself: We're done, and I'm grateful for all your help. Hope everyone enjoys the weekend. I understand the ski area may open tomorrow. I suppose you'll be there, Wayne."

His status as an expert skier was a perfect topic to distract the professor, and so the others drifted off as he answered Loretta with details about how the manufactured snow—which made such an early opening possible—would affect his style. Julie remained to hear the lecture, but was grateful when Loretta cut it off by saying she was due back at the high school to finish the work she had interrupted to come to the meeting.

"Very good," Wayne said to Julie as the two of them left the conference room. The phrase struck her as a substitute for the pat on her head she sensed he would have preferred to offer, but she accepted it and returned her own effusive thanks for his help.

"Happy to be of service," he said as they left the building. He turned right to go to his car. "That's what trustees are for, you know. I do have some further thoughts on that matter of crime and induced demand. Perhaps we can get together next week."

Before she could respond, Reiter was off at his usual brisk pace, oblivious to any response he engendered in others, satisfied with his own superiority.

Julie headed to her office, exhausted.

CHAPTER 23

Sitting through more than two hours of a meeting and watching Loretta ward off Wayne wasn't the kind of work that most people thought of as exhausting. Raking leaves or gardening or cutting firewood would normally come to mind. While Julie was grateful that her profession made only modest physical demands, emotions had a physical impact, and she didn't mind admitting to herself that she felt drained.

But it was Friday, her work week was nearly over, and Rich would probably be on the road right now. Last weekend's truncated time together in Portland seemed so long ago, and she looked forward to uninterrupted time—two nights and most of two days to relax and be just themselves. When she had asked Rich on the phone Thursday night how he wanted to spend the weekend, he had said "I just want to be with you," and Julie felt the same. It was too cold to hike, and though the opening of the ski area slightly attracted her interest, she was too early in her lessons to brave what she assumed would be tricky conditions—and crowds driven by pent-up demand. So a quiet weekend around the house seemed just right to her.

Rich arrived at six o'clock, minutes after Julie got home. He had skipped lunch because of a department meeting and suggested they move directly to dinner. Rich had shopped at the big-box grocery in Farmington on the way, and began to prepare sole stuffed with crab as Julie sat at the kitchen table. Unlike her, Rich was able to cook and carry on a conversation at the same time, a skill she admired. In her rare forays into cooking, she demanded complete solitude. His report on the week was short and—like the week itself, he admitted—pretty dull: meetings, classes, more meetings, a little work on his book.

"And you? Other than getting run off the road," he added.

Now seemed a good time to tell Rich about the Saturday-night hang-up phone call, something she had deliberately concealed during their nightly phone calls because she knew it would cause him needless worry. When she'd finished, he turned from the counter and stared at her.

"Why didn't you tell me sooner?" he said.

"You couldn't do anything, and it would have only made you worry. I did mention it to Mike Barlow, and he reminded me about getting caller ID. Funny how I forgot all about that."

"Not so funny," Rich replied. "But Barlow's right. When did you talk to him?"

Julie told Rich about her various conversations with Mike.

"Seems like you had more time with him than me." Rich remained with his back to the counter, looking at Julie.

"What's that supposed to mean?" she asked.

"Nothing more than what I said." He turned back to his work. While he chopped shallots and garlic to add to the crab, Julie remained silent.

"I'm always amazed that you don't need a recipe," Julie said, to break the silence.

"I have a recipe; I just don't need to have it in front of me, since I know this one pretty well. Hope you're not tired of it," he added.

Julie was grateful for the change of topic—and tone—and said how much she looked forward to the dish. The mood in the kitchen lightened, and Rich suggested they have a glass of wine before he put the stuffed sole into the oven.

"Unless you have a better plan," he said, smiling at her.

"Probably the same one you do," she said, and stood up. He did the same, they embraced, and then headed upstairs.

❧

"This is so fabulous," Julie said as she finished the last piece of the fish. It was nearly eight o'clock. "I know you missed lunch, Rich; sorry dinner got a little delayed."

"No problem for me," he said, and reached across the kitchen table to stroke her hand. "I love you. Sometimes it's just so hard being apart all week." She nodded her agreement. "So," he said, withdrawing his hand from hers and reaching for the bottle of sauvignon blanc, "tell me about your week. Other than your time with Mike Barlow, that is." He laughed, and she joined in.

"Let's go to the living room," she said. "Just leave the dishes. I'll take care of them later. And maybe we should open another bottle. It's been a long week, and I really need to talk."

They settled themselves comfortably, and Julie began to summarize what she was thinking about the missing artifacts and her various suspicions. After, Julie was too keyed up for bed; she insisted that Rich should go ahead while she did the dishes. But he chose to sit at the kitchen table to keep her company. As she stood at the sink, an idea began to hatch. The barest outlines of a plan.

"I'm going to set a trap," she said out loud, startling herself as much as Rich.

"A trap?" he exclaimed after a pause. "What kind of trap?"

Then the thoughts tumbled out, almost as if they came from someone else. Slowly rinsing the dishes and putting them into the dishwasher, Julie methodically retraced the idea. Thieves might just break into a museum and take things randomly, but all her experience convinced her that this rarely happened. Typically they came with a goal, their sights set on a particular object or group of them—maps, pottery, letters, whatever. Why? Because they knew the items were available, and valuable. So how did they know? An inside job was easy to explain: The person worked in the museum, handled the items in question, and could check auction records and other data to determine value.

But there was another possibility: Someone other than the thief or thieves knew the value and knew the items were in the collection, and then, in effect, placed an order for them. Wayne's talk on induced demand had made her aware of this approach. Julie wasn't surprised that Rich was skeptical, cautious, even worried. But as they talked, her idea crystallized, benefiting from his probing questions. They went to bed, exhausted, knowing they had all day tomorrow to figure it out.

࿊

Julie watched two figures, unidentifiable from where she was standing, as they made their way stealthily toward the side entrance of the wing. She had a vague sense they were heading toward the new Swanson building, but in the light snow that was falling, she couldn't be sure. She didn't remember hearing about any snow in the forecast.

She could tell now that the two figures were male. One carried a briefcase or some kind of satchel, and the other held a crowbar. As they reached the entrance, the one with the satchel stood back and glanced around furtively as the other applied the crowbar to the door and violently pried it open, stepping inside. The other, after a final look around the yard, followed.

She wanted to join them, to rush through the door and confront them to ask what they wanted, what they thought they were doing breaking into the Ryland Historical Society. If only Dennis Sutherland would come along—or, better, Rich. With one of them at her side she knew she would have the courage to confront the intruders. Alone, she thought better of it, and stood patiently waiting.

It seemed like twenty or thirty minutes before they emerged. She could see the satchel was full; in fact, papers were hanging over the edges of it, loose and disordered. They'll get wet in this snow, she said to herself; I have to stop them before the papers are ruined. No match for two men, one armed with a crowbar, Julie felt impotent, frightened. The intruders picked up their pace, almost running now, and Julie decided to follow at a safe distance. A pickup truck stood at the curb, and it didn't surprise her when they got into it. She heard the engine turn over and saw the truck ease away from the curb and then pick up speed as it headed south past the Common.

She had to get to a phone, but as she started back toward her office she heard a siren, distant but rapidly growing louder. She couldn't believe her good luck: It was Mike Barlow, in the Ryland Police cruiser, blue lights pulsing, siren roaring. She raced toward the street as the patrol car pulled up and, laughing now with pleasure that Mike had arrived and the thieves would be caught, she gestured in the direction the truck had taken and yelled, "That way—down the hill!"

"What hill? Julie, are you okay?" It was Rich's voice.

What was he doing here, Julie wondered. And why was Mike Barlow back at work for the Ryland Police Department?

"Julie!" Rich repeated. "Wake up, Julie. You must have been dreaming."

He was on his elbow, leaning over her. She looked up into his warm blue eyes, focusing, bringing herself back to the present. She lifted her head from the pillow, looked around the room, then back at Rich.

"I guess so," she finally said, groggily. "Wow. It really seemed to be happening, but obviously it was a dream."

"More like a nightmare," he said. "You woke up screaming, about going down the hill."

"That's where the truck went, with the thieves. And I was try-ing to tell Mike, and he was in the Ryland cruiser, which doesn't make any sense."

"What thieves?" Rich asked.

"Two of them. They broke into the historical society. But here's what's strange: It wasn't just a break-in. They had come looking for valuable papers—like someone had placed an order for them. And when they left, the papers were bulging out of the briefcase one of the guys was holding, and it was snowing and the papers were

getting wet. I think I was almost as mad about what they were doing to the papers as I was about the fact they'd stolen them."

Julie was sitting up now, her head against the headboard. Rich
was still on his elbow, but turned now to look at her.

"And I wouldn't call it a nightmare, Rich. It was a little fright-
ening, because the one guy had a crowbar—that's how they broke
in. I guess I was scared, but the overall feeling was more . . . I'm
not sure how to put it: more like working something out. Yes! It
was a sort of working out of my plan—the trap I mentioned. You
remember that?"

"Sure, but I don't see what it has to do with your dream."

"I know. It's hard to explain, but it just seemed like I was
watching the result of setting up the trap—like these guys had
been hired to steal the Tabor papers, and I somehow knew when
they would come, and I was there to catch them."

"But it was the famous Mike Barlow who rode to the rescue,"
Rich said.

"I guess you could say that."

"Is he in on this?"

"The trap?"

"Yes."

"No, I haven't said anything to him about it yet—and I don't
know if I will. In fact, I'm not sure I'm even going to go ahead
with it. I have to think about that. What do you think?"

"I think it would be nice to get back to sleep. It's three-thirty,
and I could use a few more hours. Think you can sleep?"

"I can try."

"We can talk about it more in the morning. Right now, just
forget about it—the dream, the thieves, and especially, the trap."

CHAPTER 24

After Rich left for Orono Sunday afternoon, Julie felt the emptiness of the house even more than she usually did at the end of their weekends together. This commuting is getting old, she thought. There was a time when the rhythm of their relationship actually had an appeal: weekdays of hard work in anticipation of their time together, then weekends of freedom and indulgence. Both elements had their pleasures, and each seemed to heighten the enjoyment of the other.

But increasingly she wished for an end to the cycle, an end that their marriage next summer might, or might not, bring. How they would shape their lives after that remained a topic of only occasional conversation, but unending worry. She was not about to move to Orono; Rich really couldn't give up his teaching job to come to Ryland; and splitting the difference by trying to live somewhere in between just wasn't practical. Skowhegan? No, thanks, they both said when the topic had come up.

One ray of hope beckoned: Rich was applying for a yearlong research leave, dependent on getting a grant from one of those alphabetical programs offered by some federal agency. He wouldn't know about the grant till Christmas. If he got it, the leave was assured, and his work was portable enough that they could live in Ryland—for that year, at least. So they quietly nurtured hope and agreed without talking about it to wait till he heard. Then they'd go from there, Julie told herself, whatever the outcome.

As she walked through the house after Rich drove off, Julie tried hard not to imagine the year they would have together because, if it didn't happen, she really didn't want to think about the alternative choices they would have to face, and resolve, by next summer, when they got married.

She considered working on a jigsaw puzzle to distract herself but found she didn't have the interest. Of course, she could go to her office and do some reading on the Tabor papers. Yes, she thought, that would help, but then again, a quiet afternoon at the house also had its appeal. Even though she associated the beverage with illness, she decided to brew a cup of tea and indulge herself by drinking it by the fire that Rich had started before he left. He was an expert fire starter, just as he was so proficient at many tasks that she found mysterious. She pictured herself in the high-backed chair by the fire, a cup of tea steaming beside her on the table—a cliché she wanted to inhabit. But when she went to the kitchen, she realized that her disdain for tea was reflected in the fact that she had none. A search of all the cabinets confirmed it. Determined now to act out the cozy scene, she decided to walk to Ryland Groceries to buy some tea bags.

Had it been sleeting earlier, when Rich left, and she'd just missed it? Or had it begun since? As she stepped out the back door and into the pelting sleet, Julie wasn't sure when it had begun—but she was sure she didn't like it. More than half of Rich's drive was on a winding two-lane highway favored by logging trucks, not great in any conditions, but certainly treacherous in slippery weather. Julie pulled up the hood on her parka and decided to test the sidewalk, which to her surprise was wet but not slippery. What was coming down as sleet ended up as mere water when it hit the ground. She decided not to worry as she proceeded past the Common. Not like last Saturday, she added, remembering her drive from Portland. The image of the incident came vividly to mind—and with it another image: of Dennis Sutherland, in her office, remarking about the tricky driving conditions of that day when he, too, had driven from Portland to Ryland.

Yesterday, when she had reviewed with Rich the names of those who might have forced her off the road—and who might have killed Dumont—she had at first omitted Dennis. After all, she hadn't mentioned him to Mike Barlow, since it was after her talk with the policeman that she had first learned from Dennis about his trip. But the fact had been gnawing at her, and so after she had named the others to Rich yesterday, she brought up Dennis.

"Sutherland?" Rich had said. "Now I know you're going over the deep end. He works for you—you know him. He wouldn't do something like that. I mean, why would he?"

Julie had had no good answer then, and still didn't. She picked up her pace, not worrying now about traction. It would make sense only if Dennis was somehow involved in the thefts—and the murder! And surely that couldn't be.

But then she remembered that another employee of the Ryland Historical Society had given in to the temptation to steal valuable items from the collection. Could Dennis Sutherland be repeating history? No, Rich was right, she said to herself. Forget Dennis.

She walked back up the hill with her box of herbal tea bags, kept dry in the plastic bag the cashier had insisted on putting it in (despite Julie's protest that to do so added to global warming). She felt a little warming was just what she needed to shake the chills the rain—and by now it had turned to simple rain, though cold—was inducing. Inside, she put the kettle on, took her notebook to the living room, and settled in to think about her trap—and not to imagine the road conditions between Ryland and Orono.

Rich had asked some pointed questions about her plan, which in the end, she felt she had answered. His last comment was typical: "Just be careful, Julie. You're putting yourself right in the middle of this." Actually, she agreed with him; she was in the middle, but her plan for a trap would put her there in a proactive way rather than as a passive observer.

The plan was simple: She'd write a note to the blog about the Tabor papers, noting their historical significance and hinting at their value. Then she'd move the papers from the archives to her office and see what happened. An inquiry at the archives? Questions online from her colleagues? A break-in? Who knew? She'd just have to wait to see. She would alert Mike Barlow, of course, but she decided not to tell Dennis about it. He would probably find out anyway, since it was unlikely that moving the boxes from the archives would go unnoticed.

Then what if someone tried to steal them from there, she wondered; that would be a pretty good sign that Dennis was involved. Wouldn't it? I'm getting ahead of myself, she thought. What I need to do now is write the blog entry.

After deleting some lines and adding others, she came up with the draft of an entry that she emailed to herself so she could review it in the morning.

Valuable Papers at Ryland Historical Society

Thanks to a generous relative who preserved them for many years in her house, RHS received eighteen boxes of papers from Dr. Samuel Tabor, who practiced medicine in this western Maine town for most of the first four decades of the twentieth century. Tabor was a packrat of the kind we historians love! He was also a wonderful observer and letter writer. The papers contain numerous letters to and from Tabor, documents related to his practice, and many items concerning town affairs that he accumulated as a selectman and member of various town committees. We have only begun to catalog the papers, but they are clearly of great value to anyone interested in life in rural Maine over a long and interesting period. The papers are open for scholarly use at the discretion of RHS. Please contact me directly for further information.

As she was rereading the text for the second time, questioning whether "great value" was too strong a description, the phone rang. She rushed to the kitchen to catch it on the second ring. Rich was in Orono, safe. The remains of the meals he had cooked on Friday and Saturday provided Julie's dinner, and a few more logs on the fire kept it going till ten o'clock, when she decided to call it a day.

She reread the draft of her blog entry again and felt it was right, though she resisted the temptation to post it then. Tomorrow would be soon enough.

⌘

She was in her office at eight a.m. on Monday morning, and reviewed her entry once more before posting it to the blog.

Done, she thought. Now it's just a matter of waiting. But what was she waiting for, she wondered; responses perhaps? On the blog itself—or by e-mail? Julie wasn't sure of the protocol. And if the entry did trigger interest on the part of some thief, or—and she was following Wayne Reiter's thinking here—a collector who would in turn engage a thief, what would follow from that? Since the blog was password-protected and open only to members of the Network, she intended her trap for one of her Maine colleagues. If that assumption proved wrong, perhaps the only response would be no response.

The arrival of Mrs. Detweiller diverted Julie from further thoughts about the blog entry, since they had agreed to spend the morning sorting through files. Worth Harding, Ryland Historical Society's founding director whom she replaced, had carried the museum from a collection of books and artifacts in a room of his house to its multi-building campus and active exhibits and pro-grams. He'd had a vision, and he had realized it. Julie was grateful to him for that.

But an organized person he was not. The files in his office were chaotic in the extreme. Early in her tenure, Julie had wanted to ad-dress the chaos, but so many more important tasks had distracted her. With the Society now running so well, she was gradually getting to those files, setting aside a day every month to work with her secretary, who had worked for five years with Harding, to sort through the letters, bills, notes, and general detritus that filled half a dozen file cases in Mrs. Detweiller's office. In a sense, culling them was a kind of historical research, and Julie had once considered using the material to write a history of the Society. But the arrival of the Tabor papers had provided a better research project, and now she approached the sorting of the RHS files as a chore she could face only on a quiet Monday morning after a relaxed weekend.

At eleven-thirty, Mrs. Detweiller announced that she would be taking her lunch hour to do some personal errands, and Julie declared that a morning of wading through dried and crumpled papers was more than adequate to satisfy her that they were indeed progressing.

"I'll eat at my desk," she told her secretary. "See you at one o'clock."

When she opened her e-mail before approaching the yogurt and apple that constituted her lunch, she saw the message from James Hartshorn, sent at 8:50 a.m.:

Sounds like quite a treasure you've got over there in Ryland, Julie. Good for you! Papers like that don't come along every day, and I'm sure when you get them properly cataloged they'll be invaluable. Thanks for posting the entry to the blog. Listings have been slow, but having such a distinguished member of the Network use it will encourage others. I'm sure your posting will get the attention it deserves. Thanks!

She so disliked and distrusted Hartshorn that she reread the message more times than it deserved. Was he being critical when he noted the papers were not yet "properly cataloged"? Was his description of her as "distinguished" meant to be ironic? And what "attention" did it deserve—perhaps the attention of a thief? Perhaps James Hartshorn himself? She thought she should respond briefly, but decided to read the rest of her e-mails first. Rich's was a delight, describing the befuddled student who had come to see him about a paper. To that she responded immediately. The others were nuts-and-bolts messages, several requesting school tours; those she forwarded to Dennis, who handled such matters. Just as she finished and was about to reply to Hartshorn, a new message popped up:

> *Julie: Your blog posting—nice to see that—reminded me that I've been meaning to get in touch re: a lunch in Portland. Any chance you could meet me this week? I'm booked for Friday, but any other day this week would work. If not then, maybe next?*
> *Brent Cartwright*
> *Curator, Portland Historical Society*

Okay, Julie thought; we know Cartwright reads the blog. Maybe it was indeed time she got to know him better. Her schedule was free on Wednesday, and she had been meaning to do some work at the Portland Historical Society anyway, so she wrote to propose lunch that day.

There was one other thing she needed to do before she ate her yogurt and apple, something she had thought long and hard about last night: Call Mike Barlow to let him know about the trap she was setting. Rich had urged her to do that, and she was quite willing. What she wasn't sure of was whether she should also mention her suspicion about Dennis Sutherland. Her relationship with the policeman was founded on honesty—don't hold back what you know or think. But what did she really know—or think!—about

Dennis Sutherland's possible involvement? Maybe lunch first, she thought, giving herself more time to mull it over.

She left a message for Barlow at one-thirty, and he returned her call an hour later.

"I can see it makes sense, Julie," he said, after she described the trap. "But you've got to see that it's also risky. You're potentially putting the historical society—and yourself—in the crosshairs of a thief. And possibly a murderer. Not for the first time, I should add."

"That's why I'm telling you," she replied. "And I'll keep you informed. You know I always do."

Barlow laughed. "You say that like we're longtime partners in crime. Guess in some ways we have been, and I know you well enough to realize I'm not about to talk you out of this."

"But you think it's a good idea?"

"I said I understand it, and it might work. Still . . ."

Before he could finish the thought, which Julie figured she knew anyway, she added, "And there's one other thing, Mike." After she told him about Sutherland, the line was quiet for more seconds than she liked. "What do you think?" she prompted.

"I'm not sure what to think—except that I don't like the idea of someone there at Ryland Historical Society being possibly so involved in this. Is it mainly because he has a truck and was in Portland that Saturday you got run off the road?"

"Only that. I don't have any other reason to suspect him, but you always say it's best to start with all the possibles and work down from there. And, well, it is possible he drove me off the road—opportunity and means, as you say."

"And motive?"

"Same as for anyone else who might be stealing stuff."

"Okay. Let me think about it. I'll run a check on him, see if anything pops up there, but in the meantime, be careful. Are you going to tell him about your posting on the papers?"

"He knows all about them."

"I see what you mean. Well, like I say, let me think about this. Be in touch."

Sorry as she was to complicate things, and even sorrier to cast her colleague in a bad light, Julie felt relieved that she had told Mike Barlow about her suspicions. Mainly, she told herself, because she was eager for him to prove her wrong.

CHAPTER 25

Julie had lived in northern New England long enough now to recognize how simultaneously maddening and delightful transitional parts of the seasons can be. In any week between Halloween and Thanksgiving, you could experience the lingering sun and warmth of late summer one day and then face the chill early touch of winter the next. You never knew what to expect.

Wednesday's weather was indeed unexpected—to the good. After several cool, raw days when rain and snow alternated, Wednesday was a gorgeous throwback to early fall, if not late summer. The deep blue sky was cloudless, the temperature was 60 degrees when she left home, and likely to be even warmer when she got to Portland, and some trees still sported those nearly fluorescent yellows she found so lovely. What a day for a drive, she thought, as she followed the state highway that connected Ryland and Portland—what locals called the "regular route," not the "back route," that went west of Ryland and then skirted Lake Sebago, or the "side route" that she had taken home from Portland ten days ago.

Avoiding the side route was easy; she didn't want to revisit the scene of the road incident. The back route was appealing but slightly longer, and since she wanted an hour or so to check some books in the Portland Historical Society's library before meeting Brent Cartwright for lunch, she took the regular route, thoroughly enjoying the low hills and fields along the way.

She couldn't resist thinking about the upcoming meeting with Cartwright. She recalled seeing him at the Halloween party and being struck by what she'd admitted then was a certain sexual appeal. Small in build and oddly feminine in the fine features of his face, he was still undeniably masculine. Perhaps androgynous, like boys in their early teens whose gender you at first don't register. She had said something to this effect to Rich when they had met at the Halloween party, and Rich's arch comment was "Not my type." Well, Julie wasn't sure Brent was her type either, but she did realize that she found him physically attractive.

She asked herself what she actually knew about him, other than the fact she found him, for lack of a better word, cute. She knew he hadn't been the curator at Portland Historical Society for very long, maybe a couple of years—less time than she had been at Ryland, because she had met him at a Network meeting when he started work. But somehow she gathered he was a native—perhaps even a scion of an old Portland family. Hadn't someone hinted to her that he "didn't need to work"? She couldn't recall who had said that, but its meaning was clear: Brent Cartwright had independent means, old money. With a name like that, it made sense.

But she also remembered that he had worked somewhere in the Midwest before joining Portland Historical, because when she'd first met him at that Network gathering, they had shared some remembrances of life there. Julie wasn't at all ashamed of having grown up in southern Ohio, but her education and career made her feel more East Coast. Thus, it was easy for her to relate to Brent's comments about having, as she remembered his line, "done my time in the great Midwest, in all its secondhand splendor."

Chicago, that was it, she now recalled; he had worked in the Windy City, which, from Julie's Ohio perspective, was actually a small part of the East set down in the wrong place.

But where, exactly? Somehow she thought it was the Newberry Library, that magnificent research facility. Pretty impressive, if so. He can't be a slouch if he worked at the Newberry, she thought. But why am I thinking about Brent Cartwright when I could be enjoying the scenery, she asked herself. Beats scrutinizing pickup trucks, she thought.

Julie found a two-hour-meter parking space directly in front of the Portland Historical Society and made a note to herself to top it off when they went for lunch. She headed directly to the library and spent the next hour checking some local histories to identify several of Dr. Tabor's Portland correspondents. She managed to locate four of them before she looked at the clock behind the main desk and saw it was nearly noon. The person at the desk directed her to Brent's office, which turned out to be just down the hall from the library.

"Welcome to the big city!" he said when she appeared before his open door. He rose to meet her and shot out his hand for a firm shake, a gesture Julie realized she preferred to the hugging that had seemed to become the norm even among professional colleagues. She accepted his suggestion of lunch at a Thai restaurant just up Congress Street.

"Not a cuisine we get in Ryland," she said, "and I love it. Actually, Ryland doesn't offer many cuisines," she added.

"But I understand you have your own gourmet chef," Cartwright said.

That surprised her. Had he and Rich talked about cooking when they'd met at the Halloween party? She couldn't recall, but decided not to pursue it.

"From time to time," she said.

After they ordered, Julie said she had done a little work in the library, and hoped to spend a couple more hours there in the afternoon. She wanted to put a clear limit on their time, as well as highlight her professional interests, which she was able to emphasize when he asked what she was working on.

"Those Tabor papers must be quite interesting," Cartwright said. "Glad you posted that. I wasn't sure this blog would get much attention, but if you're using it, I'm sure that'll encourage others. How large is the collection?"

Julie described the papers, and said, "Of course, I'm not sure if they're all that valuable in the way Hartshorn seemed to have in mind—you know, alerting people to things that might be attractive to thieves. They have a lot of historical interest, but as to monetary value, well, I just don't know."

"Everything has monetary value! But then, you know more about that than I do."

Julie nodded but didn't say anything.

"So how's your investigation going?" he asked, more abruptly than Julie expected. Now that they were on the topic, she welcomed the chance to find out what he knew about the Mountain Valley and Two Rivers thefts. Quite a bit, it turned out, as he mentioned the maps at Dumont's museum and the ceramics at Betsey's.

"How'd you hear all that?"

"Oh, folks talk. It's a small world, especially in this small state."

Julie saw her chance to find out more about him.

"You're a native, aren't you?"

He laughed. "Yeah, but a native of New Jersey! Like you, I'm from away. You're from Ohio, right?"

"Born there, but I came east to college and graduate school, and much as I liked growing up in the Midwest, I can't see ever leaving New England. How about you?"

187

"Who knows? I like Portland a lot, and the job is fun, but as they say, 'Never say never.' "

"You were at the Newberry, weren't you?" Julie asked.

"Briefly. Oh, here's lunch."

Julie realized that door had been closed. While they ate, she tried several times to turn the conversation back to how Cartwright had heard about the thefts she was looking into, but he sidestepped with vague comments about how museum people like to gossip.

To redirect him, she mentioned Dan Dumont.

"Sad," Cartwright said. "That's the problem with the hunting culture."

"You think it was a hunting accident?"

"Sure. What else? Now don't tell me Dan was murdered! I've heard people saying that because they don't want to face up to the fact that if you arm half of the people in Maine, they'll eventually kill someone. By accident, of course. But, like I say, very sad. He was a good guy."

"Did you know him well?"

"Only as a colleague, but I liked him."

As they were finishing lunch, he asked her more about the Tabor papers, and in responding, Julie tried to hint at their value without being specific or seeming too obvious.

"Well, I'm sure they're safe with you," he said. "You haven't had any thefts since the Lincoln letter, have you?"

"None that I know of. But we're always vulnerable; who isn't?"

"Oh, Portland Historical is a Fort Knox. Don't think anyone would try anything here, but as you say, you never know. Anyway, I'm glad we had a chance to talk, Julie. I've really been wanting to get to know you better."

Julie tried to read his face when he said it, but she just couldn't be sure if the slight flirtatiousness she heard in his words was reflected in the look he gave her.

"Getting to know each other and our work is what the Network's all about," she said in a deliberately pompous way that she hoped would shift the tone.

"True. And of course, the blog."

"That too. Can I get this?" she offered, picking up the check.

"My invitation, my treat," Cartwright said, pulling the check toward himself. "And you're a cheap date! One of the reasons I like Thai."

Okay, she thought; it's a common expression. Still, the use of the word date made her uncomfortable.

As they walked back down the street, Julie remembered that she had forgotten to top off the meter before they left for lunch, and when she saw the ticket stuck under her wiper blade, she said, "Damn! I meant to put some money in the meter. Now I've got a ticket."

"Just a warning," Cartwright said as he extracted the paper notice and showed it to her. "Portland tries to be friendly. We need shoppers. But if you're coming back to the library, you should take this and put money in the meter in case they come back and see you got a warning. Then you'd get a real ticket. Not good to be on the wrong side of the law," he added. "Not that you'd ever be there!"

Julie agreed, filling the meter before she and Cartwright returned to the Portland Historical Society buildings.

Back in the library, Julie was glad for the focus that came from tracing the names of Dr. Tabor's Portland friends—it kept her from reviewing the lunch conversation—but on the drive home she returned to it. Had she picked up anything of use?

Well, she had confirmed that Brent Cartwright had an odd attractiveness, but what else? That he wasn't from Maine. That he knew a lot about her—and a lot more than he should about the two thefts that she was, so far unsuccessfully, working on. He knew that he was interested in the Tabor papers. But really, she wondered, was any of this important? If it had not been for the small triumphs in the library and the very good Thai food, Julie was inclined to think the day had been wasted. She certainly didn't think she knew any more about Brent Cartwright's possible role in the thefts, or the murder.

Maybe, she thought, as she cruised back through the rolling hills, Rich is right when he says I try to tie too many things together: the thefts, the murder, her road incident, the hang-up call. Nothing she had observed today made any sense out of the string of events, and nothing made Brent Cartwright look like a suspect.

On the other hand, she thought, nothing made him less so.

CHAPTER 26

"How was Portland?" Mike Barlow asked when Julie phoned him from her office.

Since it was nearly five p.m. when she returned, Mrs. Detweiller had already gone for the day, but she had dutifully left a pile of WHILE YOU WERE OUT slips on Julie's desk. The one about Barlow was at the bottom, but it was the first one she acted on.

"Working on the case?" the policeman added, with his wry humor.

"Tracking me?" she asked in the same tone as his.

"Have to keep an eye on you. Look, if you've got a minute, there are a couple of things here of interest." He paused and then said, "First, about Dennis Sutherland. Clean. Nothing on him anywhere, but he does have a pickup truck. Red. You didn't say the one that ran you off the road was red, did you?"

"No, but remember, the visibility was bad. I'm pretty sure I'd remember if it was red, though. Nothing else?"

"Nope. A law-abiding citizen as far as I can tell. The second thing might be of more interest. You sitting down?"

Julie said she could if he wanted her to.

"Better do it. We've got the murder weapon."

"What?" she practically screamed.

"I'll spare you the details, but it turned up at a gun show in Newport."

"Rhode Island? That seems a long way off."

"No, Maine. We've got a Newport here, you know—you've probably been through it on your way to Orono."

Julie remembered that she had driven through it, and that it was an hour or so from Farmington.

"So how did it end up there? And how did you identify it? And—"

"I can't really go into the details, but fortunately one of the exhibitors at the gun show was using his head. He remembered getting our bulletin about the type of rifle, so he called and we checked it out. It matches."

"The dealer bought it from someone?"

"Right. That's what happens at gun shows—folks buy and sell guns. The dealer can't really tell us anything about the person he bought it from, except for a name and what turns out to be a phony address in Massachusetts. And actually, he didn't see the person; his wife bought it while he was out on the floor. However, I thought the name would interest you. Still sitting down? Okay, ever hear of a Timothy Brothers?"

"No way! I can't believe it."

"Well, it's pretty interesting, since I kind of suspect there's a connection here with the Timothy Brothers who visited the museum in York County."

"This definitely ties it all together, Mike!"

"Not sure I'd go that far, but—"

"So what do we do now?" Julie interrupted.

"We don't do anything. What I do is get some pictures from you of some of your museum colleagues and then go talk to the gun dealer's wife, hoping she'll recognize one of them."

"Did she describe him?"

"Not in any useful way—maybe young, maybe middle-aged; maybe tall, maybe not; dark hair or maybe blond, and so forth. That's typical, but a picture's a different thing. So can you get me pictures of some of the folks we've talked about?"

Julie thought immediately about her presentation at the Network and the pictures that someone took and circulated afterwards.

"Hold on, Mike. I think I can find some right now. Can you give me a minute?"

"How about you call me back?"

They agreed she would check immediately and call if she found any. It took her only a few minutes to sort through the files on her computer and find three pictures—one of her with James Hartshorn; one of Ted Korhonen, Brent Cartwright, and Hartshorn; and another of Cartwright and Hartshorn. Typical, she thought, that Hartshorn would get himself in so many pictures! She phoned Mike and then e-mailed him the photos.

"You'll let me know," she said.

"Let's see how it goes. I'll see the dealer and his wife tomorrow. So how was Portland? I meant it when I asked before."

"Because I was seeing Brent Cartwright. I did, but I don't think I know anything more than I did before."

"You think he's still a possible?"

"I can't rule him out, but we'll know more when you show them the pictures."

"Do I hear 'we' again?"

Julie laughed. "Not from me. But you'll call, right?"

"If and when I have some news. Thanks, Julie; gotta go now."

And so do I, she thought, looking at her watch and seeing that it was almost six p.m. She did have some work to do first, and decided she might as well do it at the office and leave her evening at home free. So she took out a pad and wrote "The Trap" at the top. Below that she jotted notes, randomly, and then came back to the first one: Reiter. She was convinced that to speed up the trapping process, she needed to, in his words, "induce demand" for the Tabor papers. She had posted about them on the blog, of course, but she wasn't content to wait for that to stir interest. Instead, again thinking of Wayne Reiter's comments about thefts occurring in reaction to someone's need or desire for an item, she had been thinking that her trustee might be just the person to get that ball rolling.

From his years at Harvard, Reiter was well connected in Boston. She knew he would enjoy a challenge, like being in on something. The challenge she had in mind for him was to use his contacts to get someone interested in the Tabor papers—interested enough to put out the word that he or she would welcome a chance to purchase them, however they might come onto the market. She felt sure that she could get Reiter to do that, but she was far less sure of whether she trusted him enough to bring him into her confidence, to make him a player in the scheme.

The next item on her list was moving the papers. She planned to bring them from the archive into her office, for two reasons. The first was simply that she wanted to protect them. Having described them as being in the archives, she figured a thief would go there first; by moving them to her office she could be more certain they would be safe. There was a second reason, one she really hated to admit to herself: She intended to let Dennis Sutherland know about moving the papers, and if they were stolen from her office, the finger of blame would be pointing pretty squarely at him. She really didn't want to think this way, but she just couldn't shake the notion that he might be involved.

Next, she said to herself as she scanned the list, was when. Julie knew herself well enough to understand that once she had decided on a course of action, delaying it just wasn't her style. So she was prepared to start right away, first talking to Reiter to get his help, then moving the boxes. Tomorrow didn't seem too soon for that. But there was a little problem with timing. By this time next week, she would be on her way to Ohio, to spend Thanksgiving with her parents. She would be away for six days, leaving next Tuesday to drive to Delaware to visit a friend from graduate school, on to Ohio on Wednesday, then three days with her folks before making a long one-day drive home. What if she started to set the trap right away and the thieves took advantage of the holiday, when the historical society would be closed for two days—Thanksgiving and the day after? She would be out of the picture, far away. She preferred to be close to the action.

Okay, let that be for now, she said to herself. The next item was Rich/Mike. She had already talked to both men about the trap—Rich, in some detail on the weekend, Mike, more generally on Monday. But she would have to talk with both again and in far more detail if she really was ready to move. She wasn't reluctant about doing so—well, maybe a little reluctant, she admitted. It was just that she was sure both of them would try to talk her out of it, and while she was determined that they would not succeed, she still wasn't eager to have those conversations.

When she saw it was seven o'clock, she realized she was too tired to resolve any of the outstanding questions—and most were outstanding. At least not sitting at her desk. So she turned off the lights, closed and locked the doors, set the security alarm on the building, and headed across to her house. She wished Rich would be there to greet her—and, to be honest, fix them a nice dinner.

And Tabby! She realized as she walked into the kitchen that she had forgotten to put Tabby on her list. How would she explain to the librarian about moving the Tabor papers? She could . . .

But Julie stopped herself, with the stern admonition that she was going to put all this behind her now. And see if Rich had left anything in the freezer.

CHAPTER 27

Thinking about the phone call as she was lying in bed that night, Julie laughed out loud at how obvious she had been. She knew herself to be perfectly capable of defrosting the lemon chicken left from the weekend, but since she'd needed to call Rich anyway, she had taken advantage of the matter to phone him. Once his cooking instructions were out of the way, she had turned to the real topic—her planned trap.

Rich's reaction had been predictable, but her assurance that she would bring Mike Barlow into it had calmed him down, and most of the conversation had centered on her upcoming trip to Ohio. Back in September, when her parents had invited the two of them to celebrate Thanksgiving, she was not surprised that Rich had been less than eager. Relations between him and her father were never more than cool and polite, but after they had announced their engagement, heavier frost had settled in. For various reasons, they had decided Julie should go alone, while Rich would join his family in Massachusetts; it would be, they had said then, their last Thanksgiving when they could be with their families, as singles.

After next summer, they would face the dilemma of being a married couple having to choose between families for holidays. During tonight's phone call, they had reviewed that decision, wondering if it was right. For one thing, the separate trips would add another week between their getting together, and Rich was concerned about Julie making the long drive by herself. When the call ended, they had decided it was too late to change their plans, but it had taken some time to reach that conclusion. One good consequence was that the matter of Julie's proceeding with her intended trap had gotten buried.

So, lying in bed and remembering their earlier talk, Julie felt reinforced in her decision to go ahead with her plan the next day. Thinking about how to approach Wayne Reiter turned out to be the soporific she needed to lull her into a long and restful sleep.

—❧—

When she got to her office Thursday morning, Julie phoned Reiter. Like a number of the older trustees Julie had dealt with, Reiter made a fuss about checking his schedule, implying that even in retirement his time was as constrained as it had been in his active years. Not to her surprise, he discovered he was free all morning, and so they set ten a.m. to meet in her office.

To maintain momentum, Julie wanted to deal immediately with the matter of moving the papers to her office. She phoned Dennis Sutherland and asked him to stop by, which he did promptly. Over breakfast that morning, Julie had decided to play what she thought of as the boss card: no need to explain her actions to those who worked for her; it should be enough to simply announce her intentions. In this case, at least, that worked with Sutherland, who simply said he'd be happy to carry the boxes to her office. As they went up the stairs to the library, Julie hoped the same directness would work with Tabby. It did, and within a half-hour she and Dennis had carried the boxes downstairs and gathered them in a neat pile in the corner of her office.

And just in time, because as Dennis was leaving, Julie saw Wayne Reiter coming down the street in front of the historical society, a full fifteen minutes before their appointment.

"Thought I'd just come along," Reiter said when Julie went into the outer office to greet him. "You were a bit mysterious on the phone," he added. "Sounds like you're up to something."

"That's probably a good way to put it, Wayne," she said. "I am. And I need your help." She was confident this would appeal to him.

"Well, it does seem to have some risks," he said after she had described the trap. "But then," he added before she could respond, "one always has to mind the risk-return ratio, as we used to say at the B-school."

"And I think there's a chance of a good return," Julie said. "That is, catching the thief—and murderer."

"Or thieves. We can't be sure it's a single person. Indeed, there seems to me a high likelihood that we're dealing with multiple actors here."

One side of Julie valued that "we." Another side found daunting his implication that they were in this together, though she admitted to herself that hooking him on the plan had been her goal.

"That's certainly true," she said. "Likely more than one."

"So what exactly do you see as my role in this, Julie? I gather we're not having this discussion for sheer entertainment value."

"Actually, a big role. The critical one." And so she explained.

"Well, that's quite interesting. I see you're a quick learner: induced demand. Yes. And I just might be able to help out on that. I've got quite a few good contacts in Boston—collectors, dealers, well-off types. Yes, I could imagine having a word with one or two about these papers—spread the news, as it were. Of course, I'm not implying any of them would go so far as to engage someone directly to, as it were, cross the supply-demand curves."

Reiter chuckled at this, and Julie followed the joke far enough to join in.

"No, I don't think you're part of the criminal underground," she said. "Or that you know any of them personally. I realize it's a bit indirect, but I can't think of anything better."

"Nor I, though I'll give it some thought. In the meantime, I can make a few calls, suggest that a big cache of important papers landed here, start a bit of a buzz."

"I think that's the best way, at least for now."

"Right. I should know a bit more about the papers. Could I see what you wrote on that blog?"

Julie said she'd print it for him, and as she was doing so he said, "Now I need to ask, Julie—you are going to bring the police into this, aren't you?"

"I've talked to the State Police in a general way, but I'll be more specific now. Here's the description. And we've got to keep in touch ourselves, Wayne. You'll let me know what you've done?"

"Of course. In a general way—no names, of course, until that becomes important."

"I'm going to be away next week," Julie said. "Visiting my family for Thanksgiving. I'll be gone Wednesday through Sunday, but you can always call me on my cell phone. You have that number?"

He said he probably did, but wrote it in his pocket calendar to be sure. Then he pointed to the boxes in the corner and asked, "Are these the papers?"

"Yes, but this is important, Wayne: On the blog post I said the Tabor papers are in the archives. I brought them down here for safekeeping, but it's important that a thief thinks they're upstairs."

"Got you," he said. Julie didn't think it was necessary to add anything about her suspicions about Dennis Sutherland. That is, if they were suspicions; she wasn't really sure.

"So I should get started on my part in this. I'll make some calls as soon as I can, and get back to you."

After he left, Julie sat down to think. Trap sprung, she thought. Nothing more to do—for now.

CHAPTER 28

Having a deadline always focused Julie. Not that she was disorganized or easily distracted, but she did like to have a firm date or time to work against in accomplishing tasks. Friday at two p.m. was the time she had set for herself to leave for Orono for the weekend, so on Friday morning she made the two calls on her list: the first to Mike Barlow, and the second to Betsey Bowers. Because she felt guilty she hadn't been in touch with Betsey—even though she had no reason to, since she'd made no progress on that front—Julie decided to start with the policeman and work her way to Betsey.

She wasn't surprised that Mike was less than enthusiastic about the trap she had initiated with Wayne Reiter, but as had happened on other occasions when they'd worked together, she was able to bring Mike around to see there was really nothing to lose by having Reiter spread the word about the Tabor papers.

"Just make sure he keeps you informed," Mike said. "And that you keep me informed."

"Of course, but it'll take time, I'm sure, so don't sit around waiting for me to call."

"I do have work to do," he said.

"Speaking of which, anything yet on those photos? Did the seller recognize any of them?"

"I was going to tell you. Unfortunately, no; the dealer was sure none of those were our Timothy Brothers. Probably not surprising."

"No," Julie said, "though I sort of hoped it would be that simple."

"Rarely is. Anyway, back to your little trap, Julie. If it does work, and if someone comes looking for those papers, you'll stay clear, I hope. I mean, if there's a break-in, or even any suspicious inquiries or anything, you'll let me know right away, and you won't do anything on your own."

She agreed, and Mike told her he'd keep her posted on anything else that came up with the Dumont case.

So she called Betsey Bowers and explained that nothing new had happened regarding the missing ceramics. That Timothy Brothers had made another appearance in Maine, buying a gun, was a matter she didn't feel she had to share with Betsey. Of course she understood the relevance, but Julie decided that Betsey didn't have to know that the picture was developing, at least in her own mind, of a fairly wide conspiracy involving the thefts and Dan Dumont's murder. Betsey seemed satisfied with the update, even though there wasn't anything substantial.

With those two calls behind her, Julie saw that it was nearly noon. She decided to forgo lunch and instead pack a snack to eat in the car and use the time saved for finishing some paperwork and reviewing with Dennis Sutherland the activities he would be responsible for while she was away over the weekend. By one-thirty, she had accomplished those tasks and was headed to the door, happy to think she might actually get started a bit ahead of schedule.

"She's just leaving," Julie heard Mrs. Detweiller say on the phone. She gestured to indicate she could take the call. "Professor Reiter," the secretary said.

Julie returned to her office to take it.

"Mission under way," Reiter said when she picked up. "It's a tight circle, and of course I'm pretty well known," he continued before she could respond. "Just a few calls, but I think they'll have the intended results. Don't ask," he said before she could. "Best if I keep the details to myself, but I just wanted you to know the game's afoot."

Of course he reads Sherlock Holmes, Julie said to herself. To Reiter she said simply "Thanks, and keep me posted. I'm going to Orono for the weekend, but you have my cell number. Call me if you hear anything. I'll be here Monday and Tuesday."

Even with the last-minute interruption, Julie was happy to see the clock in her car said exactly two o'clock when she pulled out of the driveway and turned down the street toward the state route she would follow for the next hour and a half, before hitting the interstate for the final leg of her drive to Orono. Every time she made the trip, she was reminded of what a large state Maine is; the Ryland-to-Orono part of it, long as it seemed to her, covered just a tiny segment. Someone had told her that you could drive from Portland to New York City in less time than it would take to drive from Portland to Presque Isle. Without wanting to test that, she was prepared to accept it as fact.

She nibbled as she drove, thinking that eating was probably as distracting as texting, a driving sin she couldn't imagine indulging in. She avoided even taking or making a voice call on the road, yet eating seemed so innocent. Driving functioned for her as a mind-clearing exercise since the focus it required freed her from thinking: about her work, about Rich and their relationship and impending marriage, about puzzles of one kind or another.

The one thing she did allow herself to think about now was whether or not she should worry that someone might try to force her off the highway. Not likely, she decided, although every pickup truck reminded her of that possibility, and on the road from Ryland to the interstate the number of pickups well outnumbered the cars.

Despite the fact that being on the interstate made it possible for Julie to cruise at a much higher speed than on the state highway, the last hour or so of the trip seemed the longest—probably always that way, she told herself, since anticipation of finally arriving slowed the clock. It was already dark when she turned up Rich's block, and she was grateful she had been able to get away early enough to make the trip mostly in daylight. He had obviously been waiting and watching, because he was beside her in the drive when she turned off the engine and opened the door. After hugs and kisses, he retrieved her bag from the trunk, and inside the house immediately suggested she accompany him upstairs to the bedroom. There was an urgency and passion to their lovemaking that both of them realized came from the fact they'd be spending the Thanksgiving holiday apart.

As they lay in bed talking, this was the inevitable topic.

"But this will be the last time, won't it?" Rich asked. "By this time next year, we'll be married, and we'll have Thanksgiving together. The parents can come or not, but we don't have to go to them."

"Or we could take turns—yours one year, mine the next, and then reverse that for Christmases?" she suggested. "That's what a lot of couples do."

"I know, but we don't have to be like a lot of couples. We're not now. A lot of couples actually live together. Are we ever going to?" he asked tentatively, hesitant to raise the issue kept in check, avoided.

"Of course we are! I don't know exactly how it's going to work, Rich, but I know we'll figure it out. But right now," she added quickly, "can we figure out dinner? I'm starved."

"Soon," he said, and reached to pull her toward him.

When they went downstairs, Rich assured her the delay had been necessary so the oven could heat to roasting level for the halibut steaks he had been marinating.

"Well, in the interest of your cooking I suppose that's acceptable," she joked.

Dinner that night seemed especially relaxing to Julie, and, as always, delicious. They kept the conversation low-key, steering clear of the matters raised by the earlier talk about future holidays—and their future in general.

Instead, they recounted how they'd spent the last week, he with complaints about his students, she with reports on unimportant but interesting aspects of the historical society.

"So no more detective work this week?" Rich finally asked as they lingered over their wine.

"Well, a few developments," she admitted, and proceeded to describe Mike Barlow's report on the photos and Wayne Reiter's call.

"I should have figured him for a Sherlock Holmes fan," she said. "'The game's afoot'—imagine actually saying that as if it were some bright new phrase of your own!"

"You didn't involve him in your plan for his originality," Rich reminded her. "He's helping you set the trap, and that's what you wanted."

"True. I just hope someone springs it."

"When you're safely in Ohio," Rich added.

"Oh, no! I want to be there. If and when someone tries to get at the Tabor papers, that is."

"Well, I hope you're not there, but we can agree to disagree. What we can't disagree on, though, is that you should head to bed while I clear here. You had a busy week, and you made that long drive, so I think you should go up. I'll join you as soon as I can."

Julie and Rich often remarked on the irony that small and rural as it was, Ryland seemed to offer more to occupy their weekends together than Orono did. But this was, Rich had more than once pointed out, because on their Ryland weekends they tended to run, hike, kayak, or otherwise do something active, because for both of them the workweek was passive, and mostly spent indoors. Orono certainly had its attractions, but Ryland's rural character seemed to offer more of the outdoor activities they craved.

At some point over dinner on Friday, Rich had mentioned that he had a plan for them for the weekend that would, as he put it, "tap the rich cultural resources of this university town."

Julie reminded him of that as they lay in bed Saturday morning, listening to the rain.

"If basketball fits your definition of culture, I can deliver on that," he replied.

"And if it doesn't?"

"I can still deliver."

Julie's dislike of basketball was an oft-mentioned point of difference between them. Rich adored it and followed both college and professional teams, but Julie said that she'd prefer watching paint dry any day. Neither considered the difference of opinion a source of real tension, but on a rainy November day in Orono, Julie didn't see herself sitting in an arena watching Black Bears hoops. And said so.

"Well, I do have an alternative—or actually, an additional event, since the game isn't until this evening. This afternoon I have a lecture for us to attend. Surely that qualifies as culture!"

"Not if it's about basketball."

"Try ceramics—eighteenth-century English ceramics, to be precise."

"Fascinating!" she said jokingly.

"And here I thought you'd be eternally grateful to me for providing a touch of the exotic. You're sure not showing your gratitude."

"I could," she said.

Later, over their leisurely breakfast, Rich explained that the university's gallery was opening a new exhibit of ceramics; the lecture, to be given by a noted expert from University College London, was the kickoff event.

"It should be fun, Rich. I mean that—I don't get much in the way of intellectual stimulation, and I really should learn more about ceramics. You remember that's what was stolen from Two Rivers?"

"Yes—part of the reason I thought we should go. Still no news on that?"

"No. As a matter of fact, I just talked to Betsey Bowers this week to let her know it seems like a dead end. I didn't mention Timothy Brothers and his appearance at the gun show, but until I figure out who he is, the connection isn't going to get those ceramic pieces back."

"Maybe the lecture will give you a clue."

"Right! I'm looking forward to it, Rich—it will be a nice break."

"From running the historical society—or solving mysteries?"

"Both. What time is the lecture?"

"Four o'clock."

"And the game?"

"Seven."

"Sounds tight. I wonder if we can do both?"

"Doubtful. Would you mind if we just went to the lecture and then went out for an early dinner afterwards?" Rich said, with a knowing smile.

"I can live with that."

CHAPTER 29

The crowd entering the lobby of the gallery surprised Julie, but as Rich pointed out, a rainy Saturday in Orono didn't offer much competition. They joined the others in wrestling their umbrellas closed and depositing them in the racks outside the door to the lecture room. By the time they entered, the only available seats were near the back, but Julie said she preferred sitting there anyway, to get a better view of the screen. The lecturer, so obviously English in his tight black suit and narrow tie, was prancing about in front and consulting with someone over the operation of the controls for the projecting device.

"Wouldn't it be nice just to see an old-fashioned slide show?" Julie asked Rich after they took their seats. "I'm sure it'll be PowerPoint, and I'm sure there will be problems." Rich nodded in agreement.

A woman moved to the podium, welcomed them, and proceeded to give an introduction that said more about her than the speaker, who stood nervously to the side, awaiting his turn. Once he got past his acknowledgment of the introduction, apologies in advance for his lack of familiarity with the projecting technology, and preliminary explanations of his topic, he quickly settled in to what Julie admitted to herself was a lucid and interesting summary of the development of ceramics in eighteenth-century

England—something she knew very little about, and found engaging for that very reason. Even so, as he spoke, Julie occasionally found her mind wandering to those missing items at Two Rivers Museum.

And then she spotted him—or his head, at least. Julie was sure James Hartshorn was sitting near the front, twisting from time to time and nodding at points the speaker was making. She leaned over to whisper to Rich to see if he agreed on the man's identity, but Rich whispered back that he had only met Hartshorn once, and hadn't paid attention to the back of his head. A dark look from a person in the row ahead of them who turned to express displeasure at their whispering ended the conversation.

Julie was sure it was James Hartshorn. Maybe not surprising, since his museum was only an hour or so away from Orono, but still interesting, she thought. Was Hartshorn a ceramics guy? She didn't know, but she knew she was going to ask him.

When the talk ended, the speaker agreed to answer questions, and for the next fifteen minutes, people gave mini lectures from their seats, showing off their own knowledge more than asking the speaker to display his. Finally, the woman who had introduced the talk stood up and suggested that if others had questions, they could come to the front and ask them individually. While a handful of people made their way forward, like salmon swimming upstream against the current, most of the audience flowed to the rear.

Julie kept her eyes on Hartshorn to make sure he didn't disappear into the retreating crowd. Then his eyes met hers, and the awkward smile that came across his face left Julie puzzled: Was he happy to see her? Embarrassed? Just surprised? She wasn't sure, but when he waved to indicate he'd catch up with her in the lobby, she concluded that at a minimum he wasn't trying to hide from her. Well, how could he?

"How lovely to see you, Julie," Hartshorn said when she and Rich worked their way over to him at the long refreshments table. "And Rick, is it?" he asked, turning toward Rich, who quickly corrected him. "Of course, of course. And you teach here, don't you?" Rich admitted he did. "Which is of course what brings you here, Julie," Hartshorn continued.

"And what brings you?" Julie asked, more abruptly than she wished.

"Ceramics. I'm quite mad about it, as our English speaker might say. Are you fond of it, too?"

"Oh, I like to look at ceramic pieces, but I'm pretty ignorant—don't know a thing about glazes or any of the technical stuff."

"One doesn't need to, really," Hartshorn said, implying, Julie felt, that of course he knew quite a bit about glazes and might, if prompted, proceed to inform her.

"But I suppose it would help," Rich interjected, "although the lecture was pretty interesting, even to me."

"It was, wasn't it?" Hartshorn said. "He's really tops in the field, our speaker. When I saw the announcement of the lecture, I said I just had to come over to hear it."

"You're not far away, are you?" Julie asked.

"An hour as the crow flies, but nearly double that if you're not a crow," he answered, laughing at his effort at wit.

"Does Down East Historical Society have a good collection—of ceramics?"

"A few items of interest, but a lot of the kind of stuff we all have—bowls, pitchers, the sort of thing our generous donors feel we couldn't do without. Probably about the same as Ryland."

Julie nodded her agreement.

The sherry and nibbles on the table beside them were now under steady and aggressive attack, and Rich suggested they should get something now before it disappeared. She declined, but

Hartshorn was eager, and he and Rich decided to push through the group in front of them to retrieve something. Julie said she'd retreat to the other side of the lobby and await their return.

As she did, she brought to mind what Mike Barlow had found out about Hartshorn's alibis: He had said he was working at Down East when Dan Dumont had been murdered, and that he was driving home from Portland when Julie had been run off the road. So no help there. But his interest in ceramics was interesting. She decided to use it to probe his awareness of the missing ceramics.

"Two Rivers, without a doubt," he replied, when, as the three of them sheltered in the corner with drinks and plates, Julie asked where he thought the best ceramics collection in the state was. "You've seen it, of course," he said. "Mostly American, but as I recall, they have a few choice English items—a nice pitcher, I think, late eighteenth century. Possibly more."

Or used to, Julie said to herself, since she remembered clearly that one of the missing items was a 1798 pitcher, made in England but featuring an American packet boat.

"Anything like that in your collection?" she asked.

"Not that fine, I'm afraid. I'd be delighted to have it, or anything like it, but Down East doesn't have much of a collections budget, and of course, nice pieces don't come on the market that often anyway."

So stealing them would be the best approach, Julie thought.

"I've got a few in my own personal collection," Hartshorn continued, "not at the historical society. A very nice creamer, a set of teacups, a few other pieces."

"You're a private collector, then," Julie said.

"Oh, on the most modest scale! Back when I had a full-time job that actually paid me, I dabbled a bit, picking up things here and there. But I'm hardly a 'private collector.'"

"Do you still collect?"

"Haven't bought anything for myself in years, since I came here. If anything came my way, I'd want it for Down East anyway. How about you, Julie? Do some buying for yourself?"

Julie explained that at this stage in her career, she didn't have the time or money to pursue any personal interests, but that if she did, she would focus on papers and letters rather than artifacts like ceramics.

"Fits your historian's interests," he said. "Easier to read the past from documents, I'm sure. But remember that unlike you, I'm not a trained historian—or a trained museum professional of any kind. Just a retired old software engineer trying to manage a struggling historical society in the boonies."

While she knew that this self-deprecating remark was offered to encourage a spirited rebuttal, Julie passed.

Hartshorn broke the brief silence: "Of course, you and Betsey Bowers are true professionals. And doing some work together, I understand."

Was he aware of the missing ceramics at Two Rivers and her work in trying to find them? Julie just couldn't be sure, but she was sure she didn't care for the look on Hartshorn's face—narrowing his eyes, staring directly into hers, almost as if he was daring her to admit something.

"Not really" was all she could come up with.

He paused, but continued the penetrating gaze. Finally he said, "I see. Must have heard that wrong."

She let the conversation pause again, and then Rich asked Hartshorn if he'd like to make one last run on the refreshments table. Hartshorn demurred, saying it was time he wound his way home.

While Rich moved toward the table, Hartshorn said, "Don't care to drive in the dark. Always dangerous, especially at this time of year."

Again that look. Julie wondered if he could be sending her another message, a reminder of when she was forced off the road. But then he smiled and said, "So glad to have a chance to catch up with you. Pleasant surprise. Staying on for the holiday?"

Julie said she was driving to Ryland on Sunday and then heading to her parents' home in Ohio for Thanksgiving.

"With Rich?" he asked.

She explained they were doing the parental visits separately this year. "So next year you'll face the young-marrieds dilemma," he said. "Oh, I remember that well. My wife refused to make the drive to Maine back then, and her family was so close in New Jersey. Those do seem like ancient days. You're lucky to be young and just starting out. Well, I really should be off. Tell Rich I said good-bye. Hope to see you both again soon."

Then he was gone.

Rich returned just in time to see Hartshorn leave.

"Grilled him, did you?" he said with a smile.

"I think I was the one being grilled," she said.

"About?"

"Let me think about it."

"Find out anything?"

"I'll give you the rundown over dinner."

"Unless," he said, "you'd rather take in a hoops contest first and catch a late bite at home."

"Not on the cards, Professor. You owe me a fancy meal at one of Orono's swanky restaurants."

"Your town, your choice."

"Actually, there's a new bistro I've heard about. Okay with you?" She agreed. "A nice quiet place for you to reveal the solution to all the items missing from Maine museums."

❧

"I really should have come to Ryland this weekend," Rich said on Sunday afternoon as he carried Julie's overnight bag to her car. "You've got a long drive coming up this week. You shouldn't have had to make this one, too."

"It's not a problem, Rich. I like driving, you know that. And I'm breaking up the Ohio trip. Everything will be fine. Did you . . . ?"

"Here it is," he said, handing her a bag. "I made a few other items and froze them, so with the leftovers from Friday, this should get you through till you leave."

"Nothing like meals on wheels, especially when you provide the meals and I provide the wheels."

They embraced, and Julie got into her car and rolled down the window so Rich could lean in for a final kiss. "Be safe," he said. "And call. A lot."

Julie said she would. Then she started the engine, backed out of the drive, and headed for the highway. Despite what she had said to Rich, she was not looking forward to the longer drive later in the week, but thinking about it actually made the current drive seem less daunting. At least the weather was good—dry, cool, sunny. Not, she said to herself, like the day she drove home from Portland and got forced off the road.

No reason that should happen today! Well, maybe one, she admitted to herself. Her talk with James Hartshorn. As she had told Rich over dinner last night, Hartshorn's interest in ceramics, his hints about Julie's awareness of the Two Rivers thefts, and that she might be working on them, and then his comment about the dangers of driving. James Hartshorn had certainly moved himself higher up on her list of suspects. When she told Rich that he'd changed the topic to the lecture they had just attended, she understood that this was his way of warning off further talk about her investigations. So she had taken the hint and said no more.

It had been a fun weekend and a nice visit all around, but now she was on the road and alone and had time to think about where the various matters stood. As much as James Hartshorn now seemed to stand out as a suspect, Julie didn't want to ignore the others—Cartwright especially, but Korhonen as well. She recognized that limiting the list to her Maine colleagues wasn't necessarily justified. Thieves didn't have to reside where they worked. And then there was the question of whether the thefts were directly linked to Dumont's murder. Coincidences did happen.

Except for the weather, nothing seemed clear to her. So maybe it would be better to focus on other matters, she thought: the long drive to get to her parents' house, the visit itself, the inevitable talk about the wedding, the question of what she and Rich would do after the wedding. No, thinking about any of those topics didn't appeal, either.

Maybe she'd just put the radio on, relax, and concentrate on driving. She knew Rich would approve of that.

CHAPTER 30

It was never what you remembered or expected, Julie said to herself, but what you forgot or didn't expect. And in this case it was Connecticut. Pennsylvania she remembered well, and was therefore not frustrated by its length as she drove home from Thanksgiving. She had left her parents' Ohio River town at mid-afternoon Saturday to split the return drive into two manageable pieces, stopping that night at a rural motel on Interstate 80 two-thirds of the way across Pennsylvania's length. Between there and Maine for her Sunday drive lay only small states, or small pieces of larger ones: Connecticut, a slice of Massachusetts, an even smaller slice of New Hampshire, and then Maine itself. But why had she remembered Connecticut as small? Around Hartford she decided she had had enough of it, though she knew it would be more than another hour before she hit the Mass Pike at Sturbridge. So here she was, putting in her time, and as usual when she drove, she couldn't help using it to review and preview.

The review was mixed. Knowing it was the last Thanksgiving she and her parents would spend together before her marriage, they had all tried too hard to make it resemble the many holidays of her childhood, while ignoring the obvious fact that she was a grown woman with a career and life elsewhere—and an impending wedding that at least her father didn't fully welcome. Her mother accepted the wedding, but regretted its location and her lack of control over it. Ignoring that particular elephant in the room had created other tensions, though Julie credited her parents with doing their best to be cheerful and to keep the focus on their holiday traditions.

Sneaking off to her old bedroom to make calls to Rich at his parents' home in Boston made her feel like an adolescent, and he had concurred, though his reminder that this was the last year they'd have to do it provided some comfort. Still, the predominant sentiment she felt as she added the miles that took her farther from Ohio and closer to Maine, was sadness.

To offset that, she decided to shift from reviewing the past to previewing what lay ahead: the resumption of the work she loved as director of the Ryland Historical Society, the upcoming board meeting and Victorian Christmas celebration at RHS, a long Christmas holiday with Rich—and, of course, the tangle of thefts and murder that she never mentioned to her parents but that came too often into her mind as she helped to prepare and enjoy the Thanksgiving feast with them and the various relatives and friends who joined them.

As she thought about it, she felt confident that the strategy of laying a trap to induce a potential theft of the Tabor papers still made sense. There were aspects she needed to work on, but at least it was under way. And then there were the suspects to review—the list hadn't changed in her mind, though she was beginning to feel that Sutherland's name didn't belong there.

She was able to shoot through the backup at the Sturbridge tolls because of her recent purchase of an EZ Pass; nonetheless, traveling on the Sunday after Thanksgiving was, as Rich had said more than once, less than a good idea. When after another three hours she crossed the bridge at Portsmouth and saluted the WELCOME TO MAINE SIGN at its halfway point, she surprised herself with the catch in her voice when she said out loud, Home! Well, a few more hours of driving, she realized, but at least she was in her home state.

❧

Much as she would have liked to sleep in on Monday after the long drive, Julie expected to pay a high price for her absence from the historical society, and so set her alarm to make sure she would get to her office early. To her surprise, when she sat down at her desk just after seven-thirty, it was about as clean as she had left it last week. She credited Dennis Sutherland for that. The former assistant director had seemed to enjoy leaving messes for her during her then-rare absences, and before Dennis arrived, when Julie was doing both jobs. Mrs. Detweiller, rather than pitching in to relieve her, became even less efficient. Of course the Thanksgiving holiday meant things had been slow anyway, but Julie was still grateful to Dennis for handling things.

She found only routine correspondence and two call slips on her desk. One asked her to phone Wayne Reiter. The other, dated Friday, listed Ted Korhonen. She recognized Mrs. Detweiller's handwriting: "He says it's very important." She decided it was probably too early to return either call, but Korhonen's intrigued her, so she thought she could at least phone and leave a message. She was surprised when he answered on the first ring.

"I'm so glad you called. Your secretary told me you were away, and I was almost going to ask if I could get in touch with you wherever you were, but decided it wouldn't be fair to bother you. Anyway, we had a break-in here."

"What? When did it happen?"

"Thanksgiving Day."

"Anything stolen?"

"A painting."

"Have you called the police?" she asked.

"I'm going to, but I wanted to talk to you first. Should I call that friend of yours—the Statie? I figured since he's sort of working on all this, that would be better than the county sheriff."

"You better just report it the normal way," Julie said. "You really should have done that earlier."

"I know, I know, but it's all been really upsetting, and I kept thinking that I should talk to you before I do anything else. I didn't want to make an official fuss if it wasn't necessary."

"I'm sorry I wasn't here," Julie said, "but it is necessary." She wondered why she was apologizing. Korhonen was a grown-up who knew enough to report a theft when it occurred, and not wait for days for someone to return his phone call. But then Julie remembered Betsey's similar reluctance to report thefts. She just couldn't understand why museum professionals acted that way, but so be it. "What happened, Ted?" she asked.

Korhonen told her he had gone to the museum on Friday morning to do some work on a new exhibit and noticed that the side door was unlocked. Inside, he wandered around, checking on things. Although it was nothing obvious, he still felt something was wrong.

"You know how it is, Julie. You just have a feeling—something out of place, something not quite right. Anyway," he continued, "I went out to the room where I'm setting up this new exhibit, and as soon as I got there I realized it was missing."

"The painting?"

"Right. God, I'm so upset. It's a terrific landscape, a real treasure. A pretty famous Finnish painter, but you wouldn't know him. No one here does, but he's very famous in Finland, and it's a valuable piece."

"What's it doing in Maine?"

"Oh, a gift from a local guy whose parents, or maybe grand-parents, bought it back in the homeland. He decided it was too valuable to keep in his house down on the lake, so he gave it to us a couple of years ago."

Julie quickly consulted her memory and couldn't recall any-thing.

"I never saw it," she said. "Did you put it on the new blog register?"

Korhonen hesitated before answering.

"No, as a matter of fact, and I'm kicking myself that I didn't. I did list it on the insurance coverage, so at least that's okay. But I feel just sick about this. The hardest part is going to be telling the donor."

"That's all the more reason to report this right away, Ted—for the insurance company, and so you can assure the donor you're handling it the right way. Can we come back to the door—you say it was unlocked?"

"Yes, and I just can't explain that. I was there on Wednesday. Left around six p.m. or so, and I'm absolutely sure I locked up."

"No security system?"

"Alas, no. I guess I'll have to look into that now, even though the horse is already out of the barn."

"And you didn't go in Thursday?"

"Thanksgiving Day? No. We're closed until Monday."

"And no one else has a key?"

"The chairman of the board, just as a precaution, in case I misplace mine, or if someone needed something when I'm not around. It's not a great system, but we're a small outfit. You know that."

Julie did. It was an all too familiar story with small museums.

"Have you talked to him yet?" she asked.

"The chairman? No, not yet. I wanted to talk to you first, since you know all about this kind of thing. But I'll call him. And I'll call the sheriff instead of your friend."

Julie told him she'd think about whether to alert Mike Barlow, but that in the meantime the sheriff was the right one to call.

"Let me know if anything comes up. And good luck, Ted. Maybe it'll all get sorted out."

But in what way? she asked herself after the call. She'd had no idea that Korhonen's museum owned a valuable painting, and he hadn't put it on the blog register. So all of a sudden, the painting goes missing? And presumably this happened because the door was unlocked—not broken in, not tampered with. Assuming everything he had said was true, why in the world had Korhonen not called the county sheriff to report it—and inform his own board chair? None of it made sense, unless you factored in Ted's haplessness.

But maybe, Julie thought, it made a different kind of sense—a red herring. The more she thought about it, the more the craziness of what Korhonen had told her seemed to add up to a diversion, a way to direct attention away from . . . Well, from what? She had to think about that.

But before she could, she heard the phone and realized that Mrs. Detweiller was not at her desk. So Julie picked it up.

"Back at your desk, I see," Reiter said. "Good holiday?"

Julie said it was, and asked about his.

"Kids and grandkids overdoing the turkey," he said. "But I did have an interesting call, which is why I'm phoning."

Julie listened as he summarized the conversation he had had on Friday, with "one of his Boston contacts." The person, unidentified in what Julie knew to be Reiter's favored way of enhancing the drama, had circulated the information about the Tabor papers and had gotten some strong interest, also from an unidentified person.

"Quite excited, apparently," Reiter said. "The inquirer said that documents of that sort would find a ready market among his clients, and he asked for details—more than my contact had, of course."

"Of course," Julie repeated. "So where does it stand?"

"Just there. I told my contact to tell the person that he—or it could be she, I suppose—should get in touch with you directly. You see my point?"

"I'm not sure I do."

"Simple; if you get a call, then it's legit. If not, we may have stirred interest in, shall we say, a less than reputable person. Someone who might decide to take matters into his—or her—own hands."

"To try to steal the papers?"

"Exactly. So the trap is set. Or it might be. I thought you should know."

When Julie probed for further information, Reiter invoked the confidentiality of his contact and ended the call with an abrupt command: "Keep me informed."

About what? she wondered. If she got a call from someone about the Tabor papers, that would be easy. But how long should she wait for that before deciding a vanload of thieves was on its way to Ryland to steal them? And if that was the case, what was she supposed to do about it? Wait, she told herself.

"Oh, there you are," said Mrs. Detweiller, standing at the open door to Julie's office.

"Indeed I am," Julie responded, wondering exactly where Mrs. Detweiller thought she might be. "How was your Thanksgiving?"

"Busy. And yours?"

The question didn't invite a long answer, so Julie said simply that she had had a good visit with her parents, and left it at that.

"Looks like everything's under control here."

"Yes. Dennis handled things in your absence," she said, emphasizing the last word.

"I'll catch up with him when he gets in," Julie said. "If you see him first, would you ask him to come in? I'm just cleaning up some correspondence now. I don't have any appointments today, do I?"

"No. You wanted to keep your schedule free," the secretary said, again emphasizing the last word, as if to indicate that a free schedule was a sure sign of slacking off.

Nice to be back, Julie said to herself.

CHAPTER 31

A few minutes later, Dennis Sutherland appeared at her door. They exchanged stories about their respective Thanksgivings, she thanked him for minding the store, and he reviewed what had happened while she was away.

"Quiet," he said. "A few visitors on Wednesday and Friday. Saturday was fairly busy—folks bringing in the grandchildren to get them out of the house, I'd guess."

"Shop sales?"

"Decent. We're pretty much on track there."

One of the things Julie liked about Dennis was that he perfectly understood the financial importance of the museum shop, unlike his predecessor, who had always projected disdain for that part of the operation.

"Actually, maybe a little ahead," he added. "I'll have to check the weekend take. But of course, the big season is coming up."

The shop made more than a third of its revenues in the month leading up to Christmas, and Dennis had increased the inventory in anticipation of increased sales. In the past, Julie had been reluctant to pay for so many items so far ahead of when they would be sold, but Dennis had convinced her that the investment was worthwhile. Last year's results had proved him right, and she had authorized even larger purchases for this season.

"Victorian Christmas should help a lot," Dennis said. "If we pack the place again this year, folks will head to the shop for last-minute gifts."

Victorian Christmas was an event she and Dennis had introduced last year. It was an open house two weeks before Christmas, and featured holiday decorations in all the period rooms, cookies and cider, docents dressed in costumes, caroling, a tree lighting—the sort of event designed to lure skiers and other weekend visitors, and at the same time, bring together the trustees and other volunteers for a holiday thank-you. It had worked brilliantly. She and Dennis hoped to make it even bigger this year by adding a small musical ensemble to play in the background, an appearance by the high school choir, and heavy publicity via flyers distributed at the ski area. Julie continued to resist Dennis's suggestion of a Santa Claus, even though he offered to take the role.

"I'm still thinking about that," she said when he raised the matter. "It just doesn't feel authentic to me, but we can talk more about it. One small idea I had was to invite the History Network.

I don't know how many, if any, would come, but I thought it would be a nice gesture."

Dennis agreed. "Helps showcase RHS."

"Right."

Julie didn't mention the other reason: bringing some of her professional colleagues to the event would give her a chance to think about their possible roles in the museum thefts. She couldn't explain to herself exactly why that was so, but she sensed that if a few of them turned up, it might signal interest in RHS's collections—interest in more than just viewing them. Although her idea was vague and probably not very promising, Julie still thought it was worth doing, if only, as Dennis had said, to show off her museum.

"I'll use the Network e-mail to invite them," she said. "Anything else about Victorian Christmas we should discuss?"

Dennis said it was under control, but he would continue to nag her about Santa Claus.

As he left, Mrs. Detweiller came in to say that Ted Korhonen was on the phone.

"Sorry to bother you again, but I wanted to let you know that I took your advice right away and called my board chair and the sheriff. I feel a lot better about all this now, but I'm still really upset about the painting. It's such a beautiful piece."

"Tell me more about it," Julie said.

Korhonen described the painting—a large oil landscape of a winter scene in Finland, by a painter Ted said any Finn would recognize immediately, though the name meant nothing to her.

"Trust me," he continued. "He's major. This was worth a lot. I still can't believe it's gone."

"I don't understand why you didn't put this on the blog, Ted."

"I don't either! It's the most valuable thing we have—or had. I should have listed it, but with the holiday and all, I just didn't get around to it."

"But don't you think you should alert the Network about it now—in case someone tries to sell it to one of the others?"

"How likely is it that some historical society in Maine would buy a Finnish painting? It'll go national, I'm sure. The sheriff said he'd get it listed on some national database right away. But I suppose it wouldn't hurt to notify the Network. I'll do that, Julie. Meantime, have you talked to your policeman friend?"

"I'll call him later today and let him know what happened."

"Thanks, Julie. I really appreciate your support on this. Maybe it all fits together somehow—the painting, along with the other things you're working on."

After the call ended, Julie pondered that, remembering something her father had said to her over the weekend. They had been working on a jigsaw puzzle together as they had done so often when she was younger, no doubt the source of her interest, and her father had said that sometimes pieces of puzzles fit puzzles other than the one you're working on. The remark was applicable to the fiendishly difficult puzzle of a Turkish carpet they had been tackling, but it struck Julie as having deeper resonance. Maybe Ted's painting was part of her puzzle—but maybe it wasn't. Maybe it was a piece of another one, one she knew nothing else about. That was something to talk to Mike Barlow about, she thought, and decided not to postpone calling him.

She was forced to leave him a message, so had no further reason to put off the other things she needed to do, starting with the e-mail invitation for Ryland's Victorian Christmas to the Network.

By mid-afternoon, Julie hadn't heard back from Mike Barlow, but every other item on her list had been crossed off. She decided she needed a run to clear her head and to give her body the stretch it needed after so much confined time in the car. Even Mrs.

Detweiller's obvious disapproval of her early departure, conveyed solely through body language, didn't deter her.

CHAPTER 32

Julie had two big events on her work calendar between Thanksgiving and Christmas: the fall meeting of the board of trustees at the end of the week following her return from Ohio, and, a week after that, Victorian Christmas. In and around preparing for and carrying out those events and doing her daily job, she had to find time for holiday shopping. So an easy month ahead, she said to herself Tuesday morning—unless, of course, something new emerged about the thefts and murder.

Mike Barlow had phoned her at home the night before, and she'd passed on the information about the missing painting, which he took without comment, except to ask if it had been reported to local law enforcement. He had nothing to tell Julie, and the call was quite brief. It all seemed too quiet, though she knew that could change at any time, especially with regard to the Tabor papers. She just had to wait patiently to see if anyone called about them—and, if not, to see if anyone took more direct action.

At three-thirty p.m. on Friday, the trustees began to gather in the meeting room of the Swanson Pavilion. Howard and Clif Holdsworth were already there when Julie entered, even though the meeting was, as always, scheduled for four p.m. The tray of cookies lured Howard and Clif as predictably as a cheese-baited mousetrap, and, as always since she had introduced the custom, the competing tray of fruit remained untouched until Dalton Scott entered and picked up a bunch of grapes. Henry LaBelle, the board's solicitor and secretary, came next, and joined Dalton at the fruit tray. As if voting on which side of the board they belonged, Ann Gibbons and Wayne Reiter paused briefly before making their choice—Ann to the fruit, Wayne to the cookies. Howard surveyed the group and announced that they might as well begin since everyone was assembled, except for Loretta Cummings, whose duties at the high school rarely allowed her to be present on time, a fact Howard drew attention to, as he routinely did, by saying that no doubt Loretta would be coming along soon.

After review and approval of the minutes of the last meeting—surprisingly to Julie without a single correction—the board turned to Holdsworth's treasurer's report. For him, this was no doubt the highlight of any meeting, but for Julie, Dalton, LaBelle, and perhaps a few others, the real highlight was the verbal fisticuffs that inevitably followed the treasurer's line-by-line reading of the budget report, when someone would move for approval and Clif would counter with the assertion that his report required not approval but acceptance, a substitution they all knew Clif was willing to explain at considerable length.

But on this occasion, Dalton, perhaps as drugged as everyone by Clif's mind-numbing reading of the figures, immediately moved acceptance of the report. If Clif was happy with having won the battle without even taking to the field, he didn't show it, and Howard quickly thanked Dalton for his motion and got a second from Mike, and a unanimous vote.

"Excellent as always," the chair said to Holdsworth. "Now the next item of business—"

"—is my late entrance, as always!" Loretta Cummings finished. "Sorry, everyone. You know what happens to me at school," she continued, taking her seat beside Henry LaBelle.

"Glad you're here, Loretta," Howard said. "We're just turning to the main item, so your timing is impeccable. Julie will update us on the collections matters."

Julie reminded them that a small working group had been set up to develop a formal policy for de-accessioning items from the collection and to recommend the creation of a collections committee to implement it. It had been left to her to consult with Wayne Reiter, the impetus behind the move, and to draft a policy. Discussions with Wayne since then had tended to detour into the matter of the thefts and, ultimately, to the scheme for setting a trap for would-be thieves. The draft Julie had presented to Wayne some weeks ago remained, as he put it, under review, and she had not wanted to provoke him by pressing. So now she faced the dilemma of having to come to the board empty-handed.

Before she could say anything, Wayne Reiter jumped in.

"Let me just preempt Julie for a moment," he said. "As you may recall, I was one of several trustees tasked with assisting Julie in the development of a formal policy on de-accessioning. You may also recall that I was probably the one most responsible for pushing this matter in the first place, because of my eagerness to have us clean up our collections. Well, I stand before you to confess my guilt!"

Julie had once speculated to Rich that Wayne Reiter probably wished he had pursued an acting career, to which Rich responded: "Hasn't he? That's what professors at the Harvard B-school do: act." And, Julie now thought, even trustees of the Ryland Historical Society could do the same. Reiter continued.

"Julie did her best to move me to action so we could present a formal policy today, but my confession is that I failed to respond to her gentle pressure, and the result is that we are unable to do that, although I believe Julie stands ready to review the work she did—and excellent work it is. Julie?"

"Well, since Ann and Loretta are part of the task force, I'd like to ask them to comment first."

Ann Gibbons said they had had a good meeting, and that she was comfortable with leaving the drafting of the report to Julie, with Wayne's help. Loretta agreed, and asked Julie to give an overview. This took her less than ten minutes, and answering a few questions took another five. Howard brought the matter to a close by saying that the board looked forward to receiving the official recommendations at its next meeting.

"And hearty thanks to you, Wayne, for heading us down the right path here," said Julie, adding silently to herself, "And getting lost at the end of it."

"Now, Julie," the board chair continued, "I'm sure we'd all like to hear about the plans for the big event."

After several years of board meetings, Julie knew she should realize that what most—not all, of course—of the trustees expected of such events was a pleasant few hours of sociability, with just enough attention to real matters to convince them they had done their duty. Serious substantive issues like collections management were, she knew, several notches below top priority for most of them, and so the ease with which they skated over the delay on that front shouldn't have been a surprise. She knew that what they really liked was to discuss public events, digging into logistical details and offering suggestions, some couched more like directives, but she was still surprised at the gusto with which the trustees now tucked into the plans for Victorian Christmas.

Clif Holdsworth began: "A very nice affair, last year, but I'd like to repeat what I said then: I don't see why we have to get into all that other stuff—Kansas and Three Kings and so on. It's called Victorian Christmas, isn't it?"

"Kwanzaa, you mean," Loretta Cummings interrupted. "Not Kansas. And I think it's entirely appropriate that we honor other cultures, Clif."

"You would," he said testily. "I mean you have to at the school; that's a public institution, and I understand you don't have any choice. But the Ryland Historical Society is a private institution, and if we want to celebrate Christmas, well, why not? How many Muslims and African Americans do we have in Ryland, anyway?"

"Not many. Not enough, I admit, but I think it's entirely right for us to recognize that other cultures have similar traditions," Loretta said, "not the least of which is Hanukah."

This was a fight Julie was content to watch rather than join, but as she waited for another trustee to weigh in, she was tempted to say something. Dalton Scott, usually quiet at meetings unless the discussion involved architectural issues, came to her rescue.

"You're certainly right about our white-bread population, Clif, but just because we don't have Muslims or other religions at the event doesn't mean we should ignore the traditions they celebrate. We're a historical society, after all, and we have exhibits on logging and farming, even though you can count on one hand the number of active loggers and farmers in the area today. Maybe the lack of people different from us obliges us to make a special effort to celebrate other cultures—for the sake of those white kids who will grow up here not knowing about anything else and then move to Boston or New York and have to learn about others."

To Julie's surprise, Ann Gibbons actually clapped her hands.

"Right on, Dalton! We need to be inclusive, to stretch our minds, to expose our kids to other ideas and traditions. That's our mission, isn't it?"

Howard said, "Any other views on this?"

Clif, who had been sitting with his arms folded and staring at the ceiling, said, "Well, I'm in the minority here, being a native, but I'm not going to take a stand. The only thing I'd ask is that we consider having a visit from Santa Claus. Isn't that a tradition our children should understand?"

Julie glanced at Dennis Sutherland, who as a staff member, never spoke at board meetings except in response to direct questions.

He returned her look with one that said 'I didn't put him up to it.' Both of them smiled. Julie knew when to retreat.

"That's a fine idea," she said. "As a matter of fact, Dennis has mentioned this because a couple of the visitors suggested it to him last year. I've been going back and forth on it, but you've convinced me, Clif. As long as others agree, of course."

"I take that as agreement," Howard said before anyone else could speak. "Now, who would like to play the role? Wayne?"

"Not enough padding," Reiter said, proudly rubbing his slender waist. "Not that weight is a requirement for the job. But shouldn't we have a Santa that looks like one?"

"I suspect you can get padding wherever you rent a costume," Henry LaBelle said. "Why don't we leave it to Julie to find an appropriate Santa?"

"Delegation of authority—quite proper," Howard said. "You'll handle this for us, Julie?"

She said she would, but couldn't help adding, "Of course, if any of you would like to volunteer, just let me know. I can keep a secret."

The goodwill that her comments engendered was quickly picked up by Howard, who liked to conclude on a positive note.

"Excellent. I believe we've settled that. Is there anything else about Victorian Christmas we should discuss?"

To Julie's relief, there wasn't, so Howard quickly announced adjournment.

"Looking forward to seeing you all there," he added. "I'm sure it will be another great event for the Ryland Historical Society."

꧁꧂

Back in her office after the meeting, Julie was preparing to leave for the day when Dennis Sutherland appeared at the door.

"I really wasn't behind that," he said.

Julie laughed. "I know. Clif is Clif, but it worked out, Dennis. I really don't mind having Santa Claus. Would you be interested?"

"I've got the heft, but I wouldn't want to take the job from someone else. It might be good to have someone other than staff or trustee—that way, no one would know who it was."

"Any suggestions?"

"I was thinking about Rich."

"Rich? He's too thin."

"But as Mike said, you can get the padding with the costume. No one would guess it's Rich."

"Least of all Rich! Well, maybe I'll ask him. He's coming this weekend," she added, remembering how much she was looking forward to his arrival in another hour. "Sure, I think I'll ask him."

After their long period apart over the Thanksgiving holiday, suggesting the Santa role for Rich was not at the top of Julie's priority list for his weekend visit. Since his priority fit hers, it was almost eight o'clock by the time they came downstairs and went into the kitchen to start dinner. He had stopped at the large grocery store in Farmington to buy haddock—the only fresh thing they had, he apologized, but added, "I'll try to spice it up a bit."

"You're good at that," she said. "Can I do anything?"

"Just give me a few minutes to make the sauce, and then we can have a glass of wine while it cooks—it's really simple."

Fifteen minutes later he joined her in the living room, carrying two glasses of wine and a bowl of nuts.

"So tell all—we've got a lot to catch up on," he said.

She recounted her drive and Thanksgiving visit in greater detail than their recent phone calls had allowed, and he filled her in a bit on his family time in Massachusetts.

"And you had a board meeting today, right?" he asked.

As she started to answer, the timer bell in the kitchen went off, and Rich announced dinner was ready. At the table in the kitchen, he said, "So I started to ask about your meeting today."

"Nothing big," she said, "although there's one matter that involves you."

"Me?"

After she raised it, he said, "Why not? Sometimes I feel a little out of place at your events, so this would give me something to do."

"You'll be Santa?"

"It'll be fun. How's the haddock?"

"Just like you, Rich—better than I deserve!"

CHAPTER 33

"Every hour on Saturday and Sunday has forty-two and a half minutes, whereas hours during the week have, on average, sixty-eight minutes."

"On average?" Julie asked.

"Right. Monday hours are a little longer," Rich answered. "I'm surprised you've never heard about this, you being a PhD and a museum director and all."

Julie tried to keep a straight face to match Rich's, but she couldn't resist laughing when she asked: "Do your students have any idea that you're nuts?"

"Some. Well, maybe most. But they're sort of stuck with me."

"Like me. I do think you're right about weekdays versus weekends. Where did this one go?"

"Once you understand the differences in minutes per hour, all becomes clear."

Even more than most, this weekend had seemed to vaporize. It was nearly four o'clock on Sunday afternoon when they sat at the kitchen table, talking about its rapid ending and Rich's imminent departure for Orono.

"So let's look ahead," he said. "Next weekend you're coming over, and then I'll be here the following weekend, white beard and fake belly at the ready."

"Then the next weekend we both stay put, but the one after that is Christmas, and I'll be with you in Orono. Are you going to keep the Santa costume?"

"Only Santa knows, and Santa is a pretty secretive guy. But I'll get a tree and put up lights and turn my digs into a holiday wonderland for you. Meantime, I better hit the road."

After he had left, Julie mused on how dependent she was on Rich's steady, careful ways, always planning, always looking ahead. Well, that and more. The next few weeks, she knew, would be busy with final plans for Victorian Christmas, but Rich's outline of the next month helped her put things into a framework—and reminded her how much she was looking forward to the holidays, especially spending time with him. Focusing on that, she figured, would help her work through the time between, not, she realized, unlike a child who sees Christmas looming but can't quite imagine how she's going to hold on till it comes.

At her desk on Monday morning, she thought about how little she actually had to do for the Society's holiday event. Thanks to Dennis's good work last year, the details were quite under control. Victorian Christmas had already become what they both now called one of Ryland Historical Society's two signature events, the other being the Fourth of July concert. They neatly divided the year, each creating its own enthusiasm and momentum, reminding the community of the Society and its important local role. What either had to do with the core work of a historical society was not something Julie cared to dwell on. "Hey," Dennis once said, "we're in the entertainment business, you know. Like Disney." To that she had considered several possible responses but said nothing. There really wasn't anything wrong with entertainment, she rationalized, as long as its effects supported the serious work of teaching history that she wanted RHS to be known for.

So aside from consulting from time to time with Dennis about specific matters, Julie found that her work that week was routine and not terribly engaging. At the back of her mind, she was preoccupied with thoughts about trapping the thief, but her daily workload was keeping her too busy. She did have a conversation with Wayne Reiter on Wednesday—or really, she answered his brief interrogation about whether she had had any calls concerning the Tabor papers. She hadn't, and his response—"That tells you something, doesn't it? Keep me informed"—didn't in fact tell her much. If Reiter's supposition was correct—that no inquiry meant the papers were at risk for theft—she should be more worried than she actually was. Having moved the papers to her office, she decided the only thing she needed to do now was to remind Dennis to keep an eye on them over the upcoming weekend, when she would be away and he would be on duty. It would not be necessary to tell Mrs. Detweiller to secure the office; there were some things she could count on her secretary to do, locking the office being one of the prime ones.

The week went quickly, but as explained by Rich's bizarre theory on the shorter hours on Saturdays and Sundays, the weekend in Orono went even more quickly. Somehow without realizing how it had happened, Julie found herself back at her desk at the Ryland Historical Society the Monday morning before Victorian Christmas. The first thing she did was to check that the boxes holding the Tabor papers were still securely stashed in the inner closet of her office. To an untrained eye, they might look like a stack of yellowed pages; but to a historian, this kind of primary source material was invaluable. The thief seemed to know the difference. Besides, they were the best bait she had available.

Content that the papers were undisturbed, Julie walked over to Dennis Sutherland's office in Swanson Wing to get his report on the weekend.

"Quiet" was his simple description. "Very little traffic—I suspect folks are holding off till next weekend. And everything's okay there, too," he added. "All the publicity's out, it's on our website, musicians and the choir are set, food is on order. All we need, I guess, is good weather. Oh, and Santa Claus."

"I can guarantee the latter but not the former. What does it look like for Saturday?"

"Well, we'll know on Saturday, but the forecast is for clear and dry—no snow. A little white stuff might add atmosphere, but I'd rather have safe roads."

Julie agreed, and added that the lack of snow for the past month had surprised her.

"New England weather," Dennis said. "Maybe we'll have snow for Christmas."

Thinking of her drive to Orono for the holiday, Julie silently wished otherwise, but kept the thought private.

"So all in all," Dennis concluded, "we're in good shape. It should be a great day Saturday."

❧

Saturday morning, Dennis's prediction appeared to be coming true. Temperatures in the 40s and bright sunshine, she noticed as she left Rich at the house and went to the historical society; she guessed that would bring out a good crowd. Although the event didn't begin till two p.m., Julie and Dennis had agreed to meet in the large exhibition room at noon to check final details. The harpist and flute player were setting up in the corner, and Julie spent a few moments helping and thanking them. Tables were set up along the walls, and the caterers from the Ryland Inn were arranging trays of snacks and cookies.

"It's sort of like a play, isn't it?" Dennis said to Julie as they surveyed the scene. "Getting the stage ready," he added.

"Well, you told me we're in the entertainment business," she responded.

"Another opening, another show!"

"How many do you think we'll have?"

"Last year I counted seventy-five, but the word's gotten out about it, and the weather's great, so I'd think at least a hundred, maybe more. I told the Inn to prepare for a hundred and twenty-five, so we'll either be eating cookies through New Year's Eve or madly running to Ryland Groceries to get more. By the way, how many of the Network folks are coming?"

"Just three," Julie said. "Ted Korhonen, Brent Cartwright, and Betsey Bowers. Frankly, I'm surprised that Brent and Betsey are coming, since it's somewhat of a long drive for them, but of course, Ted is close. Anyway, it was really a gesture, just to let them know what we're doing."

At that moment the director of the high school choir approached Julie and asked about the timing of their performance.

"The harp and flute will play in the background for an hour and a half," Julie told her. "Then if the choir could assemble and begin around three-thirty or so, that would be great. Santa Claus will come at four-fifteen, so it would be good if they could lead into that with 'Santa Claus Is Coming to Town.' People will start slipping out around then, at least the older ones, and Santa will finish a little before five."

"Sounds good," the young woman said. "I told the kids to be here by three, so we should be fine."

Julie wasn't surprised to hear Clif Holdsworth's voice as she turned from the choir director.

"Pretty thin turnout," he said. "Seems like we had a lot more last year."

From where they stood, Julie could see the clock high above the door at the end of the meeting space. It was precisely two o'clock. She would have loved to point out to her board treasurer that it was a bit early to judge the crowd. She would also have loved to note that Clif always arrived early when goodies were on offer, lest others get to the best first. But she made neither of those comments, instead saying, "Have you seen the cookies, Clif? They're really cute this year, and there are plenty of them. Come on over and take a look."

It was not at all difficult to persuade him to join her in survey-ing the tables heavily laden with trays of frosted cookies in the shapes of Christmas trees, Santa, reindeer, and sleighs.

"I suppose someone needs to be first," he said as he reached for two of the reindeer.

"And the punch is over there," Julie said, gesturing to the bowl. "Excuse me a moment, Clif," she added. "I see a couple of people I need to welcome."

She wasn't surprised that Betsey Bowers and Brent Cartwright entered together because she had e-mailed them after they had separately responded to the invitation and suggested they could share a ride, Betsey being in York and able to pick up Brent in Portland on the way.

"It's so nice of you to invite us," Betsey said. "And to suggest sharing a ride. That made the trip easy and gave us time to talk. I haven't been to Ryland in ages, and I'd forgotten what a lovely town it is. And such a pretty ride to get here."

"I'm glad you could come," Julie replied. "This has become a really good event for us, and I'm happy to have some of my colleagues join us. Glad you could make it, Brent."

"Wouldn't have missed it," he said. "As I was telling Betsey in the car, we really all ought to do more of this—bringing Network members to our events. It sort of helps give us ideas for our own shops."

"Well, your Halloween party sets a pretty high standard," Julie said.

"Thanks. Nothing like wearing a costume to take us out of our humdrum museum lives."

"You could have worn yours," Julie said. "Every party needs a Henry Wadsworth Longfellow."

Cartwright laughed.

"The only person in costume you'll see today is Santa," she added.

"What? You mean it's not going to be the real Santa?" he said with feigned disappointment.

"You'll have to wait and see."

"Any other Network folks coming?" Betsey asked.

"Only Ted Korhonen. I probably should have connected the three of you, since you went right through his town, but since he's so close I didn't think about it. Come on over and help yourself to some goodies before it gets crowded. We're expecting a hundred or so."

After leading her two colleagues to the food and introducing them to Howard Townsend, who had a plate of cookies and a glass of punch and was eyeing the sandwiches, Julie circulated around the room, greeting volunteers and members, making other introductions, directing traffic, and encouraging people to inspect the ornaments on the large Christmas tree. When she spotted Ted

Korhonen by himself, she made a point of greeting him and moving him over to where Brent and Betsey were standing.

Ted was shy and not likely to strike up a conversation with people he didn't know, so she was pleased to see the smile on his face when he saw two colleagues. Although she hadn't talked to him recently about the painting stolen from his museum, and was eager to, she also knew this wasn't a good time. She recalled that he was going to post something about it on the Network's blog but couldn't remember seeing it. So maybe Betsey and Brent knew— or maybe they didn't. In either case, Julie decided to say nothing unless Ted did first.

After she had brought them together and was about to move along to continue working the room, Ted surprised her by asking if they might take a look at the Tabor papers while they were here.

"Sure," she said. "When this is over, if you don't mind hanging around."

"Great," Ted said. "I've been eager to see what you've got since that post went out. How about you two?"

Betsey said she'd be interested, but Brent seemed less enthusiastic.

"But if you want to, Betsey," he said, "I don't mind waiting a bit after the party. Just so we're not too late leaving. I have something going on in Portland this evening."

Brent's lack of enthusiasm to stay long enough to look at the papers gave Julie pause, since he had mentioned his interest to her before, but she assumed his need to get back to Portland trumped that now.

In any event, she didn't have time to think more about all that because the high school choir had just broken into "Santa Claus Is Coming to Town" as Santa himself came bounding into the room, shouting "Ho, ho, ho" to the delight of dozens of squealing children.

CHAPTER 34

Rich O'Brian's reputation as an energetic and engaging teacher was known to Julie as long ago as their time together in graduate school at the University of Delaware. That he had been nominated for an Outstanding Teacher award at the University of Maine twice already in his short time there was not a surprise.

But people who didn't know him well found his teaching reputation a contrast to his quiet, restrained manner and his deference to others, especially Julie. So the Ryland people who knew Rich were startled to discover Santa's identity after his rollicking, ebullient performance that extended the Victorian Christmas celebration well past its announced closing. There were still too many young children waiting to sit on his lap. He patiently dealt with the crowd, making it nearly six o'clock by the time the last youngster got her chance with the jolly old man.

The room was nearly empty save for the three members of the Maine History Network, who had gathered in one corner to wait for Julie to close the event. Finally joining them, Julie apologized.

"So who is that masked man?" Ted asked, grinning.

"Rich. My boyfriend. You've met him."

"He could do it for a living," Betsey Bowers said. "I'm impressed."

"Well, he's a great teacher," Julie said with pride, "so I guess it sort of makes sense."

"Yeah, we all know teaching is acting," Brent Cartwright said, with an edge that Julie didn't like. But she resisted responding and said they could go look at the Tabor papers now that her duties at the party were done.

"If you still want to," she said.

They agreed, though she did notice that Brent checked his watch, no doubt thinking of his need to get to Portland.

"We can do it quickly," she said, and then led them from the building and across the small campus to her office.

"Upstairs?" Ted asked when she had entered the security code and unlocked the building.

They were standing in the space where at one end the stairs ascended to the library and at the other, a hallway led to her office. Ted had been to the library on several occasions.

"No, I've got the papers in my office right now because I'm working on an inventory. In my spare time, of course."

The others, familiar with the multiple demands on a museum director, laughed.

"Is that safe?" Betsey asked. Her own direct experience with thefts no doubt made her especially sensitive on that score, thought Julie.

"Perfectly," Julie said. "The security on the whole building is strong, so my office is as secure as the library upstairs. Come on in," she added as she guided them past Mrs. Detweiller's desk and then used another key to unlock her door.

"And there they are." She pointed to the boxes. "Not too exciting to look at, but there's a lot of great stuff in there."

She spent a few minutes enumerating the kinds of items—letters to and from Dr. Tabor, clippings from contemporary newspapers, records of the Ryland Town Council—and then reached in to retrieve one especially interesting item that she had been working on, Tabor's diary. Holding out to them the small leatherbound notebook, she said it was one of more than a dozen, covering the years of the Depression.

"That's what I'm really interested in," she said. "How a small rural community like Ryland experienced the Depression. He was such a keen observer, and his diaries are just full of great little details that really add color and life to it all."

"Too bad Jim Hartshorn couldn't see this," Betsey said. "I know he's quite interested."

"I didn't realize that," Julie said.

"Oh, yes; after you posted that message about the papers, he wrote to me to ask if I had seen them or knew anything more about them. I wouldn't have thought they would be his cup of tea, but, well, you can never be sure. I'm surprised he didn't talk to you about them, Julie."

Except for a shrug, Julie didn't respond to that. But she certainly registered it.

"Well, we should be going, let you get on with things," Ted said. "You must have a lot of cleanup after that party."

"You're all welcome to look through these anytime you like," Julie said. "They're a treasure trove, and it's going to be a long time before I can really master what's here."

"Thanks, Julie," Brent said. "For the party, and this special look. I'd probably like to come back and spend some time with them. Will they stay here in your office?"

Julie paused before answering.

"For now. But if any of you want to work on them, I can have some boxes taken back upstairs to the library where there's room to spread out. Just let me know."

"I can't imagine how valuable they are," Ted said. "You should keep them wherever they're safest."

Julie realized that Ted was as sensitive as Betsey when it came to missing items and would like to have talked to him about the painting, but knew this wasn't the time.

As the group was exiting her office, Rich appeared, without his Santa suit. Julie reintroduced them, and they took turns congratulating him on his performance.

"Hope you hang on to that costume so you can play Santa for your own Christmas together," Brent said. "Will you be here for that?"

"No, we're going to celebrate in Orono," Rich answered.

"A nice long break, I hope," Brent said.

"Longer than usual," Julie replied. "It'll be good to get away for a bit, and Rich has promised the best Christmas tree he can find."

"Will RHS be open while you're gone?" Brent asked.

"Sure. Except for Christmas Day and the day after. I've got great staff to cover."

"Lucky you. Well, if you don't mind, Betsey, I think we should get on the road. Thanks again, Julie. It was a great event."

"Thanks to you!" Julie said as she kissed Rich once they were alone in her office, after her colleagues had left. "You were the hit of the party, you know."

"Just acting," he said. "That Cartwright has a way with words, doesn't he? Somehow I don't think he's a big fan of academics."

"I think he's mostly a fan of Brent Cartwright," Julie said. "But who cares about him? You really were fantastic, Rich. I'm afraid you're going to have to sign up for Santa duty for all of our Victorian Christmases to come."

"Talk to my agent. Do you need to clean up over there? I can help."

"You've done enough today for the Ryland Historical Society, but if you really insist."

When they got there they found that Dennis and a handful of hearty volunteers had already done most of the cleanup, but Julie and Rich helped with the rest, and when everything was in order, they headed to her house.

"I found that pretty interesting," Julie said, sitting at the kitchen table as Rich extracted items from the refrigerator to begin preparing dinner.

"Afraid you've lost me."

"Hartshorn. What Betsey said about him. He didn't mention his interest in the Tabor stuff to me, but apparently he made a point of telling her. That's pretty interesting."

"Why?"

"Because none of the stuff Reiter did with his Boston friends has prompted any legitimate interest in the papers, which Wayne interprets to mean they might be targeted by people with an illegitimate interest. But now here's Hartshorn telling Betsey he's interested—and not saying anything to me."

"So you conclude from this that he's likely to steal them? Or have someone else steal them for him? He's got to figure that if he talked to Betsey she'd tell you—now, or maybe after a theft. That doesn't make sense to me."

"Yeah, I see that."

She sat silently for a few minutes while Rich continued assembling items by the stove.

"Remember when we saw him at the lecture in Orono? He seemed to know that I was helping Betsey with the thefts at Two Rivers."

"Can't say I committed that conversation to memory, but I'll take your word for it. So what?"

"Not sure. I should talk to Betsey to find out more about Hartshorn's interest in the papers. I didn't feel I could do that with Brent and Ted right there, but I'll call her tomorrow."

"Sounds like a plan. Meanwhile, would you care for a sip of something while I chop these 'shrooms?"

"And here's another interesting thing," Julie said after Rich had poured them both a glass of pinot noir and toasted the success of Victorian Christmas, and she, the triumph of Santa. "Brent made a big deal about where I was spending Christmas and how long

RHS would be closed for the holiday. Doesn't that strike you as funny?"

"It strikes me as a pretty normal bit of chitchat, but I suspect I'm missing something that you have penetrated in your customary way and determined was making 'a big deal' about it."

Julie laughed and said, "Is it time for me to leave the chef to his devices while I go work on a puzzle?"

"I'm always impressed by how readily you pick up on hints," Rich said.

After they had eaten Rich's vegetarian pasta and were sitting at the table in silence, he said, "So, I know your mind is churning. What are you thinking?"

"Still stuck on Hartshorn, I guess. Or really, the Tabor papers. You know, they're sitting there like bait while we wait for someone to pounce, but nothing is happening. I have this funny sense that someone is circling out there, I don't know who, as we wait for the papers to lure them in."

"Are you thinking they're not safe in your office?"

"No, they're as safe there as anywhere, but it's getting to me."

"You're looking for action," he said, and gave her an odd look.

"Maybe you are right," she replied. "It's been a long day. I can clean up here if you want to head to bed."

Rich yawned in a completely fake way and said that sounded like a good idea. "If you can clean up fast," he added. "Or better yet, leave everything till morning."

"Sounds good to me," she said.

"Shall I greet you in my Santa suit?"

"That wasn't exactly what I had in mind."

"You're right—definitely too kinky. Let's go."

CHAPTER 35

Discussing Rich's suggestion that they go on a hike that day provided an excuse to linger in bed Sunday morning far later than either was accustomed to.

"There's hardly any snow," Rich said, "so it won't be a true winter hike, but that's a good way to work up to one."

"Assuming I want to. Work up to one, I mean."

"If you're not going to learn to ski, you better find some form of exercise to get you through the cold months," Rich said.

"Different from . . . ?"

"Well, there's that, but then when you're here by yourself you know you need to do something to relax yourself, and you really can't run safely with snow and ice. You don't have to decide on winter hiking versus skiing or anything else. I'm just proposing a simple hike. With so little snow, it'll be like a fall one except for the temp."

"So we dress warmly? That's the only difference?"

"Right. What do you say?"

"I guess I can't think of a reason not to, except that we could stay in bed a little longer."

"I didn't mean we had to leave right away."

Later, as the coffee brewed and Rich was scrambling eggs, Julie said, "Here's another reason to delay: I really have to call Betsey Bowers today. I need to find out about Hartshorn and his interest in the Tabor papers."

"So how long can that take? You can call after breakfast while I clean up, and then we can head out by late morning."

"I suppose so, but . . ."

Julie didn't finish her thought because the phone rang.

"I can't believe this, Betsey," she said, once she'd learned the identity of the caller. "I was planning to call you today. No, it's not too early, but we're just about to have breakfast. Could I call you back in twenty minutes or so?"

"That's amazing," Julie said to Rich. "Betsey sounded excited. Maybe she remembered something else about Hartshorn."

"You sure you want to take time to eat?"

She said she did, but she realized she was eating faster than normal, distracted by the call and eager to return it. Rich said he'd clean up while she called from the living room.

"I'm sorry I bothered you so early," Betsey Bowers said, "but I just had to tell you. One of our ceramics has turned up!"

"Where? How? Tell all."

"Well, when I got in last night from your party—and thanks so much for that, by the way; it was really fun—there was a message on my machine from Lucy. You remember Lucy Bodewell, my curator? Well, she was working yesterday, but it was slow and she started surfing the web, looking for ceramics. That's something she does regularly—not to try to trace our missing items, but just to see what's on the market, who's selling, how the prices are. In any case, she stumbled on it—the 1798 pitcher with the packet Portland on it. You remember it? It's definitely the rarest of the items that went missing."

"So where is it?" Julie asked, understanding Betsey's excitement but frustrated not to get the details.

"In Baltimore, or at least offered for sale by a dealer there, as 'newly in stock.'"

"And you're sure it's yours?"

"Lucy came over last night and we went online and checked it out together. We're absolutely sure."

"Amazing! What are you going to do now?"

"Well, I don't know for sure. That's really why I called you, to get your advice. I was thinking about getting in touch with the dealer directly, but Lucy didn't think that was a good idea."

"I agree. I think you should call the cops, Betsey. Report this to the one you made the original report to and let them handle it. I've forgotten who that was."

"The York County sheriff's office."

"Okay, I'd call them right away and let them handle it. They can have someone in Baltimore check it out. I don't think you should try to contact the dealer. Maybe he has it legitimately—or at least thinks it's legitimate—but I'd still let law enforcement take the next step."

"That sounds like good advice, Julie. Thanks. Maybe I should wait till tomorrow, since I doubt the detective I talked to before would be on duty on a Sunday."

"Probably not, but I'd call the sheriff's office today and at least leave the message so you'll be sure to get someone on it tomorrow."

Betsey agreed, and promised she'd phone Julie on Monday to keep her informed.

While she was taking the call in the living room, Julie hadn't heard Rich go out, and so was surprised when she went back to the kitchen and found it empty. Assuming he had gone upstairs to take a shower, she pursued him there, but with no luck. As she was coming back downstairs, she heard him in the kitchen.

"I figured you decided to leave early for Orono," she said when she came into the kitchen and found Rich holding four ski poles. "But you decided to go skiing instead," she added.

"Hike, but we can use these. I put them in the car just in case I could persuade you to ski, but they also help with hiking. Anyway, what's up?"

Julie quickly told him.

He was silent for a moment.

"So what do you think?" she probed, unsure if his silence reflected lack of interest or something else.

"Well, it's a breakthrough, isn't it? I mean, a stolen item has actually turned up, and not in Maine, which sort of—"

"—confirms Reiter's idea," Julie finished for him. "That's exactly what I was thinking," she continued excitedly. "It means that these thefts are part of a planned campaign."

"You're way ahead of me there. I was going to say that it means at least this one piece found its way to a dealer pretty far away. That doesn't mean it's part of some larger 'campaign.' Don't stolen items often end up with dealers?"

"Sure, but I just have a hunch this is beginning to come together."

"Well, it's almost ten o'clock, so if we're going to get in a hike, we better get ourselves together."

"I really wanted to call Ted Korhonen," Julie said. "About that painting."

"Fine. Maybe I should be heading back to Orono."

"Sorry, Rich. No, we'll hike." Julie knew Rich's anger rarely surfaced, and when it did, it was of the quiet kind—not with heat but with coolness. "I'm looking forward to it, really."

"I don't want to interfere with your detective work," he said. "I've got plenty to do at home."

"Rich, don't be mad at me. I said I'm sorry, and I mean it."

"I'm not going to enjoy a hike if you're going to be worrying about Ted Korhonen and that damned painting. Or some ceramic pitcher in Baltimore."

"I won't. Promise. I really do want to hike. What should we wear?"

As they gathered clothes, Julie sensed that Rich was still quietly angry. She tried to engage him by asking about the route, but his response was curt. And when she asked if she should wear hiking boots, he said simply, "Whatever you like."

Julie knew that the hike was going to be a failure if she didn't clear the air now, and so she said, "Rich, it's my fault, and I'm sorry, but hiking isn't going to be any fun if you're stewing. Can we talk about it, now, before we go?"

The conversation took only ten minutes or so, but when it was over they both felt relieved, though it had been tough. Rich enumerated the ways in which he felt Julie was, as he said, taking advantage of his goodwill and willingness to subordinate his interests to hers. She tried to assure him that she didn't mean to do that, but recognized that she had a tendency to push, and that when he didn't push back she kept going.

"So what do you want me to do?" he asked. "Play the heavy? Insist on your doing whatever I want? That's not who I am, Julie, and you know that."

"Well, what should I do? I'm not a mind reader. If I want to do something and you don't, you have to tell me. That doesn't mean you have to play the heavy. It just means we need to be more open."

"And have a fight? I don't like to fight, especially with the woman I love and want to marry."

"That's your family talking, Rich. You've told me how your dad's ruling everything drove you crazy and that you don't want to be like him. So maybe you go too far the other way, letting me go too far, but then you get mad at me for doing it."

"Okay, Dr. Freud, you have me there. My dad was always the boss, ordering all of us around, and I hated that. I don't want to be like him—which is probably how many sons feel. But I'm sorry if you feel you have to read my mind. I should be more open about how I feel on some things, but it's not easy."

Julie came to him and pulled him toward her.

"Rich, I love you, and I'm so sorry I take advantage of you. I can say I'll try to be better, and I mean that. But you have to help me. You have to stop me when I'm using you. Yes, I know I do, but if you don't push back, I'll keep doing it." She pulled his head toward her and kissed him. "Okay?"

"Okay. I'll try. So . . . want to hike?"

"Absolutely," she said. "Where are we headed?"

In the car on the way to Mount Brill, the tension of their conversation gave way to easy banter, and by the time they reached the trailhead they were both focused on the hike. While they were making a final decision about what layers of clothing would be appropriate, Julie said, "Rich, I'm so glad we cleared the air, but just one more thing: You said earlier I was the woman you wanted to marry. At the risk of opening things up again, I just want to say I'm the woman you are going to marry. Next summer. And it makes me feel so good, so warm inside just to think about it."

He kissed her and said, "Same. Now, let's put on plenty of layers. The first part is straight uphill, so you'll be thinking we're overdressed, but on the way down you'll thank me. You might want to tie that parka around your waist for the first part, though."

Rich's description of the first section of the trail was quite accurate, and by the time they reached the top, both were sweating. The views, however, made up for it. From the rocks at the top of the trail they could look out over the river as far as the next town to the east, and in between were lovely peaks with light snow at the tops.

"I was beginning to wonder if we'd see any snow for Christmas," Julie said. "I guess this will have to suffice for now."

"Just a light dusting, but it's pretty. I think I heard somewhere that we might be in for a big snowstorm around Christmas. I meant to mention that."

"They're usually wrong about tomorrow, let alone two weeks away. I'll be in Orono, whatever the weather. So where does the trail go from here?"

Rich had explored Mount Brill before on his own, and had been meaning to bring Julie in the fall, when the foliage would have been spectacular. Although that hadn't happened, he had considered it a good bet for a winter hike, since the absence of those lovely leaves actually meant better views.

"Basically over the top," he answered. "We follow along for a mile or so across a flat stretch to a viewpoint overlooking Ryland, then it's downhill from there back to the parking area. The viewpoint should be a good place for lunch. It'll take a half-hour or so to cross the top. Sound okay?"

She said it did, and they started off. After stopping halfway so Julie could put on the parka that she'd tied around her waist, they reached the outcropping of rocks that indeed gave onto a clear view of Ryland, up the river. They ate mostly in silence, admiring the view, but as they were finishing Rich said, "Not to raise a sore point, but why are you so eager to talk to Ted Korhonen?"

"We don't have to talk about it now."

"No, it's fine. I'm interested. I know you said last night that you didn't think he had posted the missing painting on your Network blog, so is that why you want to talk to him? Or does it have to do with this pot of Betsey's showing up in Baltimore?"

"It's not exactly a pot. It's a ceramic pitcher with a painting of a ship on it. But anyway, no, that doesn't have anything to do with Ted. Or at least, I don't think so! It's what I mentioned last night: Why is he keeping the fact of the stolen painting such a secret?"

"You think that's meaningful?"

"It just troubles me. I might have missed his posting, so I should check out the blog again before I call. But that's for tomorrow."

"Or after I leave this afternoon, you just might sneak back to the office and do a little sleuthing."

"So the trail down is pretty steep," Julie said, standing up to signal the end of the conversation.

"I just wish you weren't so subtle," Rich kidded. "But I get the point. Onward!"

CHAPTER 36

Julie had been brought up to believe that the reward for a job well done was, to put it as her father did, "just that—a job well done." In his academic world that measure no doubt made sense, but when Julie moved from studying to managing—from being a graduate student in museum studies to running a historical society—she had learned that the reward for a job well done, when others did it, was the application of heaps of praise. She wasn't sure exactly how she had developed this understanding. It probably began during some of her internships, maybe reinforced by her old mentor, who had plenty of practical experience along with his academic knowledge. Or maybe it was instinctive, an intrinsic trait that suited her better for leading an organization like RHS than for following Rich's path toward the classroom and library.

Whatever its origins, Julie's awareness of the need to praise others had led her from the beginning of this job to spend plenty of time doing so, an approach that had won her strong support from staff and volunteers.

So on Monday morning she made a point of circulating among the people who had made Victorian Christmas such a success. She started with Dennis Sutherland, visiting him in his office, and then moved through the volunteers in the museum shop, period rooms, and exhibits. Mrs. Detweiller was last, because Julie had begun her congratulatory tour before her secretary had arrived. She was also the hardest to thank, because normal human emotions seemed to be generally missing from her makeup.

But this morning was different. After thanking her for all of her hard work organizing the event, Julie was surprised at Mrs. Detweiller's response.

"Your fiancé was really the star," she said. "He just threw himself into the role, didn't he? The children were so happy."

Julie agreed, but repeated her gratitude for the secretary's role.

"It was my pleasure," she responded. "The whole event was quite a triumph. You should be very happy, Dr. Williamson. RHS is lucky to have you—and Rich, too."

Julie couldn't believe her ears. Though her secretary still insisted on the formality of the title, the sentiments she expressed were beyond anything she had said to Julie in all the years they had worked together.

"That's so kind of you," Julie said, "but it was all of you—you and Dennis and the volunteers—who made it happen. I really appreciate it. I do think it was a great success."

"It couldn't have been better," Mrs. Detweiller said. "I just hope we can live up to it next year."

Ah, Julie thought, now there's the real Mrs. Detweiller, already anticipating the prospect of a lesser event, maybe an outright failure, in the future. Still, she was pleased, and when she sat down at her desk to review her schedule for the next two weeks, she realized that with Victorian Christmas behind her, the days ahead looked fairly uncomplicated.

RHS's annual fund, which provided over a third of the Society's income, was already slightly ahead of budget and needed only modest attention—a few reminder phone calls to donors who always waited till the last weeks of the year to contribute. The exhibit schedule for the new year was set, and Dennis had the details under control. One program for January still required fine-tuning, but she realized that this could be wrapped up in a few days.

Confident that her work was well under control and that she had done her duty in thanking people for their hard work, Julie felt she could afford to take some time to tie up the loose ends of her thinking from the weekend, starting with Ted Korhonen. After reviewing the Network blog long enough to satisfy herself that he had indeed not posted anything about the missing painting, she phoned him.

"I just didn't want to draw attention to it," he told Julie when she asked why he hadn't alerted people to the theft by posting a note. "I did report it, just like you suggested, but I figured I'd let the cops work on it."

"But the point of the blog is to bring in other museum people to help. You know, they might see or hear something that the police could use."

"I suppose, but I think I said this before: I'm pretty confident that not many museums in Maine, except mine, would buy a Finnish painting, so I can't imagine a thief would try to sell it here."

"Okay, Ted; you may be right about that. What kind of museum would buy it?"

"Who knows? Like I said, it's a gorgeous painting, but American museums just don't collect Finnish stuff as a rule. More likely a private collector. That's what I told the deputy sheriff, and he said he'd make a note of that when he passed it on to the art-theft database."

"Have they done that?"

"Hope so. I haven't checked."

Julie was about to suggest that he ought to, but the whole conversation was bothering her, and she wanted to think it through before saying any more to Ted.

"Well, I just wanted to find out what's happening. I didn't really want to bring it up when you were here with the others on Saturday," she said. "Good luck," she added to end the call, but Ted had more to say.

"Thanks again for inviting me—and for letting us see those papers. I'm thinking I might try to come up and spend some time with them if that's okay. I'm curious about whether this Tabor wrote anything about the Finns around here."

"I haven't found anything yet, but then, I really haven't gotten very far yet. You're welcome to come anytime."

"Maybe after the holidays. Things get pretty slow around here in January. I'll give you a ring. Meantime, keep your eyes on them—they really do look like quite a valuable collection."

When Julie reviewed their conversation after the call she was struck by Ted's interest in the Tabor papers, and especially his description of them as valuable, something she was pretty sure he had said on Saturday as well. Maybe there were some references to Finnish immigrants, but she couldn't quite believe that possibility explained his interest. And she was still bothered by his apparent casualness about the stolen painting: the fact that he hadn't followed up on his report, and his unwillingness to alert members of the Network.

She just couldn't shake the feeling that there was something strange about the whole thing. Could it mean that Ted himself took the painting, to sell it, or maybe just to add it to his own personal collection? If either of those things were true, did it also mean Ted was involved in the wider situation: the thefts at Mountain Valley and Two Rivers? Maybe even Dumont's murder?

As she was turning these thoughts over in her head, Mrs. Detweiller knocked at the door and stepped in.

"You've got a school group, Dr. Williamson. The bus just pulled in, and you're supposed to take them through the museum."

Julie had forgotten that she had agreed to do the tour and talk today, to give Dennis a break after his work on Victorian Christmas. She thanked her secretary, put on her coat, and headed over to greet the middle-school class.

❧

On Tuesday, Betsey Bowers phoned to tell Julie that the police in Baltimore had gone to the dealer who advertised the pitcher and learned that he had obtained it from a source in Boston. When he was told the item was potentially stolen, he had expressed shock and quickly agreed to take it off the market and secure it until Betsey could confirm it was indeed the one stolen from Two Rivers. She and the dealer exchanged photos over e-mail, resulting in the dealer agreeing to return the pitcher.

Meanwhile, the authorities in Baltimore alerted police in Boston, who were asked to investigate the person who had sold it.

"But I'm not sure when that will happen," Betsey told Julie. "Somehow I don't think an eighteenth-century pitcher stolen in Maine is going to go to the top of the priority list for cops who have to investigate murders and whatever down there."

Julie agreed that it might be a while before anything useful happened, and asked Betsey to keep her informed. "At least you're getting one of the items back," she added. "And it's possible when they close in on the guy, they'll find the others."

A few minutes later, Julie realized that she didn't in fact feel confident about this possibility. If one item from the Two Rivers theft had already been moved, it was likely the others had, too.

She phoned Betsey back and suggested that Lucy should keep searching the web for them. Betsey said she was already doing that, but without any luck so far, and that she would alert Julie if anything turned up.

After her calls with Betsey, Julie realized she hadn't talked to Mike Barlow recently. She knew that if anything had developed he would let her know, but the news about the stolen pitcher gave her an excuse to phone him.

"They've got more cops than they know what to do with down there," Barlow said after Julie had told him about the recovered pitcher and its source in Boston. "It's all because of the unions," he continued. "They have to find jobs for everyone's brothers and cousins, and so the unions bargain for lower hours and that creates cop jobs."

"So you think they will pursue this," Julie concluded after a pause, as she tried to figure out the relevance of Mike's rant.

"Sure. Like I say, they've got the manpower for it."

"Well that's good. Do you by any chance have——"

"A Boston contact? I can give it a shot. I've met some folks at law enforcement conferences. But, unlike the Boston PD, the Maine State Police are understaffed, and I do have a few little chores to do here. But I'll look into it, Julie. I'll let you know."

She thanked him and decided that he was too busy to talk any longer, even though she really wanted to discuss Ted Korhonen and the missing painting. So she ended their call with further thanks and then phoned Wayne Reiter to let him know of the latest developments.

Like Mike Barlow, the former professor seemed preoccupied and listened in a desultory way to her report. She tried to focus him by ladling on the praise: "You were really right on this," she said. "It does seem like a commercial operation, just like you said."

"Of course," he replied. "Now I've got to go, but do keep me informed."

Saying she would, Julie hung up and sat quietly for a few moments before laughing out loud. I'm like a little kid who can't find someone to play with me, she told herself. So she decided to play by herself. The Tabor papers can't turn me down, she thought as she glanced at the boxes in the corner of her office.

CHAPTER 37

On Thursday, Julie again felt like a child, this time because she was looking ahead to Christmas and wondering if it would ever arrive. A week from today she would be driving to Orono to spend the holiday with Rich. At this point it seemed like it would be a very long week.

The historical society was quiet. No school tours were scheduled till January, because the kids were hunkered down and, like Julie, counting the days. The few tourists in town were skiers whose interests were firmly focused on the mountain. Locals were finishing their shopping and decorating and, aside from a few who came to buy gifts in the museum shop, weren't inclined to spend precious pre-holiday time at the museum. The volunteer crew was accordingly reduced, and so the only people around the buildings aside from Julie were Dennis Sutherland and Mrs. Detweiller. Tabby insisted on coming in to work in the library, but her presence was rarely apparent because she came and went quietly and stayed exclusively upstairs. Julie made excuses to go there to check on one thing or another, brought to light by her reading of the Tabor papers, but the older woman resisted Julie's invitation to come downstairs to her office.

"I'm busy here, Dr. Williamson," Tabby told her, and Julie sensed an implication that the rest of the staff would do well to follow her example.

During her first Christmas season at RHS, Julie had taken the staff for lunch at the Inn on one of the quiet days ahead of the holiday closing, and the event had become an instant tradition. Because so much attention this year had been focused on Victorian Christmas, she hadn't set a date yet for the lunch. As it turned out, the only good date for all of them was the coming Monday, which left the rest of the week quiet.

It was the weekend that Julie really dreaded, because she would be alone. Rich was staying in Orono to finish reading papers and exams so he could submit his grades mid-week, in time to clear the decks for Julie's Christmas visit.

Julie surprised herself by how easily she got lost in the Tabor papers during the next two days. By Friday afternoon, she had added many pages of notes from the letters and clippings—about the way the Depression had affected Ryland, specific and moving details about bank foreclosures, the vast increase in families applying for aid from the town, patients requiring treatments for which they sadly could not pay. Dr. Tabor never turned them down, and Julie wondered how he had been able to meet his own financial obligations, admiring him for never complaining.

Not eager to go home to face the long weekend alone, she was still reading papers when Mrs. Detweiller came in to say she was leaving.

"Oh," the secretary said. "I didn't want to interrupt, but Chief Barlow called earlier. I told him you were busy, and he asked that you call him back when you had a chance."

Although she would have jumped at the chance to talk to Mike, Julie decided not to say so. Instead she thanked Mrs. Detweiller, and reminded her of the planned lunch on Monday.

"I don't know why I still call him 'Chief,' " the secretary said in a distracted way, ignoring the lunch reminder. "I still think of him that way."

"I'm sure he wouldn't mind," Julie replied, picking up the phone to return Mike's call. She left a message saying that she'd be in her office till six p.m., and at home after that.

The news of his call deflected her attention from the papers, but she shuffled through them for another hour, realizing she should stick it out till six in case he called.

At five-forty-five the phone rang.

"Keeping cops' hours, I see," Mike said when Julie answered on the first ring. "You used to close down at four-thirty. Putting the screws to the staff now?"

Julie laughed and explained that she was the only one around, and that was because she was doing some research as a way to avoid going home. "Rich is in Orono, and I'm going there for Christmas," she added, "so I have the weekend to myself. I'd rather be here working than at home doing jigsaw puzzles."

"Makes sense," the policeman said. "And since you mentioned puzzles, here's one for you: The guy in Boston who sold the pitcher to the Baltimore dealer seems to like Maine, because he's been sighted here a couple of times. That's a hint."

Julie paused, pleased that their relationship was still good enough to encourage Mike's teasing.

"So how many guesses do I get?" she asked.

"No guesses. Just one name, and you should get that right the first time."

"Someone I know?"

"No clues. Your time's running out."

"Okay. It can't be Korhonen or Cartwright or Hartshorn; since they live here, you couldn't say they were sighted in Maine."

Before she could continue Barlow said, "You're a good lis-
tener—picked right up on that word. You should be a detective,
Julie. But you're stalling. Shall I tell you?"

"I don't believe it!" she exclaimed after Mike revealed the
name. "Timothy Brothers again! So who is he?"

"Can't say. All I found out is that the dealer in Baltimore
named a Boston dealer as the source of the pitcher, and that guy
told the Boston cops he'd bought it from Timothy Brothers. You
probably won't be surprised to know that the phone number and
address this Brothers guy gave the Boston dealer turned out to be
nonexistent."

"Did you tell them about Brothers signing in at Two Rivers
and buying that gun at the gun show?"

"Sure, and they said thanks very much, and I'm sure they'll put
that in their case notes and deposit same in a file folder that won't
be opened again."

"But it's a big break, Mike. It ties things together, doesn't it—
the thefts and the murder."

"Ties them to a phantom. Who is Timothy Brothers?"

Mike's question hung in the air. It was of course the right question, and if Julie had an answer, she could see the whole puzzle
solving itself. But all she could say was "I don't know, but when we
figure that out, we'll nail him."

"We?"

"Well, Dan Dumont's murder is still your case, Mike, and now
we know the murder is tied in with the thefts, and . . ."

Before she could finish the policeman said, "I know the murder's my case, Julie."

This was an old issue for them, going back to Julie's first year
in Ryland when Mike was chief of police and the two of them
had become entangled in Worth Harding's murder and the theft
of documents from RHS. Julie understood that Mike had police

authority and resources and that she was a civilian with no standing. But Mike also understood that Julie's skills at detection, intuitive and imaginative, were beyond his own. Although they made a good pair, acknowledging this was still difficult for him. And Julie was reluctant to push it, instead allowing it to continue unresolved—so long as he didn't shut her out completely. Light treatment was best.

"I like to be a good citizen, Mike, and since I know a little bit about thefts from museums, I'm happy to pass it along to you."

He laughed, as she'd hoped he would, and then he said, "Well, I appreciate that, and I value your knowledge. Just wish you could tell me who Timothy Brothers is."

"I'll let you know when I figure it out. Meantime, if anything else turns up, let me know."

"So you said you're going to Orono for Christmas?" he asked, to change the topic.

She said she was, and asked about his plans. He told her, and then added that he hoped the weather predictions would turn out to be wrong.

"What predictions?" she asked.

He told her that a major blizzard seemed likely for Christmas Eve.

"Hope it holds off," she said.

"Well, you know the weather people; they hype everything. Just keep an eye on the forecasts and don't take any chances driving. I've got to go now, Julie. If we don't talk before, have a merry Christmas, and the same to Rich."

The call over, Julie had no reason to linger in her office. She reluctantly turned off the lights, checked the security system, and headed home. She called Rich, who knew about the storm prediction but reminded her of what Mike Barlow had said about how weather forecasters on the radio and TV had a stake in hyping the news. He said he had to get back to his grading, and asked how she would spend the weekend. The question gave her the chance to tell him what Barlow had learned about Timothy Brothers.

"So I'll probably spend my time trying to figure out who he is," she said.

"If that's what you'll be doing, you might want to think about getting a life," Rich said, a smile in his voice.

"I'd have one if you were here," she said.

"Hey, you know I'd rather be with you than reading these undergraduate essays, and I wouldn't be good company for you when I'm doing that. But my grades will be in on Thursday, you'll be here, and we'll have the long Christmas holiday together. Look, Julie, you shouldn't spend your whole weekend thinking about thefts and murder."

"Oh, I was kidding—a little bit. No, I'll do some other stuff. Maybe I'll go back to the museum and tackle more of those papers. Or work on a puzzle. Yeah, I think I'll definitely do that. I have that Winslow Homer painting you got from the Portland Museum—remember?"

"The one with the waves hitting the rocks?"

"*Weatherbeaten*, it's called. Good title. Anyway, yes, I think I'll get to work on that tonight. So don't worry about me trying to solve mysteries. The puzzle will be enough mystery for me."

After the call, Julie fixed herself dinner, selecting from the items Rich had thoughtfully stocked the freezer with last weekend. She watched a British comedy on Public Broadcasting as she ate, feeling vaguely that she may have seen it before.

She put the dishes in the dishwasher and started it, then retrieved the puzzle from the closet and spilled out the pieces on the table in the living room she reserved for such activities. It really was a gorgeous painting, she thought, as she examined the cover of the box—a huge white wave striking reddish rocks with a fearful force. Gorgeous and scary, she thought: Homer never underplayed the power of nature.

She followed her usual approach of finding pieces of similar color that she knew belonged together: She piled bits of wave to one side, rock fragments to another, the troubled sky in another. As always with her, working on a jigsaw puzzle was all-consuming, blocking out other thoughts and causing time to pass unobserved. When she realized the sound of the dishwasher had stopped, she looked up at the clock and saw that it was almost ten o'clock.

Glancing at the separated piles of puzzle pieces, for a brief moment she considered sitting down to begin assembling the sections. But she was tired, and tomorrow—and the day after—needed some focused activity.

It'll keep, she told herself, and went upstairs to bed.

CHAPTER 38

The white pieces, gathered in the upper-right-hand corner of the table, were so intensely, unnaturally white that they seemed to glow. The brown ones, in the lower left corner, were just the opposite—pale and washed out, a brown so light it was almost neutral.

Julie knew both colors were wrong, so wrong that they must be from a different puzzle, probably not even a famous painting, since no good painter would have used such awful colors. But how had that happened? Had someone switched puzzles on her? And if so, why would they do that? Well, she thought, she would just have to work with the pieces she had, even though she knew she could not construct *Weatherbeaten* out of them. It was a different puzzle, and she had no clue as to how she should proceed.

Julie woke feeling as frustrated as she had been in the dream. The clock on the bedside table said two-forty-five, an absurdly early hour to wake. Of course she would get back to sleep eventually, but she was still annoyed. Maybe, she thought, she let herself get too deeply involved with puzzles. If she just turned off her mind, or focused it on something else, maybe she could get back to sleep.

The more she tried to redirect her thoughts, the more they returned to the puzzle—especially to the fact that without the picture to guide her in the dream, she had no idea what to do with the pieces. Sort of like her real-life mystery, she thought. She had pieces, but not the whole picture. Julie decided to turn them over in her mind, mapping their shape and color, in the hope that they would start to create a scene.

There was Dan Dumont's murder, the theft of maps from his museum, the thefts from Two Rivers, the recovered pitcher, and the painting missing from Ted Korhonen's museum. Across all of them was the presence of someone named Timothy Brothers—or at least calling himself that. She was certain the name was fake.

But then she realized that Brothers wasn't connected to Korhonen's painting—at least, not so far as she knew. Well, in any case, here were the pieces, but where was the picture into which they should all snugly fit? Puzzle people had to work in one of two ways: fitting pieces to a picture you knew, or fitting pieces until they became recognizable as something. While she considered herself pretty good at doing jigsaws, Julie recognized that she was best at using the first approach. With other puzzles, like those involving thefts and murders, she had to use the other approach—building the pieces into something, creating a picture that she didn't have a sense of as she worked.

But was that true in the current case? I'm not going to think about that, Julie told herself, checking the clock to see it was now just after three. I'm going to think about something else entirely, and I'm going to get back to sleep, and then in the morning, I'm going to think about all this again.

When the creeping clock had only advanced to three-forty-five, after what she imagined was several hours of shifting and turning, she had a passing thought that she should just give up, get out of bed, and try to salvage the day. But when she awoke later at seven a.m., she was happy that she hadn't acted on that earlier impulse. Interrupted though it was, the sleep had been restorative, and when she dressed quickly and went downstairs, she was happy that the colors of the puzzle pieces were right and would, with a little work today, get shaped into the Homer painting.

And it was that puzzle she planned to work on—not the one with the murder and the thefts. And Christmas shopping.

Julie really found shopping unappealing. It wasn't that she didn't like the things shopping yielded. As a museum director, after all, she lived a life in which objects played a very large role, albeit items that told stories of the past. But going to a mall or a discount district like Freeport or North Conway and spending the day trudging from store to store to find the right pair of shoes or the perfect serving dish or whatever—that she simply couldn't do.

As strongly as she felt about shopping in general, like most Americans, she simply could not resist the commercial pressure of Christmas that required everyone to seek and give gifts to others. She had used her Thanksgiving trip to Ohio to transport Christmas gifts for her parents, so that was one duty crossed off. Really, she had only one other: to buy things for Rich. In her first year in Ryland, she had gently scotched gift exchanges among historical society staff and volunteers—a difficult move, since the former director had encouraged it. In place of that tradition, she had substituted a lunch and accompanied it with a no-gifts policy. She was well aware that this had made her a bit of a Grinch in the eyes of some, but since she'd made other changes, this one seemed rather small, and happily, it stuck. So it was only Rich she needed to shop for.

Just a week now from the holiday, she regretted that she hadn't shopped for him earlier, as she had for her parents. But last-minute shopping was another American tradition she realized she would have to observe.

Over breakfast, she made the outlines of a list: a sweater, new hiking boots, and certainly books. The outdoors shop at the lower end of Main Street would supply the first two, but books presented a challenge, since Ryland's only independent bookstore had closed last summer, crushed by online sites. She really hated those monsters—the big one, especially—but feared that she had no choice but to go online and hope she could find books for Rich that could be delivered in time. She realized that the time to get anything delivered was quite short, since she planned to drive to Orono on Thursday.

Then she remembered the used-books shop that had opened a year or so ago about thirty miles away, on the road to Portland. That's perfect, she thought. Rich can get new books in Orono, but some old volumes, perhaps about Maine history, might be just the thing. Browsing in a quaint store among dusty books suddenly seemed to her a perfect way to spend part of her otherwise-unoccupied Saturday.

After breakfast she walked to the outdoors shop and quickly found a nice wool sweater, made by a local craftsperson, and bought a gift certificate for a pair of boots, since Rich would have to select the right ones in his size. She also bought some stocking stuffers—a small compass and two types of insect repellent—and a new trail guide that she could wrap as an under-the-tree present.

Feeling energized by her early success, she walked home to get her car for the drive to the used-books store, deciding she would add lunch at a diner on her way home as motivation to complete her shopping first.

The store was just as she'd imagined: dark and crowded, with books everywhere, filling fragile shelves and stacked in piles on the floor like those geological shapes in caves that she could never remember the names of. The owner directed her to the area where Maine history volumes could be found, warning her they were in less-than-perfect order.

"Some of it's by county, and some by dates, but the fact is, there isn't any real pattern," he said. "If there's something specific you're looking for, I might be able to find it," he added, but she sensed from his hesitance that might was the operative word, so she said she'd just browse a bit.

She was not surprised to see that town histories predominated, and she tentatively selected two of these—one of Ryland, and one of Orono. A charmingly illustrated book on steamboats on the Rangeley Lakes was too good to pass up, and an early-twentieth-century trail guide to the White Mountains was a perfect fit for Rich's hiking interests. Four books seemed enough; she didn't want to overdo it, but digging through the piles provided its own pleasure. She decided she might as well sit down on the floor among the stacks and continue to browse, vowing not to buy but just to look, since, after all, Maine history was now a professional subject for her.

A voice interrupted her. "Scouting for the collection?"

Startled, Julie looked up, and as often happens when someone appears in a place you haven't seen him before, it took her a few seconds to place Ted Korhonen.

"Christmas shopping," she said with a laugh as she stood up. "I decided to buy Rich some Maine books. I've never been here before, but it's fun."

"You never know what you'll find here," Ted said. "It's a short trip for me, so I stop by pretty regularly."

"Scouting for your collection?"

"Finnish things do turn up."

"But not paintings?" Julie asked.

As soon as the words were out of her mouth, she realized it was a stupid question, but seeing Ted reminded her of the missing painting and his reluctance to alert the Network to it. She just couldn't explain this to her own satisfaction.

"He doesn't deal in paintings," Ted said in a tone that Julie thought was intended to shut down that line of conversation.

"No word about it yet?" she asked, unwilling to let it go.

"No. So what did you find for Rich?" he asked.

She showed him the volumes she had collected so far.

"Nice," he said. "I shouldn't interrupt you."

"I should really stop," Julie said. "This is the kind of thing that doesn't have a natural end. Did you find anything?"

"Not yet, but I've only been here for ten minutes. The museum's closed now through the first of the year, so I've got plenty of time on my hands. In fact, I was just thinking, even before I saw you, that I might call to see if I can come over in the next week to look at those Tabor papers. I know you're going to be away, but will RHS be open over the holidays?"

It was a perfectly natural question, Julie recognized, and she had mentioned spending Christmas in Orono when Ted was at the event. Still, Julie couldn't help but think that Ted seemed awfully focused on the papers and on her absence from RHS in a way that signaled something more—what, exactly, she didn't know, but it troubled her.

"You're welcome anytime," she said. "But if you could pin down a day and time, I'll be sure to have the papers available, even if I'm not there."

"Still keeping them in your office?" he asked.

Julie paused before answering, remembering that at Victorian Christmas Brent Cartwright had made a point about the papers being in her office rather than in the archives. Ted had been a part of that conversation, and she was trying to recall whether he had said anything on that score. She couldn't remember, but right now he was definitely honing in on their location. Why did he care? she wondered. Then she realized that she hadn't responded, and so, avoiding a direct reply, said, "Just let me know when you'll be coming."

Ted said he would, and they exchanged Christmas wishes before parting.

After she had paid for the books and taken them to the car, she saw that it was almost one-thirty. She had spent more time there than she had planned, but knew the diner on the way back to Ryland served all day. She felt she had earned a good lunch.

Although she had brought the newspaper to read, after she had ordered, she found she couldn't concentrate on it because thoughts of Ted Korhonen kept coming to mind. There was something about him—the missing painting, his refusal to list it on the blog, his interest in the Tabor papers—that bothered her. When her chicken wrap came, she tucked into it, realizing how long ago her light breakfast had been, and how hungry she was. But even the wrap couldn't get her mind off Ted.

On her drive home afterwards, she tuned in to the Saturday opera on MPBN, but after fifteen minutes she found herself bored with it, and changed the station to a rock one. The first thing she heard was a weather forecast warning of the possibility of a major snowstorm for Christmas. Just when it would hit and how severe it would be, the forecaster said, was unclear at the moment, because the various models were not in agreement.

"But it could be a big one," he concluded. "Stay tuned."

She would indeed, Julie said to herself. A big storm that might hit just before Christmas, maybe even while she was driving to Orono, warranted her attention. And at least for a few minutes, it gave her something to think about other than Ted Korhonen.

CHAPTER 39

Squirrely was the word Julie's father used to describe how he felt when he went from task to task, unable to focus.

"I'm just feeling squirrely today," he would say when she was a young child, staying close to him on weekends or over the long summers when teaching didn't occupy him. He might spend a few moments in the garden and then go into the garage to clean something on the workbench, and after that, suggest they walk into town for ice cream. She had laughed at the image: her father as a fat gray squirrel dashing about, hiding or looking for nuts.

When she grew up and had her own squirrely moments, Julie realized that she shared with her father a minor anxiety disorder, nothing clinical and rarely lasting long—maybe even, she came to believe, a good trait that caused her to look for new challenges. After a point early in their relationship when Julie told Rich, who was the opposite of a squirrel in every way, he adopted the word and didn't hesitate to apply it to her when her restlessness was on display.

So on Sunday afternoon when they talked on the phone, he understood when she said: "I spent a few hours at the office with the Tabor papers, and then I came back here and worked on the Homer puzzle, and after that I took a walk. But I'm still restless."

"Squirrely," he corrected her.

"Exactly. I can't really focus. I guess I'm just so eager to get through this boring week and come to see you for the holiday."

Neither of them mentioned the predictions of an impending nor'easter, but both realized that the possibility contributed to her restlessness. For the rest of Sunday, Julie avoided the radio and television. On Monday morning, she didn't even tune in to the Portland station she usually had on as background during breakfast.

But such avoidance was immaterial once she got to the office and Mrs. Detweiller greeted her with the dire pronouncement: "A really big storm."

Ignoring Julie's expression, she continued: "That cute young fellow on Channel 6, Keith—well he sounded pretty sure. Probably Friday, but maybe even the day before. Isn't that when you're driving? Maybe you should go earlier, Dr. Williamson."

If she thought the holiday lunch at the Inn would ease her concerns, Julie was proved wrong, since Mrs. Detweiller had become fixated on the weather and returned to the forecast at every lull in the conversation. "Keith says . . . ," she interjected, as if the young weatherman—Julie agreed there was something lovable about his boyish enthusiasm for all things weather—were present at the table, or at the very least, a close friend with whom she was in regular contact. So while the lunch was modestly pleasant, Julie returned to her office in a state of increased anxiety about the storm. Before she could even try to settle in, Mrs. Detweiller came to the door to announce that Rich was on the phone.

"I'm sure it's all hype," he said, after explaining that he, too, had been hearing doom-filled forecasts, "but I really worked hard this weekend and my grades are almost ready. I can get them in tomorrow and drive to Ryland on Wednesday—that's well ahead of any storm, if we even get one. So you can just sit tight there and stop worrying about the weather. We'll celebrate Christmas at your place!"

"Are you sure?" she asked, hoping her relief wasn't too obvious. "I don't want to be a wimp."

"Of course you're a wimp. But won't this be better? We can stop worrying about the snow and just enjoy it."

"That would be great, Rich, but I'm always doing this to you—making you change plans and do things my way. And what about the tree you got?"

"Well, I have to confess, I haven't done it yet—planned to go out today. Can't you get one in Ryland? I can bring the lights and decorations, and we can have a trim-the-tree party for just the two of us on Thursday while the snow piles up."

The speed with which everything changed when even a small decision was made amazed Julie as she sat quietly at her desk after the call. Ten minutes ago she had been in a panic, for which she realized she had unfairly blamed her secretary, and now she felt almost giddy about the new plan. While the clock had seemed to run at half-speed for the past week, it cranked to double time for the rest of the day, and Tuesday. She got a lovely balsam spruce at the stand near the high school on Monday evening and wrapped the presents she had accumulated over the weekend. She found that she could even watch the forecast on TV and actually enjoy the growing hype. When Rich arrived late Wednesday and they unloaded the decorations from his car, she felt that Santa Claus had come early.

The first flakes began to fall early Thursday morning. The current prediction was for accumulations of six to eight inches by the end of the day, then a pause before the second wave hit overnight and brought up to two feet more before winding down Christmas Eve. Ryland Historical Society had been scheduled to be closed Friday through Sunday, but Julie decided on Wednesday to close at the end of the day, since the combination of the holiday and the storm would mean even less traffic at the museum than had occurred the first few days of the week.

So, Rich told her Thursday morning, she had no excuse to go to the office, no reason not to plunge headfirst into the holiday. Besides, he said, they needed time to talk about plans for next year.

"You got the grant!" Julie exclaimed once he'd filled her in. "Why didn't you tell me?"

"I just found out yesterday before I left Orono. Yes, I got it, for the full year. After this May, I won't be teaching again for fifteen months."

"That's just so great! You should have told me as soon as you heard. Or last night, even!"

"I wanted to keep it a secret," Rich replied, "tell you in person. You're happy, aren't you? Though it means you may have me underfoot all next year."

"Are you nuts? Of course I'm happy for you—for us. You know what it means, Rich: Now we don't have to think about who lives where."

"In our first year of married life," he interjected.

"Exactly. Wow! I would have had a bottle of champagne last night if I'd known! I'll go down to Ryland Groceries and get one now, for tonight."

"Actually," he said, "I did bring one—a really expensive bottle—but I wrapped it as a present." He pointed to a package under the tree. "But I suppose we could break it out tonight if you really insist. Or we could wait till tomorrow night—Christmas Eve. That's when you open presents, isn't it?"

"My family did, but we can wait till Christmas day if you want, for the rest of the gifts. The champagne comes out tonight, whatever we decide about the others."

"Start our new Christmas tradition," he said. "Whichever way you like."

"To be discussed," Julie said. "Meantime, how about a walk in the snow while we can?"

The snow was steady but gentle, and for the next two hours they circled through town, up the long hill and back, down toward the river, then back to the Common, where they paused to survey the scene. Ryland was a fairy-tale Christmas village, holiday lights on all the houses around the Common, lighted trees in front of the Inn.

CHAPTER 40

Julie was glad they had agreed—and so easily—on adopting Rich's family tradition of opening presents on Christmas morning. They brought coffee to the living room and set about the task, one reaching for a gift to hand the other, then waiting till the recipient expressed pleasure and thanks and then exchanging roles, till the scene under the tree turned from one of brightly wrapped packages to a pile of wrapping paper at one side and gifts lined up on the other. The last one Julie opened was—no surprise—a puzzle.

"Not very imaginative, I know," Rich said.

"No, it's great! The Longfellow House," Julie said as she opened it. "*Weatherbeaten* really was a challenge, and I'm definitely ready for a new puzzle."

She paused briefly, staring at the picture on the box. "The windows here don't seem quite right to me. I thought there were four on the third floor, but the box shows five." She held it toward him, and Rich agreed there were five. "I'm probably wrong, but I thought the house had five on the second floor and four above that." She closed her eyes and was silent for a few moments, a technique Rich recognized as her usual way of trying to call up a visual image. "No, I guess it's right—must be five. Did you get this from the Portland Historical Society?"

"I think Santa probably got it there, since they own the house."

"You never know where Santa shops, but maybe I'll just check PHS's website and see if it has a picture of the house. I'm sure it does. But that can keep. We should have a proper breakfast first. Was that part of the O'Brian tradition—a big breakfast after you opened presents?"

"How'd you guess?"

"Don't you remember that I'm a puzzle solver?"

"And detective," he added. "Let's eat. Shall I see what I can do with the fresh sausage and eggs I brought with me?"

Over breakfast they heard the town plow at work and went to the front window to watch it make its way slowly up the street. Rich suggested that since the snow had now stopped, he should shovel the walks, but Julie countered by saying they could do the work together and then take a walk.

They returned a while later, tired from tramping through heavy snow after shoveling, but excited by the lovely winter scene and the pleasure of exercise in the crisp air. Because they had eaten a late, and large, breakfast, they decided to skip lunch and have an early dinner. Rich had put the turkey in the oven before they'd gone out, and the smell of the roasting bird was already permeating the room.

"Smells like Christmas," Julie said.

"Or Thanksgiving," Rich said.

"Both, and it's great. Let's just relax and while away the afternoon. Maybe I'll take a crack at the puzzle, but let me just check the website for the Longfellow House first."

Unable to resist a book, Rich was happy to lie on the couch and thumb through the ones Julie had given him to decide which one to begin reading first. Julie was using her laptop at the table in the kitchen. How much time elapsed as he browsed books and she websites he wasn't sure, but he knew when the quiet period ended, because Julie sprang out of the kitchen like a rabbit pursued by a dog, exclaiming: "This is unreal! Absolutely unreal!"

"Okay," Rich said calmly, "I'm sure it is, but perhaps you could just bring me up-to-date on what it is that's unreal?"

"Long story or short?" she asked, as she began pacing around the living room.

"Your choice."

"Maybe in between. I'll spare you all the details, butI looked up the Portland Historical Society website, to check on the Wadsworth-Longfellow House."

"Number of windows on the third floor?" Rich interrupted.

"Five. So I was wrong. Anyway, you know how it is with web-sites: You get on one and get onto another, and before you know it you're down a chute and not sure how you got there."

Rich nodded; it was a familiar problem.

"So somehow I got onto a site about Longfellow."

"Makes sense," he said.

"Sure. They own the house. I remembered that I had done a search for 'Timothy Brothers' back when his name surfaced because of Two Rivers—you remember all that?" He nodded, and she continued. "Okay, that was in my search history, and somehow I hit it up."

"For Timothy Brothers?"

"Yes, and up came a Longfellow poem. Let me get my notes so I get this right."

Julie ducked quickly into the kitchen and returned with a pad.

"Okay, the poem is called 'The Sicilian's Tale; The Monk of Casal-Maggiore.' It's in *Tales of a Wayside Inn*. I read the poem, and it's actually kind of funny—about two monks, one of whom is named Brother Timothy. He's a crude guy who likes pranks. It's sort of complicated, but the long and short of it is that this Brother Timothy pretended to exchange himself for a donkey, and the donkey got named Brother Timothy, and—"

"Makes perfect sense to me," Rich said, rising from the couch. "Can't say I'm very knowledgeable about old Henry Wadsworth, but it sounds like the kind of stuff he wrote."

"You see it, don't you? I've got to call Mike Barlow."

"On Christmas, to tell him about a Longfellow poem? Now I'm not sure I'm really following."

"Rich, it's all coming clear now. The guy who signed in at Two Rivers as 'Timothy Brothers' and who dealt with the Boston dealer under that name—he's someone who knows Longfellow! And how many people do? Well, people who work at the Portland Historical Society, in the Longfellow House, must know his poems."

"And no one else does?" Rich said, to stop her. "Not like English professors or graduate students writing a dissertation, or just someone who likes old poetry? Your Timothy Brothers has to be someone who works at PHS? I think that's a bit of a stretch."

"Brent Cartwright," she said. "Everything points to him. I've got to call Mike right away."

Rich followed Julie to the kitchen, knowing there was nothing he could say to deter her from making the call. He stood across the room from her as she dialed.

"Mike. This is Julie Williamson. I know it's Christmas, but I had to call because I've found out something really, really important about the case. I'm home for the rest of the day. If you get this, can you please call me at home? Anytime. Thanks, Mike. And, oh, Merry Christmas."

"Well, that will make his holiday," Rich said when she hung up. "I noticed you didn't tell him the whole thing revolves around a Longfellow poem. Guess that would have been too much for him to handle. He's probably having a nice Christmas dinner and doesn't want to interrupt it to call you, and I can't say I blame him. Maybe I should be checking on our dinner."

"Great," she said. "Can I help? I'm just so excited, Rich, but maybe if you give me something to do, I'll calm down."

"While you wait for Barlow's call? Sure, why don't you set the table? I'll just start the vegetables and we can eat in a half-hour or so. Think you can hold out?"

"A glass of wine would help."

"More than a glass, I think," Rich said, and reached for a bottle to uncork.

CHAPTER 41

Julie and Rich considered it fortunate—and certainly a good omen—that among the many things large and small they had in common was a preference to begin dinner no earlier than seven-thirty and no later than eith-thirty. That habit had gotten Julie into trouble with Ryland folks, who almost to a person considered it close to sinful to sit down for dinner later than six, but when she ate alone during the week she held to it, just as she and Rich always did when they were together.

So finding themselves clearing the table at six-thirty after a long and leisurely dinner struck both of them as odd. But as Rich said, holidays allowed for different behavior.

"So let's really go wild here and let me do the dishes while you relax," he said. That she had sat through the meal without once glancing at the phone was, he added, much to her credit, and an-other reason she deserved to be free of the washing up she usually did in return for his preparing the meal.

His work at the sink was interrupted by the phone. Julie flew back to the kitchen to stand beside him as he was about to answer it. He handed the portable to her, and when she said, "Oh, Mike, thanks so much for calling back," he gestured to her to take the phone into the living room. She was finishing the call ten minutes later when he came in to check.

"So?" Rich asked.

"Well, I think Mike may share your skepticism a bit, but he also seemed to understand that this could be a breakthrough. It took a bit of explaining to get him to see it."

"And what did he see?"

"That this Brother Timothy, Timothy Brothers thing has to be more than just a coincidence. Everything points to Cartwright. I know I can't prove that, but I really do believe it, Rich. And I think Mike agrees, at least to the extent where he's willing to check it out."

"And how is he going to do that? Track him down on Christmas and interrogate him about his knowledge of and interest in Longfellow poetry? 'Okay, Mr. Cartwright,' he'll say. 'Do you know anything about a certain poem in *Tales of a Wayside Inn* that may have given you the idea of a false name?' Something like that?"

"Doubtful. Actually, we agreed that it was going to be tricky to pursue this, but we're both going to think about it and get in touch tomorrow to see if there's a way to follow up."

"We? You and the state cop are going to corner Cartwright and put the screws to him? I somehow don't think so."

"Well, we're going to think about it. That's all. Do you have any suggestions?"

"As a matter of fact, I do. Why don't I pour us another glass of wine, and I'll sit here and read one of my presents and you sit there and work on the Longfellow House puzzle, and maybe between the wine and the puzzle you'll be hit by a brilliant solution, at which point you can call Barlow again—at midnight, let's say— and the two of you will roar off through the snow to Portland to capture the villain. How about that for a plan?"

Rich was happy that Julie accepted the first part of his sugges- tion, and for the next few hours they sat quietly in the living room, engaged in their pursuits to the degree that they spoke only occa- sionally, and never about items stolen from museums—or a murder.

⌘

"So why is it called Boxing Day?" Julie asked when they woke the next morning.

"The Brits call it that," he answered. "Since I'm an American historian, I don't have to know that sort of thing."

"My dad always made a big deal of it, wishing us a happy Boxing Day, but I never really understood it. Something about putting presents back in their boxes, he said, and we always had a special breakfast—eggs with tomatoes and sausages and mush- rooms, very British."

"I'm afraid I can't do that—we ate the sausage yesterday. How about hot oatmeal? That sounds pretty British to me."

During the night they had heard the plow at work, and after breakfast Rich went out to see if the walk needed further shovel- ing. When he came in to report that there had been no new snow and that the sun was out, he suggested a long walk to work off the effects of yesterday's feast. Julie resisted his idea to drive out to the hill north of town with their snowshoes because she didn't want to be away from the phone that long, in case Mike Barlow called. So they decided on a walk in town, agreeing they'd limit it to an hour.

As they were coming back up the street by the historical soci- ety, Julie said that she ought to call the contractor who plowed and shoveled for the museum to remind him that it would reopen on Monday, and that he needed to be sure everything was cleared by then.

"He's probably got his hands full," Rich said, "and it is Sunday, after all."

"And Boxing Day," she added. "But that's his job. I'll call when we get home. Let's go around the back way," she added.

Rich followed as she led the way outside the new wing, following the unseen sidewalk now covered in snow. She planned to cut across in front of the wing, loop past her office, and emerge above it by her house, which they could head to without the benefit of a sidewalk, since the snow required the same effort regardless of the surface underfoot. But as she approached the main building she stopped suddenly. Rich bumped into her and said, "Hey, I almost knocked you down. What's up?"

Without speaking, Julie pointed at the deep footprints that came in from the other side and led up the stairs to the entrance.

"Look at these," she said quietly, but with an edge to her voice.

"Weird," Rich said as he traced the tracks to where they ended on the small entrance porch, directly in front of the door. "Maybe I should just go check the door."

"It was probably Dennis, coming in to check on things," she said without much conviction.

"Sure, but why don't you stay here and I'll go see if the door is unlocked."

"We'll go together," she said firmly.

They stepped into the tracks and walked up to the entrance porch. Rich reached for the door and after a few turns of the handle, found it was secure.

"Is the alarm on?" he asked.

Julie looked at the pad and saw that it wasn't blinking, which meant it had been disarmed.

"Strange," she said. "I don't know who was the last to leave, but we all know to arm the system when we do." She reached into her pocket and extracted a ring of keys that included the ones for her office as well as the house. "Let me do it," she said. "It's sort of tricky."

Rich stepped aside as Julie put the key in and turned it and then opened the door.

"You stay here," he said as he started in.

"No way! I'm right behind you."

When they stepped inside they saw the empty reception area with Mrs. Detweiller's desk. The only light came from the sunshine outside. It was quiet. Rich started to move across the room toward the open door to Julie's office when she grabbed his arm.

"I'm sure I left my door closed and locked," she said in a whisper. "I always do."

"Okay," he whispered back. "You go back outside and wait, and I'll check it out. Maybe you just forgot."

"No, I closed and locked it—and I'm coming with you."

Rich turned to ask her again to withdraw, but before he could get a word out, a figure came running from Julie's office, turned to the right to pass them by, and headed to the entrance.

"Stop!" Julie screamed.

Rich turned around to pursue the figure as it rushed through the open door and onto the porch. Rich followed, with Julie immediately behind. The figure jumped from the porch into the fresh snow and began sprinting away. Rich was right behind him as the man increased his speed, now retracing the tracks he had apparently made earlier. A fast and experienced runner, Rich came within a few feet of the fleeing man and was reaching out to grab him when he stumbled and fell sideways in the snow.

Julie nearly stumbled over Rich but managed to veer off to avoid him and then increased her speed so she came up directly behind the fleeing man. She reached out to try to grab him but instead pushed him just enough to knock him slightly off balance. As he tried to right himself, Rich came rushing past Julie and threw himself hard at the man, hitting him from behind and dropping him into the snow.

"Stay there!" Rich screamed at the man as he rolled to his side in an effort to stand. Rich dropped down on top of him and pulled his arms behind him. Out of the corner of her eye Julie spotted the snow shovel that stood outside the door on the entrance porch and raced to retrieve it. Breathless now, she rushed back and handed the shovel to Rich, who inserted the shovel's handle between the man's back and his pinned arms.

"Call the cops!" Rich yelled to Julie, and to the man, "If you try to move, I'll put the other end of this over your head. Be still and you won't get hurt," he added, in as threatening a voice as he could muster.

As Rich stood guard, Julie rushed back to the office and called 911. Identifying herself as the director, she explained that a break-in had occurred at the historical society, and that she and a friend had caught the intruder and were holding him outside. When the operator advised her to be careful, Julie said they would, wondering to herself why the advice was even offered.

"So get someone here as fast as you can," she urged, and the operator promised to do so, again advising caution.

During the short time the call had lasted, Julie had surveyed the room for another possible weapon, but saw none. She did spot a coil of rope—really, just a heavy cord that they used to bundle boxes. Grabbing it, she raced back outside, and as Rich kept the man pinned down with the handle of the shovel she looped the rope around his arms. Rich then pulled it tight to the handle. Julie had an image of the intruder as a trussed turkey.

"Turn him over," she yelled at Rich. "I want to see Cartwright's face."

Rich rolled the trussed man over so that he looked directly up at them. But it wasn't Brent Cartwright. She had no idea who he was.

CHAPTER 42

In Orono, Rich told Julie later, it would have taken an hour to get a cop on a Sunday, after a snowstorm, let alone the day after Christmas. Exactly how long it did take before they heard a voice and looked to see a young uniformed officer racing toward them through the snow, his gun in hand, wasn't at all clear, then or later. But like everything that had happened since they'd terminated their leisurely walk with the discovery of the footprints, it seemed to be happening in fast-forward.

It wasn't the Ryland chief Julie expected but a county deputy sheriff, and at first glance Julie thought he looked about eighteen, though she was sure no one that young could be employed as a cop, carrying a gun. The officer identified himself as Deputy Conyers before barking orders to the man lying prone on the ground. In just seconds the intruder was in handcuffs, the cord Julie had used to restrain him, removed. Conyers told the man to remain on the ground and then used his handheld radio to request assistance. Julie noticed that he kept his gun at the ready the whole time.

The deputy instructed them to go inside and leave the job to him while he awaited backup. Although always responsive to an official order, Julie dearly wanted to remain in place to ask the man his name. Rich guided her inside, and while they stood at the open door watching the scene outside, she told him she wanted to call Mike Barlow. She quickly turned from the door and picked up the phone on her secretary's desk.

"Hey," he said, gently pushing her hand back down so the receiver remained in place, "that's not your job. Not now. Let the sheriff handle this. They'll talk to us after they get him out of here, and you can talk to Mike then."

"Okay, you're right. I just want to know who he is."

"My guess is we just met Timothy Brothers, but let's see what happens. Right now it sounds like the cavalry's coming."

The sound of a distant siren was interrupted by a closer one, and then the two of them played in counterpoint until they both came to a loud end.

"They must be out front," Rich said.

As they watched from the entrance porch, two uniformed men—a state policeman in blue and one in the drab brown of the county sheriff's office—bounced through the heavy snow toward where the young deputy stood guard, both holding guns. The one in brown seemed older and took control. The state policeman frog-marched the man back through the snow toward the front of the building. The younger officer, Conyers, gestured toward Julie and Rich, and after a brief conversation, he started toward the building as the older one headed out front.

"I need to get some information," Conyers said as he stepped onto the porch. "They're taking the suspect to the county lockup, but all we have so far is your call to 911. That works for a B-and-E charge for now, but I need to get your statements. Can we go inside?"

As they started in, Rich thanked the deputy for the quick response, and Julie added that she was surprised that Ryland police didn't come. Conyers explained that the county sheriff covered for Ryland on holidays, and that he was, luckily, quite close when the call came in, as were both his superior, the chief deputy, and the state policeman.

"Good luck all around," he added. "Now if I can just start with your names," he began after pulling out his notebook.

Seeing that Julie was impatient and wanting to stop her from talking about Barlow, Rich responded for both, giving their names, explaining their relationship, how they came across the break-in, and how they apprehended the suspect. Conyers wrote quickly, but not quickly enough for Julie, who said that someone needed to call Detective Barlow of the State Police.

"This involves other related cases that Mike Barlow knows about. He really should be notified."

"Julie," Rich said with some annoyance, "let the officer do his job."

"I'll be sure to pass that on," Conyers said. "I knew Detective Barlow when he was the chief here, and I'm sure my boss will get right on to him."

When the interview ended, Rich and Julie left the historical society and returned to her house. While Rich read in the living room, Julie busied herself in the kitchen, and when he went to check on her, she admitted that she was merely killing time by rearranging the contents of the cabinets.

"Like Garrison Keillor says about Lutherans," she said when he questioned her intentions. "Their treatment for depression is alphabetizing the spice rack. But then I'm not depressed, and the spice rack is pretty thin, so I'm just reorganizing stuff."

"While you wait for a phone call," Rich added.

"You might say that. I'm assuming the deputy got in touch, but if Mike doesn't call in an hour I'm going to try him. Do you think we can make another meal from the Christmas feast?"

"That was my plan, unless . . ."

The ringing phone stopped him, and when he heard Julie say Barlow's name he retreated to the living room. She joined him shortly and reported on the call.

"His name is Kevin Jeffries. He lives in Boston. No record. So right now they've just got a B-and E-charge, enough to hold him while they try to find out more."

Rich easily read the disappointment on Julie's face.

"Look," he said, "I understand you're mad because it wasn't Cartwright. You had yourself convinced that he's the one. You even said his name when we had him pinned. But it's not. It's this guy Jeffries. Still, you should be happy—your trap worked! He took the bait. You solved it, Julie, and I'm willing to bet this Jeffries is a serial thief who specializes in stealing from Maine museums. That would solve the other thefts, too."

Julie nodded, reluctantly. "If he admits to them. Yeah, I know you're right. It's the logical conclusion . . . but, well, I just thought . . ."

"You thought your guy Cartwright was the perp, but look at it this way: you figured out the whole thing, just not the name of the guy who did it."

"Okay, okay." Julie held her hands up in mock resignation. "I solved it. So where's that leftover feast you promised? Thinking about all this is making me hungry."

"I thought maybe a turkey curry. But that's takes a bit of time. Mind waiting?"

"I can occupy myself with a puzzle."

"Don't you always?"

⌘

Rich was glad that while he was cooking Julie remained in the living room, though he knew the downside was she would keep mulling over the idea that Cartwright was involved in some way. She hated to let anything go—and she really hated being wrong.

When he called her to the kitchen to eat, she seemed content, and for the first fifteen or twenty minutes of the meal she talked about other things, making Rich hope that she had accepted the fact that Jeffries was the thief and that he was now under arrest. But when he got up to dress the salad she returned to the topic.

"The more I think about it, the more I think I need to talk to Mike about this."

"Julie, it's the holidays. He's got his life, and they've got the thief, and now you need to relax—and take credit. After all, your trap worked," he repeated.

"I won't call Mike, but he said he'd call again if something else came up."

By the end of the evening Julie's disappointment grew. There was no call from Mike. Despite the fact that Jeffries had been caught red-handed, she couldn't let go of the idea that Brent Cartwright was involved, and she hated the thought that she had been wrong. More than that, she hated that Rich knew she had been wrong, even though he was trying hard to avoid the topic entirely. She almost wished he would just say it: Julie, you were wrong. That wasn't like Rich, of course, but she knew that if he didn't mention it, she would keep worrying the issue. Either way it stood between them, so she raised it herself.

"You think I was wrong," she said, startling him as he lay on the couch reading one of the books he had received for Christmas.

He put the book aside and sat up.

"All I said was that your analysis was right, that your trap worked, and that they caught the thief. It just happened to be someone other than who you suspected. Everything else was right. You should be proud of that."

Although his words were meant to be soothing, they had the opposite effect on Julie, who suddenly found herself angry at Rich, even though she knew down deep that the person she was truly mad at was herself.

"Okay, let's drop it," she said. "But admit it, you think I got it all wrong."

"No, no! I just said you got it all right—or almost all. I don't want to fight about this Julie. It's been a long day, and we're both tired, and the whole scene today was pretty scary. I'm exhausted, and I think you are, too. Let's just go to bed and get some rest and see what tomorrow brings."

Julie knew very well that everything Rich said was true. But she also knew that sleep was an unlikely outcome for her.

"I don't want to fight either. It's been a great holiday, and I don't want to spoil that. But I don't think I could get to sleep right now. Why don't you go ahead to bed, and I'll just read down here and join you later?"

Rich knew her too well to object, and so he went upstairs.

Julie paced around the room for a bit, wrestling with an idea that finally became too large to ignore. She opened her laptop, brought up the search engine, and typed in "Kevin Jeffries."

⌘

Rich's had slept so deeply that he hadn't noticed when Julie joined him, but when he woke and saw that it was almost seven a.m., he felt her beside him. She was now in that same almost coma-like state in which he had spent the night. He got up quietly to avoid disturbing her, threw on slacks and a shirt, and went downstairs to start the coffee. Fifteen minutes later she appeared in the kitchen while he was refilling his cup.

"Nothing like the smell of java to rouse me," she said.

"Sorry. I didn't want to wake you, but I was ready for this," Rich said, holding up his cup. "Let me pour yours."

She gratefully accepted the cup, took a long swallow, and said, "I'm sorry about last night. You were right that I was mad, mostly at myself."

"That's okay."

"But I was right," she said, grinning over her raised cup.

"About?"

"It all. Cartwright. Start some toast and I'll explain."

CHAPTER 43

"So," Julie said as she spread peanut butter on her toast, "I just couldn't get to sleep last night, so I did some searching on the web."

"About Cartwright?"

"No. Kevin Jeffries. And guess what? He worked in a library in Chicago for a couple of years."

"Good for him. I'm sure lots of people did—probably still do."

"Don't make fun of me, Rich. Yes, lots of people worked in a library in Chicago. Including Brent Cartwright! And at the same one! And probably at the same time, though I'm not absolutely sure of that. Cartwright told me he worked there before he came to the Portland Historical Society, but he didn't say exactly when or for how long. And I couldn't figure out from the website when Jeffries was there. You know how these pages don't get updated, and so you're not sure about time, but there is no question that Jeffries was an archivist there."

Rich looked at her without speaking for a few long seconds. Then he sighed and said, "Why do I think I know where this is going?"

She laughed. "Maybe because you know me so well?"

"That must be it. Okay, go ahead."

"So I'm thinking that it's too much of a coincidence, both of them working at the same place. And now they're both in New England, and things get stolen from Maine museums, and—"

"And you just can't get past the idea that Cartwright is in this. Tell me again why you think so."

Julie reviewed her suspicions, beginning with Dan Dumont's memorial service when Cartwright appeared to know about the map thefts and Julie's efforts to help Dan. Then there was the conversation at the Portland Historical Society's Halloween party, and his interest in the blog. Julie reminded Rich that she had put Cartwright on the list of possible suspects when she was run off the road, but that Barlow had determined that he didn't have a truck and was visiting friends in Boston at the time.

"But it was the lunch I had with him in Portland that really got my attention," she continued. "The only specific thing then was his interest in the Tabor papers. I remember driving home and thinking that there was just something not quite right about him—the way he deflected talk about his earlier career, a sense that he was doing folks a favor by working at PHS. I just don't know how to describe it to you, Rich, but he made me uneasy. And then when he came to the Christmas party, he kept focusing on the papers, especially where they were located. So now Kevin Jeffries shows up to steal them. Doesn't it all sort of add up?"

Rich sighed and said that maybe it did to her but that he wasn't convinced.

"And I doubt Barlow will be either," he added.

"Now you're reading my mind. I really need to talk to Mike about this."

"What do you think he'll do? Go see Cartwright and say 'We know you worked at the same library in Chicago that Jeffries did and so you two must be in on a scheme to steal artifacts from museums.' That makes a lot of sense."

"Don't be silly! Of course he can't do that, but I have an idea. I'm going to call Mike and see what he thinks."

"Do what you want, Julie. I can't stop you, but I think you're wasting your time as well as his. They've got Jeffries. Let them take it from here." But Rich knew very well that Julie was going to have to play this through her way. And he also knew himself well enough to know that he'd go along with it, however reluctantly.

It was nearly noon by the time Julie connected with Mike Barlow, and when she came into the living room to tell Rich about the call, he knew at once that she was happy with the outcome.

"I think Mike shares your opinion that I'm being bull-headed about this, but he finally agreed to give it a try. What convinced him, I think, is that Jeffries isn't talking—just won't say anything, and his lawyer was right there with him. So they're sort of stuck. They've got him for a simple breaking and entering, but since we stopped him before he could grab the papers they can't even charge him with theft. And the ceramics and the maps are probably long gone by now. So, pulling it all together, and maybe even connecting it to Dan Dumont's death, just isn't possible right now. That's why I think Mike eventually agreed with my plan."

"I'm glad he knows what it is. Wish I did."

"I was sort of formulating it this morning while I was waiting to hear back from Mike. It's really simple. If I can talk to Cartwright, I can tell him about Jeffries and make it clear that I know there's a connection between them. I can shake him up, maybe even suggest that Jeffries identified him as a partner or whatever. Anyway, he's not going to reveal anything to Mike, who really doesn't have grounds for even interviewing him. And even if he did find some way, Mike can't make up a story about Jeffries without opening himself up to an entrapment plea. I don't have that problem. I can shake Cartwright up and get the whole story. What do you think?"

"You don't want to know, but let's leave it at that. Where do Barlow and I fit in?"

When she finished fleshing it all out, Rich was no more convinced. He agreed to do his part so long as Barlow was fully apprised. Julie assured him that Mike already agreed, and so the next step for her was to set up a meeting with Cartwright. She accomplished that with a single phone call.

"Trap number two is set," she told Rich. "Tomorrow in Portland."

"Yes, and you're the bait," he replied, looking sour.

CHAPTER 44

After the first twenty minutes or so of the drive, Julie realized that the hour-and-a-half trip was going to feel like twice that if she didn't do something to break the silence. They had already experienced some delays because of plow trucks, but it wasn't the road condition that troubled Julie. It was Rich. He had been cool last night after her call to Brent Cartwright yielded a lunch date, and had insisted on driving her. This morning had been a little better, but he remained distant. Julie decided she had to say something.

"Look, Rich, nothing is going to happen, really, but I'm thinking we should change the plan slightly: you should join me for lunch with Cartwright."

The atmosphere in the car changed completely. They became, as Rich put it, partners in crime. All that remained was to have Barlow agree.

When they met the state policeman at the Portland police station an hour before the lunch, Barlow's relief was evident.

"I think that's a great idea," he said to Julie and Rich. "I was thinking about it myself but didn't want to get between you two. Let's review."

Julie had told Cartwright on the phone that she was coming into Portland to do some post-holiday shopping, and he had replied that he was more then happy to meet her. He had suggested a restaurant on Custom House Wharf, a classic waterfront dive that he liked. Although Julie hadn't mentioned Rich at the time, she didn't think his presence would surprise Cartwright, nor would it interfere with their plan: to tell Cartwright about the arrest of the intruder.

Barlow and a casually dressed state trooper would linger undercover outside the restaurant, along the wharf by the fish store, to trail Cartwright when the lunch was over. The hope was that Julie's revelation would scare Cartwright into action.

"It's a very popular place," Barlow said, "and there are always folks coming and going, so he shouldn't be suspicious. We'll stay with him to see what he does."

"What if he just goes home and makes a call to someone?" Rich asked.

"That assumes there's someone else, beyond him and Jeffries," Barlow said. "And that could be. I got a wiretap order this morning, so we'll know who he calls, if anyone."

"Looks like we're good to go," said Julie. Looking at her watch, she added, "We've got fifteen minutes. Should Rich and I head over?"

Barlow suggested that he and his colleague would go right away so they could identify Cartwright when he arrived. With the picture he had downloaded from the Portland Historical Society's website, he was confident they would recognize Cartwright, but wanted to be early enough to do that so they were sure to follow the right person afterwards.

After the two policemen left, Julie and Rich walked around a few blocks in the Old Port to kill time and then headed the short distance to the wharf.

"Nervous?" Rich asked as they stopped to cross Commercial Street.

"More like excited. It's coming together now, I just know it."

Rich didn't respond as they crossed the street and headed down the narrow route that was really a wharf, the fish market on their right, and the restaurant almost directly across from it.

"The deck's the really fun thing," Brent Cartwright said as Julie and Rich, in response to his wave, walked toward him across the nearly empty restaurant. "But of course, not at the end of December! I still like the place, though—an authentic waterfront dive."

If he was surprised to see that Rich was joining them, Cartwright didn't show it.

Rich said he had been there before, in the summer, and so knew about the outside seating. Julie confessed this was her first time. They talked a bit about the decor, the lack of customers, and the restaurant's history before settling in to study the menus the cheerful waitress brought.

"So it's shopping that brings you to the big city," Cartwright said after they had ordered. "Cheers," he said before they responded, raising his beer glass to them. "I assume Santa made his way to Ryland and brought you some cash to spend on the post-holiday sales," he continued. "But then, Saint Nick had already been there, as I remember. That was a terrific party, by the way."

"And a terrific Santa," Julie said. "How was your holiday?"

After a brief description of his quiet day spent with friends, Cartwright asked how the storm had affected Ryland, and Julie saw her opening.

"Well, it was a pretty wild time, as a matter of fact. Ryland was basically snowed in, but one visitor got through. Yesterday. To the historical society."

"You were open?" he asked.

"No, but that didn't stop him."

Their food arrived, and Julie carefully studied Cartwright's face to see if her statement had gotten his attention. He calmly began to salt his french fries and asked what she meant.

Rich kept his eyes on Cartwright but couldn't read anything either.

"He broke in, and Rich and I happened to be walking by and caught him. Red-handed. He's in the county jail now."

The waitress came by to ask how their food was, and her presence stopped the conversation. But, as they later told Barlow, both Julie and Rich noticed a quick change in Cartwright's demeanor. He reached for a fry, then put it down, then looked out into the distance. He still didn't speak, so Julie prompted him.

"We think he's the one who's been stealing artifacts from all around the state. You know all about that, of course."

"Guess we all heard," Cartwright said, playing with another fry but stopping short of eating it. "So," he said, "do you know who he is?"

"Yes. His name is Jeffries."

The name hung in the air until Cartwright abruptly stood up and excused himself, saying he needed to go to the restroom.

"Should we do something?" Rich whispered.

"I don't think so. If he leaves, Mike will see him. I don't want to give anything away. He'll probably come back, because he didn't take his coat," she said, pointing to the heavy parka on the back of Cartwright's chair.

"He might be willing to give that up."

"Give what up?" Cartwright asked as he resumed his seat.

"Your coat," Rich said. "We wondered if you were planning to leave without it."

"I just needed to use the toilet. Actually, I'm not feeling so good. Too much holiday cheer yesterday. I should probably go home," he added, reaching for the parka.

"But we haven't told you about Jeffries yet," she said, without taking her eyes off his face. "He says he knows you."

Julie didn't consider the lie important. It was one she could tell, unlike Barlow, and so she used it. And got a response she hadn't expected.

Cartwright stood up, pushed his chair aside, and without saying a word headed quickly for the exit.

"Get Mike," Julie said to Rich, who had jumped up and followed Cartwright to the door. "Hold on," Rich yelled, but Cartwright hurried through the door, turned right, and was headed toward Commercial Street, almost running now. Then Rich saw Barlow and his colleague step directly in Cartwright's path.

"Mr. Cartwright," Rich heard Barlow say as he put out arms. "I'm Detective Barlow of the Maine State Police. I think we need to talk. Will you come with us, please?"

Cartwright took one glance behind him, sweeping the alley with his eyes as if it might reveal an escape, then looked down at his feet and nodded once. The two cops flanked him and took him away, Cartwright stepping meekly between them.

Julie appeared at Rich's side, and they stood in the alley watching until Cartwright was loaded into an unmarked car parked at the corner. After a few minutes, Rich broke the silence.

"Look at those." He pointed to a pile of lobster traps in front of the seafood store.

"What?" Julie asked. "What are you talking about?"

"Those traps. Familiar?"

"I still don't follow."

"Well, you set another trap, didn't you? And it worked."

Julie laughed, and Rich joined in.

They returned to the restaurant to finish lunch. Julie poked at her quesadilla with little interest as Rich happily consumed his lobster roll.

"So you think he'll come clean?" she asked.

"Who knows? Guess it depends on how Barlow handles it. Unlike you, he can't tell Cartwright that Jeffries fingered him, but I'm willing to bet your detective friend will find a way to get him to talk."

"And if not?"

"Don't know. Maybe they can use the old prisoner's dilemma. You know: keep the pressure on as the two of them try to figure out whether the other one confessed and just hope one actually does. But that's Mike's job now. How about you? Want to head home?

"You've got to be kidding, Rich! Let's hang out here and see if we can get in touch with Mike later. I've come too far now to just walk away."

"So, a little post-Christmas shopping?" he asked.

"There's really nothing I need, and to tell you the truth, I've had it up to here with things—stolen things, things that might get stolen, even things given and received. No, I'm not talking about any specific Christmas gifts. Just things in general. How about a walk instead? I'd rather have views than things at this point."

CHAPTER 45

And so they made their way along the walk toward East End Beach, a path made treacherous by the tramped-down but as yet unplowed snow.

"Cities don't know how to handle snow," Rich observed. "I'll bet everything in Ryland is clear by now, and we had a lot more snow there than Portland got."

Nonetheless, the walk was still enjoyable—invigorating in the crisp air, beautiful with views out over the harbor to the closest islands. When they reached East End Beach, they decided to go up the hill and circle back via the sidewalk of the Eastern Promenade, paralleling the walk but from a greater height—and, Rich said, with the possibility that the walkway there would be better. It wasn't, and they occasionally had to resort to walking in the street, but the views were even better from this perspective, and they proceeded almost entirely in silence, processing the earlier events in their own ways.

When they got back to the Old Port, Rich said he was happy they were staying in town that night instead of driving back to Ryland, a drive that promised to be made slower by continued plowing. Julie had suggested they stay at the bed-and-breakfast they had been to in the fall, but Rich said he wanted to splurge. So they booked a room in the old armory that had been renovated into a very nice hotel, where Rich had once attended a conference. That it was only a few blocks from the Portland police station made it easy for Julie to agree, despite the price.

"Think of it as another Christmas gift to ourselves," Rich said after they checked in and stood admiring the lovely woodwork of the reception lounge. "And it's not a thing," he pointed out.

It was only a bit after three p.m., but Julie decided Mike Barlow must have had plenty of time to interrogate Cartwright.

"I'm going to call him on his cell," she told Rich, but he persuaded her to give it another hour.

"He knows where we are, and if he has something to tell you, he'll call. Remember, Julie, he can't reveal much. Despite what you think, you're not a cop. Cut him a break and don't push."

Ten minutes later, the phone rang.

"I'm just wrapping up here, Julie, and I've got to get back to Augusta," Barlow told her. "I can talk for a minute, but remember, I can't say too much."

Anything he could tell her would be welcome, Julie said.

They agreed to meet in ten minutes in the reception area downstairs. "If we can't find a quiet space there, we can come up to the room," she said.

The room was deserted, and they moved two chairs to face a couch in the back, far from the check-in area and away from the route any other guests might take to the stairs.

"You know I have to be discreet," the policeman said when he arrived. "Even though you've been in this up to your neck, I have to protect the case. I can give you just a general overview—no details. I know that doesn't make you happy, but it's the best I can do."

"Maybe you can answer a question or two?" Julie asked.

Barlow laughed. "Maybe. Depends on the question, of course. So the gist is that your friend Cartwright just broke down and confessed, to a lot; don't ask me exactly what. He really crumpled. Didn't want a lawyer, waived his Miranda rights, agreed to full videotaping. I really had the feeling he wanted to get it all out—to purge himself."

"He told us it was a relief, when he started crying," Julie said. "He's usually so buttoned up and smug that I was shocked. But I guess it was all just too much for him."

"And when he heard from you about Kevin Jeffries," Barlow said, "the floodgates broke. Anyway, you were right about the Chicago connection. Seems Cartwright had some problems at the library where he worked there—I have to check that out, so right now I really don't have any more details. Whatever it was, Jeffries knew and basically blackmailed Cartwright into running the operation here."

"Did he track Cartwright down in Maine, or did he sort of send him here?" Julie asked.

"Don't really know. Point is that Jeffries was the center of the thing. He took orders, based on what Cartwright knew was available, and then he probably did the actual thefts, though I'm not sure about all of them. More to check when I interview Jeffries."

"So it really was a business organization, just as Wayne Reiter guessed."

"Hey, to one degree or another all crime is a business—theft particularly"

"Sure," Julie said, "but in this case—well, I guess you'd call it marketing, advertising available items and taking orders for them—and then taking orders and delivering."

"I think it's called 'fulfillment' in the marketing world," Rich added.

"Could be," Barlow said. "Look, I really don't have a lot of time, and I think that about covers what I'm allowed to say."

"Are you open to a few more questions?" Julie asked.

"Such as?"

"Well, the murder is number one on my list. Did Cartwright say anything about that?"

"Or who ran Julie off the road?" Rich asked.

"What I can tell you—and this may cover both questions—is that we know Jeffries has a truck that matches your description.

It's possible that a rifle was found in the truck—lots of folks with trucks have guns, you know. Just speculating, of course."

"Got you. But I wonder why Jeffries killed Dumont—if, in fact, he actually did."

"If he did, as you say, that's something we'll have to pursue. Maybe Dumont found out and confronted the person who ended up killing him, or maybe he was a part of the organization and wanted out or something like that. All speculation again."

"Of course," Julie said. "But you don't think Cartwright killed Dan?"

"Let's just say that if you're part of a criminal conspiracy and murder results from that conspiracy, you have a lot to answer for. That's not up to me."

"I understand, Mike, but I'm just curious about how you read Cartwright, in general."

The policeman paused and glanced out at the room for a few seconds before responding.

"Hard to say. He seems like a good guy gone bad—smart, nice-looking, respectable, working at a job he was good at. Whatever happened in Chicago that sort of lit the fuse on this, well, I can't say. But then it spiraled down from there. He got deeper and deeper into it and probably couldn't see a way out. When we told him we were holding Kevin Jeffries's for the break in and attempted theft at the historical society, he just cracked and everything came out. That's about all I can say."

The three of them sat in silence before Rich said, "I don't know about that. He made choices at every step. Okay, one step led to another, but why didn't he just say no at some point? Like when Dumont was killed; surely he could have come forward then and confessed? But he didn't. I don't think we should be too sympathetic to him."

"Not for me to say," Barlow said. "Look, I need to go. That it?"

"One last question," Julie said. "Ted Korhonen; any reason to think he was involved?"

"That reminds me: I need to call him to say that when the Massachusetts police searched Jeffrie's house, they found a painting. Quite a nice one, I gather. It seems to match what you told me, Julie, about the one stolen from Korhonen's museum. I'm sure Korhonen will be happy to get it back."

"You're saying it was stolen, not that Ted stole it?"

"Right."

"I'm glad to hear that," Julie said. "Mike, I really appreciate our talk."

"Which never happened," the policeman said.

"The very same. Thanks!"

CHAPTER 46

Near the end of January, on the third call from Wayne Reiter in just over a week, Julie came as close as she ever had to losing her temper with a trustee. His interest in the cases, he told her, stemmed from his thinking that he might, as he put it, "write them up" in the form of a business school "case."

"Two different meanings of the word, of course," he said, "but I do think I was right from the beginning about this business of crime, and students might benefit from learning more."

Sensing that her tolerance for Reiter's pompousness was declining rapidly, Julie agreed in a perfunctory way that the cases might hold some interest, but she told him, as she had twice before, that she didn't have any further information.

"I would have thought you'd be all over this," Reiter said. "You have a reputation for solving crimes, but it seems like you've dropped the ball this time."

This was the part of the conversation that Julie nearly responded to with an outward burst of the anger she was feeling inwardly. But checking herself, remembering that Reiter was, after all, a trustee of the historical society, and it was her job to be ever so nice to each and every one of them, she paused and counted silently to ten before saying, "Well, Wayne, I do have some familiarity with crimes, but I don't have a lot of experience with what happens afterwards."

He accepted her distinction and cut short the call. As she sat at her desk, Julie realized that the anger she had managed to suppress was really not directed at Wayne Reiter but at herself, because the explanation she had given him was correct: The two murders and related thefts she had helped investigate previously had simply resolved themselves. In both cases, the guilty parties had confessed, and she'd had sufficient knowledge of what had happened to make her relatively uninterested in the details of any subsequent legal action.

But the current situation was far different! There were too many pieces of the puzzle, and she dearly wanted to put them together so she could see the whole. The big matter, of course, was Dan Dumont's murder, but there were other, smaller factors that she also wanted to understand—from why she had been run off the road to how Kevin Jeffries had gotten the security code that allowed him to break into RHS on Boxing Day. And of course, Brent Cartwright's involvement in all of these facets of the case still remained unclear to her, as did the role the blog had (or hadn't) played in the thefts.

The fitting together of these pieces wasn't going to come quickly, or simply. When she pushed Mike Barlow for answers, he reminded her that the wheels of justice turn at a different pace from the wheels of investigation. Three trials would eventually bring the facts into view.

The first, locally—for Jeffries, on the break-in—was scheduled for early February. Julie had been asked to be ready to testify if necessary, though Mike had told her its purpose was really to keep Jeffries in jail while the murder remained under investigation. In fact, the bigger purpose was to pressure Cartwright, charged as an accessory, to provide evidence against Jeffries in the other matters. The Two Rivers thefts would be tried in York County, although that was being deferred, since the central focus was Dumont's murder, and that trial would be in Franklin County, probably in the summer, if Cartwright indeed offered enough evidence to ensure the right outcome.

Julie continued to badger Mike Barlow in the weeks leading up to the local trial, but his response was always the same: "I'll let you know what I know when I can." A week before the trial, an assistant district attorney phoned to verify that she would be attending, and to ask her to come to the office to preview her testimony. When Julie asked if it was likely she'd be called, Lisa Grover, the assistant DA, told her that she was still in discussion with Cartwright's attorney about a potential plea bargain. Grover hoped this would be sufficient to make Jeffries's attorney agree to a plea that would ensure Jeffries would be held for the murder trial in the summer. She said that such outcomes often didn't happen until the last moment.

"If he pleads before," the young woman told Julie, "I'll be in touch. But for now, we have to assume it's going to trial, and we need your testimony."

Julie asked if Rich would also be called, hoping he might, since such a summons would easily excuse him from some classes and allow for more time together in Ryland, but the DA said that his written testimony would suffice. Julie's eyewitness account and her status as director of the historical society would be more than adequate.

Julie had the feeling that she was something of a pawn in the game the prosecutors were playing, but she agreed to come to the DA's office two days before the trial. Late in the afternoon on the day before she was to go, Lisa Grover called to say that the preview session would be unnecessary.

"Cartwright is talking," she told Julie. "Looks like he's giving us enough to put Jeffries in big trouble, so we're asking the judge to defer the B-and-E trial. Then it all goes to Franklin County, and that's where the real action will be. I don't know if they'll need you up there, but I'll be passing along all of our case material, and they'll get in touch if they do."

So much for seeing the judicial system at work on a firsthand basis, Julie said to herself after the call. But at least now she might be able to get some answers to her questions, so she called Mike Barlow and left a message asking for him to call her back.

He did so the next day, confirming that Cartwright had indeed made a deal, agreeing to provide strong evidence against Jeffries in return for his own guilty plea on the charge of being an accomplice to theft.

"He'll get some time for that," Barlow said, "but probably less than a year—and certainly a whole lot less than if they charged him with being an accomplice in the Dumont case."

"So did he point to Jeffries for the murder?"

"That's my understanding."

"Can you tell me anything else, Mike? Like, did Cartwright explain about who ran me off the road, and how Jeffries got the security code, and—"

"Hey, this is still under investigation, and you know I have to be careful. Let me check with the assistant DA down there and see if she'll talk to you about what Cartwright said. I'll call if there's anything I can tell you. I've got to go now."

Julie was surprised when that afternoon Mrs. Detweiller told her she had a call from Lisa Grover. It took her a moment to remember that Grover was the assistant DA.

"Detective Barlow told me you're interested in a few matters," Grover began. "The investigation is ongoing, as you know, but we had to file information related to the plea, so I can try to answer some questions if they don't go beyond what will be public shortly."

As the conversation proceeded, Julie felt she was in some sort of amateur play in which the lines were being written as the actors spoke. She asked, Grover hesitated, she rephrased, Grover half-answered, she probed, Grover again hesitated. It took almost twenty minutes, but when the call was over, Julie had at least some of the answers.

It was indeed Jeffries who had forced her off the road. Cartwright had alerted him to Julie's interest in the thefts after the Halloween party in Portland, and Jeffries had apparently come up with the idea of throwing a scare into her to deter her from pursuing the matter.

"Cartwright admitted it was a dumb idea," Grover had said, "but with Jeffries, we're not dealing with a genius."

Cartwright had played a more direct role in the RHS break-in. After Victorian Christmas, he had lingered to watch Dennis Sutherland punching in the code and then provided it to Jeffries. Julie hadn't realized that Cartwright had remained afterwards, but she could imagine how it happened. And as to the blog, Lisa Grover said she didn't have much on that from Cartwright's plea, but did think that it was intended to help identify potential items to steal.

"It's a little murky as to whether it actually worked," Grover had said, "but certainly Cartwright intended it to be a source for him and Jeffries."

Cartwright's own involvement, she had revealed in response to several efforts from Julie to pin it down, resulted from Jeffries's blackmail.

"He knew about Cartwright's problems in Chicago and used that knowledge to pressure him," the assistant DA said.

When Julie asked about the "problems," Grover explained that Cartwright had been dismissed from his job when some items had gone missing.

"No charges were filed, and I gather it was a bit ambiguous," Grover said, "but whatever Jeffries had on him was enough to make Cartwright cooperate."

This confirmed what Mike Barlow had hinted at back in December after he'd arrested Cartwright.

The other matter Julie had raised with Grover was the involvement of Ted Korhonen. On that front the answer was clear: Cartwright had said nothing about the man or the painting missing from his museum. Julie was relieved.

So it now came down to the murder of Dan Dumont, and on that front Grover had nothing to offer.

"That goes up to Franklin County. I can't say any more about Cartwright's information on that, but—just speculation, you understand—I'd say that the case is pretty strong. With what we've learned, I'm guessing Jeffries's attorney will be in serious discussion with the DA there."

Julie realized that the final big piece of the puzzle wasn't going to fall into place until the summer trial—if there even was one.

⌘

In late May, Julie learned that a trial was indeed scheduled for the third week of June. That was cutting it close, since their wedding was set for July 14, and Julie's mother planned to come to Ryland two weeks ahead to work on final details.

Because she had promised to keep Wayne Reiter informed, she phoned him, and he suggested they drive to Farmington together to attend. The day before the trial, she phoned the court to be sure that it was going to happen, and was told that it was.

"To be accurate," the clerk said, "it's scheduled. We never know what's going to happen, but the judge and jury are set to go at nine-thirty tomorrow morning."

Wayne offered to drive, and they arrived at the courthouse at eight-forty-five after a harrowing drive that made Julie regret she had agreed to go with him. She could understand that he was proud of his 7 Series BMW, but she was tempted to point out that the two-lane roads between Ryland and Farmington were not the Autobahn.

"Perfect car for these roads," Reiter had said more than once when he noticed her grabbing hold of the door handle as he took turns at sixty-five miles an hour.

When they entered the courthouse, Julie immediately recognized the man standing with two others to the left of the entrance to the main courtroom. Although she hadn't seen him since she and Rich had apprehended him outside the historical society on Boxing Day, she had no doubt that it was Kevin Jeffries, aka, Timothy Brothers. He was talking earnestly to the two men, presumably his lawyers.

She felt awkward, not knowing whether he recognized her, but realizing that the discussion among the three was quite animated. Jeffries kept shaking his head, and at one point he started to walk away, but was confronted by a uniformed sheriff. Of course, she realized, he had been brought from the jail and was being allowed to meet his legal team here. When she nudged Reiter to move away from the scene, he said, "Typical—this is how it goes, you know."

"How what goes?"

"I think it's called 'making a deal on the courthouse steps,' though of course we're inside and not on the steps. But this is how it happens—the last-minute deal, keeping the pressure on both sides right up until the start of the trial. I'll make a note of this for my little case study."

When Reiter sat down and began to type into his tablet computer, Julie walked back to the entrance, feeling like the scene that was unfolding was not really something she should be a witness to. When Mike Barlow came through the door, he nearly ran into her, but she was glad to see him.

"Figured you'd be here," he said. "Looks like they're working on a deal," he added, and gestured toward Jeffries and his attorneys. One of them left and headed into the office labeled DISTRICT ATTORNEY.

"And it doesn't look like Mr. Jeffries is happy about it," Julie said, glancing over to see that Jeffries had separated himself from the second attorney and was standing silently next to the officer. "Should we be here?" Julie asked.

"It's a public space," Mike responded. "If they do their business here, they have to accept that they'll be seen. This is pretty typical. I forgot that you haven't been to a trial before."

She confirmed that this was her first time. "What do you think is happening?" she asked.

"I'd guess his attorneys are telling him they can cut a deal with the DA if he pleads to a lesser offense than murder in the first degree, and I'd guess that he doesn't like the deal. His guy is going in to see the DA to talk it over, but that's probably really just to put Jeffries under a bit more pressure to accept. It's all a dance, and the defense and prosecutors have practiced it many times. They know that in the end they'll both get what they want."

"Whether Jeffries wants it or not?"

"Whatever."

At that point Wayne Reiter walked over to them, and Julie introduced them. As Reiter began a mini lecture to Mike on the business of crime, they had to step aside to let a number of people come through the entrance, looking unsure of where they were going—or why. Mike spoke to a couple of them and directed them to the room at the far end of the corridor.

"Jurors," he said to Julie and Reiter. "They're the real victims of the judicial system. They'll be herded into that little box of a room to sit around for who knows how long while the lawyers go back and forth on a deal, and then someone will tell them that the trial is off, but not to worry, because they're still on the hook to hear another one. It's sad, really."

"I've never been called for jury duty," Reiter said.

"Consider yourself lucky," Mike replied.

"Well, they probably wouldn't take me anyway—too educated, I suspect."

As Julie considered whether she'd want Wayne Reiter sitting on a jury that was trying her case, she noticed that Jeffries's attorney had come back into the corridor to speak to his client, who sat down on a bench and put his head in his hands. She and Reiter and Barlow couldn't help watching, and after a few moments, Jeffries stood up and shook his head, not side to side but up and down this time.

"They've got a deal," Mike said. "Not much use in hanging around here. Want to get some coffee? I'll meet you in a couple of minutes—just want to go have a quick chat with the DA first."

CHAPTER 47

Julie and Wayne took a booth at the back of the cafe located a block down the street from the courthouse. Mike joined them there ten minutes later.

"Why do I think you might have a few questions for me?" Mike asked after the waitress had brought them their coffee. Before Julie could reply, he said, "Okay, I can tell you what Cartwright said. The deal, by the way, is that Jeffries pleaded to aggravated manslaughter and will probably get ten to fifteen. The case against him is pretty strong, but proving murder might have been a stretch, since most of the evidence is from Cartwright's testimony, and we don't have any proof about what actually happened out there in the woods. Jeffries claims he was defending himself against Dumont, and there's no one to say he wasn't. Anyway, here's the long and short of it: The DA cleared my telling you, since it'll all be in the record eventually."

Years of pulling information together for the sake of developing a coherent narrative and then telling the story on the stand had made the detective concise. He told his story simply and quickly.

"After Dumont talked to you that Tuesday, Julie—when he said he wasn't sure where the idea of a statewide blog had come from—he remembered that Cartwright had been the one to mention it at your Network meeting. Apparently he spent that afternoon digging around in the library, and noticed a couple of visits from one Timothy Brothers. He also found there were a couple of other items missing, either letters or maps; Cartwright couldn't remember which. In any case, Dumont made notes on these in a file on his laptop labeled 'Maps.' We found that, by the way, but I couldn't tell you at the time."

"I understand," Julie said. "So then . . ."

"Well, that evening—this is the night before the murder—
Dumont called Cartwright from a pay phone at a diner where he
was eating, because he'd apparently left his cell phone at the office.
The phone records we checked back that up. He told Cartwright
that he remembered it was Cartwright himself who had told him
about the statewide blog at that Network meeting; he also mentioned the missing items, and asked Cartwright if he saw any connection. I guess Cartwright got real scared at this point, or that's
what he told us, and the name of Timothy Brothers in the visitor
log made him realize what was going on."

"You mean he didn't know that this Brothers—Jeffries—was
actually stealing things, whether or not it was based on the blog?"
Julie asked.

"That's roughly what he told us. In any case, Cartwright told
Dumont on the phone that night that he had an idea about who
this Timothy Brothers was, but that it would be better to talk
about it in person. So Cartwright offered to come to Farmington
the next day and meet Dumont."

"So Brent was there on Wednesday?" Julie said.

"Hold on. No, he made the arrangement, but claims he didn't
go, and we can't prove it one way or the other. What Cartwright
says he did that Tuesday night after talking to Dumont was to call
Brothers in Boston. We confirmed that from his phone records.
At that point Jeffries took over, drove up to Farmington, and met
Dumont at the place he and Cartwright had discussed—a pull-
off not far from where Dumont's body was found. Well, you can
guess the rest."

"But wasn't Dumont surprised to see Jeffries there if he'd
planned to meet Cartwright?"

"Probably, but that's something else we don't know. What we
do know is that Jeffries claimed Dumont had accused him of the
thefts and attacked him, and that Jeffries acted in self-defense

when he shot Dumont. Of course, that doesn't make any sense at all. We surmise that Jeffries had bought the gun at the gun show earlier, had it in his truck—yes, the one that ran you off the road—and planned to kill Dumont because what he knew would blow the whole scheme wide open."

Wayne Reiter, uncharacteristically, had been silent as Barlow told the story. Now that it was apparently over, Julie, too, went quiet for a bit, digesting. Finally she said, "And you're sure Brent Cartwright wasn't involved in the murder—that he wasn't there when Dan was killed?"

"Like I said, we can't prove that he was, but we did keep the charge of accomplice to murder hanging over him, since he was the one to put Jeffries on to Dumont. And of course, that's what made Cartwright so cooperative—if you can call it that."

"So what happens to Brent now?" Julie asked.

"Not up to me. He's got charges against him here and down your way, for the B and E, but the two DAs will have to work that out, and honor the deal they made for his evidence. He'll get some time in prison, I'm sure, but on the whole, he's come out of it pretty well, considering his role."

Julie agreed, though there was a side of her that felt Cartwright was getting off too easily, no matter how much prison time he would earn. If it hadn't been for the way he directed Jeffries to the various items, Dan Dumont would be alive today.

"Mike, I'm grateful to you for all of this," she said.

"I know you like to see all the pieces of the puzzle come together, Julie. If I hear anything else, I'll let you know, but I think this pretty much wraps it up. Thanks for all your help. Much as I enjoy working with you, however, I hope we're not back in business together anytime soon."

Julie laughed, and said she was going to be a bit busy. When Mike looked at her quizzically, she reminded him of the wedding, to which he had been invited.

"Geez, I almost forgot," he said. "We'll be there."

"We?" Julie asked.

"I asked Tara to come with me. You remember her—Tara Bolduc, the policewoman here in Farmington. The invitation said 'and guest,' so I figured it would be okay. Matter of fact, I want to go by the station here to bring her up-to-date on all this, since the locals have been following it at a bit of a distance. If you'll excuse me, I'll see you in a couple of weeks. Should be fun!"

Julie couldn't believe that Wayne Reiter was still quiet. She feared she'd pay the price for that on the drive back to Ryland.

"We should be hitting the road," she said to him.

"About that blog, Julie," Reiter said once they were settled into the comfort of his luxury BMW. "I'd like to ask you a few more things, for my case study."

"You know, Wayne," she replied, "I don't think I want to talk about it just now, or even think about it. My mother is coming in a couple of days, and she's going to drive me nuts with all the wedding details. I'd like to focus on dealing with her, and looking forward to the wedding. I'm going to forget about thefts and murder and blogs and anything connected to them."

"Your choice," he said. "Somehow I don't really see you forgetting about those things for long."

"No doubt you're right, Wayne, but for the time being, consider me off duty. And hey, if you want to drive home as fast as you drove here this morning, this time I won't complain."

"Right," he said, pushing the pedal down even further.

Julie leaned back, smiled, and decided to enjoy the trip.